G000134725

**Kit Whitfield** was born in West ... Wiltshire and London, where she no... son in a neurodiverse family. She... (published in the US as *Benighted*), ... Authors' Club Best First Novel Award and ... Waverton Good Read Award, and *In Great Waters*, which was nominated for the World Fantasy Award. Her fantasy duology *In the Heart of Hidden Things* and the sequel, *All the Hollow of the Sky*, are published by Jo Fletcher Books. You will find her on Twitter @KitWhitfield.

## Praise for Kit Whitfield

'Power struggles, violence, mistakes and responsibility are threaded throughout the story. John is a strong, nuanced protagonist whose sound heart gives this book its warmth, even when things start to go wrong. Whitfield's world-building is detailed, the magic of this story is enticing and I found plenty to enjoy in this book'
**Beth O'Brien, *Disabled Tales*, on**
***In the Heart of Hidden Things***

'As powerfully intelligent as it is entertaining, Whitfield's marvellously assured fantasy debut leads the reader into a mysterious world of fairy-smiths, weaving a gripping tale of trespass, revenge and responsibility'
**Waterstones on *In the Heart of Hidden Things***

'A very engaging novel'
**SFcrowsnest on *In the Heart of Hidden Things***

'Takes a traditional genre and changes it into something extraordinary'
**Kate Atkinson, author of *Shrines of Gaiety*, on *Bareback***

'An impressive debut'
**Tananarive Due, author of *African Immortals*, on *Bareback***

'Resonates with real issues of power, responsibility and blame'
**Lisa Tuttle, *The Times*, on *Bareback***

'A powerfully intelligent novel'
***Independent* on *In Great Waters***

'Whitfield shows undoubted powers of imagination and talent'
***Daily Mail* on *In Great Waters***

# IN THE HEART OF HIDDEN THINGS

## KIT WHITFIELD

**Jo Fletcher**
BOOKS

First published in Great Britain in 2022
This paperback edition published in 2023 by

Jo Fletcher
BOOKS

Jo Fletcher Books
an imprint of
Quercus Editions Ltd
Carmelite House
50 Victoria Embankment
London EC4Y 0DZ

An Hachette UK company

A CIP catalogue record for this book is available
from the British Library

ISBN 978 1 52941 491 2
ebook ISBN 978 1 52941 489 9

10 9 8 7 6 5 4 3 2 1

Typeset by Jouve (UK), Milton Keynes

Printed and bound in Great Britain by Clays Ltd, Elcograf S.p.A.

Papers used by Jo Fletcher Books are from well-managed forests and other responsible sources.

To Nathaniel, my darling.

Wherever you are, my love is with you.
Wherever I am, my love is with you.
I will always, always love you.

Some writers have maintained that the luck associated with the horse-shoe is due chiefly to the metal, irrespective of its shape, as iron and steel are traditional charms against malevolent spirits and goblins ... In certain countries blacksmiths and farriers have always been credited with supernatural faculties.

*The Magic of the Horse-Shoe, With Other Folk-Lore Notes*
Robert Means Lawrence

Sometimes I wouldn't speak, you see,
Or answer when you spoke to me,
Because in the long, still dusks of Spring
You can hear the whole world whispering ...
Everything there is to hear
In the heart of hidden things.

'The Changeling'
Charlotte Mew

# PROLOGUE

At the centre of any village stands the smithy, where you can expect deals to be shaken on and conflicts to be shaken out, but if you need fairy-smithing, you must travel the miles to Gyrford. At the time Jedediah Smith held the forge, he and his kin had been master craftsmen in that trade, father to son, for longer than anyone could recall – and it just had to be hoped that each new son would have a head on his shoulders, for if you need fairy-smithing, you need it badly. When you're trying to till the earth and the stones sit up and argue with you, or you enter your dairy to find something untenable stirring the curds with long green fingers, it's a time for iron: the People abhor it, and a skilled farrier might be the only thing between you and disaster. We build our houses with sense and geometry and plough our fields with toil and patience, and all the while, a blink away are the People, dancing and tearing, gifting and stealing, snatching up fury and scattering light, feeding on air.

You do not war with the People unless they war on you, but if matters edge towards a precipice, the fairy-smith will be the one to fight for you. That is, if a fight cannot be avoided, and

1

certainly they preferred other means: Jedediah on the grounds that only a fool borrows trouble, Matthew on the grounds that fighting is a sad business, and John – well, they were worried about Johnny. And even John wasn't to blame for the deaths that autumn, not really; he wouldn't have wished anyone an end that bloody. But sometimes, if you are not to be crushed, you need a fairy-smith at your back.

This is what a fairy-smith would tell you, if you were so new to this part of the country that you needed telling. What they might not tell you is that there are times when the People may be the least of your troubles. The day Tobias Ware came running out of the forest, Black Hal's scorch on his soul, dancing with dazzled, sidelong glee at the presence of so many friends whose eyes he couldn't meet, the boy himself wasn't able to picture any greater threat than the chance that somebody might snatch the dripping quarry from his tender hands. And folks who didn't know better might think that the People had already done more than enough to him. Tobias didn't understand laws, or landlords; he only understood the snap of twig and the green whisper of frond on frond and the glinting, shattered sun that yearns through the canopy.

So those who did understand other matters had to stand by him. The laws are made by and for the grand folks, and there is no known way to settle the grand. We sweat over our work and speak good sense to our children and live as we can, and beyond us are the folks who do not choose to have mercy. The smithy stands at the centre of the village, and someone has to man it.

2

## CHAPTER I

John Smith was entirely too interested in the forest. It was sensible and well-kept, and there was nothing in the glowing canopy above them or the froth of bracken around the track to suggest mischief. But it was too quiet. Woods are the marketplace of birds and beasts, and on any common day you should hear a chatter of song and contest above your head, but as they walked, the world around them hushed. Up ahead, oaks rattled their frilled leaves against one another, and the ivy shuddered on its stems; as the men neared each branch, the green scraps stilled as if checking themselves. The tree trunks around them were pearled with lichen, and moss glowed like embers on the bark, and when anyone spoke, the clumped tendrils hunched down like mice flinching still at the sound of a footstep.

This was the sort of thing that tended to distract John more than either his father or his grandfather, who were at that point deeply absorbed in conversation with the customer. And it must be admitted that the boy did have a somewhat vague look on his face. Matthew would have been inclined to humour his son; Matthew was a man who'd humour anyone on God's earth as long as Jedediah wasn't watching. Jedediah was, though, and so Matthew held his tongue while Jedediah turned and snapped at John: 'Have you ears, boy?'

'Of course I have,' said John, offended. 'I don't see why you have to scold me with empty questions, Grandpa, and I don't think you need scold me at all, while you're about it.'

'Then you can use them or I'll see to it that they ring,' said Jedediah. This threat made about as much impression on John as a stone skipped across a lake: Jedediah was held in respectful awe by folks throughout the county, and the fact that neither his son nor his grandchildren feared him in the least was among several creditable truths about himself that he was at pains to disguise. 'Listen to what the man has to say.'

'The man', in this case, was Franklin Thorpe, a favourite of the Smiths', who was usually very sure on his feet amidst the trees: he'd been a forester since his teens, and loved the work because it gave him good, long hours to walk the woods with no one shouting at anyone else. He turned to promise that it was quite all right; Mister Smith and John had always sparred with energetic spirit and no real heat, but Mister Smith became sharper when he was worried, and elder farriers have a lot to worry about, even without their grandsons going drifty-headed in the Bellame woods. Franklin hated to see Mister Smith ill at ease, and at that moment, his desire to smooth things over distracted him so much that he took an unfortunate step askew of the regular path.

John exclaimed, 'Stop!', but just as Franklin's foot came down, there was a sharp flicker in the air, just a little flutter of pressure, as if something around them had laughed in a voice that could be felt rather than heard. Franklin froze.

'Wait there,' Jedediah snapped, and then, as John drew near in utter fascination, looped an arm around his waist and gestured Matthew to help Franklin.

'Grandpa, let me go, I'm the one that spotted it!' John protested, putting up a real struggle rather than a token one. Jedediah, for all his fifty-eight years, had arms like steel wires, and John wasn't quite able to free himself, but there was a definite contest going on as Matthew went to Franklin's side as soft as he could, and examined the danger.

Franklin's boot had come to rest in the centre of a small circle: white puffballs, smooth as velvet and domed as cathedrals, stood in a fairy-ring just wide enough to form a foothold trap around a careless man's step. The People are known for their caprice, but they live by laws of their own; understanding those laws – at least, so far as it was possible to understand them – was as much at the heart of a farrier's trade as the glowing forge. Some of their laws were more predictable than others, though, and it didn't take a farrier to know that breaking the bounds of a fairy ring was enough to provoke endless enmity.

'Oh dear,' Matthew said, crossing himself briefly. 'Well, lucky you're with us. You've iron hobnails in your boots, yes?'

Franklin nodded, about as calmly as could be expected. 'Good man,' Matthew said. 'Now, let's see . . .'

The People within the ring were not inclined to come out and negotiate, probably because of the iron in Franklin's boot. Franklin turned his pockets inside out without being told – an old trick to allay the People when they looked like they might get after you; Franklin hadn't followed Jedediah so many years for nothing – and Matthew worked at the earth around the sole, knotting in flowers. After a minute or so, he began to hum a weaving chant, not so much for fey purposes as because he could still hear John and Jedediah in dispute over whether Grandpa should let John go. Any good farrier can work amidst distractions, and Matthew was good, but when it's your own son, there's a hook in your heart that pulls even the most dedicated attention astray.

'Johnny,' he said, looking up, 'I've a task for you. I reckon we could do with some lives here; snails, I'd say. Can you find me seven of them?'

Jedediah released his hold as soon as John stopped struggling – the boy was quite capable of hurting himself if he was really determined – and John, at once brightened by the prospect, said, 'Of course, Dada. There's an old log fallen just thirty-odd paces back, it was quite crowned with mushrooms, I reckon that—'

'If you can reckon that your father told you to do something, and do it,' Jedediah interrupted, 'you'll stun us all. Go on with you.'

John took off, and was back again within two minutes, his hands cupped lovingly around a cluster of shells. The snails he'd found were beautiful creatures, six of them dark-banded with a bark-and-cream spiral, and one gold as a buttercup; Johnny had an untaught sense of what was good to pick for such cases.

'All right.' Matthew had been kneeling for some time before he spoke again, and Franklin, increasingly unsteady as he strove not to overbalance, had had to prop his arm against Matthew's back, but the weight of Franklin left him entirely untroubled. Matthew was six foot four with shoulders massive even for a smith, and widely regarded around Gyrford as a formidable fellow you'd better not cross. This was less to do with his true nature than with the fact that folks feel safer when their fairy-smith is fearsome, and with the additional fact that shyness may be mistaken for leashed power when the mute fellow in question can lift a grown man with one arm. In truth, Matthew was a quiet, pious soul who lived in fear of small doorways and formal occasions, and was generally happy to let his father do the talking. That Franklin had known him so long and trusted him well enough to lean on him without asking was a positive comfort; folks being afraid of him made him shyer than ever.

'Start on the Lord's Prayer, Franklin,' Matthew told his friend in a voice more affectionate than quite befitted his authority as a farrier averting disaster. 'Keep it in a whisper as you lift your foot, just a little, not all the way out.'

The People had mixed opinions about religion, and what the ones in this fairy ring would make of it, Jedediah, watching from the sidelines, wasn't sure, but it was never a bad idea to give them some kind of show of ritual; even if they didn't understand its meaning, they tended to love ceremony for its own sake.

Franklin lifted his foot, and Matthew's fingers worked fast, fixing a fine garland in the shape of the boot-sole printed into the earth. Within it, enclosed by the confines of green leaf and late bloom, he placed the snails, the gold one at the toe end and the rest ranged around. Franklin tried not to wobble; falling now might mean his life if he smashed the mushrooms, and he'd prefer not to crush the snails either, if he could avoid it.

'So now,' Matthew said, giving Franklin an arm. 'Step away,

and you should be . . . yes, that's it, good man. There you go.' Franklin's foot came free, and nothing pursued it; the air didn't pleat.

'Are you well?' Jedediah asked, hastening over to brush Franklin down, although he hadn't got any mess on his clothing.

'Quite all right,' Franklin said, accepting the pats for what they were, 'thanks to your good care. I'm sorry to put you to trouble. That was very foolish of me. You know I know better than that.'

His tone was so apologetic that Jedediah rounded on John, who was crouched down, gazing intrigued as each of the snails stretched out its pearly neck, bowing needle-fine eyes down in prostration to the lords of the circle. 'Never fret yourself, Franklin Thorpe,' Jedediah said with the bite of relief in his voice. 'You were only put off your stride by young Stare-Eyes there, who has more use for his tongue than his ears, by the look of things.'

John was, indeed, staring; his gaze was so intent that he didn't appear to have heard them, until Jedediah tapped him on the head, at which point he turned round and announced, 'If I did that to anyone, Grandpa, you'd say I had bad manners.'

'I might say more than that,' Jedediah said, with more fatigue in his voice than anger; John could hold his opinion against all comers.

'That's all right, Mister Smith,' said Franklin. 'I am sure Mister John is a sharp young lad.'

The fact that Franklin called him 'Mister John', along with the fact that he picked and dried berries from the woods and often had a handful of such sweetmeats to share, had long since bought John's loyalty. 'I am glad to listen to Mister Franklin Thorpe,' he announced with dignity. 'I hear nothing but the best sense from him.'

'I can only say,' Franklin intervened with some haste, before Jedediah could comment on John's lofty air, 'that I'm grateful as always for your kindness. Thanks, Matt.'

Matthew smiled, and, a little flustered at gratitude that felt much deeper than he deserved for so minor an assistance, said, 'So, this business of the hedge we talked of before – well, before just now. You didn't go too close?'

'No,' Franklin said, as willing as Matthew to get back to the reason he'd called them to the forest in the first place. 'I'd rather trust your judgement, by your leave.'

'You did right, Franklin Thorpe,' said Jedediah. 'Fewer limbs would be scattered to the winds if more folks would come to us before trifling too close. John, do you pay heed?'

'Yes, Grandpa,' said John, peeved at being nagged. 'Mister Thorpe says something is talking in the bramble hedge and he didn't go near it.'

It wasn't that John couldn't use his common sense – at least, not if he made the effort. But some places are feyer than others, and the woods always belong more to the People than the folks. In such places, John had an unfortunate air of fascination that his family were at pains to chastise out of him (when the 'family' was Jedediah), justify as a wisdom and perception beyond his years (his mother Janet, who was commonly regarded as flighty), or find some explanation to excuse, anything that could be grounded in sane, sensible reasons (Matthew). Nobody liked to consider that the boy might be anything other than a sound, iron Smith, struck out of the family mould with both feet firmly planted on mortal soil. The Taunton incident was in the past, and John was a good boy, really he was, and that was all there was to it. Things happened in the world that couldn't be taken back, and what you made of them was who you were, that was Jedediah's dictum. John could still be made a fairy-smith. It could be done.

As the three men tramped along the track and John hurried after them on legs he would never acknowledge as small, he was paying attention, but only with half his mind. This was the first time he'd been allowed into the Bellame woods, or indeed any-where the People were more than usually active, and he could not quite stop seeing it. The light fell through the leaves in wavering casts, tinged with dust and soft as water, and it was quiet in a way that wasn't quite peaceful.

'This is the hedge,' said Franklin, soon enough, and Jedediah stopped and looked at the offending property ahead.

'And the Ware farm on the other side, with Chalk Lane beyond.' It wasn't a question: he knew the land around his smithy like the surface of his anvil.

'Ooh!' John exclaimed before anyone could stop him. 'I don't suppose the bush is leaning Black Hal's way?' He dropped down on the ground, examining what appeared, at first look, to be a fairly normal bramble – albeit one that stood in a gap in the hedgerow, holly and hawthorn straggling smashed branches either side. The fact that the barrier was broken through caught Jedediah's attention more than the bush itself, which is why John was already nudging the bush with his nose, crooning a soft little howl to it, before Jedediah was able to collar him.

'What, I beg to know,' Jedediah said, with the strained steadiness of a man trying to stay reasonable, 'do you think you are about, boy?'

Matthew stood stricken, and Franklin made an effort to employ his huntsman's experience of fading into silent obscurity against the green background. Perhaps the boy had only been playing, overexcited at the chance to see something new. The sight of him crouching, crook-limbed and wordless, was not an attempt to mock or mimic the Wares. That was the disturbing thing: that the boy had so suddenly dropped into a stance he'd had no chance to learn. They'd seen it before, but Johnny was only being himself.

'I just thought,' John said, squirming against Jedediah's grasp of his shirt as if it were an innocent tree branch that had happened to snag him, 'that if it was, perhaps it might rather hear a bay than a word.'

Jedediah looked to Matthew, who was better at keeping his temper.

'Johnny, dear,' said Matthew, 'listen to me now. You must not act on rash guesses like that. We're on fey ground here. The kind friends might see what you did there and take it amiss.' It was always wiser to refer to the People by some polite turn of phrase when they might be listening, and Matthew's advice was correct. It also had the advantage of avoiding any reference to how like Tobias Ware, just for a moment, John had looked.

Jedediah swallowed. There was that oddity John had just performed, and there was also something about the hedge, something that he didn't want to discuss in front of a chatterbox child who couldn't be relied on not to say the wrong thing in front of the wrong hearer. Jedediah didn't like to be unfair, but he was deeply worried about something, something more than John's apparent wildness, and it was with a resigned sense of strategy that he said, 'No sense at all. First knock a man off the path, now this. Get yourself killed, carrying on that way, boy. He's not ready to see the People up close today, Matthew. You take him off and see if you can talk some sense into him.'

'Grandpa, I want to see it!' John protested.

'Now, Johnny, be a good lad,' said Matthew. 'We'll get some oak twigs and show you how to make a Mackem knot. That's useful knowledge.'

'I'm ready!' John insisted. He was a sunny-tempered boy and seldom shouted, but his grandfather's apparently capricious refusal really did sting him. 'I've worked hard for a *very* long time and even Grandpa said I was shaping well last month . . .' There had been many more admonitions since, but John's memory for a compliment was much longer than his memory for a criticism. 'Mister Franklin Thorpe, wouldn't you rather have three farriers' opinions than one?'

Franklin Thorpe glanced with some discomfort between the tense men of the smithy. He knew more than most the worries Matthew and Janet had about young John, but it wasn't his place to say anything. Mister Smith wouldn't; he was blunt about folks' mistakes, but he left their sore spots alone, and Franklin had never heard him say anything truly wounding in his life. And this could cause a wound. John was so bright and full of himself; so different from how Franklin had been at ten years old, battered and exhausted with fear, or how Matthew had been, earnest and anxious and too responsible for his age. And from the little Mister Smith had said of his own childhood, that hadn't been the happiest either; he was the son of a foreigner from over the county border who never got fond of his new neighbourhood, and hadn't much liked Jedediah either, for growing up so thoroughly a Gyrford man. It had taken them this long to produce a boy who really enjoyed his boyhood, and Franklin could understand why none of them were in a hurry to mar his blitheness.

'Well, Mister John,' said Franklin, 'if I'm to have one man's opinion, I can think of no better man than your respected grandfather. And if there's a chance of harm, I wouldn't like it to befall you. Suppose you stay here with your father and work on that knot of yours, and when we come back, I give you some of my dried currants? I know I have some in my pocket.'

'Would you have given me any if I hadn't been told to stay here and wait?' John asked; whatever his faults, he wasn't easily fooled when it came to bribes. 'Because if you would, I don't see that's a reason.'

'Well, you have a point,' said Franklin, whose own father had called him stupid many drunken nights when he was a boy. 'But I meant to give you some, and send some home with Matthew for your sisters, and share the rest with Francie. I reckon if you oblige your grandfather, I'll just save Francie's share and give you mine.'

'Oh.' John thought this over. Francie was Franklin's grown-up daughter, or at least, grown-up by John's standards. He didn't want to deprive her; she was just about the only member of his family who never scolded him. Well, not blood-kin, but Mister Thorpe was sort of an uncle; John only called him 'Mister Thorpe' because it sounded more grown-up than 'Mister Franklin'. All the Smiths were persistent in trying to teach John manners – which were easier to explain to him than the nebulous rules of common sense – and Jedediah was particularly firm that Mister Thorpe should never be addressed with anything less than perfect courtesy. John liked to protest, meanwhile, that he would have been polite without being told; he thought very well of the man.

Fever had taken Franklin's Sarah six years ago, so now he lived alone with Francie. The name had been Sarah's idea, as she had found her soft-spoken husband so gentle, temperate and constant that she would have named a dozen children after him had she had the opportunity. Providence not having granted her siblings, Francie was much attached to the Smith children, and all four of them, John included, returned that affection. Put to the test, he was heroic enough to love her passing the love of currants.

'No, thank you,' John said, his generous intention only slightly marred by a note of excessive magnanimity. 'I am sure Francie would not wish to eat currants alone, and would give to you of her share. I shall take only the currants you first earmarked for me and no more, I thank you, Mister Franklin Thorpe.'

Jedediah's glance towards Matthew was wry, but Matthew gave his father back an earnest smile: the boy might have a questionable head on his shoulders, but surely his heart was sound.

'That's a good thought, Johnny,' said Matthew. 'Come, I saw a comfortable stump back there. Now, can you find me some narrow twigs and peel them? I'll race you: first to find five. Go!'

Franklin and Jedediah waited until they were entirely alone before they spoke again.

'A fine boy, your grandson,' said Franklin, with the air of a man cautiously putting out his hand to a mastiff.

Jedediah didn't answer. His face was grave.

'If I can help, in any way . . .' Franklin went on. The boy had looked queer in that moment, there was no question of it. Franklin had grown up in a house where his father beat his mother at night and his mother railed at the world during the day, and the great resolution of his life was that he would speak civil to everyone and give no folks cause to shout at anyone else. Jedediah's frequent threats to John would have made him flinch, coming from another man, but Jedediah was different. Jedediah had dressed some of his bruises when he was a child, found quiet moments to help him learn his letters when there was no peace at home, slipped him food on the days when his father drank the money, sheltered him when he was afraid to go home. It had been Jedediah who had a discreet word when the master forester's horse needed shoeing, and suggested that there was a young lad named Thorpe in the village who was bright and biddable and wouldn't be sorry to live away from home, and Jedediah who paid for the articles of apprenticeship and gruffly refused any talk of repayment until Franklin was truly prospering.

When Franklin's Sarah died, it was Jedediah who'd sat up with him; Jedediah had been widowed young, and knew better than anyone how long the nights could be. And he knew, too, what it was to be a father when loss overwhelmed you: after Mistress Smith died, Jedediah's family, certain that no solitary man could manage a five-year-old boy, had all pressed him to foster Matthew on some female or married relations. Jedediah had refused every offer. He wouldn't part with his son, and he'd never raised a hand to him. Of course, Matthew had been a lot more docile than John, but if John ever got more than a light swat, Franklin would have been astonished; the boy was afraid of nothing.

Franklin had never been permitted to thank Mister Smith for his kindness – the man was uncomfortable with personal compliments – but he would have broken his bones for Jedediah, or any of his kin and kind. That included his slightly worrying grandson.

'If you want my help, Mister Smith, you have only to ask,' Franklin ventured.

Jedediah shook his head. 'It's the Wares need help today, man,' he said, pulling himself together. 'This is their boundary hedge, yes? We'll think of them for now.'

Franklin would have liked to offer more, but he'd revered Jedediah four full decades, and was in no hurry to outgrow his faith that the man knew best. Deep within Franklin was the conviction that he could never repay Mister Smith's many generosities; all he could do was try to be the man Mister Smith would wish him, which meant being willing to serve others ahead of yourself. It was with quiet obedience, then, that he added, 'I've not spoken to the Wares about it yet. But it troubled me. Soots wouldn't go near it, not within ten feet.' Soots was

Franklin's dog, a flop-eared, black-speckled lass with a happily ugly face, a nose that could follow a day-old deer track through a rainstorm, and a healthy caution of the People. Dogs, in general, were uncomfortable with things fey, but Franklin had trained Soots with impeccable patience, and her utter worship of him kept her from turning nervous. If she was so frightened of this thing that it was kindest to leave her behind, it was a dismal sign.

Jedediah accepted this with brief nod, and stooped to examine the bush. At first glance, it was common bramble, with wide-palmed leaves and long-leggity stems lolling this way and that. That was ordinary enough: throughout the hedgerow, twigs intertwined to make a good, solid barrier between the farm tenanted by the Ware family and the woods exclusive to Lord Robert and his guests. But the bush stood in a gap – and it had been recently transplanted. The earth around it was still churned; you could see where boots had stamped it down. It was a big bush to have dug up and moved, though, and a particularly spiny one; setting it here couldn't have been an easy task. Something had broken through the hedgerow, and these spines had been put here by someone very determined to plug the gap in the hedge. But they hadn't been left alone since then; down on the ground, some of the branches were trampled.

Jedediah rubbed at his forehead with a cold hand. This did not look like good news. A bush where the People hunched down and argued over the berries, or a bush that pulled up its roots and ran out to dance in a midnight glade; those things he could manage easy enough. In itself, a fey bush wasn't much of a problem. If the only problem was the bush.

Reaching into his pocket, he pulled out his iron glove. This wasn't really a glove, but a loop of worked iron to slip over the knuckles: you knocked on the earth or the stones, and listened to hear if anything shrieked within. It wasn't a failsafe way to find the People, but it was a good beginning, and it had the advantage that if anything streamed howling out of a tree trunk or dashed up from the soil in a shower of blinding gold, you were well equipped to land a good punch. Jedediah knocked and listened. He poked the earth, then pressed the iron against a leaf.

The entire branch squeamed down, and there was a sound from inside, something between a snarl of fury and an indignant yelp.

'Ah,' said Jedediah. John staring at every twig he passed might have been excessive, but fey bushes were bread and butter. 'Well, there's your talker.' He took from his pocket a small chain, link on iron link, and laid it round the base of the bush with a swift, practised swoop.

The twigs rattled against each other with the sound of snapping teeth.

'If it were just a bush in the forest, Mister Smith,' said Franklin Thorpe, sounding less confident than usual, 'then of course I'd leave well enough alone. The Good Neighbours must live somewhere. But you see, this is a boundary hedge. And the truth is, Mister Smith . . .'

Jedediah had been tapping his iron glove against the spines with the air of a man shooing a chicken off its nest, and not really listening to Franklin. It was Franklin who jumped the highest, therefore, when the top of one of the stems cartwheeled down off the bush in an explosion of thorns and outrage and made a dash towards the offending men.

It might have gone ill with them if it wasn't for the chain surrounding the bush, but as it was, the bundle of limbs stopped at the iron boundary and chattered in a series of vindictive clicks, each as dry as the snapping of a twig.

Jedediah looked down at it with a cautious regard. It was a thin thing, really, armed and legged with more or less the right number of limbs, albeit with a profusion of thorns on them and more angular air than was proper. Perhaps for the purposes of conversation, it had taken to wearing a blackberry for its head, and the beaded surface was giving it trouble as to the number of eyeballs it should settle upon.

'Good day, kind friend,' he said. 'I hope you do not quarrel with your neighbours here.'

The thing bared its thorns at them.

Jedediah sat back on his heels. You don't shoe horses by losing patience with them, and you don't deal with the People if you can't wait. 'Good day, kind friend,' he said again with no rise in his tone. 'I hope you do not quarrel with your neighbours here.'

'Neighbour ash, neighbour rat, neighbour holly, neighbour neighbour neighbour . . .' Its voice was as thin as its limbs, a hoarse, piercing creak.

'Your neighbours the men,' Jedediah said. 'I hope you do not quarrel with your neighbours the men.'

'Neighbour ash, neighbour rat, neighbour holly, neighbour fox.' The little thing was not one of the People's freest talkers; it was gathering words together with evident effort. 'Neighbour man no. Neighbour ash, neighbour rat, neighbour bush find us at.'

Franklin Thorpe stood behind Jedediah. His hands were in his pockets, so it was hard to explain exactly why it felt so much as if he was wringing them.

Jedediah put his gloved hand behind his back. 'Answer questions, kind friend, Iron will go and trouble end,' he said. He was not devoted to poetry, unless it had a good tune to go with it, but some People found it easier to follow you when you spoke in rhyme, and any forge kept a few quatrains amongst its equipment. 'You say yes, you say no, Smith and iron away will go.'

'No,' said the little thing, which at least proved it understood what he was getting at.

'You had an ash tree for a neighbour?' Jedediah asked.

'Yes.' The thing shook what were more or less its arms.

'And a holly bush, and a place where a rat lived?'

'Yes.'

'Do you mean to quarrel with your new neighbours?'

'Neighbour ash, neighbour rat!' The voice was rising. 'Neighbour runner broke twig mine is!'

Jedediah gave a harsh cough. Things were becoming clear to him that he wasn't happy about. 'Will you keep from quarrels with men if you go back to your old neighbours?'

'Yes.' The blackberry head bent on its stem; several seeded bobbles attempted to blink. 'Neighbour ash. Neighbour runner broke mine twig mine!'

Yes, that was the thing he needed to talk through with Franklin, and he didn't like it at all.

'Very well,' he told the little thing. 'We shall put you back.'

'Broke mine twig mine is mine twig!' Now the idea had been

touched upon, the thing was getting angrier and angrier. Jedediah could see the trampled stems, and the breaks were recent.

'We put you where you wish to live, you live in peace and you forgive,' he said. This was a rhyme that just occurred to him; sometimes you had to improvise. 'You hurt the neighbour men, we dig you up again.' The scansion wasn't very good, which irritated him: he did not like to produce poor work.

'Neighbour ash, neighbour rat,' said the little thing. Then it spat, and flurried back into a branch.

Jedediah stood up, dusting his hands. 'Well,' he said, 'that's a nothing job. Folks dig up a bush in the forest without checking it, they anger the People, the People come bother them. Fools' work.'

Jedediah was not an easy man to mislead, nor a comfortable man to be caught misleading, and his searching stare was giving Franklin a little trouble. Now he had shown Mister Smith the ground, it wouldn't be difficult for him to put things together. A boundary hedge with Lord Robert Bellamy's woods on one side, and the Ware family on the other; a hedge that had been broken through, then broken through again.

Jedediah and Franklin might walk the Bellame woods unchallenged — it was Franklin's place of work, and the whole county was Jedediah's, private property or not — but the same could not be said of most common folk. There were necks unbroken in Gyrford this day because Franklin Thorpe had had a quiet word in the ears above them about keeping off rich men's land, and since he wasn't above a little charity when it was poach or starve, he had managed to spare his fellows a great deal over the years. But hangings still happened. Franklin couldn't stop them all. Neither could the Smiths, although there had been times when a man spent a night in the forge and nobody had asked him any questions about why he was on the run. If you could keep out from under the eye of the grand, it was best for everyone.

And that worked as well as it could, so long as the fellow Franklin needed to help could hold a conversation. But both of them knew about Tobias Ware.

'I reckon you're an easy man on trespassers, Franklin Thorpe,' said Jedediah.

'I – I hope I do my duty by my Lord Robert,' Franklin said, a little louder than necessary.

'I hope you do,' said Jedediah with dry emphasis. 'And I know you know the grand folks are well enough in their place, so long as they let the common folks alone. And Lord Robert needn't know every footstep that falls in his woods uninvited, eh? It's not a forester's duty to hang more souls than he must.'

Franklin said nothing. The lord of the manor handled the People the way he handled everything else on his estate, which is to say, he expected his servants to tidy trouble out of his way. It was not an approach to life Franklin could understand, but it did make it possible to hide things from the man's august notice.

'Forgive me,' said Franklin. 'I – I did not feel the village the place to tell you all.'

Jedediah thought back. Franklin had arrived with his usual quiet courtesy, and they'd been alone for most of the conversation. But yes, now he thought of it, there had been a man passing the smithy door as Franklin began explaining the case. It was

Ephraim Brady, out on his way somewhere. Wherever he was headed, it wouldn't be to anyone's good: Ephraim Brady was a landlord in the area, a money-lender, a man with a long pocket and a stony smile, and nobody who crossed him profited by it. His house stood opposite the Smiths' in the village square, a finer place by far than the small stone cot that had birthed this white-lipped man, but no one thought of him as a neighbour. He was up at dawn and out about his business, and if you saw him standing still, it was to talk trade, and you must just hope that the trade wouldn't touch your livelihood.

Ephraim Brady was quite capable of turning in a trespasser to collect the reward on him, and he had a grudge against the Smiths to boot. Last month he had been on the verge of turning out some of his tenants, Joey and Liz Sheppard and their children, because they had fallen behind on their rent. The Smiths investigated and found a nest of stone-eyed, grey-furred intangibles in the roof of their goat-house, which had been drinking up much of the goats' milk and sadly interfering with the production of cheeses for market. Ephraim couldn't quite afford to alienate the fairy-smiths – he had too many properties needing management – so when Jedediah had presented him with a large bill for the trouble of transplanting the nest, along with some comments on the false economy of delaying calling them in for so long, he had paid. The next day, the Sheppards had somehow been able to pay their debt. Nobody had said outright that Jedediah had passed the money along, and he was brusquely emphatic that the Sheppards not show him any gratitude. But making a man pay his tenants' rents out of his own pocket – which was how Ephraim undoubt-edly saw it – was not the kind of thing he would forgive.

All of which was bad enough, but worse, he owned property near Chalk Lane too. This was partly his domain, and he was not a light-handed landlord. The less he heard about anything, the better.

Jedediah regarded Franklin with weary approval. 'Just tell me a lie another time,' he said. 'You know I won't think you false. If the Wares can't ask me themselves, someone should. Better I hear it before that landlord of theirs does, God help them.' 'That landlord' was Roger Groves, a colleague of Ephraim Brady and not much the better man. 'Tell you what, if it's about Tobias, come in the smithy and say there's an oak that needs—'

He did not finish the sentence. There was no yell, no snarl or sob that broke into their conversation. It was just a patter of feet, a swift, soft lollop across the echoless earth of the forest that you'd hardly hear unless you were listening. The steps came to a stop just behind them, and when they turned to face the woods, there stood a boy, bright-eyed and all alive, twigs in his hair and scratches up his arms, and his face smudged with days of earth. He gave them just a glance, more at their mouths and their hands than at their eyes, then ducked himself to a sideways stance, standing rocking on his feet, half-turned away, his shoulder raised like a protective wing.

Jedediah looked at him for a long moment. Then he made a gesture to Franklin.

Franklin cleared his throat and spoke. 'Good day, Tobias dear,' he said.

Tobias Ware didn't turn at the sound of his name, but he sidled up towards Franklin and rested a head against his shoulder just for a second, kissing the air with a light chirruping sound. Then he dodged away, grinning at the ground. Franklin had met him before, and had always been at pains not to hurt him; to Tobias' understanding, this made him a beloved friend. The grin slid across the boy as fast as a gleam through a cloud, lighting him up, and he smiled towards the earth, as if confiding in it his pleasure at being greeted.

Franklin spoke softly: 'I see you are on your way home, Tobias. Shall I take you to your brothers?'

When Franklin said 'brothers', Tobias bounced on his heels a little, a half-skip of contentment. He had no notion, Jedediah thought, which direction to aim his love, but he was joyful, alert, full of delight at the pleasant folks around him.

There was a dead rabbit in his hands. It hung there, limp-furred, dry-eyed, unmistakably poached: a death warrant dangling loose, broken paws. The boy's mouth was smeared with blood, smiling calm as an angel as he ducked his head to tear dripping pink strips of flesh from its open throat.

It was not the Wares' fault that they lived beside Chalk Lane. Poor tenants live where they must, and the land they farmed was well enough – but Chalk Lane was a place no one walked alone, and the two families at each end, the Porters to the west and the Wares to the east, did not like to speak of it.

When the sky was grey and clouded it was no worse than dingy: a raggedy ridgeline track with cart-ruts rubbed into the white, fractured earth, with a stripe of grass down its centre where the wheels did not go, and bracken thickening on the verges. In the daytime, the view was fine, with acres falling either side of you and a froth of trees on the horizon, but when the dark closed in, it was dizzying: you walked atop it like a fence, and the weight of the world slipped down away from you in all directions, and the wind blew without let or mercy. It was a wide road and stony underfoot, but always felt as if you might overbalance – and if you fell in the dark, you could never be sure how far you'd tumble or where you'd fetch up when you stopped.

This road was the haunt of Black Hal. That was what folks

called him: the great dog that ran along the path, the People's dog that under a rising moon slipped his collar and went loping along the gusty tops. Fire struck from his heels, they said, and his eyes were the red of coals: in the dark, travellers saw two round blazes, big as cups, coming towards them with a four-point patter of flashes below. Those burning eyes wept flames, tumbling globes of red streaming back from his head it as it blew in the wind. On brighter nights, folks swore, they could see the whole of him: a huge black hound, face contorted in a gargoyle snarl, ragged pelt thick as thorns, and, either side of his chest, a set of flayed ribs, a skinless hatching of gleaming white and twitching red, through which could just be glimpsed the jerk and pulse of his thick, heavy heart.

It was considered extremely ill luck to see Black Hal, and not just because the sight of him was enough to whiten your hair. There were People who could lay curses that followed you all your life, and People who'd hurt you then and there, and Black Hal was one of the latter. He was seen seven times a year, reckoned from one Michaelmas to the next, though exactly when he'd appear within that year was anybody's guess – and while most of those times he just ran by, leaving a shaken and older mortal behind him with a tale to tell that nobody in the neighbourhood wanted to hear, history showed that he would and could kill a man. There had been mauled corpses found, mawfuls of throat torn out and blackened prints in the chalk around them. Jedediah's father had witnessed the last of these, and while a garrulous man, he had never liked to describe the look on the victim's face.

This was the road that led up to the Wares' home. Why Black

Hal always ran along Chalk Lane and never anywhere else was one of those questions there was no point in asking: the People have their notions, and while some of them can be persuaded, some hold to their habits with implacable fealty. Black Hal was one of the latter, and there was nothing to do but keep out of his path. Jonas Ware was a thin, pressed, careworn man, with no wife left alive, but four sons to help him work the land and no fortune to leave to any of them. They were good lads, and no one had any ill to say of them – except for the existence of the youngest brother.

Tobias Ware was eleven years old and had said nothing all his life. He worked, when he had a brother there to show him what to do, and he had a strong back and was willing in spirit, but he was wild in his mind: he slept outdoors, no matter the weather, and fought like badger if anyone tried to drag him back in; he'd eat only raw meat and berries, no matter what dainties were laid before him; he had nothing to say to anyone. It was his bad luck that he'd been born one dark autumn night after his mother took fright at the sight of Black Hal running past their gate, and there was no doubt it had affected him, but he was a good lad; he smiled when his father and brothers petted him, he hurt no one as long as they didn't break in upon his attention too sudden, and the Wares, who were an affectionate family, spoke of Tobias as kindly as they spoke of their other brothers, saying only that we all have our ways and Toby had his.

No one had heard tell of him trespassing; for all most folks knew, Tobias never left the farm. But when Jedediah and Franklin finally got him back to the fields where his brothers and father were working – Tobias didn't follow instructions, but Jedediah got behind him and walked slowly forwards, and Tobias had sidestepped and jinked his way back onto his homestead to avoid Jedediah coming too close – Jonas Ware dropped his hoe at the sight of his son and gave a moan of dismay.

'Toby!' he exclaimed. It was just that, one word, but Tobias gave a small shriek and dashed sideways.

The Wares all froze. Then they looked at each other and, with the regularity of folks taught by hard practice to hide their feelings, gathered their faces into careful smiles that wouldn't frighten their boy.

Peter, the oldest of the brothers, went up to him. 'Toby,' he said, in a voice almost calm and very quiet, 'it's all right. Nobody's cross. It's all right. What have you there? Let Peter see.' Peter's own face and arms, Jedediah saw, had some scratches upon them, as if he'd carried a thorny bush recently.

Tobias didn't meet his brother's gaze. Instead, he whirled round and threw the rabbit high in the air; its tattered limbs splayed out in a giddy arc before landing back in his grip. Tobias gave a grin towards his hands, and hurled the rabbit up again.

'I found your boy,' said Franklin, with a very careful manner. 'He was lost, I would say. And he had – found a dead coney by the wayside, I would say. I thought it best to bring him home, where he must wish to go.'

Jonas couldn't speak; his eyes were locked on Tobias and Peter. Tobias flipped the rabbit again; little scatters of flesh were landing on his face as it spun, and he picked them off and licked them from delicate fingertips. Then, with a silent giggle, he tossed it towards Peter.

'Ugh, no, Toby!' said Peter, making a wild grab to remove the thing from Toby's reach. 'No thank you.'

Tobias grinned again, and edged up to Peter. With his eyes, shining brilliant with love, fixed on the ground, he reached out for the rabbit and pushed it up towards Peter's face.

'No, Toby,' said Peter, spluttering a bit, 'I don't want any— Toby, no— Toby—' But he was smiling; Toby's gory ministrations were so full of generous mischief, so earnestly set on sharing, that Peter couldn't keep from catching his grin, even with this gutted mess before his teeth. 'Peter don't eat raw coney, Toby-rascal,' he said, with a helpless laugh that suggested years of experience had worn away his talent for disgust. 'Ugh. No thank you.'

'No doubt that is the way of it,' said Jedediah. 'Lost. Found a coney. But Jonas Ware, I would like a word with you about your hedge.'

The story, once Jonas Ware had steadied his nerve to tell it, was not that surprising to Jedediah. Toby had taken to wandering; they had tried to keep him indoors at night, but when they locked the door on him he screamed without stopping, and had gashed his wrist deep when he finally broke through the panels and made his way back outside. The hedgerow had not been enough to hold him in. A few months ago he'd ripped right through it, and no matter how many times they'd patched and planted, Toby just kept breaking out again.

Yes, Mister Smith, he did get hurt. Jonas acknowledged it with a kind of braced desperation in his eyes. Most days Toby was covered with scratch marks thick as lace, but he never minded it. He would be out in the forest. They couldn't talk him out of the wish. Jonas Ware stood before Jedediah, waiting in defensive exhaustion for the scolding, but Jedediah didn't deliver one. He recognised the voice of a man doing his best, and when Jonas said they couldn't stop Tobias, Jedediah could hear that he was speaking the literal truth.

Yes, Mister Smith, Jonas confirmed as Jedediah moved without comment to the next question, they'd planted the new bramble. They'd dug it up from the woods. They kept planting new brambles, but they didn't grow fast enough to keep him out, and Toby would always get past them.

Yes, Mister Smith, they knew the bush they'd planted had some tenant in it. They thought that perhaps Toby mightn't like to pass it.

Jedediah sighed. 'Well,' he said, 'he passed it all right. Now the thing's angry your boy broke its branches. Guesswork's no way to handle the People. You can unsettle a whole forest that way.' Jedediah could have said more on that subject, but he didn't want to. John's stareyness when they'd walked through the woods was still troubling him; while Jedediah disapproved of woolly-headed notions, plain experience reminded him that when John got like that, it was usually in a disturbed spot. Forests could take it amiss if their People were tugged around; this little thing in the bush wasn't much, but uprooting any of the People willy-nilly could upset a place. He shook off the thought; there was no point beating a downed man, and besides, it led down paths of thought about John he preferred to avoid. 'Courting trouble, you were, Jonas Ware,' he said instead. 'We'll need to put it back while there's still time to make peace.'

Jonas Ware looked at the ground. 'I – no doubt you are right, Mister Smith,' he said.

Jedediah looked at the man who hadn't dared ask for his help. He'd put a fey bush on his boundary and taken his chances rather than send to the smithy, where he could be overheard, and only when that hadn't worked . . . had he begged Franklin Thorpe to be the man to bring them, or had Franklin offered? A forester coming to complain of a talking bush somewhere in the woods would attract no attention whatsoever. Jedediah had to admit it was neatly done. He wasn't going to say that, though; if they hadn't been lucky enough to pick a bush with a small and stupid inhabitant, they might be dealing with two problems now instead of one.

Ten years ago, Jedediah would have scolded them roundly. Today, he looked at Tobias, who was crouching on his heels and butting his head against Peter's legs as if making conversation with his brother's knees, and sighed.

'Another time,' he said, 'ask Franklin Thorpe to come for us before you go digging up bushes. He won't mind. You ask him, you hear?'

Jonas looked at him with a tired light shining from eyes the depth and shade of Tobias'. 'Excuse me, Mister Smith,' he said. 'Sometimes – sometimes there is much to do, and I do not like to trouble men.'

'Never mind that,' Jedediah said. 'Now I'm here, we'll talk of why you really called me here. Let us speak plain now: you need to keep your boy out of the woods.'

Jonas looked uncertain as to whether to smile or cry. 'We do, but I – I do not know such a thing can be done,' he said. 'You are right, Mister Smith, but Toby – Toby has his ways, you know, he has his little ways. And for your fee, you see . . .'

Jedediah cleared his throat with a fierce blast of sound. 'I'll tell you what,' he said. 'It's such as we haven't tried before. Chance to learn. We'll try this and that, not charge you for the work. Just for the plain iron. Won't come to much. I'll send my Matthew to move the bush tomorrow, when young John isn't around to chatter of it.' The last thing he felt like doing was giving John a chance to converse with the bush; not here, not on this farm. 'He'll come by after. See if we can keep your boy home at night.'

John had scowled a little when Grandpa left him behind, but Matthew was well used to coaxing his son, and not above scattering some excess praise to get his attention, so fairly soon John started enjoying his woodland lesson. A Mackem knot involved plaiting twigs into a complex twist that would, at least in theory, entertain the People enough that if you passed through their land and left it behind they'd see you as a courteous visitor – though Matthew could be frustratingly cautious in how much success he promised with it, saying nothing more emphatic than, 'Well, I've never known it do harm, Johnny,' and 'It's done some good in times before now, at least when the trouble wasn't too great.' The air in Bellame woods was soft as cream and the silences came and went like gusts of wind, and it was an interesting background for a boy of John's tastes – and besides that, he got to lean his cheek against his father's shoulder and rest for quiet moments in the confident knowledge that Jedediah wasn't around to tell him to stop dawdling. John liked to take his pleasures where he could find them, including getting cuddles, and was too cheerful to waste his time with sulks when the offending party wasn't there to witness them. But that didn't mean he was forgetful, and when Jedediah reappeared with a tired-looking Franklin Thorpe in tow, he sat up straight and said with an air of haughty forgiveness, 'You may note, Grandpa, that I have not come to any harm or committed any foolishness when your back was turned. No doubt that will astonish you, but the fact speaks for itself.'

'Hush your plainting,' said Jedediah with a preoccupied air that disappointed John's hopes for a proper set-to. 'Matthew, listen now.'

Matthew gave John a surreptitious pat, but sat up with habitual obedience.

'The Porters aren't a long step from here,' said Jedediah. 'That boy Tobias Ware got lost today.'

'Oh dear,' said Matthew. He almost asked whether they should look for him, but there was a slight emphasis on the word *lost*.

'Yes,' said Jedediah. 'Unlucky. Lost. No one's fault.'

'Why are you talking so short, Grandpa?' said John. 'There's no one around to hear if you mean to say more than you're saying.'

Jedediah gave John a look that failed to subdue him, and turned back to Matthew. 'He's back now,' he said. 'Franklin Thorpe, I think we'll be done with you today. You can go. We'll just stop in on the Porters on our way home, see if Tobias happened to be down their way. I'll wager he went visiting them. That'll be where he was.'

'Oh.' Matthew was reticent in speech, but he was not slow on the uptake. Struggling to find words that reconciled his Christian duty to truth with the demands of his trade, he ventured, 'Oh, I see. I, well, I shall not dispute you, Dada. I was not there to see, of course.'

'Can I meet Tobias?' John asked, with hope undimmed by past experience. Almost nobody met Tobias except Franklin and Grandpa; the boy wasn't exactly hidden away, but he was said not to cope well outside his home. John had a natural curiosity to see everything and anything fey, and the fact that his elders were determined to shield him from all the really interesting examples frustrated him: he was surely supposed to be learning the trade, and even if he was only an apprentice, John was quite sure he was a clever one who could manage such sights.

'We'll to the Porters,' said Jedediah without turning his head. 'Good day to you, Franklin Thorpe.' As dismissals went, it was not the harshest Jedediah could give, and Franklin took the point.

'Good day to you, Mister Smith, Mister John,' he said. 'I am sure you will be proved right. See you, Matthew – Thursday, yes?' The two often went fishing for their Friday supper; neither had brothers or sisters, and Franklin considered Matthew's friendship not the least of Mister Smith's gifts to him.

'Wait a moment!' John protested. 'I thought you had some currants for me.'

'Oh,' said Franklin, turning. 'Indeed I do. I beg your pardon for my bad memory. I thank you for the reminder. Yes.'

John grabbed the currants before any further odd moods

could take the grown-ups. 'I don't know why you should all stare at me,' he said. 'I said nothing silly.'

Matthew patted John on the shoulder. 'Come along, Johnny,' he said. 'Maybe the Porters' little boys would like to meet you.'

The Porters were within walking distance, but the Smiths had left their horse and cart tethered at the other end of the woods, so there was nothing to do but go back for them and drive up Chalk Lane. Being shod every fortnight by way of practise for John had obliged Dobbs, the mare, to develop a philosophical nature, and all the Smiths had learned to handle horses around the age they'd learned to handle spoons, so between the resigned beast before the cart and the skilled drivers atop it, rides were usually peaceful affairs. But as the cart rolled along, Dobbs was skittish, shying at every gust on the path.

Chalk Lane was not unpleasant of a morning; the fields either side of them waved and shimmered as if giant fingers of wind were stroking the green grass, and the air was fresh and brisk as river water. Matthew concentrated on keeping Dobbs steady so they could finish the journey as quick as possible, while John scanned the white road for any sign of footprints.

'Dada,' he said after a while, 'Mikey Nobbs said he saw Black Hal last winter. He called him a devil dog.'

John spoke more in speculation than in fear of the infernal, but Matthew flinched. 'Johnny, do not say such words, not on this road.'

'But that's what I mean, Dada,' John insisted. 'I think some-one ought to tell Mister Nobbs he's a fey dog, or he'll get into trouble mixing them up.'

Jedediah was smoking his pipe, or rather, he was trying to draw some smoke from it; the wind kept puffing it out. The contest was not putting him in a good temper, so he merely said, 'Watch yourself, for pity's sake.'

Matthew confirmed his father's comment, albeit more gently. 'John, the kind friend who visits this road has his own ways, and folks who live near know to abide by them. We must all pay heed and take care.'

'I know, Dada,' said John. 'But I think it is interesting he burns the chalk, at least. Think how hot his feet must be! But you know, all the stories I heard, folks only talk about feeling the wind cold. You'd think they'd have felt some heat coming off Bla— from the kind friend. Since he's full of fire, you know.' He had seen Matthew's shoulders start to hunch up as he said the name, and it was quicker to use the preferred term than to listen to another explanation about respect and knowing one's limitations.

The boy's resistance to feeling overawed was something Matthew was secretly glad of, being a quality Matthew was not heavily endowed with himself, and he didn't like to suppress it too much. 'That is a thought for another time, but a good one,' he said. 'But perhaps we should not speak of our kind friend on his road, out of manners, eh, Johnny?'

'Heed your father,' Jedediah added. 'We've enough bluster up here without you adding to it.' It was, indeed, becoming a rough journey; the wind pressed harder and harder the longer you travelled down the road. It wasn't a stormy day: the clouds drifted above in no apparent hurry, and out at the horizon, trees put their heads together in an unshaken line. But up here, it blew hard enough to slap the shirt against your chest.

'One day,' John informed his grandfather, 'I shall be a master farrier and a great man, and you will have to listen to me talk instead of telling me to stop all the time.'

The Porters had been on good terms with the Wares for years, both families being agreeable, honest and of the opinion that if you had a few extra turnips or cheeses, it was only right to share them with your neighbours. And if it had been only Sukie Porter standing at the gate, the Porter homestead would have been a cheerful sight: it was a well-kept place, and Sukie Porter, who stood at the gate, was well kept too; her hair was still fair and showed remarkably little grey for a woman with two young boys to run after. Paul Porter had never been anything but a good husband to her, albeit a short-spoken one: his method of proposing had been to say, out of nowhere on a Sunday walk, 'Like to marry? I'll love you.' That was more or less the last time he'd talked of love, but he'd said 'Good cooking' over every meal, and 'Very fine' when she'd dressed for church on Sundays, and 'There now' at every worry she'd expressed, and he'd been a patient and gentle father to their boys.

Today, though, her hands were clasped in a gesture awkwardly close to wringing, and the reason was clear. She was speaking to two men the Smiths knew all too well.

Roger Groves, thickset and jovial, leaned against the gate with comfortably crossed arms. He was the Wares' landlord, a man who occupied that most dire space for his common neighbours: near grand, but not so near that you were beneath his notice. Some branch of his family led back through uncles and cousins to the Bellamy clan, but the Groveses were not folks of title and politics. They were owners of land, and collectors of rents, and within that sphere, they lived just as they pleased. Not being fully grand himself, Roger had enough shrewdness not to ape grand manners. Instead, he tended in the opposite direction: he could be as coarse as he liked, and he'd still be third or fourth cousin to the grand, and folks would just have to put up with it. Roger Groves was, by repute, a slightly less gripping landlord than the man who stood beside him, but the price of his patience was that you had to treat him as a gentleman even while he was scratching his arse at your kitchen table.

As to his companion . . . Jedediah needed a moment to make sure that nothing showed on his face. It was Ephraim Brady.

The Smiths were not easy folks to prey upon: they owed nobody rent and were masters of their trade, and if they hadn't cared about the lives of their fellows, Ephraim would have been easier for them to ignore.

But it was not in his nature to be ignored. There had been that incident in Stanford, a year ago now, when Magpie Tilly had grabbed his purse and made off with it. Everybody knew that Tilly wasn't clever; she'd been born out of kilter and had been sitting in fields chattering to the People, or thieving any shining object that took her eye, for fifty-odd years. How touched she'd been when she began life was anyone's guess; there were so many ways of being touched, from mild eccentricity to maddened frenzy, to, in at least one case Jedediah had encountered, growing a full head of feathers and ending every conversation with the suggestion that matters should be referred to 'our elders in the cloud-nooks'. You could never assume you knew about them all.

But Tilly was certainly touched enough, and her decades conversing with the People had made her more so. The Smiths should have been told of her years ago, and if they had been, they might have done something for her.

But nobody did. She was a nuisance and she hadn't kin or fortune, and her neighbours never quite bothered to do more than give her some spare crusts to live on. She didn't spend the coins she stole, just played with them, and mostly folks took them back and, according to their natures, shook a finger at her or kicked her in the ribs. But for that theft, a case was made to the judge that a known vagrant and robber had taken a respectable man's purse in broad daylight, and it was Ephraim Brady who made it.

Tilly was in a pauper's grave now. She had leaped from the gallows towards the bright, golden sun.

And these days it was known that scattered wits bought you no mercy if you robbed Ephraim Brady. He could walk into any village in the county in the knowledge that his purse was safe. If Tilly been a less touched woman, no doubt there would have been more outrage over it, but the first the Smiths heard of it was when Roger Groves joked in their hearing that his friend Ephraim Brady had made the magpie fly.

These, then, were the men Sukie Porter faltered before: her neighbours' landlord Roger Groves, who was grinning broader the more she fidgeted, and her own landlord Ephraim Brady, who stood rigid as a fence post and about as yielding, listening with merciless courtesy as she stammered. Coming as they were with the aim of appealing to the neighbours of Tobias Ware, the Smiths couldn't have chosen men they less wished to see.

'. . . of course, sirs, if you wish,' she was saying, 'only my Paul, my husband, sirs, and my boys are busy about the milling just now, so I do not know if . . .'

'Come now, Sukie,' said Roger, as if jollying her along. 'Surely your men can spare a little time for poor hagglers like me and my friend Ephraim here?'

Sukie flinched. 'Indeed, sirs,' she said. 'I . . .'

'*Mistress* Porter, oblige me, please,' said Ephraim. Ephraim Brady wasted words with scarcely more grace than he wasted money, and the clip in his voice sent Sukie's hands twining round each other as if each was trying to hide behind its fellow. There was a particular bite on the word 'Mistress' that made Jedediah give an extra shake of the reins to encourage Dobbs to close the gap between them. The Porters, like many village couples, had never quite got around to wedding in the church; they had lived together as man and wife for a long time and everyone common considered them married in the eyes of God – Who was, after all, not so unobservant as to miss their mutual devotion and faith – but the more doctrinal were inclined to regard such unions as lax. And Ephraim was doctrinal. He always had been, and had grown more so as he began, in his teens, the serious business of buying and selling. It had been a great financial advantage to him when it came to trading with church lands, and a fall from grace would have entailed a serious blow to his purse, but it was sincere for all that: if he looked at his books, Ephraim could no doubt find calculable proof of Divine favour. Jedediah described as him as having contracted with God for a life of gain in exchange for the leasehold on his soul, and while such impious sarcasms made Matthew nervous, it was certainly true that Ephraim did not expect the lax to prosper. And since it was possible to find laxity in almost everyone he turned his eyes upon, his own contributions to their downfall were evidently within the Divine will.

'Now then, Ephraim Brady,' said Jedediah as the cart pulled up. 'Interrupting your tenants about their work, are you? That's no way to get the profit made.' Jedediah had a general respect for all those who worked hard, but since hard work was no way to protect yourself from Ephraim, and since dragging rents out of those who'd had a bad year required only the labour of mis-placing your kindness, Jedediah made an exception for him, and took a certain pleasure in speaking slower than necessary when addressing him, just to waste a little more of his time.

'Good day, Mister Smith,' said Ephraim. The matter of the Sheppards had clearly rankled with him, but there had been nothing he could do about it: a man must be free to set his own prices and do what he liked with his own profits, or else how was someone like Brady to thrive? So he had, for once, been forced to swallow a defeat. No one doubted that he disliked the taste of it, but he made a point of speaking with frigid courtesy to everyone higher than a tenant; his tone to Jedediah now was terse, proper, frozen with dislike. 'Mister Matthew Smith, good day to you.'

'G-good day, Mister Brady,' Matthew said awkwardly. He and Ephraim were much the same age, and might have been playmates as children if Ephraim had ever had much inclination to play. In their very early years, though, before Ephraim had learned to guard his tongue, he had been disputatious in contests, and prone to accusing Matthew of thinking himself

better than others because he was the farrier's son. This charge
upset Matthew quite a bit at the age of four, when he felt unable
to deny that he'd rather have the home and parents he did than
anyone else's, and it upset him still more after his mother died,
when he lived his days in the smithy under his father's patient
eye, learning and learning as hard as he could to fill up the great
aching gaps in his heart, and resting upon his growing skill and
usefulness as a solid comfort. To be 'Mistered' instead of called
by your Christian name, by a man who could remember you
sucking your thumb, was a truly uncomfortable experience,
but Matthew could think of nothing to do about it except be
polite in return; after all, pride was a sin, and it was true, he was
glad to be the farrier's son. 'How do you today?'

'I have work to attend to,' Ephraim said, making no attempt
to hide his displeasure at its interruption. 'Mister Roger Groves
here wishes to view the property.'

'Been trying to buy it for years,' said Roger Groves with
expansive enjoyment. 'Right on my rounds, this place, convenient as you like. The mean bastard won't sell it. You know,
it's taken me this long just to get a look round the place?'

'You are pleased to joke,' said Ephraim without expression. 'I
am glad to let you see. I doubt we can agree a price that would
content both of us, but you may view if you wish.'

Sukie Porter covered her mouth. When properties changed
owners, tenants did not always go with them, and finding
another mill was no easy prospect. It would not be beyond
Ephraim Brady to frighten his tenants with the possibility of a
sale just to stop any murmurs when their rents went up next
quarter-day, and it certainly wasn't beyond Roger Groves to

take time out of his day just to enjoy the sight of a good wife biting her lip. That would explain why they were wasting time dallying by the road instead of just marching into the property.

'Well, Mistress Porter,' said Jedediah. Ordinarily he exercised the fairy-smith's privilege of calling everyone, grand or common, by their full name, but he was damned if he wouldn't be civil to this poor woman being badger-baited at her own gate. 'I wish only a quick word with you or your man, if you please. Perhaps Ephraim Brady and Roger Groves might walk in while I speak with you.'

Roger Groves looked a little disappointed at the game ending so soon, but he shrugged, hawked onto the ground, and sauntered in, Ephraim Brady walking beside him on steady legs that could match any man's stride to perfection. 'Pleasure to talk to you, Sukie,' Groves said. 'Always good to see a woman obliging to her man. That's how you get fine sons, eh?'

He gave a bark of laughter, and Sukie a nervous smile; Ephraim, however, didn't stop walking, and his stiff back gave no indication that he'd heard. There was no gain in rising to the gibes of wealthy men, and Sukie hadn't been the only target of that one. Ephraim had made a careful marriage, but had no children to his name. And however little he liked it now, it was a contract he couldn't break: they'd been married in a church, and neither Ephraim's business dealings with the clergy nor his own treaty with the Deity would have allowed him to prosper as a publicly divorced man. He did not speak of the subject, but as the years wore on, he had become less and less willing to be reminded that he had a wife living, eating at his board and sheltering under his roof and yielding no return of heirs on the investment. Nobody of less weight than Roger Groves joked about getting sons around Ephraim Brady.

There was a long, miserable silence.

'Never you fret, Mistress Porter,' said Matthew, having rather an anguishing wrestle between his compunction and his shyness. 'I'm sure all may be well.'

'Thank you, Mister Smith,' Sukie said to her shoes.

'The man's all talk and roar,' said Jedediah. 'Nothing better to do than come and trouble folks. Put it out of your mind, Sukie Porter. Now, we have just a word for you. You know the Wares, of course?'

'Oh,' said Sukie, struggling to obey Jedediah's instruction to put the thought of terrifying landlords out of mind. 'Yes. I hope they are well?'

'Well enough,' said Jedediah. 'That boy of theirs, Tobias, you know him?'

'Yes, indeed,' said Sukie; having trouble getting off the subject of Roger Groves, she cast her eyes around. A sleek-striped cat with a particularly cynical cast of countenance was stalking past, and she turned aside and lifted it up, fondling its ears and crooning a soft, shushing noise to it.

John, who liked cats, reached out a hand for it to sniff, and Jedediah said, 'You have coneys about your place, I suppose? Now and then?'

The cat gave a little spitting *prrt* sound, apparently scorning John's friendship, and Sukie said, 'Well, not so many. We have Puss, you see, we have him to hunt for us.'

'Now and again, though,' Jedediah persisted. 'I'm sure. Tobias Ware was visiting you lately, I'm sure he was.' Imposing this tale on the Porters was necessary if they were to avoid risking Tobias' neck, but the fact that he was doing it just when Sukie Porter had her own troubles to worry about nettled Jedediah's conscience and made his voice rather harsher. 'Caught a coney last night. He'll have caught it here, I reckon, going after those fine cabbages and turnips you grow, yes? I'm sure you saw him this morning.'

Sukie Porter was not a woman who could afford to offend anyone. 'Oh,' she said, churning her fingers through the cat's plush stripes. 'I – I suppose so.'

'Thought so,' said Jedediah. 'Saw him going after a coney in your garden. Helpful of him. Not a talker, that boy, couldn't ask if he could take it home for the family pot, but you wouldn't have minded. Glad to help a neighbour, I'm sure.'

Sukie's fingers were evidently working Puss' fur more for her own comfort than the cat's, as it gave a displeased snarl and twisted itself down to the ground. 'I – I know I am glad to help a neighbour,' said Sukie.

'Not,' said Matthew, who really couldn't endure the white look on her face, 'that any man is likely to ask. Only we may say you have coneys here? Or that you cannot swear that you never have coneys, Mistress Porter?'

His voice was gentle; the only woman in the world, as far as he was concerned, was his beloved Janet, but every now and again bystanders entertained themselves by speculating as to which of his female customers Matthew Smith might be stepping out with, speaking so soft to them as he did. There had been an incident last month when young Abbie Price was affrighted by the People's work in her kitchen – they had cleaned it up handily, but unfortunately had also tidied up the bread by unpicking it one crumb at a time and rearranging it in an image of her own face – and her husband had ended up wanting to fight Matthew. There really had been nothing between Matthew and Abbie – he had only meant to reassure her that she needn't take the image too seriously, as it was probably one of those times when the People took a fancy to making themselves useful and doing folks' work for them, and the fact that the bread-icon was so terrifyingly unflattering would be more to do with the People's notions of what a face should look like than any aspersion on her beauty. To Matthew's profound dismay, Thomas Price challenged him to a fistfight one Sunday after church on account of those comforting remarks. Matthew was head and shoulders taller than Thomas, and had a terror of hurting the small; he would have much preferred to let himself be knocked down, but as Jedediah had known him a long time and pre-emptively banned such a measure, he was forced to block punch after punch until Thomas grew tired enough to listen to explanations. Since Matthew did not find it easy to consider himself handsome, despite Janet's festoons of praise on the subject, he had not drawn from this the lesson to avoid speaking tenderly to women.

Perhaps fortunately for her marriage, if not for her present happiness, Sukie was too distraught to hear anything more in Matthew's tone than reassurance. 'I certainly cannot say there are never coneys here,' she said. 'At least not before Puss catches them. And Puss must sleep sometimes.'

'That is good to hear,' said Matthew, warmly enough that Jedediah gave him a glance: Roger Groves and Ephraim Brady were heading back their way, and the last thing needed was for either of them to get the notion that Matthew was flirting with other men's wives.

Sukie Porter swallowed. 'Well,' she said, 'you must give my best to the Wares, and to Tobias.'

'Tobias Ware?' said Roger Groves. 'Has that idiot of mine been bothering folks your way?'

'Dada, is Tobias Ware an idiot?' John demanded. If he was, John thought, he'd rather like to meet him. John had a fondness for the kind of folks Matthew referred to as 'not clever', which the older Smiths tried to consider the sign of a caring temper, rather than any sense of kinship.

'Tobias Ware's been giving no trouble to anyone,' Jedediah told Roger Groves, giving him a look that most other men would have felt scrape against their skin. It might be just a landlord's way of talking, but Tobias wasn't Roger's possession. Folks spoke of the touched, sometimes, as if they were livestock. Jedediah's own mother had been somewhat touched – nothing like Tobias, but what you might call innocent-minded, if you had manners and didn't know her well enough to describe the shades and subtleties of her confusion – but his anger wasn't entirely personal. Or at least, taking it personally was a farrier's job, whether it touched his kin or not. He had never liked such talk, and he liked it even less after steering the boy back home and seeing the look of miserable love on his father's face. It was easy enough to laugh at Tobias when he was just a rumour, an oddity you vaguely knew was living under some poorer man's care. Jedediah had felt tired after just a few minutes of trying to direct the boy without frightening him; what it must be like to care for him every day was quite the thought, and what it must be like to be him was something he couldn't imagine. But the boy was something to himself; he must have been. He couldn't speak what was in his heart, but that didn't mean he didn't have one. Jedediah thought of that bright smile, that happy bounce as Tobias heard someone talk of his brothers.

*That idiot of mine.* Jedediah reminded himself that it wasn't politic to box the ears of wealthy men.

'No, no,' said Matthew, in greater haste than he intended. 'He just has his little ways, that's all.'

'His ways with other men's game, I hear,' Roger said, laughing heartily as he said it.

The Smith men went still. Neither of them looked at the other.

'I wouldn't listen to gossip too hard if I were you, Roger Groves,' said Jedediah. His voice was careful. 'Why, if you listen to gossip, you'd think my Matthew was meddling with Thomas Price's wife.'

Ephraim Brady remained impassive — marriage in general was an unwelcome subject with him — but Roger gave a shout of laughter. 'Oh, I heard that story,' he said. 'Folks laughed over it as far as Grenmere. Silliest fight I ever heard of. Really, Jedediah, you ought at least to teach your son to throw a punch if he's going to go casting eyes at pretty girls.'

'It was much talked of, yes,' said Jedediah, with a mildness any who knew him well would recognise as the mark of bitter antagonism. 'I suppose we must live to be laughed at.'

'Well,' said Roger, measuring amusement in his voice, 'sons are what they are, I suppose. Idiots after game, or walking backwards through a fight, or – hey now, how's that grandson of yours since his mother took the People's touch? Any uncanniness on him, now? That'd be a trouble for a farrier all right.' He grinned, baring teeth of a bold, uneven yellow.

John felt a moment of giddiness, not entirely due to his father swinging him right off his feet and bundling him into the cart.

'Come along, Johnny,' said Matthew. He spoke with a slight tremor in his voice: Janet's little difficulty was not something to be discussed – or at least, not in front of the Smiths – and they had never talked of its implications in front of Johnny himself. Nobody had, until this moment.

There was a silence, longer than it should have been. Matthew's hand tightened on John's shoulder.

'John is everything he should be,' said Jedediah in a voice that would have frozen mead. John was too astonished at the compliment to think of a retort of his own to add. Grandpa had never said anything that nice about him in his entire life.

## CHAPTER 3

When John was born, they gave him an extravagantly sensible name, but by that time, the damage – if there was damage – was done.

It wasn't really his mother's fault. Janet was an affectionate woman who'd fight a wolf for her children if need be, and the worst you could really say of her was that she was fanciful. And neither Matthew nor Jedediah ever blamed her; Matthew adored her, and Jedediah allowed no one to criticise 'the girl' in his presence. The incident was just one of those things. Folks aren't always sensible. But once one of those things happens, even fairy-smiths' power is limited. You just have to hope it goes far enough.

Matthew had fallen in love with Janet the moment he saw her. He had been called to the dairy of Middle Latchton because something had developed a habit of getting into the creamery and turning things a range of startling colours. Nobody minded the churns themselves being decorated, but their contents were another matter: you cannot sell blue butter, and the visitor had a very decided preference in that direction. Dogs had been set, guards had stood over the door, and all that anyone could report was a shimmer of light that skimmed up through the brass keyhole, and a little voice piping through the door, a sweet, strange tune along the theme that, 'Blue is blue, so blue is blue.'

That day, Matthew Smith, twenty years old and big as a hill, eyes downcast when he passed a stranger and a sack of iron on his back, walked the three miles from Gyrford to Middle Latchton, his mind mostly on the subject of colours. Regular blacksmiths used cold iron to keep the People out, but fairysmiths dealt in alloy and tint, twist and compound, and since the little visitor was intransigent in favour of blue, Matthew wondered all the way down the road whether a blue sheen on the metal of a new lock would make the visitor decide that the dairy was now blue enough. Or would that just act like a lure to a fish, a glint of colour it wouldn't be able to resist? From reports he'd heard, he suspected the latter was more likely: the People could be volatile, and a frenzy of blue from an over-excited visitor was not the kind of thing a good farrier asked his customer to cope with. At least blue milk could be thrown away, whereas a blue village hall or a blue sexton would be a permanent nuisance.

But in that case, should he choose another compound, maybe an orange sheen, the antonym of blue? Matthew did not consider himself artistic, though he had a deep love of music, a decorative knack with wrought iron, and a fondness for fine embroidery that he kept to himself for fear of looking unmanly. These, though, he mostly felt were a tribute to the beauty of the world rather than anything in himself; he had that keenness of admiration for those he *did* consider artistic that suggests a pulse of responsive talent in a man's soul. But artistic or not, you do not become a fairy-smith unless you have a decent grounding in colour and iconography, and Matthew could identify a colour's complement with impeccable precision. An orange-tinged lock might repel the visitor, he reflected, but then, it might also enrage them, or send them shrieking into the bell tower or the cow barns or some other even less convenient location, and then Middle Latchton would have a bigger problem on its hands than just changing a lock: the People sometimes took it hard when they decided you were ungrateful for a favour. No, it was probably safer to leave colour of it when the visitor was this enamoured. Matthew was fond of blue himself; a blue sky or a blue flower after the rippling orange glow of the forge all day was like washing his face in cool water. Perhaps he was not the right man to involve himself in the visitor's predilections anyway.

It was while his thoughts were running along these shades that he found himself approaching the Middle Latchton creamery, and there, at the door, sat a girl who made him stop so suddenly that the sack clattered against his back. Janet Patmore was the dairyman's daughter and had been set there to watch for the coming fairy-smith, but at the sight of her, such a practical explanation didn't occur to Matthew: his attention caught and snagged and tangled irrevocably round the cream-skinned, brown-curled girl with the bluest of eyes, eyes so utterly blue it was as if his own thoughts had leaped from his head to look back at him from her pretty face.

Janet was not, in fact, keeping watch for him, although she

was supposed to be; she had set her heart on a walk through the meadows that morning and was out of temper to be put to something so dull. She had sat sullenly on a stool in front of the door and prepared herself to meet this coming smith with a distant hauteur that she had recently learned about in a romantic poem her cousin Bessy had taught her, and which Janet had been rather hoping for an opportunity to try out. It had been a long wait, though: Janet's mother Elizabeth was an active, housewifely woman who finished her chores fast and could never relax unless everything was running slightly ahead, and Janet had been shooed out the door well before anybody but Elizabeth Patmore could possibly have thought it necessary. As a result, Janet had sat on her stool practising elegant arrogance and languid dismissals until her mind had wandered.

It's rather hard to stay interested in pretending to dismiss everything – you end up with nothing much left to think about – and by the time Janet had dismissed the cows, the door, the beech tree growing beside the dairy and a passing blackbird, she had started to move on to other fancies. There were daisies growing in the verge beside the dairy, and with no one around to call her a baby, Janet had gathered a bunch, wove them together with some dandelion clocks – she had clever fingers, as her mother would admit, no matter how silly her head might be – and created for herself a limp and delicate crown. Humming a little tune of coronation, Janet laid the diadem on her head, and took to nodding this way and that, graciously admitting the previously dismissed blackbird to her presence.

Of a sudden, though, the little bird dashed up from the ground in a burst of feathers and fluster, and Janet turned in shock to see what had frightened it: a big man in hobnail boots who stood staring at her without saying a word.

The dandelion clocks had shed their fluff. Matthew saw the bright-eyed girl, flowers melted across her hair, and his heart gave a little thump.

'I'm Matthew Smith about the locks, Miss?' he said. It was a plain statement, but it came out as a question because there were other things he was aching to ask her.

His boots were dusty, but his face was handsome, and Janet wasn't quite sure which to notice. She lifted up her chin, remembering that she had meant to practise her hauteur, and, with an attempt at fine carelessness, said, 'Ah yes, I believe my father is expecting you.'

'A-are you Miss Patmore, then?' said Matthew, feeling that he'd give more or less anything to hear her first name, to watch her lips shape the sounds of it. Her pose had impressed him: she struck him as a spirit set apart. But those blue eyes, and the down strewn across her head as if she'd just woken in a tumbled feather bed, seemed in that moment almost shockingly intimate. Matthew was a virtuous man, on the whole, but the airy manners and spilling hair together had well and truly overthrown him.

'I am Miss Patmore,' said Janet, trying an arch of her eyebrows.

'I'm Matthew Smith,' said Matthew. He wasn't sure how else to offer himself.

'Yes, you said,' said Janet, suddenly losing interest in the game. If a man just kept greeting her politely, there wasn't much she could dismiss, and really it was rather nice to be looked at with such admiration. Perhaps if Matthew had been an ill-favoured lad it might have gone worse for him, but she was noticing more and more that he had a fine face, and his eyes were more intelligent than his actions just at that moment.

'Well, Dada will be pleased to see you, we've had blue milk for a week and he's started talking every night about what kind of a world it is when a man can't even have his milk left alone, and it's really not very cheerful. Not that I don't sympathise, of course,' she added, 'because we do need our milk for the butter and such, but Dada does seem to be taking it to heart. It was the same when we had a rat trapped in the kitchen and we couldn't find it for days, and it chewed all the way through the wainscotting after we sent the dog in after it. Dada talked all the next day about how he'd have been only too happy to let the – well, I won't say what he called it, but to let the *certain* thing out through the door without it chewing good honest wainscotting to pieces. So I do hope your lock will do the trick – though of course,' Janet reflected, remembering that she'd decided to be elegant today, 'we may call upon your services again if it does not.'

'I – I'd be happy to do anything to oblige,' Matthew said. 'If – if only you'll tell me your name. '

Janet, seeing that neither her chatter nor her lady game had stopped this tall young man from staring at her with open fascination, dropped both and looked at him for a long moment. He looked back at her. Matthew had the sense that he was gaping, and maybe he was, but he was also listening. Janet had seen her conversation deter more than one young swain, and it wasn't happening here. The many things she had to say were flowing past Matthew at speed, as if she were shaping her thoughts on the air, and he felt there was something lovely in it: it was like air he could move through, air he could breathe in. Also she was sparing him from having to find something long-winded to say himself, and the pleasure of being there, just standing there with this girl talking to him so free and vivid, overcame his shyness enough that he smiled. Matthew's smile was very sweet, when it could be brought out, and his eyes were green and dappled and alight, and they were entirely for this girl sitting on the stool, and it was that unwavering gaze, that interest set upon something other than her affectation of the moment, that started to pull her heart towards his.

It is not surprising news that a romantic girl might spur an enchanted man to speech, and Matthew's heart was quickly so full that he proposed out of sheer awkwardness. A few months after meeting her, there came an afternoon when Janet wound haws into her hair and talked with animation about the bright tips of gold on the edges of the clouds, and the desire to have her for his own possessed him so thoroughly that he simply couldn't think of anything else to say.

'I do love it when the clouds are burnished so,' said Janet, who in Matthew's gentle company was becoming more relaxed and occasionally able to enthuse about something without striking an attitude. 'I feel like I've never seen such pure light.'

'I – I love you,' said Matthew. He hadn't meant to be so blunt, but he had to say something, and if he didn't get this off his chest, he might never find words for anything ever again. 'I love you, Janet. Will you marry me? Please?' he added, worried that he wasn't asking right; there ought to be fine words for a laughing, talking, be-petalled girl such as this, but he wasn't finding them. 'I swear I'll be a good man to you all my days. You are the most beautiful girl in the world, and the brightest and the best, and if you marry me I'll do all I can to make you happy, and – and—'

He stopped. Janet's face was glowing more brilliant than the sky.

'I am sorry,' he said. 'Should I stop talking and let you answer?'

Janet flung herself into his arms and kissed him, and Matthew's world spun, and a little while later he pulled away long enough to say in a slightly slurred murmur, 'Janet, but does this mean you will?'

So Matthew was quickly betrothed, and Jedediah said nothing worse than, 'Well, if she's what you like . . .' This did not hurt Matthew's feelings: his father's fondness for him, while deep, had always been more a matter of deeds than words. Since the death of his wife, Jedediah had settled down to life with a stiff resolve that impressed the village and discouraged the glad eye of even the most flirtatious of girls, even for such a prize as the master smith of Gyrford. He raised his only son with unbending dedication for his welfare and gave no indication that he'd ever heard of speaking soft to anyone, but while he'd never felt able to remarry himself, he didn't believe in putting obstacles in the way of a genuinely fond couple. Life was hard, and you couldn't get away with being a fool, but that didn't mean fathers should be making it harder than it had to be.

He thought Janet a little silly, but she had some wits when she chose to use them, and she wasn't hard-headed enough to be marrying for position or hard-hearted enough to be leading Matthew a dance. Jedediah didn't reckon it was his job to withhold his blessing if the boy really wanted her. Terse assent was all Matthew had expected, and he was so grateful for it that he told Jedediah he was the best of fathers, and Jedediah scowled and told him to get on with his work.

There was no suggestion of setting up a new household: the smith's cottage and the smithy were part of the same establishment – had to be, for no good farrier strays too far from his eternal-burning forge – and both the practicality and the prestige made it impossible that Matthew should live anywhere else. A fairy-smith not living in the smith house would be like the parson preaching his sermons in the alehouse: unorthodox to the point of blasphemy, and liable to provoke riotous thinking in those who depended upon such men to be a steadying influence. In theory, Jedediah might have moved out, but Matthew was too dutiful to suggest it – indeed, the notion of home without Jedediah's pensive frown at the dinner table made him rather nervous – and Janet, on the day when they were discussing future arrangements, was having one of her angelic days and professed herself uplifted by the thought of being a prop to the dear old man. (Jedediah was, at that point, all of two-and-forty, but to be fair to Janet, elder farriers hold the common right to talk to anyone like a naughty child, and the venerable Jedediah was not the most restrained elder farrier in history when it came to exercising that right.)

The dear old man, meanwhile, reminded himself that a man

should be fond of his wife and that was what mattered, and determined to make the best of things with this new daughter-in-law — or, as he referred to her in his less patient moments, 'that girl of his'. And undoubtedly she made Matthew happy, for which Jedediah could forgive a lot. She wasn't a bad mid-wife either, which was fortunate: living at the centre of the village in a house anybody could knock awake at any hour, it was the custom for a farrier's lady to learn how to ease a child-bed, and babies being particular darlings of the People, it was always felt safest if you had the luck to be attended by a woman of iron. Janet was not exactly the implacable pillar such a phrase suggested; she was, though, one of those mortals who can find drama in the snap of a daisy-stem but face a real crisis with steady hands. She quickly proved more popular with the women of the village than Jedediah had expected, which he took largely as a confirmation of his long-cherished belief that Matthew was a sensible lad whose heart would never really lead him wrong. It was only her more domestic virtues that were at fault — but that is an 'only' easier to overlook in one with whom you don't share your board.

Janet could cook more dishes than either of the Smith men, but when Jedediah or Matthew boiled eggs, they boiled them well. Janet's pies had a tendency to be served with their ornate edges coming unrolled and a scattering of scraped-off soot spangling their domes; her vegetables were grown with tender love while her pottages condemned them to a pauper's grave; her soups and stews were distinguished from each other in name only, and her baked apples more often ended up consumed by the compost heap than by her menfolk. She could keep a room clean enough, for her mother had drilled her from an early age, but she had a tendency to pile up furniture and clamber to the top to declaim the latest poem; she could knit warm enough clothes, if you didn't mind a spider-trail of ladders; she could even embroider, in her way. This last was the only time Matthew had truly struggled to indulge her: Janet was fond of embroidering grand animals, wolves and hawks and griffins, but lacking the patience to compose them in full, had a tendency to use her thread to sketch them in outline and then fill in the shapes however seemed best at the time. While Matthew saw it as a sign of her higher nature, and perhaps a mind that saw things too vivid for thread to capture, it would have been too much for his father to see such tangled creatures laid alongside his lost wife's neat stitching, so Matthew always found other, more important uses for them.

Jedediah made no open comment on these vagaries at first, merely looking at the upside-down chairs and the dishevelled pastry with single and expressive grunts. By the birth of his first grandchild, however, he had grown enough used to Janet, and enough able to approve of her as a mother, if not as a housekeeper, to feel able to relax into some franker expressions of his opinion. Finding himself attached to the little girl with an affection that surprised his customers somewhat, and Matthew not at all, he took to calling her Annie Molly – a name which, to Janet's great annoyance, Anemone answered to with perfect willingness. He was also entirely on the child's side, and if she ever got under her mother's feet, Jedediah was inclined to say, 'Let her be. The Lord knows we're resigned to your cooking now.'

Celandine and Vervain followed, a pair of twins Jedediah

humoured under the names Andie and Fannie, revising the nickname of his eldest granddaughter to plain Molly to avoid confusion, and Matthew and Janet remained as much in love as ever. If Jedediah was partisan towards the children, Janet stayed fascinating to Matthew. Children added flesh to her hips and stretch marks to her belly, but as Matthew caressed her with uncritical passion, Janet decided she would regard the marks as variegation, like the streaks that bloom on a crocus petal come spring. Every girl likes reassurance, though, so she told Matthew of this idea, and Matthew felt himself to be in a dell of pleasure, shaking his head in bemused satisfaction that he had married a woman with such a remarkable mind.

Within the home, then, matters were domestic enough; Janet and Jedediah might have quarrelled without Matthew's peaceable presence between them, but as it was, everyone rubbed along. Janet did have the spirit for a good quarrel, though, and it was thanks to this that their only son ended up with such a workaday name.

Really, it was the Tauntons who started it. The Patmores were decent folk, but Janet was possessed of two unfortunate cousins: Michael and Adam Taunton, who were twins, as like as two chestnuts and as ill-suited to each other's company as any two men living. It's an unfortunate truth that we don't always get along with people exactly like ourselves, especially when they share our faults. Adam and Michael Taunton were both stubborn, high-handed, and incapable of believing that they'd ever lost an argument.

The incident would never have happened, and John would

have been nothing to worry about, if only the Tauntons' father had made a will. Benjamin Taunton had been an absent-minded man who paid less and less attention to his sons the more they quarrelled, and when he died intestate, his land fell to common custom and passed on to the oldest son. This was Adam, by twelve minutes – quite a big enough margin to justify the inheritance in his eyes. Michael, however, was equally determined that their father had always meant to divide the property, and could argue his case with equal righteousness: Benjamin had never said anything to contradict the notion, never having said anything of his intentions at all. These being their relative opinions, they had a bone of contention to worry between them until one or both of them died.

Michael stayed on the land and worked it; to leave would have been to admit defeat. But when Adam told Michael to plough from left to right, Michael ploughed from right to left, and when Michael told Adam the white cow needed a drench, Adam would call in a neighbour just for a second opinion, and then when the neighbour agreed that Michael's plan of a herbal draught was a good one, Adam would inflict a black draught on the animal just to show that he was his own man. Farms do not prosper under such circumstances, and the Taunton brothers considered themselves most unlucky souls.

All of which would have been the common troubles of fallible mortals, but the Taunton farm also possessed something uncanny: a circle of oaks in which the People danced. On certain nights, shrieks of delight and the sound of clattering cymbals could be heard, and the odd neighbour swore they'd seen little men dancing in a circle, not so much holding hands as tangled together at the wrists like clumps of bindweed. The occasional cat disappeared after hunting squirrels up the oak trees, and old Barney Hyde was much put out when his prize sheepdog wandered into the circle and a few weeks later gave birth to a litter of two-headed puppies with voices like screech owls and silver, unblinking eyes; the creatures were useless for herding and all had to be drowned, and the dog moped for weeks and chewed up Barney's boots.

The Tauntons weren't stupid, though — or at least, not *that* stupid. They knew perfectly well that felling the People's trees was only inviting vengeful spirits to step out of their circle and make trouble. A few years before Matthew had met their pretty cousin, they had come into the smithy to ask Jedediah for assistance.

'We'll have them felled,' said Adam, giving Michael a glare intended to be silencing.

'I say no need,' said Michael, who had come along, he was glad for everyone to know, to make sure there was no double-dealing from his rogue of a brother. 'I say we iron the ground around and they'll stay within.'

Adam turned and glared at him. 'Do you speak for the farm, Michael Taunton?'

'Do you provoke the People just to spite me?' Michael flashed back.

'Do you speak for the People now too? I say again, who owns the farm?'

When the Taunton brothers got to arguing they could go on all day, having an evenly matched rhythm of speech that could swing from insult to insult as regular as a treadle.

Jedediah did not feel called upon to put up with such goings-on in his smithy. 'You are neither of you farriers, nor wise men,' he snapped. 'I shall decide, and you shall abide, or find your-selves another fairy-smith.' Since no other fairy-smiths were to be had within thirty miles, this was only a way of putting his foot down. For a moment, the Tauntons were united in offence against him, but in this imperfect world such happy unities were not made to last, and by the time Jedediah came to tackle the place, they were on the outs again.

To deal with a grove, you must first place iron bands around the trees, and fell them only after they are shackled. This will hold for a while, but iron rusts and must be maintained. If you can keep the People out of the grove for seven years and seven days, they generally take the point, but if you let the iron fail before then, you can expect worse than thorns in your bed and blood in your porridge: you can expect the People after you with all the fury of a stolen home, and they will seize you so thoroughly that it's a matter of priestly speculation whether even your soul will be able to escape to Heaven. Certainly your body is unlikely to be found, at least in any form your own mother would recognise.

Jedediah therefore shackled the trunks with care and super-vised as Adam did the felling. Ordinarily he would have felled them himself, but he'd burned his hand on one of Janet's more exuberant pies the previous night, and wasn't about to break his blisters for such a tiresome customer. The axe whistled through the air with a sound too shrieking; the blade stuck in the wood and creaked too loud and too deep as Adam sweated to work it out; the rush of air as the trees fell was too much like the sound of a sob. Adam chopped and tugged and laboured in silence. When he finished the felling, he looked at Jedediah for a long moment and said, 'If my lazy brother would help, this would have been done the sooner,' and that was the last time he spoke of that day, ever.

For a few years, the shackles held. Matthew and Janet lived happily, raising their children and quietly hoping that the next would be a son, flowers though their little girls undoubtedly were. But the Taunton farm struggled under its two owners: quarrelling is a luxury that a farm with only two men to work it cannot afford. Weeds crept in from the verges and calves were born dead when each brother insisted it was the other's job to go and attend a difficult labour, and there was even the autumn when some fungus got into one of the fields and several families suffered ghastly visions with their bread before anybody realised what was going on and demanded their money back.

None of this had anything to do with the stump circle. If the People are displeased, they can wreak plenty of havoc with your land, but this, as Jedediah observed, was just a case of bad farming. Calves born with eyes all down the ridge of their spines, cattle leaping fences to climb trees, ears of wheat fruiting with red towers of lolling tongues rather than good yellow grain: *those* were signs that the People were at work. The fungus was unlucky, but messy fields and neglected stock were entirely the fault of mortal men and nothing else.

'They could have left the trees alone if they were only going to keep quarrelling about them once they were down,' Janet said. 'Anemone, your sisters are climbing on the chairs. Go and help them up or help them down, one or the other.'

'I heard Walter Stryde say they blame the circle,' Matthew said, quietly lifting the twins down to safety.

'No,' said Jedediah, a drawn-out, final syllable. 'Those rings will hold a little longer. And if they wear, they should speak to us.'

'Walt said they say the job was money wasted and money robbed.'

'Walter Stryde chatters like a jay,' said Jedediah. Foolish folk said foolish things and you'd never get on in life if you cared about all of them, but he was growing thoroughly tired of the whole Taunton nuisance.

'Well, I like that!' said Janet. 'And them running their own farm to ruin and blaming my family for their own mistakes! I'll tell them what I think, that's what I'll do.'

'Don't worry yourself,' Matthew said, taking her hand.

'Worried, I am not. Angry is what I am. The two of them are born liars and fools and the world should know it.'

'Take your sisters off to bed, dearie, I'll be up to tuck you in,' Matthew told Anemone, giving her a kiss on the top of the head; preferring not to take sides regarding the girls' names, he usually addressed his daughters as 'dearie' when Jedediah and Janet were both in the room. 'Janet love, silly folks aren't worth your care. The world knows the Taunton men are no farmers.' He appreciated her loyalty – it was nice to have a wife who got angry on your behalf, especially when you were not very good at being angry yourself – but the Tauntons were not the men to take a scolding from a woman quietly, and if they carried the quarrel back to the smithy, there was the alarming chance he'd have to start quarrelling himself.

'Well, the world should know they are worse than that,' said Janet.

'Let them look for other farriers if they find us so dishonest,' said Jedediah, his voice a deep rumble like the rattle of an old bridge. 'Those shackles will need repair a year-odd from now, and then we'll see if the Smith family are so low in their eyes.'

Janet did, in fact, seek out her cousins the next day to give them a piece of her mind. She encountered one of them in the lane, carting a load of hay along with a sullen face, and hailed him at once: 'And when that horse of yours needs shoeing, cousin, will you say your new fine smiths are robbers too?'

'Go home, Janet,' returned the cousin.

'You and your brother have been slandering my Matthew's name, and you deserve every piece of your misfortune for it!' Janet shouted, causing the horse to shy a little as she ran after the cart in pursuit of her offending relation.

'If your Matthew cannot speak for himself and sends his wife to do it, you married a fine man,' came the snapped reply from atop the driving seat. In fact, the complaints had been almost entirely against Jedediah, but it was Matthew Janet adored, and if she was going to bring him into it, the Tauntons were not the men to leave him out.

'My Matthew is a finer man than the two of you together and ten more!' Janet yelled. It was dawning on her that she might indeed be exposing Matthew to accusations of hiding behind her skirts, and her voice was a little too tearful to carry much weight. Of course Matthew stayed out of quarrels: that was because he had too beautiful a nature to stoop to them, but men so low as her cousins would certainly not see the manliness of being above petty strife.

'Hah,' answered her cousin. 'Your Matthew is welcome to you, girl, and your pack of girls with you, Nettle and Dockleaf and whatever you call them.' Janet was sensitive on the subject of her girls' names and the family knew it. 'You tell him when he can hammer out a straight deal or a straight poker, then honest men will call upon him for business.'

Pricked on the raw, Janet hurled the irrevocable insult that most folks had better sense than to commit. 'You are as bad as your brother!' It was probably Michael she was talking to, but she wasn't entirely sure. Janet had a moment of doubt as to whether the accusation would stick on that account, and then, fired by a sense of injury to her whole beloved household, she grasped that confusion as an inspiration. 'Michael, Adam, I cannot say who you are! You are just alike and every bit as bad, and one of you would be two too many! No wonder you do so badly! I cannot tell one knave from another!'

'Out of my way, woman!' shouted probably-Michael, and swung his whip in her direction. It missed her, fortunately – she wasn't actually in his way and he had already overtaken her – but his face was thunderous and he gave the horse a vicious swipe that sent it cantering down the road in bewildered alarm, leaving Janet shouting names after him.

It might not have been Janet who put the idea in Michael's head. But the fact remained that not long after, the two brothers turned up at church, each swearing that he was Adam Taunton, that the farm was his, and that he was accursed with a lying brother trying to steal it from him.

Land rights are life blood, and with no order followed by anyone and the fields neglected, the Taunton farm was beginning to go wild. And bad work spreads: neighbouring farms were complaining about the floating dandelion and thistle seeds that drifted across from the unweeded fields. The fences rotted, and when Jack Styles' cows broke one of them and wandered onto the Taunton property, there was an even worse quarrel: the Adam Taunton he encountered accused him of damaging the crop and demanded compensation.

Jack was outraged, but just before he could begin to argue in earnest, the other brother came down the lane and Jack appealed to him. This, alas, made things even worse. That brother took one look at the situation and said only, 'Michael, I told you that fence needed mending.'

'Adam! Adam! I am Adam, you lying bastard, and well you know it!' screamed the first Taunton, to which the second shrieked, 'Michael, you are a liar and a thief and you shall hang for this one day!' and the two of them fell to a hysterical fistfight in the midst of Jack's startled and galloping cattle, and Jack had to drive them home himself. It took him a long, sweating time, and when he left, the two brothers were still scuffling on the ground.

The truly unfortunate thing was that they really were alike. It must indeed have been infuriating for the real Adam, but the maddened rage with which each of them spoke to the other was identical: either Michael Taunton was a splendid liar or he was simply enacting something that seemed true to him – that the farm really should be his, youngest or not. Probably there were small and intimate differences, a mole here, a freckle there, but nothing showed on their hands or faces, and the Tauntons were such quarrelsome wretches that nobody had ever drawn close enough to them to note any more private distinctions. As Janet was careful not to say these days, subject as she was to many dis-approving glances in the village square for connecting the Smith family to such disreputable cousins, there really was no difference between them except a Christian name.

Matthew, meanwhile, was truly alarmed. The war of iden-tity had been carrying on for months, and during that time winter had come and gone – a cold, wet winter with great sleet-ing gales and clinging mists, the very kind of season that most rusts shackles in a grove.

On an early spring day, he pulled together all his courage and knocked on the Tauntons' door.

One of the brothers opened it, a ragged, rough-bearded man now; the smell of old sweat rose around him, and rotten food, and trapped air. 'What do you want, Matthew Smith?' he demanded.

Matthew balled his fists in his pockets, and drew a deep breath. 'It's coming on time we repair the bands on your oak trees,' he said.

'Come back for more money?' jeered the brother at the door, and at that, another figure appeared, as ragged and stinking as the first.

'Yes,' the figure said. 'You're right, we should do it.'

'No thank you,' his brother said, his voice rising.

'The grove needs repairs!'

'The grove will hold, Michael Taunton!'

'Michael Taunton, you're a fool as well as a thief!'

'I – I can do it myself,' Matthew said. 'I can come tomorrow.'

'Trespass, is it?' said one of the brothers.

'The man can come!'

'Just let me view the shackles,' Matthew pleaded. 'You may be sorry if you let them break.'

'Yes.'

'No!'

'This is my farm and I say he comes.'

'You say *nothing*, Michael Taunton!'

Matthew turned and fled. As he hurried home, the wind beat around his ears and the birds screeched over his head, and the ground beneath his feet had a sense of sinking, as if he might drown in his own footprints. It was almost certainly nerves – his father often told him not to fret, and Matthew felt the advice was warranted – but something was going to have to be done. Behind him, the coppiced grove waited in the dusk.

Janet regarded Matthew as a man of near-miraculous strength and fortitude, but he looked so worried when he arrived home that night that she was truly affected. Soothing him with tender words and telling him not to worry about a thing did nothing to dent her view of him as indestructible, but she wasn't about to let her knavish cousins upset her Matthew any further. Not if she could avoid it.

That night, she spoke to her father-in-law.

Jedediah puffed on his pipe, and Janet, who had sneaked from her bed leaving her husband to the sleep of the innocent, dropped stitches left and right as she knitted a scarf for Celandine. They spoke, and they considered, and they made decisions. After that night Jedediah still called his grandchildren Molly, Andie and Fannie, but he no longer spoke of Janet to anyone as 'that girl of his'. He called her 'the girl': it was a distinction easy to miss, but he always abided by it.

Matthew rose the next morning, looked through the window, and remarked in an anxious tone, 'The day looks a bright one.' Bright days, around Gyrford, were cold in early spring, and cold weather could snap worn iron.

'It should be beautiful,' Janet said. 'I'll be glad of some good drying weather.' Laundry was not one of Janet's interests in life, but she had a plan in mind and meant to look very guileless indeed.

It was so unlike Janet to enthuse about drying that Matthew turned to look at her, more anxious than ever. 'If the Taunton circle breaks, it could be trouble for all of us, Janie.' His tone was more explanatory than reproachful: of course Janet knew that, but she had an interesting mind that didn't always keep track of regular matters, such as the People's propensity to burn houses and blight stock if they were out of temper with you.

'Perhaps,' said Janet, in a tone of sincere trustfulness, 'you might talk to one of them. Perhaps he would see reason from you.'

Matthew chewed a dented thumbnail: smithing left none of his nails quite straight, and when he was worried he bit them anyway. It was sweet of Janet to think he could talk anyone into reason, but he felt it more a sign of her loyal nature than her ability to judge his talents accurately, and the prospect of talking any more to one of those furious men rather quailed him. 'They call us robbers and trespassers, though,' he said. 'They would not listen.'

'Not together, perhaps, but one of them alone without the other to quarrel with?' Janet pursued. 'It was more your father they were calling robber. You offered without talking money. Perhaps they might listen to you. You're so good at being peaceful, Matthew, love.'

Matthew did not want to talk to either Taunton, but he couldn't quite bear to disappoint his wife's high opinion. 'I – I suppose I might try,' he said.

'I think you should take him some of my best cider,' she said. Cider, being a substance that thrives on being left alone for long periods, was one of the few domestic stuffs Janet made well. 'In fact, I think you should take a big jug of it, and go for a long walk tonight. Perhaps if you happened upon Michael and got him drunk, he might make some mistake. That would solve everything.'

Matthew was big enough to absorb large quantities without unsteadying himself too badly, but he had always been a little timid with alcohol. The idea that a man might grow drunk and talk seemed eminently likely to him. 'Perhaps I might,' he said.

Janet put on her most sinless face. 'Let me give you a jug of it,' she said. 'I think you might take it over tonight and share it with whichever one you meet first. Tell them the jug is from me to make amends for any hard words I might have said to him, and . . . and that I shall send another to his brother next week, but that I thought he would enjoy it more alone. Take him for a walk with it.'

'I will,' said Matthew in admiration. If there was one thing guaranteed to get a Taunton to leave his land, it was the prospect of enjoying a gift he might otherwise have to share with his brother. The prospect of cider now, and the chance of appropriating his brother's jug next week if he kept this week's gift a secret, would be irresistible. 'I will tell him not to tell his brother we are sharing it tonight.'

'Matthew, you are clever,' said Janet.

'It was your idea, my love.'

Janet put on her most naïve smile; she felt a pang of conscience, but only a slight one. Matthew had too gracious a nature to make a convincing liar, and after all, he would enjoy her cider.

The day passed in activity: Jedediah and Matthew worked at the forge, and if Jedediah was taciturn with his son, it was nothing very unusual. Janet stitched away at a new sampler, and when the children asked what she was doing, she snatched it away and told them to go and play. The cider sat in the pantry, cool and safe and delicious, ready for its evening walk.

Matthew was used to rising with the sun, and late nights were a little difficult for him; by the time he reached the Taunton land, he was rubbing his eyes. As he approached the farmhouse he was very worried: how could he knock on the door and invite one out but not the other? But luck was with him, for as he made his way up the path, a sharp voice above him shouted, 'Who is it on my land? I've a guard dog!'

Matthew, who knew that the Taunton's dog was the sleepiest beast ever to doze away an opportunity to show its valour, squinted up into the dark branches overhead. In amongst them sat the scruffy outline of a man. 'I have cider from Janet,' Matthew said. 'What are you about, up in that tree?'

'Better a tree than share a roof with a rascal,' came the sullen reply: evidently the battle for possession of the house had been lost, at least for the night. 'How much cider?'

Janet Smith might not have been good at hiding her feelings, but she was good at hiding herself: a childhood of slipping away from chores to play pretend in the woods had made her soft-footed and surprisingly patient. Matthew did not realise at the time, and neither did his Taunton companion, that her eyes watched them from behind the hedgerow, watched them as they walked down the road, passing the jug between them. Janet waited until they were well away, until the sound of their voices had almost faded – a relief to her ears, as neither Taunton brother was a tuneful singer and, mixed with Matthew's sweet-timbred bass and earnest attempts to keep some kind of melody going, the noise was not at all agreeable. After a while, all was quiet. It was then she slipped up to the circle.

It was beautiful in the moonlight. The stumps had grown new branches straight up from their cut edges, slim as wands and close as water-weeds; the grass, sleek with dew, glistened grey and luscious as cobwebs. Janet listened, hearing the soft rush of wind behind her and, before her in the circle, the softer silence, as if sounds were cushioned within it and left no echo.

She wore iron bracelets around her wrists, and at the sight of the trees they grew heavy on her, dragging her arms towards the earth. The chill of the metal pressed against her skin, and more than anything she wanted to pull herself free of it, to cast the bracelets away and warm herself within that ring of wood where the sounds were so gentle and the wind wouldn't reach her.

Janet was a fanciful woman, but she was no fool, and she left the bracelets where they were. Straining against their weight, which felt greater every second, she reached an arm forward and tied her cloth to the branches of the nearest oak. A cold wind blew behind her, and the fabric rose upon it: it snapped in the air and then hung, twitching in the centre of the circle like a pennant.

There, that was done.

Damp sweat on her skin, cradling her wrists to keep them up, Janet slipped back a few yards: there was a good hedgerow nearby, and she hid herself behind it. Drawing a deep breath, she let out a high, fluttering cry — not a word, not a song, not the sound of an animal, but an eerie noise that fell between folk and beast and People and could have been any one of them. Her mother might have known it — she had invented it as a little girl to frighten her Mama, although she had given it up after the second spanking — but her Taunton cousins had never been her favourite playmates, and they had never heard such a sound in their lives. Janet drew breath again, and shrilled her alarm across the air.

As she watched, a single, ragged figure came from the house at a half-run, stopping at intervals to put a hand on its chest, as if torn between the need to know what had made that weird cry and the fear of seeing it. But it came: Adam Taunton or Michael Taunton, one or the other, came up to the circle. What he saw there was not Janet, crouching her hawthorn screen, but only a white stream of cloth, floating on the air between the trees. With an unsteady hand, he snatched at its far end and drew it to him like a fisherman reeling in a line.

It was a bright night, with moonlight enough to see. Janet saw the figure stand for a few moments, head bent over the cloth, before he turned and ran. He did not read it aloud – nobody but a madman would have – but she knew he had seen what she, with swift rough stitches, had sewn into it that day:

PEOPLE TRAPPED BY AXE'S STROKE

ADAM TAUNTON FELLED THE OAK

IRON BAND AND AXE'S BLOW

ADAM TAUNTON WILLED YOU SO

Janet was not much of a poet, but the man ran as if he had read his death stitched into the cloth.

It was on that night, Janet always believed, that John Smith was conceived. Naturally it wasn't a subject they discussed with her father-in-law, but later she had time to worry. She ran into the house chilled to the bone, with the dew of the Taunton farm still on her skin and the thrill of victory singing in every vein, and Matthew was very, very drunk. They didn't mean to beget an heir, or not especially, but giddy nights are giddy nights, they'd always suited each other, and there aren't many ways to celebrate in the dark. It wasn't exactly like conceiving a child in the shade of a sarsen stone or the centre of a dancing grove, but there was a shadow over the bed nonetheless.

The smithy's work began at dawn, but that morning the family were a little late. Matthew Smith rose smear-eyed and sore-headed, fully expecting his father to scold him for debauchery and feeling rather a poor figure: Adam Taunton – or at least the Adam Taunton he had brought the cider – had drunk a great deal and said even more on the subject of his brother's knavery, stupid farming and general unfitness to own so much as a garden, and the fact that he called his enemy 'that Michael' could have meant anything.

He turned to Janet, feeling that now he was himself again he ought to apologise for his lack of success with her cousins, but while he muzzily remembered her being very lively the night before, she now looked to be unwell: her shift was damp, her hands and feet were frozen, and she was mumbling that she was a bold venturer and would rise again.

Since she was clearly unfit to stand over any pots, Matthew resigned himself to another day of bread and cheese, tucked the blankets close around her, looked in on the still-sleeping girls, and made his way out to the smithy in a state of hazed discomfort. He found his father already there; the forge was brisked up and shaking the air with its heat and several lengths of iron were already resting amidst the coals.

'Good morning,' Matthew said doubtfully.

'Morning, son,' said Jedediah.

Matthew hardly knew how to answer; it was very unlike him to stumble into the smithy with an obvious hangover, and even less like Jedediah not to comment on it. There was nothing for it, Matthew felt, but to work very hard, do nothing sinful, and hope that next time he looked up, everything might have steadied itself. He went to the forge and made to draw out some of the irons.

'Leave that,' Jedediah said. 'Go and work on the Harrisons' door-knocker. How's your Janet this morning?'

'I — I think she might have taken cold,' Matthew said submissively.

Jedediah grunted, and fed the fire. 'She's a good girl.'

This, Matthew felt, was too strange to cope with, but before he could think of anything to do about it, there was a flurry at the door, and in ran a man, a man soaked with dew and ragged from head to toe.

'Adam Taunton, is it?' said Jedediah sourly. A handful of folks had seen the running man, and were crowding around the door: Joseph Harrison the baker, who'd be wanting to retrieve his loaves from the forge's embers, young Bet Tarbott, the wheelwright's girl, and Rob Dawson, who apparently had nothing better to do than idle around the forge this morning.

'Not Adam,' the man said. His voice was a little shaky; it might only have been the effect of running. 'Michael Taunton, I am.'

There was a ripple from the watchers at the door, and Matthew looked up, too amazed to speak. Jedediah, though, didn't turn. He stood before the forge, adjusting one of the irons within it, unwavering in the blast of heat.

'Well then,' he said. 'What do you want, Michael Taunton?'

'I want you to come and repair the bands in the stump circle.' The man's face was shadowed, and his hands gripped tight at his sides. 'I will pay your price. Can you come today?'

'Repair the bands?' said Jedediah. There was no movement in his voice at all. 'A right thought. You are Michael Taunton, then?'

'Yes, but Adam will—'

'I'd come for either man,' said Jedediah, unflinching. 'But you are Michael?'

'I . . . I am.'

'A man should tell the truth,' Jedediah said. 'Even late in the day. Shake hands with me on it, and I'll mend your bands.'

The man took two steps forward and reached out a cautious grip. Faster than falling, Jedediah grabbed the outstretched hand and, with his other arm, whipped an iron out of the fire and sank the tip into the other man's cheek. There was a soft hiss and a whisper of smoke, lost under the sound of the scream.

'Shame on you, Adam Taunton,' said Jedediah. 'I would repair your bands. But to call yourself Michael to set them on your brother? That shames you.'

'What— What did you do?' asked Joseph Harrison at the door. He had done business with Jedediah for years, and was the only one at that moment self-possessed enough to speak.

'Some foolishness,' said Jedediah. 'The girl put a flag into their stump ring last night saying Adam Taunton cut it down, and only this one knew of it. I knew if I saw him today, it would be Adam. If it was Michael, he would have left the bands to rot. Well, now we can tell them apart.' He held up the brand.

Glowing at the tip of it, about the size of a fingernail, was a tiny triangle, a little like a capital A. 'It's time we put an end to this. War on each other, if you like,' he told Adam Taunton, 'but when you provoke the People and neglect to keep the iron in place, you war on us all.'

'You have killed me!' shrieked Adam through his hands. 'The People – you have killed me!'

Jedediah shook his head in disgust. 'Not you, nor your brother either, Adam Taunton. What great fool thinks the People can read?'

The affair of the Taunton inheritance was news around the county before the week was out. Michael Taunton was arrested, but eventually let free when Jedediah pointed out that Adam was equally guilty of lying as to who he was. After much dispute, intervention by the sheriff, and some naming-no-names remarks from Jedediah to the effect that he wouldn't serve the stupid, the farm was partitioned, leaving the brothers to get on with farming their own strips in uncontradicted solitude and fight over the boundary for the rest of their lives. Adam, as the elder, never forgave the sheriff for giving him the slightly smaller western half – but then, the stump circle was on the east.

Matthew was somewhat hurt to discover that his wife had misled him, and more disturbed that his father, who'd never so much as slapped him in all his life, had taken such drastic measures. Jedediah told him curtly that those who haven't the stomach for brands should be glad to be kept out of it, and then, relenting a little, that it wasn't as if he'd cut the man's head off: he could count a dozen worse scars on Matthew's own arms got in the course of everyday work, and he'd never heard Matthew make a fuss about any of them. Matthew was not disposed to doubt those he loved, and by the time Janet was well enough to reproach, he had come around to thinking that he was glad he hadn't had to stamp a hot iron on anyone and maybe he should just stick to admiring those cleverer than himself. As to his father – well, Matthew would rather get a burn on his own skin than watch it happen to another man, but perhaps if he worked hard, they could see to it that no one else would have to get hurt. That was, after all, a farrier's calling.

So much is to say that the Smiths were well able for troublesome customers, and that with Janet carrying another babe in her belly, things seemed all right. Things generally do, until the day they aren't.

One day, Matthew entered the house and found Janet crying with a lap full of fabric.

'Janet,' he exclaimed, 'whatever ails you, my love?'

Janet held up her sewing in a shaking grip. 'The cloth prickled in my hands,' she said, and for once, she was too dismayed to lavish further words on the situation.

Matthew examined the piece with dawning horror. The cloth ran damp and smelled of cold earth. Her thread had taken root on the weave, and sent up tiny branches from every stitch.

'Did . . . did you not wear iron bracelets when you went to the stump circle?' he said, unable, for once, to keep the anguish from his voice.

'I did,' said Janet, looking down in despair. Then she wailed:

'I'm sorry, I'm so sorry! I was told to sew with an iron needle, and I forgot! I used the bone one . . .'

The People may not be able to read, but they do appreciate gifts. Sometimes, the gifts they give back are not ones you want. Ever after, when Janet tried to sew, the thread kindled into thorns, and the bone needle warmed and pulsed; held up to the light, you could see the blood flowing through it.

Matthew looked at her work. 'What were you trying to do?' he asked, aghast.

'It — it was for Anemone,' Janet said in a small voice. Matthew held the thing to the light; just within the tangle of thread-fine stems, he could make out the gleam of anemone petals.

After that day, Anemone Smith was known as Molly Smith to everyone. The twins, who were wayward and spoke their own language to each other, had taken to calling each other Celdie and Vevie; Jedediah discarded his nicknames of Andie and Fannie, and everyone adopted the names the girls chose — after all, there was no such thing as a celdie or a vevie growing in the fields to interest the People. But the child in Janet's belly, the child with her touched blood flowing through its veins? Everyone knew what had happened to Tobias Ware: it had only been four years since he was born howling, gazing at anything in the world but the face of another mortal soul, choking on bread and eating earth and more afraid of a closed door and a warm bed than of a black, star-seared sky. The shield of flesh a mother keeps between her child and the world means nothing to the People: the babe lies within it, skinless and ready to take imprint.

★

Janet always believed she was carrying a boy. She had expected this every pregnancy, impressed as she was with her husband's virility and certain he must beget sons of his own breed, but on this occasion, she turned out to be right. Before she had started with the sewing, she had been thinking in terms of calling him Linden or Alder, but after a swift birth and an armful of blue-eyed, pearl-skinned, perfect baby, there was no question but that he must be kept safe — even, if need be, from his own disposition.

So it was that John Jedediah Smith raced into this world. It was a sensible name, intended to begin a sensible life. And he wasn't entirely worrying: his wayward interests and stubborn nature might just be his way of taking after his mother. His mother before her brush with the People, that is. And — which they had tested the moment Janet wasn't looking — he at least didn't recoil from the touch of iron.

You just can't know everything. There are so many ways of being touched. John could be fine, or he could be feral, or he could be anything in between. All they could do was wait, be alert to any sign, and keep him from wandering. If they could make him safe, if they could feed his wits with good sense and try to unknot their own hearts every time his attention flickered away from the mortal path . . . he could be all right. If they could keep his feet on the ground.

It wasn't one of those things they talked about. Jedediah had spent most of Matthew's childhood trying to keep his son from worrying too much; he'd been twenty-seven when his Louise died, and too appalled to cry. He'd bent his life around that loss, trying to keep Matthew from despairing of a world that could snatch away those you loved best, tearing out your heart for no reason at all. And hard though it had been, it had made sense: parents expect to pick up their children when something knocks them down. But how do you stop a boy running joyful through the world, and tell him that there might be something wrong with his joys? John never thought there was anything amiss with him; he was always sure he was right, and that other folks just hadn't understood why yet. He had a faith in himself that none of them could bear to break.

The Smiths were, by Gyrford standards, lenient with their children – though Jedediah would have had sharp words with anyone who suggested such a thing of him – but it was a dark world beyond the glow of the forge, and they'd hoped and hoped that they could keep their young ones warm. John might grow out of his oddities, or he might grow into a better understanding of them. There would be time enough to wait, surely, until he was old enough to carry the weight of his own heart. And there might have been, if only Roger Groves had ever in his life both- ered to keep his mouth shut. Or if there wasn't Tobias Ware, ready to die of his own innocence and teach John a terrible lesson about what can happen to boys who don't know better than to follow the things that delight them the most.

Jedediah and Matthew Smith sat up late in their smithy with their small heir banished to bed, discussing the matter of Tobias Ware and how to keep him from wandering into a hangman's noose. They never mentioned John. It was important work in itself: the Bellame woods were not an abandoned place where a wild boy could roam. Lord Robert had many men who minded his game, who gathered his wood, who hunted as guests on his property. One day, the man who found Tobias with stolen meat dripping down his chin would not be Franklin Thorpe. A hanging now and again was a fine way to remind the common folk to stay off land the grand folk claimed for themselves, and Tobias' touched state would be no protection; if anything, those who didn't know the Wares might be relieved that the commoner chosen to be a severe example hadn't been a proper boy.

So measures would have to be taken. Tobias must be persuaded, or forced, or enticed, or something, anything, that would keep him out of the woods.

And if it could be said that they talked the matter over long after hours, and with far more labour than a master craftsman usually gives to a customer who can't pay – well, farriers are responsible for all the souls that come to them for help, else there's no point in being a farrier. That was all there was to it. Good neighbours must stand together, for there's no knowing what the future might hold for any of us.

## CHAPTER 4

John was supposed to be coming straight home; he'd had a small order to deliver, and Dada had made him promise he wouldn't dally. Everyone had been making him promise things, the last day or two, and it was troubling him. They'd started when Roger Groves said that thing about him, about how he might have the People's touch on him.

Which couldn't be, surely. Mama had her problem, but it was entirely her own; he could sew, a bit, and nothing went vernal when he touched it.

But then, folks said he looked like Mama. He had her hair, and her ears, and her blue eyes rather than Dada's green ones, and while he was hoping he'd inherit his height from his father – Janet hadn't much height to inherit – John wasn't unfamiliar with the idea that he was, as folks tended to put it, 'his mother's son'.

John was skilled for his age when it came to ironwork, but the methods by which you make a baby and bring it safe into the world were a little hazy to him – and certainly neither Janet nor Matthew intended explaining to him that he'd probably been conceived on the same night she'd courted the People; that was more than a boy needed to know. But then, folks could be touched for all sorts of reasons – and they didn't always know it themselves. Old Becky Barnsdale from Kidmere, for example: she saw nothing unusual in setting out her table for herself and her guests, the latter consisting of two pine cones, a mouse skeleton, and a small heap of rags she addressed as Mister Tom Timble, and in her case, Dada had said it was best not to argue with her as she was doing no harm. All they'd done was let the neighbours know that if anyone hurt or troubled Becky, the Smiths would be back to see about it – 'see about it' being a more daunting phrase when spoken by Jedediah, especially as when he said it, he made sure to be standing next to Matthew, whose arms looked particularly brawny when he was hugging himself at the awkwardness of confronting folks. Becky thought she was untouched too.

But then, he knew it wasn't usual to eat dinner surrounded by forest debris.

Nobody had ever before called him anything worse than naughty, and naughtiness didn't worry him. John wasn't given to soul-searching and bobbed through life buoyed by the assumption that God probably liked him rather well, that whatever sins he committed were surely minor misdeeds or justifiable improvisations that wouldn't provoke more than a divine grumble, followed by fond forgiveness, not a wild hunt and a bad end, and that anyway Grandpa and Dada kept him so busy he hardly had time to do anything really bad. But feyness was something else. You could be as good as gold, and yet not as sound as iron.

★

'All right, Johnny?' Matthew had asked him when they were home from the Porters'. This was the kind of question Matthew often asked – he was one of those fathers who bestows pats on whichever child he finds himself passing – but it wasn't the casual note John was used to, and he regarded his father with suspicion.

'If I'm not,' he said, 'will you scoop me up like a kitten again? I don't think it's dignified for a farrier, Dada.'

'I'm sorry about that, Johnny,' Matthew said, at the same time Jedediah said, 'Mind the charm, boy, it'll melt into the coals.'

John retrieved the charm, which was glowing hot but not as near melting point as Grandpa said, and held it out for Matthew to strike. 'Why should you bundle me away from Roger Groves?' he demanded over the rhythmic clang of the hammer and the work tune Matthew was, unsuccessfully, attempting to get started up. Matthew sang beautifully within the smithy – although he dried up the moment a stranger came in – and John usually enjoyed harmonising along, but now he persisted: 'Don't hum over me, Dada, I asked you a question.'

'Don't pelt a man with questions while he hammers,' Jedediah said, his tone only a little tauter than usual. 'Your father doesn't need his fingers broken. And mind your manners.'

'I'm all right, Dada,' Matthew said, straightening up as the light went out of the iron. 'Back in the forge please, Johnny.'

'I know that,' John said, swinging the tongs over the coals with practised confidence, 'but you don't answer me. Why should Mama's hands say anything about me?'

'Mister Groves isn't the wisest of men, Johnny,' Matthew

said, glancing at Jedediah and finding no helpful answers in his fixed expression. 'Best not to argue with him.'

'Well, I can't with my head under your arm,' John persevered. 'But what have Mama's hands to do with it?'

'Oh, that,' Matthew said, waving 'that' away with an uncomfortable gesture. He should talk to John about it, he really should – but now? There were other touched folks John could get to know, folks who knew the touch sat upon them and had learned to live with it. There was Bobby Leaton, Sukie Porter's great-uncle, who insisted he could talk to foxes, but declined to translate what they said because he was an easily embarrassed man and their conversation was apparently mostly about eating, coupling and who had pissed where. Or there was Joanie Harris, whose pregnant mother had pruned a tree and accidentally dislodged a nest of eggs as blue and gleaming as a sunlit lake; out of the egg she cracked hatched a set of lipless teeth made of pearl-white feathers that snapped and swore her babe would never walk on the ground. Joanie was all right, as long as she wore her tall shoes and you didn't mind a woman of thirty who insisted on climbing trees. If John thought himself fey, if he brought the subject up, they could let him meet Bobby or Joanie, and let him see kindly folks doing well enough.

But not the others.

Matthew thought of his grandmother, who couldn't tell where she ended and others began, who was hurt by every scratch and graze on another body's skin. Or of Timothy Halter, who'd carried so many whispering things under his writhing scalp that in the end, he'd killed himself. They should have trepanned him, risks and all; that was on their souls till Doomsday. Or Tobias,

who couldn't take a walk outside his own garden without running into danger; Tobias, who couldn't speak; Tobias, whose
neck they might not be able to keep out of a noose. If Johnny
started thinking himself touched now, just as the People's touch
might lead to a child swinging from the gallows – no, please no.

John hadn't said he thought himself touched. He was just asking about Janet's hands. Matthew shouldn't panic and race
ahead. After all, they didn't know for certain how the child had
been shaped by his conception. They shouldn't pour too much
knowledge into him before they knew what John would be able
to make of it.

'Well,' Matthew said, as casually as possible, his eyes on the
burning charcoals, 'your mama's hands began their trouble the
same time she carried you. Sometimes folks think that affects
the baby, that's all. Roger Groves is a silly fellow,' he amplified,
the words coming out with somewhat more vigour than
Christian charity strictly justified. 'Is the charm hot yet, Johnny?'

John gazed at the iron, which sat atop the coals. Its shape was
familiar, well-wrought, but it still lay there, dark and dull
amidst the glow. 'No,' he said. It was the answer he should have
expected, and there was no reason he could give for why it felt
so discouraging. He glanced at his grandfather's tense face, his
father's worried one. He didn't mind being told to behave himself, but whatever he'd done just now, it was worse than that;
somehow, he had actually upset them. 'Sorry, Dada,' he said. 'I
do have my mind on my work.'

So when John out on his errand the next day, he really did
intend to be good. But the path had taken him back past the

95

Bellame woods. It was a shortcut to the back of the Wares' property, and the woods were green and sweet as mint, and he wanted to know something. Or he wanted something. He could have a look at Tobias Ware, surely; he would just drop in and pay his respects, ask if they had any message to send to Dada. The forest was full of bread-soft earth and cool, drinkable shadows, and he could go through it. It wouldn't do any harm.

He was a little way into it, ears alert, eyes everywhere, when he came across Francie Thorpe. Or rather, she came across him: what John was taking in was the same thing he'd felt before, when he'd gone through with Dada and Grandpa: there was something upset about the place, a rill of distress running through it, like a cat bristling its fur. This was what he was feeling when he heard a voice, and it took him a few seconds to drag his attention to the girl before him.

Of course, he didn't mind paying attention to Francie Thorpe. He'd known her as long as he could remember, and Francie – curly-headed, bright-eyed, soft-voiced and patient – used to dance him on her lap when he was very little. Francie was pretty, and scented, and everything nice; obviously she was much too old for him, but he thought that when he grew up he'd marry someone a bit like her.

So when she said, for probably the third time, 'Johnny?', he gathered his attention and made her a gallant bow.

'Good day, dear Francie,' he said. 'How charming. Also, I'm not trespassing, fairy-smiths are allowed to go places to work.'

'Of course.' Francie was a little shy with adults, but unsnubbable John Smith was easy company; the two of them had been fast friends ever since he was a bright-eyed baby who laughed with joy whenever he saw her. 'I'm a little surprised you aren't here with your father or grandpa, though.'

'I was on an errand.' John could lie with conviction when necessary, but he felt a little guilty, and it showed.

'Come on,' said Francie, acknowledging his blush without comment and taking his arm. 'Escort me to the road, will you? A farrier guide will do me good.' This was tact on her part – Francie knew the safe pathways well enough and had too much sense to stray along the unsafe ones, Franklin having carried her on his back and instructed her in good prudence since she was very little – but she had also always been tender of John's pride, sharing her father's view that it was dreadful to humiliate a child, and anyone less intimate with the woods might indeed have wandered into trouble.

'I should be delighted,' said John. 'I – you needn't tell anyone, need you?'

'What were you about?' Francie said. Her tone was gentle.

John considered. 'You won't tell anyone?'

'Not a word,' Francie assured him.

'Well . . .' John chewed his lip. Bringing it up in the smithy evidently upset his father, but telling Francie wasn't like worrying Dada. 'Someone called me fey.'

'Now, that wasn't polite,' said Francie. She said it with so little hesitation that John knew, in a painful instant, that it wasn't the first time she'd heard it.

'I thought I'd visit Tobias and see what someone fey looked like,' he said. 'To see if he looked like me.'

'Oh,' said Francie. 'Truly, dear, I wouldn't, not today. I've just come from there.'

'Ah,' said John. Francie was friends with the Ware boys, he remembered now. Janet, who loved to plan happy outcomes for everyone and didn't much censor herself before her children, had speculated whether there might be some interest between Francie and Peter Ware, but nothing had come of it; Francie spoke of them all with an affection that was warm, sincere, and nothing but sisterly. 'Is he prospering?'

Francie sighed. 'Not . . . oh, I couldn't say. But your father visited early this morning, and Toby, he didn't take it so well. I think he's had enough visitors for the day, dear.'

'Dada's here?' John said in alarm. Of all the Smiths to catch him scamping, Dada was probably the best – Janet might slap his legs, Jedediah say *very unnecessary* things – but he still wasn't eager.

'I'd head home by the Beresmere road, if I were you,' Francie said, as if giving neutral information.

John was about to run off in that direction, when he stopped. 'Francie?' he said. 'Oh, also, thank you for the help. But Francie – you don't think I'm touched, do you?'

'Why should I?' Francie said, a little too quickly. 'Who said you were?'

'Roger Groves,' John told her. Her reaction made him uncomfortable, and the fact that she relaxed when he said the name didn't quite settle him.

'Oh, I wouldn't trouble yourself about him,' Francie said. 'He likes to tug tails, that man.'

'Yes,' John persisted, 'but why call me touched? Why not call me naughty, like everyone else? You don't think he's right, do you? You didn't answer me.'

Francie had her father's face: grave, handsome, poised in habitual respect. She held it steady, and said, 'Well, I'm no farrier, Johnny. Besides, if you're good about your work and good to your neighbours, would it matter?'

Matthew Smith was not a happy man that morning. If he could settle Tobias, it would be a double good: it would protect the lad himself, and it would make all this talk about Johnny, the conversation they couldn't put off for ever, a great deal less frightening.

As his first measure, he had tried bringing Tobias one of his crosses. These were something he made more or less as a hobby, although they did a brisk sale nonetheless: a simple iron core cased into a carved oak covering, which Matthew whittled into pleasant designs as he sat at the fireside by way of a rest after a long day's work. (Matthew had a diligent disposition and a slight fear that he might be lazy, so working on a different project was his preferred way of relaxing.) The crosses were not specific to any one kind of the People, but they combined a bit of iron with a bit of piety, and were sold as a general failsafe. The fact that they were worn by many girls in the neighbourhood as trinkets was a professional gall to Jedediah, who didn't enjoy seeing good work taken lightly, but Matthew took a secret pleasure in seeing the girls happy and excused himself to Jedediah by saying that perhaps Dada was right they were foolish, but if that was so, then perhaps it was good they were better guarded against the People now, perhaps. This was annoyingly unanswerable, so Jedediah allowed Matthew to keep making the crosses and confined himself to the odd remark about not knowing he'd raised a woodworker for a son, and unnecessary reminders to spread a cloth on the floor to catch the shavings.

A cross, then, was a good place to start, and when Matthew brought one that day, Peter Ware ushered him over to a bush that Tobias liked to sit under. Tobias was crouched there, legs hinged beneath him and heels ready to spring, gnawing with expressionless attention on a twig. He had a knack to it, by the looks of things: the twist of his fingers as he rotated the thing was delicate and precise as he turned it round and round between his molars, and every inch grew crimped with texture.

'Hey now, Toby,' said Peter. 'Here's Mister Matthew Smith to see you. You remember Mister Matthew. He has something for you.'

Matthew held out the cross. Tobias didn't turn his head.

'Toby, manners,' said Peter, his voice just a little firmer. 'Mister Matthew has something for you.' As Tobias still didn't respond, Peter reached over and pulled his brother's hand out to receive the cross.

Matthew placed it gingerly in Tobias' palm, and waited.

Tobias ignored it for a long moment before bringing it to his face. He didn't look at it; he raised it up to sniff, then rubbed his mouth against it.

'Toby, no—' said Peter, but before he could finish, the cross was in Tobias' mouth. Two good bites and the wood cracked, and then Tobias was on his feet, rubbing at his lips with frantic hands and uttering a grinding wail.

'I am sorry, Mister Smith,' said Peter over his shoulder, trying to stroke the howling Tobias. 'I think the iron must have hurt his teeth—'

Tobias bared his teeth at Peter and shrieked aloud.

'Now, Toby, that is not needed,' said Peter, withdrawing his hand and holding both arms out, half in a gesture of appeasement and half blocking him from rushing at Matthew.

Matthew looked down at the scattered pieces of wood and the little iron cross glinting on the ground. He picked it up, and as he did, Tobias screamed and dashed away. Fortunately he ran around the side of the house rather than towards the woods, but Peter called, 'Excuse me, good day to you, Mister Smith!', and was running after him before any further discussion could take place.

Matthew examined the cross with a sore heart. The iron was as hard as any he forged, but he could still see the toothmarks in it.

There was still the bush to be transplanted, and that was a simple job, but it took half an hour of waiting before Peter could come back to answer Matthew's questions.

When he finally reappeared, Matthew set about uprooting the bramble. 'You remember where you found it, I hope?' he asked the lad.

'I – I think so,' said Peter. 'You understand, I do not make a habit of going in Lord Robert's wood . . .'

'Of course, of course,' said Matthew. Normally he'd be using an iron spade for the digging, but since they were trying not to upset the little thing in the bush any further, today he was using a copper one, and had to be careful not to bend it.

'I shall do my best,' Peter said. He chewed his knuckle.

'Well,' said Matthew, shaking the earth off the bush's roots, 'we shall find it together. We can ask the kind friend.'

Carrying a bramble bush is not the smoothest of tasks, but as they made their way through the Bellame woods, Matthew found himself surprisingly unscratched. The branches slumped in his arms like a dandled child.

After a while, Peter pointed: there was a little space between the trees where the earth looked dug over, and next to it, there was a holly bush.

Matthew went over and laid the bramble down. 'Step back, if you please,' he told Peter, and took the iron chain from his pocket, draping it in a circle around the bush's base.

Once it was well in place, he gave the roots a gentle tap with the iron ring he wore on his right hand for such jobs.

There was a creak of annoyance.

Matthew cleared his throat; Janet had helped him prepare a rhyme for the occasion. 'Kind friend, kind friend, Smith would have your trouble end. Here your bramble may be grown. Tell me, is this place your own?'

The little inhabitant didn't bother to unlatch itself fully from the branches; it just leaned down a few twigs and craned its berry around. 'Neighbour holly, neighbour fox!' it exclaimed with an air of cross satisfaction. 'Tuck in root and go away no neighbour man away.'

That was a yes, so Matthew duly replanted the bush. He looked around him. Had the forest been worried at this loss? Did it seem any calmer now the bramble was back? He couldn't say. The wind sighed through the leaves overhead, and everything stood still and natural. The little thing in the bush was back in his place, that was all he could be certain of.

'I'll walk you back home,' he said to Peter. 'Just so if anyone comes on us . . .' He didn't finish. A fairy-smith in the woods is obviously about his lawful business; a farmer's boy alone is another matter. Peter must have been quite desperate to have ventured this far.

They headed back to the Wares' border in silence. 'I shall keep trying with Tobias,' Matthew said after a while.

Peter nodded. 'Thank you, Mister Smith,' he said. 'Toby . . . he does not mean to be rude.'

'Of course, of course,' said Matthew. He looked around him. 'Peter,' he said, 'did you feel the woods upset when you dug up the bush?'

Peter gave a polite, awkward shrug. 'I wouldn't know about that, Mister Smith,' he said.

Matthew sighed. 'Of course not,' he said. After a moment, he added, 'Tobias likes to be outdoors, I suppose.'

'Yes, Mister Smith,' said Peter. 'Under trees, whenever he can. Or near them, at least. But we have no trees within our farm, only hedges. We could plant one, but the time it'd take to grow . . .'

'Of course,' Matthew said again. 'No, we shall do what we can. And yes, we'll plant a sapling too. Only let me find it for you this time, there's a good fellow.'

When Matthew returned home, he found his son a little flushed and surprisingly quick to obey instructions. That afternoon, though, when Jedediah went out on another job, he took him aside for a quiet word.

'Johnny,' he said, 'can I ask you something?'

John squirmed, which was odd: normally the boy was delighted to give his opinion on anything and everything.

'I don't go to scold you,' Matthew said. 'I only wished to ask. The other day when we were in the Bellame woods, and Grandpa kept telling you to pay attention. I wondered – had you something on your mind?'

The boy relaxed and looked up, his face alight at the subject. 'Well, I don't know,' he said. 'They moved a bramble, yes? Now I'm thinking the forest was worried the bush got dug up without a by-your-leave.'

Matthew felt a cold sensation seeping through his chest, as if something had been knocked and overspilled. 'What do you mean, Johnny?'

'Well,' said John, with the puzzled air of someone trying to explain an obvious thing without the vocabulary at his back, 'it was acting worried. You know, it went all quiet when we went through it, like it was hoping we wouldn't notice it and dig up more. You know. Like a mouse hoping a cat won't see it. *You* know.'

'I see,' said Matthew. He'd identified the sensation. It was his heart sinking.

'I had hoped to avoid a collar,' Matthew remarked some time later in the smithy. 'It goes against my heart to see a boy collared like a beast. But if it sits close upon him, Tobias will not be able to bite it off, and perhaps with a sapling as well . . .'

He stopped; John had made a little 'aww' noise of disappointment. While the boy had been firmly banned from accompanying his father to the Wares, he was extremely interested in the subject of Tobias, and had been listening with intent ears to the conversation. The 'aww' was because he had noticed something the men had been too preoccupied to hear: a customer was coming into the smithy and this intriguing discussion would have to be abandoned.

'Manners, boy,' said Jedediah automatically; a smith who acts disappointed at the sight of a customer has no sense at all. Then the customer stepped further into the smithy, and Jedediah came extremely close to making an annoyed noise of his own before he caught himself.

It was Ephraim Brady. The Smiths hadn't seen him since that day at the Porters, when he'd stood by and let the fear of selling to Roger Groves intimidate his unlucky tenants. Ephraim was not an unfamiliar sight in the smithy: this was where a great many deals were transacted, a smith always being a reliable witness to a contract, but Ephraim's deals were such that they never witnessed them with pleasure. The fact that the man never wasted a penny, and so seldom even bought anything from them, was an added frustration, but they could have tolerated that if his business hadn't so often been buying at pinched prices from desperate folks, or trading without regard for his tenants. Ephraim, for his own part, had no love for the Smiths even before they'd thwarted him over the Sheppards – Jedediah was not retiring when it came to showing his opinion of Ephraim's dealings – but the smithy was where everyone went with their documents, and he was not the man to let mere personal dislike get in the way of business convenience. It was, after all, not a novel experience for him to be disliked.

'Now, good day, Mister Brady,' said Matthew, seeing that nobody else was quite up to welcoming the man. 'What can we do for you today?' He said a silent prayer that it would be about regular business dealings, and not the question of what they had all heard Roger Groves refer to as Tobias' 'ways with other men's game'; that poor lad had enough problems without a man like Ephraim Brady taking an interest in him. Lord Robert sometimes gave rewards to any man who reported a trespasser, and certainly would if you turned in a poacher. It was usually a way to make yourself very unpopular with ordinary folk in most cases, but Ephraim had no fear of unpopularity, and reporting an odd boy, a touched boy, was not like betraying a real neighbour. Not in the eyes of folks who didn't know Tobias, anyway.

'I have a will to witness,' said Ephraim, handing Matthew the document. He was not inclined to waste words, and spoke with lips so taut he might be supposed to begrudge the world knowledge of such personal information as his ownership of teeth and a tongue.

Matthew held the page, scanning it, and as he gathered the contents, the prayer of thanks for it not being about Tobias died in his heart. John approached with a view to reading it over his shoulder; literacy was a required part of fairy-smithing and John was rather proud of how well he could spell out words, but in this case Matthew contrived to push him away with a pat on the shoulder, a feat honed by ten years of fathering an intrusive boy.

After he had finished reading, Matthew looked at Ephraim with an expression so woebegone that Jedediah took the will from him without a word. Ephraim Brady stood still, squandering no movement until they had both finished it.

'So,' said Jedediah after a long silence. 'I see you plan to disinherit your wife.'

'To leave my property to my brother Anthony, yes,' said Ephraim. 'You will witness.' He had the page back and signed before Jedediah could say anything else, and then proffered it for one of them to counter-sign.

The Smith men looked at each other, and for once didn't say anything when John butted in, 'Why? Has she done anything wrong? Mama says she's a good woman.'

Ephraim Brady did not bother to speak to children. 'I thank you for your time,' he said to Jedediah and Matthew.

Neither of them could return his courtesy. Everyone knew about Alice Brady.

Or rather, no one knew about her. She had lived in Gyrford ever since her marriage, but she had no friends, and what happened to her behind doors was unknown. Alice Brady had a thin face and red hands and no children and, for all her husband's wealth, counted every penny on market day. Alice Brady sat at the back of the church alone and hurried home afterwards with hardly a word to anyone. Alice Brady was seen sweeping the doorstep of her house, and almost never outside it. Janet and Matthew had both tried sending their greetings to her through her husband, but their attempts at neighbourliness had dried on the stony shingle of her husband's unblinking face – for Alice Brady was an investment her husband had come to regret.

A plain, virtuous girl in her youth, Alice had outlived her first flush without any good boy caring to court her, and eventually she had been married to Ephraim. He was twenty-five to her thirty at the time, already a gaining man with grey in his hair and steel in his eyes, and well aware that Alice, plain though she might be, had expectations of inheriting a farm from her uncle. It was likely enough: Alice's own parents had died, and she'd been brought up on that profitable land with no other children to challenge her for it.

And why shouldn't she have married him, after all? She was ready to leave home. Her uncle might dispense charities, but he expected an unceasing return of gratitude, and Alice, while she had her uses — she had a knack for accounts, and loved animals so much that she could tell the personality of every cow in his herd and coax even the stubbornest of them into a quiet milking — she also had what he referred to, with weighty disapproval, as 'a mind of her own'. Men who pride themselves on their benevolence are not always pleased with disagreement, and Alice, dependent as a child, had the improper habit of talking to him like a grown woman. Ephraim, well-looking and well-mannered, could offer her a home of her own to be mistress of.

But less than a year after they married, her uncle went on to wed a girl young enough to be his daughter, and lost no time in begetting upon her a future family that would hopefully prove more satisfactory than the niece Providence had lifted off his hands. Once the man had bequeathed the farm to his new-born son, Alice's value was badly shaken in Ephraim Brady's eyes.

Alice had worked hard for her uncle, and she worked hard for her husband. The folks of Gyrford considered her respectable, and the more romantic supposed that perhaps Mister Brady might have been pleased to marry so industrious a helpmeet. But they stopped saying that after a while. It wasn't uncommon for a man to choose a wife based on his need for a skilled pair of hands, and such brides usually settled cheerfully enough into the community – but this new neighbour of theirs was getting quieter and quieter. Ephraim Brady was not the sort who gave favours to a profitless in-law, and Alice's outraged uncle, concluding that she was an ingrate who held herself above exercising any influence with her husband, cut her off in no uncertain terms.

It was around that time Alice Brady started looking old.

More years passed. With no farm to defray her existence, his wife's dowry of flesh proved, to Ephraim, a barren bargain. Years of probably assiduous cultivation created no heir. Ephraim Brady had no sons. Alice Brady's hair was grey from root to tip, and Ephraim turned to ice before answering questions after her health.

Jedediah generally minded his own business about intimate matters, but for Ephraim Brady he'd make an exception. 'Given up on having an heir, have you?' he said. 'You don't think of leaving some portion to her nonetheless?'

Ephraim took the paper back with neat fingers. 'Mistress Brady is forty today,' he said. Distaste sat on his face as he regarded the Smiths. 'Must I go elsewhere for my witness?'

Though the look Matthew and Jedediah exchanged was quick, Ephraim could not miss the fact that they were seriously considering a refusal. It wouldn't stop him – others in Gyrford could read and write – but it would definitely be an insult, and one he wouldn't overlook.

'You don't think,' Matthew said, desperate to go all lengths now that Ephraim would be angry whatever they did, 'you might give her some property and put her aside for another wife? I – I'm sure you could, if you liked.'

Ephraim's glare was flat. 'And you a man of faith, Matthew Smith,' he said.

Impossibility stared Matthew in the face. He was fairly sure there was something in Exodus about how a man could set aside his first wife as long as he provided for her, which struck him as only fair, but being an unfortunate sinner, he couldn't remember the verse – and almost certainly, Ephraim would know more about it than him. Matthew and Ephraim were both prone to stopping in at the church for a moment of private prayer, but Ephraim never greeted him, only knelt, rigid, and exchanged whatever promises with God he saw fit. Matthew actually enjoyed prayer – he'd been told as a child that his mother was in Heaven, and while he wasn't fully aware of this fact about himself, he associated most devotions with a sense of being enwrapped in love and warmth, a hazed memory of a living shoulder upon which he could once rest his head. But as to his doctrine, it was more or less to the effect that charity, justice and honesty were all very important, which was both too simple and too personal to be up to a debate with the likes of Ephraim Brady. 'I – I don't mean to suggest sin,' he said.

'Perhaps you need be more awake to it,' Ephraim said, with genuine acid in his voice, and then he was gone.

'I – I've heard of women having children at forty,' Matthew said. His voice was so sad that John went and put his arms around Matthew's waist.

'Well,' said Jedediah, 'there's a birthday gift she won't forget.'

Matthew rubbed John's curls, more comforting himself than comforting John. 'That . . .' he searched for words that could express, within his Christian duty, his opinion of Ephraim Brady. 'That was an *ill deed.*'

It had been many years since Matthew was a motherless child, but Jedediah still hated to see him upset. Since he was too big to pick up, Jedediah could think of nothing to do beyond deepening his scowl. 'If you needed this to tell you Ephraim Brady is a knave, you must truly have sleepwalked round the village these past years.'

'Dada doesn't sleepwalk, Grandpa,' said John, who was interested in sleepwalkers and a little sorry he'd never had the chance to observe one up close.

'Hush up,' said Jedediah. 'Don't mind him, Matthew. He's just annoyed you fell asleep at his wedding.'

'Oh no.' Matthew covered his mouth. 'I didn't even remember that.' It was true: the Brady wedding had been a public event, and failure to attend would have been a significant slight. Matthew hadn't meant to doze through it, but John had been newborn and the twins still toddling, and he hadn't had a night's sleep unbroken in five years. Ephraim hadn't liked him before then, but he'd liked him even less since. There was no point apologising, though: explaining the troubles of early fatherhood would not make Ephraim Brady feel any better towards a man.

'Never mind him,' Jedediah said with stiff loyalty. 'Some folks aren't to be pleased. At least you didn't suggest he get a bastard and make poor Alice care for it. And that Anthony Brady, now: as if he needed another reason to be useless.'

'Well,' said Matthew, trying hard to be charitable, 'I've never heard of him doing a cruel act.'

Jedediah snorted. Anthony Brady was, and always had been, Ephraim Brady's one indulgence. Twelve years younger than Ephraim, Anthony had been born late in life to a mother who had expected that Ephraim would be her only chick, and her previous sadness and resignation to her paltry nest of one had of a sudden lightened to golden-hearted tenderness. One might have thought that Ephraim would have resented the arrival of this unexpected favourite, for he had been a cold boy with a head for advantage who was already known for having a bargainer's eye and no friends of his own, but even cold boys may feel the gloom when no playmates ever come to warm their days.

Mary Brady had had little time for her first son, viewing him as a sad reminder of the many brothers and sisters of his that had not outlived the perils of pregnancy and birth. But a second child was a doubling of her riches, and Anthony carried with him, at least in her eyes, all the glory of an unscathed hero escaping the fray to plant his banner on newly conquered land. While this new little Anthony was rather small for such a dramatic role, he was a sunny baby who smiled on his big brother as if he had no forbidding reputation to beware of, and Ephraim's early and tentative petting of the child had proved a successful experiment, for the boy had learned how to say 'brother' not long after 'Mama', and had swaggered in pride whenever he mentioned Ephraim's name.

Mary Brady had died still not overly interested in her first-born, although her deathbed was in a comfortable house he had bought for her. The fact that she called for Anthony, but not Ephraim, might only have been because Ephraim was prepared to visit her himself, but wouldn't let Anthony, for fear he might catch the illness that was carrying her away from them both. Not that he explained this to Anthony; he only explained it to the visiting surgeon, to whom he added with stiff courtesy that there was no need to tell Anthony any of this and upset him to no avail. Ephraim had paid for a respectable funeral for her, led Anthony away when he cried, and cared for him with the same determination he had shown all his life. Anthony always said Ephraim had been the kindest of brothers to him in their grief.

One might think a child so spoiled at home was bound for some shocks in life, but to think that would be to underestimate his older brother, for if Anthony ever found himself puzzled over how to gain a wish, you could be sure that Ephraim would wrangle a way, even out of a situation that justice might have arranged otherwise. Anthony grew up cheerful, blithe, without apparent use, and the only real love of Ephraim Brady's life.

And it was a love that Ephraim would certainly need money for. Anthony had none of his turn for traffic: he enjoyed what he had, and showed no skill whatsoever in making more. The Bradys had been working folk before Ephraim started to show his talents, and Anthony had at first been intended for a carpenter, but Ephraim had put a stop to that: he could support the family, and he would. Anthony was, as a result, a man of twenty-three with no trade, not disliked, but certainly not admired by any man. If Alice Brady had to cheese-pare and stretch to make her husband's pennies go far, Anthony did not. He lived in comfort, regarded his brother as the best of men, supposed that Alice — and indeed the county in general — must share that opinion.

Not that he heard any opinions to the contrary: being the beloved brother of a fearsome man, he was generally treated as one of those things, like a boggy wood or a temperamental bull, that folks should probably avoid on the principle of caution. Francie and he had played together as children, and Franklin remembered him as a kindly little lad, but as with all friendships Anthony had attempted, that had come to an end. Ephraim was good at finding some impiety in a playmate, some unsafeness in their home, some disrepute in their family, that made them unsuitable for Anthony to spend time with. With Francie, it was easy: Ephraim was clear that her grandfather was a known drunkard and brawler, and while Anthony had been quite attached to Franklin to begin with, Ephraim had managed to convince him that such things ran in the blood and that Franklin Thorpe was a man to be feared. By now, Francie hadn't crossed paths with him in years.

If Ephraim had set his mind on keeping Anthony in ease, then he would do it, there was no question about that. The only question was how to limit who might get ground up while making Anthony Brady more of life's fine white flour.

'I – I have another cross made,' said Matthew. 'With some of my better carving. I think I shall give it to Mistress Brady as a birthday gift.'

Jedediah gave a rough sigh. 'Go on, then,' he said. 'Give her my best wishes for her husband's long life.'

A week later, the smithy found itself with a visitor usually welcome: Bobs Hinton, a shepherd, had been friends with Matthew more or less since they could toddle. 'Now then, little Matty,' he began, doffing his cap to Jedediah with cheerful respect and giving John an affable tweak on the ear. John took this with only moderate good grace: Bobs' son Harry was of an age with John, and the two of them shared the kind of wary closeness and frequent disagreements that boys often do when they're expected to be friends because their fathers are. 'What's this to-do about you and Alice Brady?'

Bobs had been one of those lads who grows like a mushroom until he reaches about twelve years old, and then decides that moderation is the way for a fellow to live, and stops. His habit of treating Matthew as smaller than himself was not the usual Gyrford notion, but Matthew found it rather comforting. Today, though, he was suffering a dawning disquiet: this didn't feel like one of their usual laughing conversations. Bobs' habit of treating him as 'little Matty' was mostly just a game, but it also meant that he was one of the few men in Gyrford who didn't hesitate before presenting him with unwelcome news.

'What of me and Alice Brady?' Matthew asked.

Jedediah had, on Bobs' question, set down his tongs, and was now looking at Matthew with an air of exasperation so profound that Matthew reached out and patted John just to reassure himself that someone in the smithy felt approved of.

'Well,' said Bobs, helping himself to a stool and sitting upon it with his chin resting on his crook, 'word is that there's more to things than meets the eye. At least, that's what the women say to my Minnie, and Minnie says that means you've been giving her more than Christian baubles, my man.'

John looked up with the reliably upsetting curiosity of children hearing things they shouldn't, and Matthew said, 'Johnny, fetch us some more charcoal, will you, son? Who said that to Minnie, Bobs?'

'We don't need any, Dada.'

'Do as your Dada says, there's the lad,' Bobs said, giving John an amiable wink. 'We can gossip the better without your dainty young ears about.'

'We've a whole store full, I only filled it this morning,' John protested. 'And Grandpa always says you have to learn folks as much as iron.'

'John, go outside or I'll skin you,' Jedediah said, fairly mildly.

'Go on, John lad,' said Bobs. 'I'll have to sit still and say nothing till you go, and my arse isn't used to resting on a stool like this. Do it a kindness, eh?'

'The pastor says,' John observed with his most saintly air, 'that it's wicked to say untruths, and I think threats you don't mean to carry out are untruths of a kind, Grandpa.' But it was hard for him to resist the wheedling of a man who used the word 'arse' so freely. Swearing was allowed within the smithy – it's asking too much of flesh and blood to work around hammers and hot coals and never say a bad word, and under a sharp enough knock, even Matthew cursed – but still, it was an achievement that John managed to keep up his martyred air till he was out of sight, and was only heard to giggle once he was out the door.

Matthew was hasty on his return to the subject: 'Who says it of me and Alice Brady?'

'Ach,' said Bobs, scratching his beard, which was of a lengthier disposition than he was himself, 'folks about. There's Priddy Barlowe, but you know a girl can't bid a lad good evening without Priddy there to talk it up. And Ida Pearce, she had a word to say to Minnie, again, holy madam that she is. And Ida said she had it from Judith Morey, and you know Judith's Tim is after Philippa Lenden, and Philippa lives beside Annie Morris, and Annie's Luke sells to Mistress Brady at the market sometimes. Not but what Annie's got a kinder tongue than Mary.'

Jedediah laid down his hammer with unnecessary vigour. 'There now,' he said. 'Isn't that just what we need?' He felt the urge to say he had told Matthew so; he hadn't, but it all sounded so inevitable now he heard Bobs' helpful recital that it was an effort to remember that. Of course gossip flew from tongue to tongue; that was just how information got around, and it could be quite useful to drop a word in an unrelated ear when you needed to threaten someone indirectly. But this explained the looks they'd been getting all week, and now he regretted not having chastised all the customers who'd given them. If he'd known they were about Matthew, he would have.

'Bobs, there's nothing in it.' Matthew was so upset he couldn't think of a place to put down his own hammer that wouldn't look suggestive.

'Aye, sure enough,' Bobs said, with the distracted loyalty of one who hadn't given the question much thought. He had married his own Minnie because he needed a good cheesemaker for his ewes' milk and Minnie's were the best in the market; he had proposed at the selling table after a thorough tasting of wares all around the square, with the explanation that he had a house and a flock, and if he only had the face God gave him, at least it'd be something to look at if a woman ever needed a laugh. Minnie, who'd been raised a foundling and spent most of her life in a cold, damp dairy, had fallen in love with the good Providence that offered her such a chance, if not exactly with the man himself, and the two of them engaged in marriage with the spirit of two workers hired to do a proper job upon the project. Bobs wasn't given to adultery, having made an honest promise to forsake all others and so on, and regarded attention to a wife's happiness both in bed and out of it as fair dues, so while he was sometimes prone to affectionate wonder at Matthew's romanticism, and Matthew to puzzled wonder at Bobs' lack of it, the two of them were mostly in agreement when it came to husbandry. Of course little Matty didn't run around behind his wife's back; the fellow doted on her.

'But if you will give women gifts, Matty, well then. After all, that dry stick can't be much fun for her.'

'Bobs,' Matthew said, desperate enough that his voice actually rose a little, 'tell Minnie there's nothing in it.'

'Sure enough,' Bobs said agreeably. 'But you know how folks are. Myself, I've better things to do than picture you poke the fire for some other man's good wife, but I can't speak for the women, eh?'

'The man's son will be back any minute, Robert Hinton,' Jedediah said, venting his sternness on the bearer of bad news since he couldn't get to the news itself. 'Watch your tongue.'

Matthew was too happily married to mind a bawdy joke, at least a kindly-meant one, but this was not the moment. 'I have to speak to Janet,' he said. 'I have to tell her before someone else does. It's only right.'

'Aye, I reckon she'd box an ear with the best of them,' Bobs affirmed. 'But if I were you, lad, I'd keep an eye to your window. I'd not like to be the one that tells Ephraim Brady, but I wouldn't bet my back leg that nobody wouldn't.'

Janet was outraged, although she resented neither Matthew nor Alice for the scandal.

'How could anyone accuse you of such?' she exclaimed. 'Folks don't know a virtuous man when they see one.'

'Janet . . .' Matthew was not at all interested in chasing Alice Brady, but he felt a little guilty for this, having the confused sense that he was unkind to share her husband's opinion that she was not desirable. This, in turn, made him feel guilty that he was apparently harbouring disloyal thoughts towards Janet, and all in all, it was not pleasant being Matthew Smith that week. 'Janet, you know I have eyes for no one but you, don't you?'

'Of course I do!' Janet was not especially vain as regarded looks, but she considered her marriage to be a thing of sacred beauty that was obviously immune to outside temptations. 'I'm angry anyone would say such a thing of you!'

It was soothing to have his fidelity taken for granted, and Matthew sighed. 'I felt bad for her,' he said. 'That's all.'

'Ephraim Brady, indeed,' said Janet. 'I have tried for years to be friendly to Alice, but all I get is a "yes" or a "no" or an "I had better consult my husband". The woman doesn't dare speak at all. She should have a *fortune* for being married to that stoat of a man!'

'Janet, love,' said Matthew with slight anxiety, 'you do not intend to go quarrel, I hope?'

'Quarrel?' said Janet, as if she'd never heard such an idea. 'See? Now he's planting ill thoughts between us. The man is a *snake*!'

★

To get away from the rumours, Matthew made another visit to the Wares' farm. This time he brought a silver birch sapling, carefully dug up from his own back garden. It would be a long time before any tree planted beside Tobias' sleeping ken would be big enough to have any appeal for him, but birch grows fast, and anything that might compete with the call of Bellame woods was worth trying. He also brought along two collars, one a plain iron band, the other of leather studded with iron plates, which hopefully should not be too uncomfortable. Jedediah had suggested beginning with a thick leather belt hooked up to a chain, but after the crucifix incident, Matthew dared not pit Tobias' teeth against his safety. The boy could bite dents in iron: a strap of leather would give him about as much trouble as a slice of bread.

The experiment did not go very well. Tobias was resting outside in a structure the Wares had hurried together. It could not be called a cage, if only because nobody wanted to call it that: it had wooden slats on the sides and some branches draped over the top. Since it wasn't his working time, he sat within it and leaned comfortably against the bars, tapping his toes against them and tossing a stone from hand to hand with patient absorption, occasionally laughing at some particularly funny revolution as it landed. Peter reached in and stroked Tobias' hair, for which Tobias thanked him by giving his own arm an emphatic kiss without turning his head to meet his brother's eyes.

'Does he stay here at night?' Matthew asked.

'Mostly,' said Peter. 'Only he grows upset if we put a roof on it. It rains on him, and he gets sick, but he will be outside. Those branches were all I could do. I hoped he'd stay for them, but they wither, and he doesn't care for dead wood, he always knows . . . well, I shall plant the birch there. Perhaps he will like it better.'

Matthew viewed the wooden construction: it was unfortunately easy to break out of. And one little silver birch didn't seem like much of a draw against the call of the great forest beyond.

'Well,' he said, 'it is good you are trying what you can. Now, let us see if what I have today will help.'

Before he could even try the softer of the two collars on, Tobias screamed, and began clawing his own face. He carried on scratching even after Matthew backed away, saying, 'No, see, Tobias, I am putting them down. I am putting them down, Tobias.'

'I am sorry, Mister Smith,' said Peter. 'Please do not think us ungrateful.'

Matthew looked at Tobias, who had dropped prostrate and was grinding his face against the earth. 'Won't he— Won't he hurt himself?' he said in a shaky voice.

'Yes.' Peter's voice was a little shaky too. 'But scratches will heal. If I grab him now while he's upset, I think he will end up hurting himself more. I am sorry, Mister Smith. He is a good boy, really he is.'

The days that followed were a time in Matthew's life he did not like to remember. He made visits; he tried what he could. By the third trip, Tobias had taken to screaming at the sight of him.

John said several times that he would like to come. After he asked once too often, Jedediah snapped, 'The child isn't a mummer, boy. Think he's there to amuse you?'

'I never thought any such thing!' John exclaimed. Grandpa often scolded him when he hadn't been really naughty, as John saw it, but this sweeping accusation came out of nowhere. 'I'm supposed to be learning to be a fairy-smith. I'm supposed to know about touched folks.'

'Learn that folks aren't a game, touched or not,' said Jedediah. 'If you don't learn that, nothing else we teach will do you any good.'

It was so unfair that John appealed to Matthew behind Jedediah's back, but Matthew appeared out of sorts these days. All he could say was, 'I don't know, Johnny. Maybe your Grandpa's right.'

'He was unjust – and – and *ridiculous*!' John exclaimed. 'You can't be on his side!'

Matthew patted John, but he didn't feel like his usual comforting self. 'It's – well, it's a question of – I don't know, Johnny. There are folks who say touched folks like him aren't ensouled. Or act like they aren't. And – and, inasmuch as ye have done it unto one of the least of these my brethren, I think. It's a question of brethren. You can't fairy-smith without it mattering. Only I don't know what to do.'

'I don't understand you, and I don't think anyone could,' John advised his father.

Matthew sighed. 'Tobias Ware isn't very happy just now, Johnny,' he said. 'Best not to bother him more than we can avoid.'

★

Which was easier said than done. One day, when John was off on an errand, Jedediah caught Matthew leaving the smithy in tears.

'Stop now,' he said, concern roughening his voice. 'What on earth ails you?'

'I . . . forgive me, Dada,' said Matthew, wiping his eyes. 'I must visit the Wares. I had some compounds I thought I ought to try . . .'

'Stop now, stop now,' said Jedediah. 'You have got nowhere, yes?'

'I know,' said Matthew, 'but we must help them somehow. I just hate to hear the boy screaming when he sees me.'

'Enough!' Jedediah did not shout, but the word came out like the slamming of a door. 'We shall stop tormenting the boy. We shall find another way.'

Matthew stared.

'We will shore up that pen of theirs,' said Jedediah. 'Reinforce the slats if need be. It would need constant checking, but the Wares would do that. Plant a couple more saplings. Poplar grows fast too; put in some poplar. Yes?'

Matthew had never in his life seen Jedediah abandon a job like this. A farrier is supposed to be like iron in several proverbial ways, and the iron-fastness of his word is prominent among them.

'A-are you sure, Dada?' he said. 'It is what I would prefer myself. I just did not wish to fail you.'

'Fail me, nothing,' said Jedediah. 'We shall stop tormenting that boy.'

## CHAPTER 5

It was the sight and touch of iron that upset Toby. He could, it turned out, tolerate a few slats with iron cores, so the Smiths set about helping to create them. Whether those planks would actually restrain Tobias was a question they were not quite ready to ask themselves; Jedediah's rule was that for a farrier to stay in his right mind, it was best to do the work in front of him and fret about tomorrow tomorrow. (It was a rule Matthew admired very much in principle, but felt a guilty sense that, like spiritual solitude or holy chastity, it was also a virtue he lacked the fortitude to sustain.)

The Smiths were, therefore, quietly busy about their tasks when Ephraim Brady entered their smithy again.

Ephraim stared at them for so long that Matthew began to grow afraid. It was upsettingly likely, given the look of the man, that he had heard the rumours that Matthew Smith was chasing after his wife.

'Oh dear,' Matthew said. 'Good day, Mister Brady. Mister Brady, I must tell you that if you have heard talk of me and your wife, there is nothing in it.'

Ephraim continued to stare. After a long moment, he said, 'Yes. I thought I should speak to you of it. It is a hindrance to business, turning aside hints. Folks are a little slower to trade with a cuckold.'

The last word came out with a quiet venom, and Matthew floundered. There were some who thought that a woman couldn't conceive without taking pleasure in her man, and while Matthew wasn't one of them, privately suspecting it to be a tale devised by clever women whose husbands weren't paying them the attentions they should, hints to that effect probably weren't absent from the gossip – certainly not about a man who made no effort to be pleasant to anyone else. Matthew did not wish to speculate about Ephraim's personal life, but it must be an added bitterness to the man to hear his wife's name linked to a man who had demonstrably fathered four children.

'I – I do beg your pardon,' he said, feeling quite helpless. 'I – I am a married man, Mister Brady. I thought to give her a birthday gift, as I had a cross about, that is all. I mean to say . . .' He couldn't think of any further explanation without pointing out that Alice Brady badly needed some kind of consolation, given the husband she had.

'I hope you do not wish to fight me,' he added in a small voice. 'I would prefer not.'

Ephraim Brady said nothing. The look he gave Matthew was so flat that for a moment Matthew feared that Ephraim was measuring him up. Ephraim was not over-tall, but he had a wiry turn of limb that suggested any punches he threw would fly fast.

Just as Matthew was starting to shift his feet to balance

against any sudden blows, Ephraim spoke without expression. 'My wife is ugly, yours handsome,' he said. 'I have no plans to waste time chasing a rumour that will die by itself. You will oblige me if you do likewise. You give credence when you fluster so.'

'Oh,' said Matthew. The relief of avoiding a fight combined with a sense of hurt feelings on Alice's behalf – it was not really true to call her 'ugly', and certainly not kind – left him stranded. 'Well – as you say, Mister Brady. I – I am a married man myself.' The phrase carried more weight than he could quite express: Matthew was married down to his bones.

There was just the slightest twist of disgust to Ephraim's lips as he said, 'Perhaps, then, you will see no further need to visit my wife.'

Matthew cast about for an answer. Now he thought of it, calling Janet 'handsome' didn't feel like the compliment it should either. Matthew had walked out with a few girls before her, but shyness had hampered him: the safety he'd felt in Janet's lively company, the easily delighted brightness of her smile, were things he cherished – but he hadn't always had them. He remembered now, a year or two before those sweet days, where he'd been chatting with Bobs Hinton in the square about a girl – Lizzie, was it? She was something like a third cousin to Paul Porter, and fine-looking, and a good lass with plenty of friends, but he could tell she was growing bored with him, and he wasn't sure he should make the struggle to become more fascinating for her. Bobs had pointed out that she had a chest a man might walk miles to see, and Matthew, while unable to deny it, was trying to explain that he felt this was true of most girls, but that Lizzie, he wasn't sure he could fall in love with. Ephraim Brady had walked by, given both of them a look of utter dislike. 'If that's all you have to weigh up in a girl . . .' he'd said, and then he'd stopped himself, and hurried back to his business.

What answer could you give to a man who thought love and desire frivolous concerns in a marriage – but who had still spoken with the burn of envy in his voice when he heard Matthew, eighteen years old, talk of them as matters he could afford to take seriously? Matthew had never wished to be an enemy of Ephraim's, but he had a sudden, unhappy vision of himself through hostile eyes: Matthew Smith, born to a place in the world, with his home and his trade laid before him by a father who stood by him in the worst of times, with his beloved wife and his thriving children and his good friends and kindly neighbours and all the many blessings heaped upon his lap. He hadn't Ephraim's wealth, of course, but he wouldn't change places with him, not for anything – and that made him the kind of man Ephraim would not thank for pitying his wife.

Matthew was truly troubled for a reply, but before he could come up with one, there was a gurgle of laughter from the doorway.

'Well, well,' said Roger Groves. 'Always a pleasure to see my good friends discrediting themselves so thoroughly.'

'Roger Groves,' said Jedediah, 'have you business here, other than to laugh at your fellow Christians?'

Roger grinned. 'A little rumour has flown my way,' he said. 'I hear your Matthew is up and down at my farm, visiting my tenants the Wares. Now, since there are no other men's wives to tempt him that way, and I suppose he must pull up his britches sometimes, I do wonder what brings him there? I am a curious fellow, you know. Thought I'd stop in for an answer.'

'Dada, what does he mean by—?' whispered John, who was a little hazy on the facts of life, and would have liked to ask what britches and wives had to do with each other if Jedediah hadn't taken a thoughtful hold on his ear.

'Always a farrier's duty to study the People,' Jedediah said, his tone as blank as Ephraim's. 'There's a touched boy up there. I'm glad to see my son learn what he can about such folk.'

Ephraim, noticing the shift from Jedediah's usual expressive abruptness, took his eyes off Matthew and regarded Jedediah with new attention.

'Aye, indeed,' said Roger, his disbelieving grin undisturbed. 'Touched, and wandering, and on the Bellame border, more like. Well, you'll get no funds from me for it, mind you. Not my job to save their son. Let them, if they think he's worth the trouble.'

'No one asked you for funds, Roger Groves,' Jedediah said, not sorry to have an excuse to speak sharper.

Matthew, who would put up with most insults, had been struggling: it was upsetting enough to be called a lecher by Ephraim Brady, and having Roger Groves come in and make further jokes at the expense of his marriage was just a little too much. Emboldened by Jedediah's asperity, he added, 'Also, Mister Groves, I will thank you not to – er' – (remembering that John was in earshot) – 'repeat ill-judged rumours. It is not true, and it wounds my wife.'

'Oh, well enough,' said Roger, with thorough enjoyment. 'No doubt she's a fearsome figure for a little fellow like you.'

'I – I should be grateful,' said Matthew, feeling the need for forceful words, 'if you would – would *hold your tongue* as regards my good wife, sir.'

Ephraim Brady had stood quiet while this much was going on, but his eyes were alert. They took in Jedediah's efforts to steer away from the subject of Tobias Ware, and Matthew's shaky earnestness as he spoke of his good wife – the woman Matthew Smith did not regret, even while he was making efforts to cheer the life of the valueless, inescapable Alice Brady. Before Roger could make another joke, Ephraim intervened with a quick neutrality of tone. 'Your tenants have trouble maintaining their border with the Bellame woods?' he asked. From the neat propriety of his stance, you'd have thought that only Roger was present in the smithy; there was nothing to suggest he was entering on a line of questioning calculated to distress the Smiths.

'Oh yes,' said Roger. 'Nuisance, really.' He cleared his throat and spat into the corner. There was a perfectly good set of hot coals in spitting distance.

'Indeed,' said Ephraim. 'Tell me, are you still interested in buying the Porter mill from me?'

Roger looked at him, his grin widening. 'You want a poacher to report?' he said. 'Well, that's one way to get the ear of the grand folk.'

Roger had been born rich enough that the reward for turning in a poacher wasn't much worth his while, and he could have an audience with Lord Robert for the asking. Neither of these things were true of Ephraim.

Matthew and Jedediah looked at each other in quiet horror – and as they did, Ephraim flicked his eyes and caught the look.

'I have been looking for a property for my brother Anthony to manage,' he said. 'I think a farm might suit him.'

'Oh, anything will suit that boy, the way you cut it to fit him,' said Roger cheerfully. 'So now you want to sell the mill? Well, if you're interested all of a sudden, we'll have to talk again about price. Come along, my man, we'll argue down the road.'

Ephraim gave the Smiths a curt nod, and was out of the smithy. There was nothing in his stride that spoke of any wish to strike at the Smiths through their care for a touched boy. After all, reporting a poacher was a course many a prudent man might take, and a farm for a mill was a workable exchange. It might not be a bad investment.

Matthew swallowed. 'Do you think,' he said with some care, 'that Mister Brady is a man who would be – happy to spare his tenants the rope?'

Jedediah let go of John's ear and, to John's surprise, gave it a brief rub by way of making good the pinch. 'Better hurry about making those bars for the pen,' he said. 'And for God's sake, don't mention wives again in front of him. Not his that he hates, not yours that you're fond of. Kick a beehive, why don't you?'

Matthew and Janet went for a quiet walk that evening; the sun was setting watery bronze behind the steeple, and the grey stones of the church glowed near black in the dusk. Ordinarily Janet was a chatterer, folks all agreed, and Matthew found it soothing to listen to her talk. She had not been married to him this long without learning to distinguish between his silences, though, and for this evening, she was quiet herself.

As they rounded the graveyard, thick with grass and white-bloomed stones, she said, without preamble, 'Dear one, what else is troubling you?'

Matthew never doubted that Janet had an exceptional mind, but that she could apparently see his thoughts never stopped surprising him.

'Well . . .' he said, more to his hobnails than to his wife. He didn't know how to begin.

'What is it, Matthew?' said Janet. The evening started to feel colder; wind prickled the back of her neck.

'It's just,' said Matthew, still staring at the ground and speaking fast to get it over with, 'that Johnny said that he thought the forest was worried after that bush was dug up, and I know he's a good boy but it struck me odd.'

'Worried?' said Janet. Her lips felt a little chilled as she shaped the word.

'Worried.' Matthew's hands hung loose at his sides. 'Like a mouse.'

'A mouse?' Janet frowned, and Matthew shook his head, more helpless than before: he was not good at recounting the details of peculiar conversations.

There was a long silence.

'Well,' Janet said, 'he stayed under your eye, did he not?'

'Yes,' said Matthew.

'And he didn't do anything queer?'

Matthew thought of John dropping to all fours, coaxing the bush with that eerie little howl. He couldn't lie to Janet; he wasn't good at it, and it was too lonely, bringing falsehoods into the safe, warm place at the centre of his life. But she had blamed herself so bitterly for that mistake with the needle. 'N-nothing you could say for sure,' he said. 'Not as such. I was teaching him to make a Mackem knot.'

'Ah,' said Janet. 'And how did he fare?'

'Oh, he did well,' said Matthew. 'He learned fast, I think. He's good at such things.'

Janet nodded with more firmness than she felt. She could tell when Matthew was softening his account of John's oddities, but she couldn't bear to press him. He tried so hard to be a good father, to be a good man, and he was, better than she could ever persuade him to believe. If he couldn't speak on a raw subject, he didn't deserve harrying. Not for something that was her own fault. She couldn't live without his love; she just couldn't, and if she was to keep it, she mustn't overtax his forgiveness. 'There you are,' she said. 'That was fairy-smithing, right there in the woods. He did well. He's fine, Matthew.'

'Y-yes,' said Matthew. 'Yes, I suppose so.'

'Yes,' said Janet.

The two of them leaned on the graveyard wall. The cold soaked up through their clothes.

'He has his ways,' said Janet. 'But he's a good boy.'

Behind them, the sun slipped down, meshing itself in a black tangle of branches along the horizon.

In times of worry, there is nothing to do but work, and there are always folks to be served. The smiths were labouring away on their neighbour Jack Walker's horse when next Ephraim Brady came to their door and viewed the business with a steady, unamiable eye.

'You'll manage that by yourself if you have your boy to help you, Mister Matthew,' he said. 'I'd like a word with Mister Jedediah Smith, and I haven't time to waste.'

Jedediah looked at Brady for a long moment, long enough to communicate that his time wasn't any incoming man's to dictate. Matthew had been a little saddened to hear this nice mare referred to as 'that' – Bilberry, her name was, a calm, sturdy little thing of good temper, and one of his favourite patients, not least because Jack Walker's young son Sam was one of John's most forgiving playmates – but seeing his father's face set, he ducked behind her flank and called out quietly, 'Johnny, hold her hoof, there's the lad.' Matthew did not like difficult negotiations, and Ephraim Brady's negotiations had been becoming increasingly so the more they tried to come between him and the folks he stood to harm.

'If you haven't time to waste, Ephraim Brady,' Jedediah said, his voice just a little slower than his usual brisk tone, 'then you'd best state your business.'

Ephraim met Jedediah's glare. 'I'll take a bell,' he said. 'Small, thimble-sized. I'll want it by next week.'

'Wait you now,' said Jedediah, crossing his arms and leaning against the smithy door – a reclining posture he never adopted when he was actually relaxed. 'You want to order work by the inch, the weavers' house is that way. You want our work, you tell us what the job is, and then we'll decide what you need.'

Ephraim didn't waste more than a blink. 'For a collar,' he said. 'The Porters' cat is talking.'

'Oooh.' John, being a bit of a cat-lover, looked up from Bilberry's hoof. 'What's it saying?' He remembered that creature

134

from the day they had dropped in to see the Porters: it had sat in Sukie Porter's arms and huffed at him when Jedediah tried to have her say that there must exist coneys unslaughtered on their land for Tobias Ware to hunt. She had, now he thought of it, been oddly reluctant to admit that any vermin might escape Puss' grasp.

Ephraim's head turned just a fraction at John's question, but he caught it before his eyes had time to follow it, and kept his stare on Jedediah. 'Will you make the collar as well, or must I provide that myself?'

'Now wait you, Ephraim Brady,' said Jedediah. He was not a leaning man, as a rule, and was a little uncomfortable lolling against the door like this, but he was not about to move from the position as long as it made his opinion of Ephraim Brady clear. Besides that, his instincts were pricking him with a sharp suggestion that he should show as little interest as possible in Ephraim's tenants. They'd been unlucky before: Roger Groves, curse his loose tongue, had let Ephraim know they were interested in Tobias Ware, and Ephraim's vindictive interest had quickened on the subject. He might have nothing against the Porters just at the moment – they were blameless tenants – but act too partial to them, and Ephraim was capable of deciding that they were just the folks on whom to enact another lesson to the Smiths on the subject that Ephraim Brady was not to be challenged.

'The boy's right,' he continued, taking his own steady time over the words. Ephraim preferred his conversations brisk, and the learned lawyers and clerics he dealt with all rattled away like rooks; Jedediah felt no obligation to help the man depart from the Gyrford speech they were both born to. 'Tell me what the cat said.'

This was good sense — talking animals happened from time to time, and whether they might be changeling beasts, the People in fleshly guise, or just common creatures that had somehow been touched with the gift of speech, was an important distinction — but Jedediah would have contradicted Ephraim Brady about almost anything at that moment.

Ephraim didn't move, but his face became a little tighter. 'Nothing to worry you,' he said. When Jedediah kept waiting, he added, 'I trust only my own word for what it said. I heard it say that the mice in my mill were its own business and it'd catch fat mice and fatter coneys without asking any man's permission. And it said' — his face darkened at having to repeat such nonsense — 'that Little Tomkin would not bow before the prince, and the prince had ordered his ears to be taken off if Little Tomkin didn't bring him fifteen rats and a mole and beg his pardon the night of the next ball.'

Matthew prudently withdrew his pick from Bilberry's hoof, knowing John was never going to concentrate on shoeing with that kind of talk going on, and sure enough, John dropped his hold on Bilberry and straightened up. 'Goodness,' he said. 'Did it say these things out of nowhere?'

Ephraim ignored the question, but Jedediah stayed immobile until he had to answer. 'I did not witness the origin of its speechifying,' he said tightly. 'I came in during the talk of Little Tomkin and suchlike. Then I told Porter that I'd have no unkenned doings on any property of mine, and,' he added through his teeth, 'Porter said that the cat was a good beast and he begged me not to hurt it, that his children loved it and it was a fine hunter and I should consider the safety of my stores from mice. And then the animal said that the mice were all very well but that it was no common hireling and would catch coneys if it chose, and that it dearly loved a fine fat haunch fed on grass, such as noblecats should eat.' Dislike of the grotesquerie was stiffening Ephraim's every line, but evidently his memory of this politically minded mog's opinions was rather good.

John was bouncing up to ask more on the subject, but at this point there was a knock upon the jamb – more a courtesy than a practical measure, as the door stood open all day – and another man appeared: Franklin Thorpe. The Smiths had seen him fairly often these past few weeks; the containing of Tobias was a subject he was earnestly following.

If he'd come to warn them that he'd seen Tobias on the wander again, it wouldn't be the first time. The reinforced bars of the pen were holding him most nights, but what the boy lacked in speech he made up for in his ability to slip through, and once even dig under, the slats intended to contain him. Matthew had begun, meaning very well, by proposing solutions with a reassuring, 'We could just—', but by now, the word 'just' had been burned out of his vocabulary.

Jonas Ware had been nervous, at first, to explain the difficulties, and indeed, you might have taken him for the most prolix of cavillers if it hadn't been for the fact that his long and complex explanations of how Toby would react to every possible safety measure the Smiths could think of turned out to be entirely correct. Tobias couldn't bear too much iron near him, and he would dig and scrape and ferret and fret, no matter what persuasions they tried. He wanted to be out under the trees, and he was not to be turned in this relentless wish. And once he was there, he would hunt. He would run down a reason for his own hanging, and carry it home dripping blood down his guileless face.

After all this, the sight of Ephraim Brady was enough to stop Franklin in the doorway, saying nothing more than, 'Good day, all.' Soots, who was with him today, gave her tail a courteous wag and went up to sniff Jedediah's hand in greeting. Jedediah was fond of dogs, but farriers don't keep them, it being unkind to expose them to the thousand shocks and slights to reality the People inflict, and he and Soots were old friends. Seeing the dark look Ephraim bestowed on the exchange, though, she returned to her master's side, giving him the expectant gaze she gave when Franklin was preparing to arrest a malefactor in the woods. Soots was a tracker, not a guard dog, but men who disliked the sight of her master were, in her experience, up to something they shouldn't be.

John, who cared more for cats than dogs, was torn between the thought of talking cats and the prospect of Franklin carrying more of his dried berries in his pocket, and perhaps being willing to share them with a deserving boy. The latter thought prevailed on him enough that he said, 'Good morning, Mister Thorpe. How do you today?'

'In good health, I thank Providence,' said Franklin. 'A pleasure to see you, young sir. I don't suppose you'd care for some of my—?'

'Ooh, yes please!' John exclaimed, seeing Franklin's hand go to his pocket.

'Johnny,' said Matthew, relieved at the presence of someone

gentler in the smithy, 'manners, please. Don't interrupt a man who's doing you a kindness.'

'Oh, that's all right,' said Franklin, dropping a handful of delights into John's slightly sooty palm and giving him a ruffle on the head. 'It's a pleasure to see a boy enjoying himself. I hope you are well too, and you, Mister Smith?'

'We are that,' said Jedediah in something of a drawl. 'It's a pleasure to meet a customer with manners. Now, Mister Thorpe,' (absent Ephraim Brady's company, Jedediah would not have troubled this man he'd known from childhood with a 'Mister', but there was his audience to consider), 'what brings you here on this fine day? How can we serve you?'

Ephraim Brady was glaring at Franklin with a look of icy outrage. Franklin gave him a neutral, polite sort of nod, giving no indication that he might have anything desperate to communicate, and said to Jedediah, 'Nothing you need hurry yourself for, Mister Smith, thanking you for your care. It's the time of year for sharpening my tools and seeing all's right with them, and I came to ask when you'd find convenient, but it can wait. And a small commission for my daughter – one of your pretty oak-and-iron crosses, Mister Matthew, as she's quite a woman now and goes about more.' There was the shadow of a proud smile on his face. 'But that can wait too. I'll be happy to take my turn.'

Ephraim's look at Franklin was not grateful; it was, instead, a glance of speculative dislike. Franklin truly wasn't making a veiled reference to the gossip surrounding the cross Matthew had given his wife, but it would take a more amiable man to trust in that. 'Can you give me a bell, or can you not?' he demanded.

Jedediah jerked his head at Matthew, who straightened up, more in obedience to his father's wishes than from any desire to enter the conversation. Matthew hated to hurt an animal, and since he hated to argue with folks as well he was feeling almost mute with distress, but the size of him towering over Ephraim was an advantage Jedediah felt comfortable employing. 'I – I think,' Matthew managed, 'it would be best not to be too hasty.'

'Or too cruel,' John supplied, feeling no such hesitation at telling anybody what was what. 'If the cat's just talking and isn't doing you any harm, it would be most unkind to hurt it.'

Ephraim's eyelids gave a brief twitch which, in a man of more lavish movement, might have been a gesture of rolled eyes, but John persisted, 'And it's unlucky too. Especially if the cat has friends, you know, among its court or among the People, which it probably does if it's talking. You must have heard of folks that hurt animals the People loved, and the People take offence at it. You remember Mister Dalby, who shot one of Pretty Nan's coach-hares by mistake, and he had to leave the county before she did something even worse to his other leg. And he didn't even do it on purpose.'

Franklin, who had brought Bill Dalby in for the amputation, flinched at the memory, but Ephraim Brady ignored John's advice: except for his younger brother, he had shown a marked disinclination for the talk of brats since he was barely more than a brat himself. 'Mister Jedediah,' he said with cold rudeness, 'I'll have some help on that land. I've a fine offer to sell it, and if it's known there are talking beasts on it going unchecked, then Paul Porter is taking money out of my pocket, and he'll answer for it. He'll bell that pet of his or he'll drown it, or he'll know what it is to rob Ephraim Brady.'

'You could just not mention the cat,' John suggested.

That did turn Ephraim's head. He looked at John with a face of closed and absolute contempt. 'If that's the honesty of this smithy, I must look to your prices,' he said. Ephraim Brady was, worse luck, known for his strict integrity: it was against his covenant with God to be dishonest, and he could command better terms if it was known that what he promised, he performed – not to mention depriving his debtors and tenants of any hope that he might one day come a cropper in the eyes of the law. Ephraim Brady was not a fair man, but he believed himself to be a just one, and as his reputation was as good as money to him, he maintained it with close and inflexible husbandry. Jedediah had over-charged him for the Sheppard job – it was the only way he'd been able to raise the funds to settle their debt – and Ephraim had paid, but there was no doubt that he regarded setting your prices according to the means and merits of your customer as a form of double-dealing, and his resentment was all the fiercer because he confined himself to honest accounting and the single principle of charging as high as you could in every situation.

Soots gave an uncomfortable whine. Matthew agreed with her.

'Excuse me, my friends,' Franklin Thorpe intervened. 'I'm sure we all know the reputation of each of you as honest men. And an honest boy, too, I'm sure,' he added, glancing at John, who was beginning to puff up. 'We mustn't expect old heads on young shoulders now, Mister Brady.'

'My head's well enough,' said John.

Franklin passed him a few more currants. 'May I?' he said, to the forge in general, and when nobody relaxed their antagonism enough to speak, he carried on, 'It seems to me your interests are really aligned.' He spoke as one surrounded by tempers that might at any moment explode up from the brush like startled grouse. 'Mister Brady, now, wants to keep the price of his land free of trouble. Our good farriers here say that a bell by itself would have consequences hard to foresee. Now, those consequences could cost Mister Brady money too, and perhaps bring trouble to him and his into the bargain. I'd say a visit to inspect would be the shortest route to agreement, wouldn't you?'

'We'll inspect, if he'll pay for the trouble,' Jedediah said shortly. 'We do no work of that kind without we inspect anyway.'

'Yes, because that would be stu—' John began, but Franklin had slipped Matthew a big handful of currents, and Matthew stuffed several into John's mouth before he could rile everyone up again.

'Now, Mister Brady,' said Franklin, with a certain desperate calmness, 'will you say a stitch in time saves nine, and welcome their visit?'

Ephraim was used to rapid weighing of loss versus gain, and only considered for a couple of seconds. 'I'll pay for a full inspection,' he said. 'If you'll put your names to a document saying you've done it. And I'll pay for any jobs you find on it, within reason, courtier cat and all. I mean to sell this land, and I'll have it done right.'

Matthew shook his head a little. He'd always rather looked up to Franklin, who was nine years his senior, and in his baby years had seemed the most impressive friend in the world, but even so, it was very rare indeed for an argument with a customer to end with him deciding to pay you more money than he'd come in offering.

Jedediah, who had picked up on the 'him and his' in Franklin's speech, nodded. 'That's the wiser course,' he said. 'The People can take against whole families and you'll not want that.' Privately he was intending to inspect every last leaf and stone of the place, for if ever there was a customer deserving of heavy bills it was Ephraim Brady, and there was no doubt that if you wanted Ephraim to do something, a credible hint against 'family' – which meant Anthony – was the only course.

'I'll have it done thorough,' said Ephraim. 'When can you go?'

'Tomorrow,' Jedediah declared, unsmiling, and making a silent resolution that all three of them would go. It was a one-man job, but triple the Smiths meant triple the fee; that would start things off nicely. He had the feeling that the Sheppard case would not be the last time there'd be folks facing starvation because of Ephraim Brady, and the more of his money they could gather in against such cases, the better. It would make him dislike them more, of course, but their own funds weren't infinite, and there was certainly trouble on the horizon for the Wares. Whatever solution the Smiths might or not find for them, it wouldn't be helped by poverty.

There was another silence, and Matthew, in dread that it might once again fill with hostility, hastened to say, 'Well, I think you do right, Mister Brady. It's a wise thing to keep the land watched over, and it'll be known in the county that you're a man to do it.'

'Yes,' added John. 'Though if you want to protect your whole family, Mama says you should be kinder to your wife.'

He said it too late to be stoppered with currants, and it was beyond even Franklin's tact to mend. Mister Brady gave John one of the darkest looks he'd ever had in his life, and swept out of the smithy.

## CHAPTER 6

Matthew had given John a quiet warning not to chatter too much about the properties of Chalk Lane as they drove down it, as Grandpa would perhaps prefer that he didn't, and after all, John had seen it before and perhaps he'd better put his mind to other matters, eh Johnny? It was tactful advice, and John took it in the spirit Matthew might have expected: he made it about halfway down Chalk Lane before he started up with the questions again.

'Will Mister Brady manage this road, do you think?' John had just enough restraint to direct the question to Matthew rather than Jedediah, since Matthew hadn't said anything about not wanting to be questioned himself, but Matthew was driving and concentrated rather fixedly on the reins. 'He has that fine mare,' John persisted, 'but she's skittish, and look at Dobbs.' Dobbs, indeed, was not a happy creature. They were passing a crossroads, a gleaming stripe that ran down through the fields either side, dandelion clocks getting their heads snatched bald by the wind. Dobbs shook a nervous mane, and Matthew click-clicked, calling out, 'So girl, so girl, never mind, never mind.'

It was, the Smith men had to admit, a thought. Ephraim's mare was a rather nice chestnut, bought by him the previous year. It had been an accident that made her his: a young filly, she'd been intended for a carriage horse, and was just breaking to harness when her companion bolted, dragging her alongside until the carriage shattered itself against a log the horses had leaped, knocking all down in a welter of flying wood. The bolting horse had been killed, and the driver alongside him, and his widow, feeling the need to economise, had sold the surviving mare. Ephraim Brady had got a good price for what many folks considered an unlucky beast, reduced further by the dark scar that ran across her chest, and further still by the fact that she would stand on her hind legs and scream if you tried to put her in a carriage harness. She was a saddle horse now, and fairly docile – Ephraim Brady did nothing he could not do well, and he could handle a horse – but she was not exactly a calm creature. Daisy, her name was; it would seem he had let his brother Anthony choose what to call her.

'If he has sense,' Jedediah said, 'he'll cut in at the closest turning, spend as little time here as he can. And he does, bad luck to him.' On another road, Jedediah might have said 'Damn him,' but this was Chalk Lane and the wind was roaring in their ears.

'I hope so,' said John. 'It would be quite unkind to make her walk along here more than he can avoid. But he's not very kind, to want to bell that cat.'

'Nothing kind about that man,' said Jedediah. 'Don't fret before you have to. He doesn't rule us.'

'There is surely nothing unchristian about a talking cat,' said John. He had a point: the People must be fought when they wrought real danger, but things that were just a little fey were best left alone. Besides that, appeals to religion were always powerful with Dada, and John was feeling an uneasy sense that he would prefer the Smith attitude in general to be sympathetic to the touched. Of course, he was fine, but folks said things about him, and he had been a little naughty to wander into the Bellame woods before. Francie hadn't said anything, but it was slightly pressing on him, just how much he'd wanted to go. 'Nothing bad. If the cat isn't saying anything bad, I mean.'

Jedediah cleared his throat, and said, 'I climbed up into a cart, boy, not a pulpit. Leave the preaching for Sunday.' John could be puzzling, but he wasn't good at subtle hints, and there was a note of earnest defensiveness in the boy's voice when he spoke of the virtues of the fey that gave an uncomfortable twinge at his heart.

'All I'm saying,' said John, offended, 'is that he's not kind to want to bother the cat if it doesn't bother him.'

'Well, most folks have doubts about the unkenned,' said Matthew. 'I do wish to be just to the man.'

'Tell that to your wife,' said Jedediah; the thought changed his worried scowl to something almost like a grin. While he and Janet were very different mortals, Jedediah found a secret enjoyment in her willingness to abuse folks who deserved it. 'She's a cat-lover like your boy there.'

John seldom failed to notice when someone was talking about him, but for once, he'd gone quiet. He was watching Dobbs, the way she shivered at every crossroad, and listening, too, to the sound of the wind. The air rushed by them with tufts of dandelion twirling manic and lost, but they weren't following normal patterns: they slowed when they reached the space a few feet away from the road and settled into a slow, idle drift, only to be sucked back again, as if a great angry spoon were stirring the air. There was nothing fey to be seen, but this place wasn't right. It was — he searched for the right word — *hasty*. The trees alongside it were dry, cracked down their centres, without the patience of growth. It was louder than it should have been, swallowing up their voices, and while Dobbs was only going at a steady walk — Matthew wasn't letting her chance anything faster — they seemed to be travelling at speed. They weren't reaching their destination at speed; he wasn't even sure how long they'd been on their lane. But they were racing along anyway, and when he stopped to listen, he could feel his heart pound.

Paul Porter was waiting at the gate, and as the sound of Dobbs' hooves and the rattle of wheels announced the Smith cart, his two sons, Tommy and Bill, came running out to meet them.

'You haven't come to take Puss!' Tommy announced with frantic accusation. He was the older of the two, six or so, and the injustice of the world appeared to be pressing on him very hard at that moment.

'Tommy,' said Paul. He was a laconic man, though very fond of his family; it's hard to make a six-year-old understand that you can't afford to protect his pet.

'Now, young man,' said Matthew, passing the reins to John and stepping down. Handling children was generally considered his job. 'You love Puss, don't you?' Both boys nodded, blinking bright, outraged eyes. 'Well, we're here to save her if we can.'

'Puss is a he,' Bill mumbled around his thumb.

'Well, to save him; thank you for telling me, Bill. We'll have to look around the place, you see, and make sure everything's as it should be, and we'll do all we can. Now, do you think you two fine young men might show me the boundaries of this place?'

Jedediah dismounted after his son, looking around. The Porters were honest folks, tenants of Ephraim Brady: easy for him to hurt. He thought of that glint he'd seen in Ephraim's eyes, the moment he'd realised the Smiths were trying to do something for Tobias Ware. It wasn't even hostility; it was observation, mettle, a moment of decision. He disliked the Smiths already; he knew they now cared for the Wares, although God willing, not to what extent, nor how necessary their care was becoming. He had nothing particular against the Porters, but that wouldn't stop him crushing them, if it profited him; he had no reason not to. Roger Groves, now – God knows he was a callous man, but he didn't bother himself over long schemes to hurt folks. He'd keep the Porters here if Ephraim advised it. The Porters could stay in their home; Tobias Ware could still have neighbours who'd lie for him if he got out again. If they could just get through this day without adding any more souls to the lists of quarry Ephraim Brady set his sights on.

The fences of the property were well-repaired, and the kitchen garden well-weeded. The mill was clean and working, and the river clear of reeds. More than that, John thought, the place was quiet. The wind was nothing more than the occasional waver, and the ground underfoot was as solid as it should be and no solider, and nothing felt out of true. Jedediah informed him sharply that a feeling was no reason not to look about properly, giving him an uncomfortable glare besides that made John angry for reasons he couldn't quite articulate, so he traipsed about after his grandfather, but with Matthew off reasoning with the two boys and Paul Porter hovering at his gate like an anxious hen, there really wasn't much for him to do.

Jedediah was wearing his iron glove, his knuckles banded and fingers flexing as he knocked on every tree, every bush, every stone he passed.

'Watch me, lad,' he said, when John fidgeted.

'I've been watching you. Nothing's happening.'

'You want it to? Want some creature leaping out at you?'

'Grandpa, this place isn't fey. I'm sure it's not. Let's just go and see the cat.'

'Oh, and I'm your 'prentice now, am I?' said Jedediah, not really annoyed but not about to take any cheek. Or at least, none more than he could avoid. John's tongue was like a curtain at an open window: you could press it to stillness, but it'd be fluttering away again the minute you relaxed your hold.

'No, but— Grandpa!' John exclaimed, as Jedediah assumed a careful stoop. They'd reached the kitchen garden now, and he was issuing a soft tap to each neat, pale sphere in the ground. 'You are *not* about to test every cabbage!' The People could indeed infest any plant they took a fancy to, of course, but such domestic fare was not usually to their taste, particularly not on soil regularly weeded with an iron trowel. Really, there was hardly a place in the county less likely to have the People making merry in it.

'I said I'd inspect,' said Jedediah, straight-faced, 'and inspect is what I'm here to do.'

'Grandpa, those are cabbages! *Cabbages*, Grandpa!'

'You're having a jack-of-all-trades morning,' said Jedediah, not giving an inch. 'Priest on the road, now gardener. I suppose when we go to the house you'll be a builder too. Heaven preserve me.'

'Grandpa, that is not— I am—' This was so unfair that John was actually tongue-tied. How many stern remarks had he got for wasting his time or talking nonsense? How many funny looks, now he thought of it? And here was Grandpa crouched in the dirt, fey-testing an iron-tilled vegetable bed. It was an outrage.

'Better give up the priesthood, if you can't sermonise, boy,' said Jedediah. He wasn't really trying to be unkind; it was just that explaining that he intended to bill Brady by the hour, and that hours could be stretched, was not something he felt inclined to do – at least, not before the bill had been presented. Nonetheless, he had a sneaking sense that he was cutting a poor figure – it's a bad teacher who withholds knowledge – and it was making him a little sharp.

'It would take more than a priest to put up with *you*!' John exclaimed. 'It would take a *saint*!' And he stalked off to the house in utter fury at the injustice of adults.

Sukie Porter was a worried woman. Mister Brady, a man she couldn't think about without a tight throat and a churning stomach, was going to sell the mill. And he'd tell them nothing about how or when. And the boys' hearts were so set on that worrying Puss that she couldn't bear to tell them Puss was the least of what they could lose. If the mill went and they didn't go with it, there would be nothing for her and Paul to do except go to the next Michaelmas fair to hire themselves out as workers: Paul labouring on someone's farm, and her, perhaps, maiding for someone else, and the boys with her only if they were lucky. She couldn't tell them any of that, and sometimes she thought she'd never get a night's sleep again.

So when she saw the cross, sturdy figure of John Smith stumping across her garden, she called to him at least partly as a distraction. Sukie was not a schemer, on the whole, but tenants of hard men can't afford to be unworldly, and she knew that the men of Gyrford smithy could be good to folks they liked. Between her need for something to think about other than the image of her little boys walking Chalk Lane with empty bellies, and her sense that it would be better to be on the right side of the Smiths than the wrong, she called out to him, 'Good morning, young sir! Would you care to come in for a drink of cool water?'

John, who was usually hungry, would have preferred the offer of something more substantial, but he had better manners than to demand food of the potentially destitute, and anyone who called him 'young sir' was all right with him, especially after the recent iniquities of Grandpa. 'Thank you, Mistress Porter,' he said with something like a courtly bow. 'That would be very kind.'

The Porter kitchen was of a piece with the land in general: well-kept, provisioned within a hair of need, and not a bad place to sit. John resting in his chair with his cup of water before him, was feeling more appreciated as he asked, 'What is your opinion of the cat, Mistress Porter?'

'Oh.' Sukie patted her hair with a nervous hand, though as usual it was neatly bound and not about to come down. 'Well, we've no live mice in our kitchen, though he does leave the dead ones where he wills, so I can't complain of him as a mouser. And the boys are fond of him.' Her face was sad, almost tearful. 'He'll chase a string for them, and — well, boys like their laughter . . .'

'I quite agree,' said John, feeling a sense of reassuring authority at Sukie's fragile looks. 'Have you ever belled him before?'

'Oh, no,' said Sukie. 'That'd be no good on a mouser.'

'But you'd keep him if you had to bell him? If he couldn't hunt mice?'

'For the boys, yes,' said Sukie. 'But . . .' Her face flushed, and her eyes glistened.

'Yes, Mistress Porter?' John felt quite in his element: this was questioning a customer, and he was making a decent job of it.

'Well, you see, he hisses at our poker. And last night, when everyone was asleep, well, I crept down to the hearth and asked him if he wouldn't kindly wear an iron bell to save us from Mister Brady. And he said that he'd have no iron near him, and that it was ig-ignoble in me to . . . I don't think he'll wear it, you see. Not for a basin of butter.'

'I am shocked at the suggestion,' said a small voice under the table. Sukie jumped, but John felt a rush of fascination too great for surprise, too great to wonder even for an instant how Grandpa would want him to handle the situation, and instead dived down onto the floor to meet this most engrossing cat.

At a casual glance, Puss did not have much of the appearance of a courtier. He was a stripy fellow, fine-banded, with a chewed ear that suggested more of the brigand than the knight, and his fur, while sleek and trim, was short and ordinary and nothing out of the common. John stared at him for a long moment, trying to recapture the alertness he'd felt on Chalk Lane. Yes, this was a cat, and nothing about it felt exceptionally uncanny – but then, John had always had his suspicions that cats knew more than they were saying. Ordinarily they didn't talk to you, but that didn't mean they couldn't.

'Good morning, Puss,' he said. 'May I stroke you?'

'You may,' said Puss, cocking his head for the purpose. The voice was high-pitched as a toddler's and rather piercing, and it didn't match the cat's lips. Those stayed quite still, John saw, fixed upwards in a supercilious smile. Instead, the words were coming forth like birdsong, Puss just quirking his jaw up and down a little as the sentences carolled forth in a liquid flow.

'I hear there are doings at court,' said John. 'Has Little Tomkin apologised?'

'I hope you do not speak of deep matters to the undeserving,' Puss chirruped, bending a sharp green eye on John.

'Not if you aren't undeserving,' he said, having had enough high-handedness for one morning. 'I'm speaking of it to you, that's all.'

Puss twitched his whiskers with a look of annoyance. 'I'd hoped for better manners from friends of yours, Mistress Sukie.'

Sukie wrung her hands and said, 'Oh dear, Puss. I do wish you'd be a little easy with us.'

'I make allowances,' said Puss, 'but I see no reason to have my patience sported with by a stranger.' His lips stayed as still as ever, but he produced every word with the manner of one who knows his observations are a boon to the honest listener. Which, John had to admit, they were, or at least, it was interesting to be talking to him. The People vary in their speech from silent glaring to broken prattle to reeling eloquence, and Puss was as chatty as they came.

'I'd like to know,' said John, 'does it trouble you living so near Black Hal's road? I wouldn't have thought it'd be comfortable. You know, for a cat.'

'*I*,' declared Puss, throat a-flex, 'know better than to be a rash neighbour. I have studied his form well enough; the view from the roof is a fine one. Puss lives advisedly. It's the tall folks who get ahead of his teeth.' That was a phrase John had heard before: it was the common saying about Black Hal: if you got ahead of his teeth, Heaven help you. He'd run you down, and you'd never get behind his tail.

'So you and he are . . . on terms?' Black Hal wasn't technically their problem right now, but John had an interest there. Black Hal was the one who'd touched Tobias Ware, and Dada and Grandpa were worried about Tobias, and he couldn't shake the feeling that if he could understand a bit more about that young man, he might settle some nagging questions about himself. He could say to the likes of Roger Groves, No, look, this is what a touched boy is like, and it isn't me.

'I live behind his tail, and Black Hal doesn't turn,' Puss affirmed. 'But you tall folks aren't known for your nimbleness. Nor for your wit, either,' he added, flexing a speculative claw, 'or there would be no suggestion of this horrid iron.' He ended his observation with a little chatter, like the hungry clicking of a moggie unable to reach a robin on the roof.

'You see, here's the trouble,' said John. He was thinking as fast as he could. 'This Mister Brady, he says he wants to drown you if you won't wear it.'

'*Prrt*,' Puss scoffed. 'I can get behind *his* tail, I'm sure.'

Sukie Porter was wringing her hands again. John considered explaining that Mister Brady was of a different order – that you might well get behind his tail, but he'd just turn and pursue you, and keep pursuing till he caught you in his net – but nothing he had seen suggested that Puss was open to different, tailless ways of thinking.

Then again, he thought, what had happened the first time he met Puss? Sukie had been unable to tell his grandfather that there were no coneys on the property, that the gallant Puss hadn't hunted them all to extinction. Puss had had nothing to say then, except a few angry cat-noises.

John thought for another few seconds, during which Puss allowed his cheek to be tickled with an air of humouring the peasantry.

'That's what Old Tom said you'd say,' John said. He had, in fact, never met an Old Tom, but there must be a cat of that name somewhere hereabouts.

Puss put a paw up on his stroking hand, claws just beginning to prick. 'What did you say?' he demanded.

'Oh, Old Tom said that you'd run before you stood your ground,' said John. 'But then, that's what all the folks say. Us folks, I mean. Tall folks. *I* don't like to judge a cat before I see one, but the word's all around the county that you're a coward.

Why, the whole church was talking of it last week. Mister Ephraim Brady and Mister Roger Groves were especially witty on the subject.'

The sound of a growl started up in the cat's throat. 'Mistress Porter,' he said, with a slow, icy hauteur, 'what is this I hear?'

Sukie stammered, but John waved her down. 'Oh, don't ask her,' he said. 'She doesn't know what to think, for her boys, they said it wasn't true, but they were the only ones. Everyone has been saying nothing else for weeks. They quite laugh about it. It's really very funny, some of the jokes. They wouldn't say them to your face, I suppose.'

There was a burst of fur, and Puss was up on the kitchen table, outrage bristling along his back. 'If *that* is what I am to expect of common society,' he snarled, 'I regret wasting my manners on the mere herd. I shall pity your boys for their unfortunate connections, Mistress Porter, and keep them company for their own sakes, but as for the rest of you and your kin and kind, why – see if I ever waste my words on *you* again!' And in a flash of chivalric sulking, he was out the kitchen window.

John fished in his pockets. There wasn't much that he could use, but a deeper search revealed a comb Janet had given him, more to oblige her critical neighbours than because she particularly found fault with his rumpled curls. Now, not at all sorry to be rid of it, he handed the comb to Sukie Porter. 'I suggest,' he said, assuming a note of manly confidence, 'that you tell folks we gave you this comb with an iron core. Don't worry, it's just wood. But you tell folks that you combed him with this and he went silent. That should fix things. Conceal them, you know. When I first met Puss, you see, he said nothing to me, because he was offended. I think if we keep him offended, he'll stay quiet.'

Being fallen upon and kissed by matrons he barely knew was not John's favourite pastime, but he still had rather a swing to his stride as he left the Porter kitchen.

Jedediah was fond of a well-kept vegetable garden, and since John stormed off he'd been feeling almost relaxed. As he heard the clatter of hooves, though, he looked up, and his heart sank. Paul Porter was standing rigid at the gate, the image of an anxious tenant, and there, coming down the road, was Ephraim Brady on his scarred chestnut mare. His face was calm, his back upright, and beside him rode Roger Groves.

This was the time to be patient, to mollify, if Jedediah could manage it – which, he knew, was not one of his gifts. Ephraim Brady did not need new reasons to dislike the Smiths, and thence take an interest in any fey boys they might or might not care about. He did not need to decide the Porters needed punishing.

Jedediah straightened up and made his way over to the gate. A bow was beyond him, but he managed a nod and a reasonably civil, 'Good morning, gentlemen.'

'Are your son or grandson here?' asked Ephraim Brady, evidently not inclined to waste words on such fripperies as a kind greeting.

'They are,' said Jedediah.

Beside him, Paul Porter cleared his throat. From the tremor of his hands, he looked like he knew his fate might depend on the next few minutes, and it was with some effort that he managed his own contribution: 'Working hard, sir.'

'When will you finish?' Ephraim demanded. Beside him, Roger Groves gave a great, wet sniff, hawked, and spat into the ground. Jedediah had no fastidiousness for men who sweated and spat at their labour, but the likes of Roger Groves always made him straighten his back and neaten his speech.

'The grounds, early afternoon,' Jedediah said. 'The house, by tomorrow morning if all goes to plan. I can tell you now that I see no sign yet of fey business about this place. It's well-kept and well-tended.' He considered adding more, but decided against it: neither Brady nor Groves were the sort to enjoy hearing a tenant praised beyond their own interests.

'We do our best,' said Paul, striving to explain himself. 'Have to keep an eye on things. No good letting them go to rack.'

Roger Groves sucked his teeth; there appeared to be something stuck in them. 'So, you're the miller?' he said. He was looking at Paul quite closely, but out of the corner of his eye; it was apparently too amusing to bother looking at him straight.

'Yes, sir,' Paul managed. 'Paul Porter, sir.'

'Where are those boys of yours?' Roger Groves added to Jedediah, apparently taking some entertainment in leaving Paul uncertain as to whether Mister Groves had heard him answer or not. 'Not idling about, I hope? I've other business in this neighbourhood today, you know.' He gave a whistle through his teeth to denote the shamefulness of such slackness, a mocking little two-tone. This was one of Roger Groves' most irritating habits, the tooth-whistling: he had perfected it as a lad, and it was now a piercing squeak, unmusical and off-key. It was said the man would travel to hear a church organ, so it was highly unlikely he was tone-deaf: he could hear his own tuning right enough. Jedediah was also fond of music – the People are prone to singing, and it's a poor fairy-smith who can't, if necessary, sing back – and the sound of that flat, clanging whistle crawled right down his nape.

'My son's talking to Paul Porter's sons,' Jedediah said with rigid formality. 'Useful to get word of a place, and children often know more than the grown. My grandson's . . .' Curse the boy, where was he? Jedediah was about to invent a lie when he heard a cheerful chirrup behind him: 'Grandpa! Grandpa, wait till I tell you!'

'. . . that's him now,' Jedediah said. John's appearance was only half a relief: these were men who needed handling, and placating the mighty was one of John's many blind spots.

'Well now,' said Roger, viewing the small, strutting figure with a humorous eye. 'I see we're keeping cockerels these days, Jedediah.'

Jedediah had buried his wife and lost his father before he was thirty, and by now, the number of folks who still called him by his first name could be counted on one hand. He was fairly sure Roger Groves knew this, but he managed to redirect his anger onto a safer target. 'And where have *you* been?' he snapped at his grandson.

'I,' John declared, too pleased with himself to feel the sting, 'have been working on the Porter Puss. And you'll hear no more talk out of it, Mister Porter, you have my word. It was,' John added, enjoying the phrase, 'a simple job. Not a difficulty, you'll be happy to hear.'

Jedediah bent a sharp eye on him. John was given to boasting, but not to the point of claiming he'd done a job he hadn't. 'What did you do?' he said.

'Grandpa,' said John, with dignity, 'I think I had better not talk trade secrets in front of company.'

Roger gave another mocking whistle. Identifying a note by ear is one of those skills that must be learned young, and it's a skill you need if you're to check your talismans have the right ring to them, so John's pitch was as good as Jedediah's. At the shrilling squeak, he pulled a face. 'Why's he here?' he asked.

'I,' Roger said with a grin that showed his unclean teeth, 'am the man who's here to buy this mill, little cockerel. Maybe I'll buy you up while I'm at it, if you're so clever.'

John had never liked being teased. 'I am not for sale,' he declared, drawing himself up. 'But if you buy my services in the future, you'll find they answer.'

Roger Groves gave a shout of laughter, and the sound of it was loud enough that it reached Matthew round the back of the house. He'd mostly been just listening to the chatter of the two boys – Jedediah was right that it was part of good surveying to hear what the local children had to say, and while the Porter lads weren't giving him much new information, it was usually Matthew's favourite part of the business. But he'd heard that laugh before, and felt it urgent to hasten round to the gate.

'Ah,' said Roger, 'and here we complete the set. How's that wife of yours, Matthew Smith? Still got that firm chest on her, or was four brats too much for it?'

For the first time in his life, Matthew Smith experienced a genuine wish for a fistfight.

Roger grinned again. 'So, my lads,' he said, 'I've this purchase in mind. Any fey doings for me to price out?'

The look on Paul Porter's face was enough to snap Matthew back to himself – albeit with the resolution that he'd be extremely kind to Janet when he returned home – and he gathered his energies. 'I can say,' he said with an effort, 'that apart from one small problem we're here to mend today—'

'Oh, I've fixed that, Dada,' John announced.

Matthew started a little, not sure whether this was wonderful news or horrifying, but he was determined to make his point. 'Well, in that case, I can say that this is as well-kept a place as you'd hope to see. I'd like to put in my word for Mister Porter, sir, if I may. It's not every man can keep a place as clean and natural as this, and if you'll take my advice, I'd keep the miller with the mill, sir. I see nothing but good work from corner to corner.'

Roger laughed. 'Oh, you village boys know how to scratch each other's backs, I've never doubted that,' he said. It wasn't a refusal, though, or not yet, and Matthew was beginning on an explanation that he'd never vouch for a man who'd bring a neighbourhood into disrepute, when the two little boys, Tommy and Bill, hurried up.

'Dada,' said Bill, 'that man's been asking us all about the place.' He pointed at Matthew, who gave him a brief pat on the shoulder. 'Why are there more men here now?'

Roger looked at the small child frowning up at him, and grinned at the opportunity. 'Oh,' he said, 'I'm the man that's here to drown your cat.'

Bill screamed, and that was bad. What was worse was that

Tommy made a rush at both of them, and while it wasn't a real attack, just the desperate flail of a little boy with his pet facing the depths, it frighted Daisy up onto her back legs, dropping Ephraim Brady into the dust below. Matthew grabbed Tommy and swung him out of harm's way, for Daisy's hooves were lashing about, and Paul snatched up Bill, and Jedediah and John were stepping forward to soothe the panicking mare when another of her kicks caught Roger Groves' horse on the hock, and it too gave a jolt and bucked Roger Groves right off its back.

The two rich men lay frozen in the dirt while John and Jedediah talked Daisy to a quivering stop. She was shaking now, but dancing on her tiptoes rather than rearing in panic, and Jedediah's voice was smoothing her over: 'Easy, girl, easy, girl, good girl, that's a good girl . . .'

The place was very quiet. Then Bill, safe in his father's arms, pointed at the bad men in the dirt and gave a cackle of vindicated, righteous laughter.

Ephraim Brady had determined before he rose that he'd have nothing worse than a bruise or two, that no injury had come to his horse, and that therefore he'd lost nothing of consequence and could dismiss the incident. He stood, brushed himself down and offered a hand to Roger Groves.

Roger Groves liked a laugh himself, but being laughed at was something else. He took Ephraim Brady's hand and rose like a set of hackles. 'Brady,' he said, 'I'll change this well-kept place of yours for the Ware farm, if it's the farm you want. We'll close tomorrow. But I'll have the mill and not the miller, or I won't buy.'

'M-mister Brady . . .' stammered Paul, but Ephraim Brady was not a waster of time.

'Done,' he said, and shook Groves' proffered hand. 'You'll stand witness, Jedediah and Matthew Smith. Tomorrow morning in the smithy, then.'

Matthew opened his mouth, but Mister Brady had already turned on his heel. There was, after all, no reason for him not to let the Porters go homeless; it was none of his business, and if the Smiths disliked it, that was no loss to him. He reclaimed Daisy's reins with a neat touch, mounted up, and was on his way.

# CHAPTER 7

Janet Smith knew she couldn't go for a walk. It was a pity, for wandering the lanes was one of her great loves, but she would just have to be responsible today: with the menfolk out of the smithy, someone had to be on hand take messages. By mid-morning she'd attended to several customers: a new poker ordered, two sets of tools to sharpen, the sound of tiny feet up in the hayloft that appeared to be dancing a jig. It was nothing exciting, and she was feeling rather bored and distractible when the door knocker sounded again.

Her spirits revived as she answered it, for there stood Francie Thorpe. Francie was a particular pet of hers, and if anyone could cheer the day, she was the lass for it.

'Good day, Francie love,' Janet said with a smile. 'Won't you come in?'

Francie gave her a smile back as she entered. The twins had taken up juggling in the last few weeks, so the place wasn't looking its neatest, but Francie was well accustomed to Smith ways and settled down in the kitchen without comment.

'Well, my dear,' Janet said, 'I hope there's nothing dreadful that brings you to us today.'

'Oh no, Mistress Janet. Dada and I are quite all right. But he had some tools he wanted sharpened, and I said I'd be happy to take them to you, for he had to make another visit today and I know he'd like them with you sooner rather than later.' She proffered a clinking satchel.

'Now, that's good of you, to run such a long errand,' said Janet; it was quite a distance between Francie's home and Gyrford. 'Did you ride all the way?'

Francie gave a shy smile. 'Oh yes. But it was no trouble. Dada started keeping a horse for me last year. Daffodil – she's outside. She's lovely to ride.'

'Well, that is handsome,' said Janet, patting Francie's hand. Janet was immovable in her belief that no child in the country was better than her own, but it had to be admitted that between Molly's many criticisms of her housekeeping, and the twins' tendency to live less like regular family members and more like a wandering festival that happened to be passing through her house every day, there was something restful about sitting with a girl so full of obliging notions. 'Father's very proud to see him so prosperous, you know. Make sure you tell him we said so.' She delivered this instruction with a wink: Jedediah's praise tended to the sincere rather than the fulsome, and Janet felt it helpful to pass along his good opinions behind his back. 'Not but what I'm sure you deserve to do well, lovie.'

'Oh, I don't know,' said Francie, blushing a little. 'It's Dada who prospers. I just try to help.'

Janet patted her hand again, and Francie appeared to gather some courage.

'Mistress Janet,' she said, 'I — I hope not to misspeak. I should not like to cause trouble.'

Janet's hand froze over Francie's. 'Is it Tobias?' she said.

'Oh.' Francie flushed a little. 'No. No, I am sorry to— No, he is— Well, as he usually is.'

'Has he been in the woods again?'

Francie stared down into her lap. 'Dada caught him on the wander again a couple of days ago. Brought him back. I fear— Toby is fond of Dada, you know. Dada told him he mustn't go out, but, well, you know how he is. Toby hears folks' deeds more than their words, and Dada's kind to him. I am afraid Toby felt it a game of hide and seek. I do not think . . . but, no, I had something else to say.' She drew a breath, preparing herself to inflict unwanted news. 'Mistress Janet, a little while ago I found John wandering the Bellame woods. I . . . perhaps I should have told you before. But . . . well, I sent him home. He made me promise not to tell you.' Her voice was quiet. 'And I thought if I came here with no excuse, Mister Brady might – well, Dada says he has taken against Toby, and means to become his landlord, and I did not want to give him cause to look from his window and see me coming in, without a pack under my arm to explain it.'

Janet did not remove her hand from Francie's, but she sat very still. 'What was John about in the woods?'

'Nothing that I could see,' Francie said in haste. 'Nothing wrong. He said he wished to meet Toby. He just looked a little . . . um . . .'

'Touched.' The word came out so flat that Francie flinched, and Janet gathered herself. It felt like taking every part of her face and hauling it, by force, into a reassuring smile. 'No, no, I am not angry, dear. We have all seen Johnny in his starey mood.'

'He did nothing foolish,' Francie assured her, a little desperate to see Janet looking so grey. 'I would not— Well, Toby works hard in the fields; he does fine work. He lives a good life, if he can be safe.'

Janet opened her mouth to say that a touched fairy-smith was another matter. A fairy-smith must deal with the People, day after day, and it was hard enough to keep your wits even if they hadn't laid a wisp across your soul. Back when you were a babe, unborn, unthought of, unprotected, and it was all your mother's fault.

She squeezed Francie's hand. 'Well,' she said, with a brightness that was only slightly shrill, 'a starey look isn't the last word on anything. Perhaps he's only silly.'

'I couldn't say,' said Francie, looking remorseful for starting this conversation.

Janet sat another moment, then said, 'So, my love, I know you are fond of roses. Come outside with me. I have some fine climbers just now, and I'm sure you can find a good use for them.'

Francie followed Janet out of the house. Janet managed to keep up a steady stream of ideas about how best to display flowers fresh or hang them up to dry, not to mention thoughts on training, dead-heading and pruning, and as she stood in the bright autumn air, enmeshed in scent, she was able tell herself, more firmly than she had indoors, that it might not be so terrible. A little staring was proof of nothing. And here were her roses; they were blown and beautiful, whatever else the world held. Francie made an earnest effort to respond, and after a while, in the softness of each other's company, things eased a little. The two of them were engrossed in the sweet tassels of petal when another visitor came up to the house.

Francie ducked her head and concentrated on the flowers, not wanting to intrude on Janet's prerogatives, but Janet turned with resolute graciousness and said, 'Good day. How may I help you this fine Friday?' before she saw who it was.

It was Anthony Brady.

The indulged brother of Ephraim could never have been a welcome sight to any sensible villager, but nobody said this to Anthony. Lacking any trade to keep him occupied, he was prone to wandering around the place, and when he turned up, few could afford to shoo him off. Ephraim preferred Anthony to ride the countryside and had given him a good horse for the purpose, but while Anthony liked riding well enough, he liked walking too, and he was always interested to see what folks were doing.

Those he bothered might, if they were honest, admit he was a good-looking young man, though if they did, they were generally less willing to admit that he also bore a fair resemblance to his brother. Anthony was brown-headed and blue-eyed where Ephraim was stony grey, and neither were especially tall, but Anthony had the health and cheerfulness of one always cared for, and he carried his hat in his hand with the grace of a man for whom courtesy would get anything. Which, to be fair to him, it usually did.

'Good day, Mistress Smith,' he said, pleasant and only slightly less formal than befitted the dignity of a farrier's lady. 'I don't suppose you've seen my brother this last hour?'

Janet preferred to consider herself a just and reasonable woman, but really, Anthony did not make it easy when he insisted on liking his abominable brother so openly. 'That I have not,' she said, with a shortness just this side of curt. 'I know he had to meet my Matthew at the Porters' mill this morning, so I suppose he will be there, or on his way back from there. Just when, I couldn't say.'

'Oh.' Anthony bore a look of disappointment, and no sign of trying to conceal or manage it. 'I was hoping he could join me for a ride this afternoon. It's such fine weather.'

'Well, you will have to tell him when you see him,' said Janet, not feeling inclined to make any suggestions. Very probably Ephraim Brady would join Anthony for a ride if Anthony asked; unless there was money in the question, Ephraim said yes to every blessed thing Anthony suggested. It was a pleasure she didn't much feel like helping Anthony arrange, though.

'Perhaps he might be coming back this way,' Anthony proposed. 'I could wait here.'

'He might,' said Janet, 'but I wouldn't promise it. My Matthew and my John and Mister Smith will be back this way, but I don't suppose Mister Brady will have a need to travel with them.'

'Oh dear,' said Anthony. 'I don't know what I ought to do, then.' He looked at Janet with an air of appeal.

Honestly, Janet thought, even her Johnny would have better sense than to loiter around dithering. If another man had been hesitating in the square like this she would probably have invited him in to sit and rest, but she wasn't going to do that, and she wasn't going to help any Brady man do his thinking for him either. Matthew had remarked before that he thought Anthony seemed a bit lonely, but really, if the fellow insisted on being fond of Ephraim, what else could he expect?

'It is a puzzle,' said Anthony, but before Janet had the chance to throw something at him, they heard the clatter of a cart and Dobbs drew into sight, pulling after him the most doleful-looking collection of family Janet had ever seen.

'Why, Matthew, what's the matter?' she asked, dropping her basket and leaving roses, Francie Thorpe and Anthony Brady all to their own devices.

Matthew reached out to take her hand over the edge of the cart. 'Oh, dear, it's bad news,' he said. There was a certain help-lessness in his manner that most definitely did not remind her of Anthony Brady: Matthew was a man of character, and if he felt helpless, Janet was sure it could only be the cruelties of fate to blame.

'Oh, my love,' she said, 'do tell me. Did it go ill at the Porters'? I do hope you didn't have to drown that poor cat.'

'*I* fixed the cat,' John announced with some defiance. 'But do you know, Mama, that Mister Brady is just going to sell the mill anyway, and to that horrible Roger Groves, and he swears he won't let them stay there!'

Janet glanced at Matthew, who nodded in mute distress. The two of them held each other's gaze for a long moment. It wasn't just the prospect of the Porters losing their home, though Heaven knew, that was terrible enough. The Porters were neighbours who understood about Tobias Ware. If the boy was caught with a coney, Paul and Sukie would swear he'd taken it from their garden, or at least that he might have done. Remove the Porters and put in strangers, and the last line of lies that might protect Tobias from the rope was broken.

'Bad luck to the pair of them,' added Jedediah. 'Never saw two rogues standing so close together.'

'I beg your pardon,' said Anthony Brady, who had been listening to the conversation with the interest of a man not sure what else to do with his time, and now fired up in an instant of offended fraternity. 'I have nothing to say of Roger Groves, he does lack manner, but how can you call my brother a rogue? I'm sure,' he added, evidently trying to forgive those who knew not what they did, 'you'll be sorry for it when you're calmer.'

'He and his buyer between them are putting an honest family out of their living,' said Jedediah. 'Make of that what you will, and see if you're sorry for it.'

'But Ephraim doesn't tell folks what to do with what they've bought,' argued Anthony, looking a little troubled. Money and trade were matters in which he had only the vaguest ideas, but the phrase had a certain solid ring to it that suggested it had come from some other, harder-headed source than himself. 'After all, we couldn't go on if folks did that. Imagine if you told folks what to do with all the things you make for them.'

Jedediah, who sold talismans with firm instructions on what to do with them, and would stand over any buyer dim enough to need further guidance, was of the opinion that Anthony Brady was beneath dispute. He merely grunted, and gave a meaning glance at his son: Matthew was better at speaking soft to foolish men.

'We do face a sad thing, though,' said Matthew gamely. 'Your brother, now, Mister Brady, he had no malice against the Porters, I'm sure, and I'm sure he knew the value of good tenants like them. But Mister Groves, he's another matter. He . . .' Matthew struggled; speaking ill of folks was unchristian, but there was no other way to say it. 'He took a spite against the Porters, only because their children grew upset when he spoke rough to them. Now he says he'll put them off the land, where they've lived these fifteen years, and your brother is selling to him nonetheless. It's very hard on the Porters, Mister Brady.'

Anthony was not an unkind young man, and he looked uncomfortable. 'Now, Mister Smith, I'm sure Ephraim has his good reasons. There may be all kinds of things we don't understand.'

'Maybe *you* don't understand them,' said John, before his grandpa could kick him, 'but you could stop the sale if you wanted. He said he was selling it to buy land for you.'

Anthony flushed. At home, things were simple: Ephraim was the best of brothers. Out of doors, though, folks were often unfriendly; Ephraim could always find a reason to dismiss someone's judgement, but it was rather depressing, having to guard yourself against the views of everyone else. Folks seemed to like each other, but Anthony himself was outside that circle, and years of being greeted with suspicion would wear down anyone's faith in their neighbourhood. 'He said nothing of it to me,' he said, which was true enough; Ephraim's secretiveness was not a habit he relaxed even in Anthony's presence. 'I'm sure it's not as you say.'

'I don't go to argue with you, Mister Brady,' said Matthew, striving to get the subject back onto productive grounds. 'But we saw him and Mister Groves agree on it. They shook hands on the deal: to sell the mill without the miller.'

'Well, then I'm afraid that's that,' Anthony said, enough encouraged by Matthew Smith's gentler voice that he felt able to offer helpful information. 'Ephraim never goes back on a handshake.'

This was so grimly plausible that no one had anything to say. Then there was a sound from the roses, a timid, cautious little, 'Um . . .'

All of them turned to see Francie, standing quiet before the trellis of roses. Anthony stared at her, her waterfall of curls, her sweet brown eyes, the buds and leaves around her like an aureole, and everything else in the world went out of his head.

'I . . . If I may,' said Francie, rather as if she was taking her life in her hands by intervening. 'Does Mister Brady himself have anything against the Porters?'

'I – I am sure not.' Anthony was stammering, staring at the beautiful, beautiful girl who stood there so fragrant and dainty and, and . . . his eyes were ruling his mind, and he could think of no words that truly fitted such a vision. It had been a long time since Francie had crossed his isolated path, and the warm-skinned young woman before him having bloomed from the little girl he'd been half in love with fifteen years ago was almost miraculous. 'Ephraim is the best of men. He would never carry a spite. He is quite the best of men.' His voice strained with earnestness.

'Then perhaps he might have some other land that needs

tenants? Or some other way to make amends to them?' Francie was blushing herself. Anthony had his faults in the eyes of, well, more or less everyone, but Francie lived by the forest with her father and involved herself in gossip less than most. She'd cried over the loss of his friendship when they were little, and she remembered him very well indeed, and now here he was, grown and handsome, looking at her as if he'd seen a sunrise.

'I am sure,' Anthony said, eager now. He could promise this girl anything. Memories were flooding his mind: afternoons ankle-deep in water, gazing at plump tadpoles; mornings of scratches and laughter and tongues stained bright with black-berries; adventures across the fields where you could be an eagle or a dragon or a hero everyone liked. Small arms around his neck, and a face that lit with delight when she saw him. 'I shall speak to him – indeed I shall.'

'Oh!' Francie gave a transported smile. In her confusion she proffered him a rose, and as she wasn't looking what she was doing, a thorn sank into her thumb. Red drops pattered on the ground between them. She hardly felt it.

The Smiths looked at each other. Ephraim Brady might deny his brother nothing, except when it came to business, but this was not a case for hope. Roger Groves was not a man who'd let go of his spites, and he could make them stick. If Ephraim offered the Porters any relief, it would be the end of his deal-ings with Groves, and why should he take such a loss? It would only be to please the Thorpes, who were no one to him, and the Smiths, who appeared bent on frustrating him. For once in his life, Anthony Brady was going to hear his brother tell him 'no'.

John looked at Francie and Anthony, staring at each other in a most annoying way. He didn't see what anyone had to smile about.

Janet sat up late thinking. Or trying not to think, not about John. There was his starey look in the woods, but then, she liked to look at green places too. There was that thing he'd said to Matthew, about the woods being quiet as a mouse, but then, he was a child; children had their fancies. And his silencing of the Porter Puss: that was an achievement, surely. Matthew and Jedediah conversed with the People all the time. With iron and negotiation, not with gossip and trickery, but they talked.

No, she wouldn't think it. Someone needed to warn Franklin that Anthony Brady was cutting eyes at his Francie. He'd be about the forest somewhere, and Matthew would find him the fastest, but Matthew — well, he had too kind and saintly a nature to enjoy giving stern warnings. She'd send Molly, perhaps. Perhaps not John.

But the resentment of Ephraim Brady was another matter. The selling of the Porters' home wasn't done out of spite, or not in particular, but it showed one thing clear as frost on a pane: life would not be safe for any tenant of his. Or anyone else he could overpower. She'd heard of the hanging of Magpie Tilly. Some folks had nodded and said, well, what can you expect, the woman was a pest and a simpleton, and those folks were no longer Janet's friends.

Once Ephraim Brady acquired the Ware farm — and from what Matthew had said, he had set about the purchase at least partly because he'd scented that the Smiths wouldn't like it – then he could catch Toby trespassing any time. He couldn't hunt him in the woods; he was no forester or fairy-smith and would have been trespassing himself. But on a farm he owned? He could walk into the garden and plant a chair by the hedge and wait for Toby to run past him. It would be a reward for him, turning in a trespasser, at the very least. And the man would destroy someone for less than that.

Janet lay in the moonlight, and thought, and the following morning, she packed a basket of early-ripening apples and set across the square.

Ephraim Brady could afford a maidservant, but he employed no such extravagance. Alice Brady lived alone in the house all day, with nothing to do but clean and cook and make herself useful on as little money as he could possibly allow her. She kept his books for him, or at least she did when the pressure of business forced Ephraim to part with them temporarily, but for the rest of the time, she was just unseen.

In the earlier years of her marriage, she'd been more communicative, catching out dishonest bargains in the marketplace and warning her neighbours, and stopping to fuss over their dogs, but that had stopped. You never knew who Ephraim might need to trade with next, and someone having a grudge against his wife might hinder that. As for animals, the Bradys kept neither dog nor cats, and only Ephraim had a horse of his own. Alice groomed the mare, and spent a lot of time in the stable, but she never stopped to chat with passers-by, and it was Ephraim who brought the beast in for shoeing. Alice was a woman who lived within her own walls – and since Ephraim never wasted daylight sitting in his house, and didn't consider time in his wife's company well spent, it was a safe wager that he wouldn't be home.

Janet was a sociable woman, for the most part, and while her best love was wandering the lanes listening to her own fancies, she did enjoy a visit. Folks had not taken her very seriously as an unmarried girl, regarding her as fanciful, idle and unblessed with the qualities of a useful woman, and sixteen-odd years with Matthew had not dimmed the satisfaction she felt at being greeted as a farrier's lady, a woman to respect and speak civil to and make no comments to about her housekeeping and habits, thank you. With good friends her manner could be unaffected, and with the vulnerable and the honest she would go to some lengths to set her hosts at ease and draw them out on any little thing she could do for them, but it was difficult to resist the temptation to play upon the stuffier folks' patience a little bit, and Janet had been known to make entire visits where she'd say nothing more than a majestic, 'If you suppose so, dear,' or base her comments on whether they rhymed with folks' questions rather than whether they strictly answered them. It was a habit Matthew had made gentle efforts to dissuade, but since her re-enactments of the visits made him laugh against his will, he was making little headway. Visiting, in short, was a hobby for Janet, and one that she cultivated with more enjoyment of its license than acceptance of its seriousness.

But Alice Brady, she never teased. She had seen the white bloom in her hair and the lines etch in her face, faster every year, and to that woman, Janet was as close as she could be to her sincere self. But it was hard to be sincere with a woman who gave you no openings for conversation, for Alice Brady said as little as possible. She hadn't been so silent in her youth, but her youth was behind her now, and if you looked at her today, you'd see little trace that it had ever existed.

Alice opened the door a long pause after Janet's knock. Her hair was combed, and though her face was sweaty as if she had been scrubbing, her apron was snow-white. She stood for a long instant before saying, in a soft, hoarse voice, 'Mistress Smith. Good afternoon.'

'Good afternoon, my dear Mistress Brady,' said Janet. She really wished she could call this woman Alice, but the invitation had never come. 'I hope I find you hale today?'

Alice looked at her. Not a finger or hair of her body moved. 'Yes, thank you,' she said. Just that: she added nothing.

After a few seconds, Janet ploughed forward. 'I hope the cross my Matthew made for you is serving?' Her conscience, not normally an over-active organ, twinged a little bit: it was low, to try to force your way into a woman's house by reminding her of a favour, but she couldn't stand in the doorway for ever.

'Yes, thank you,' said Alice. Her voice was hushed, as if she wasn't in the habit of raising it to a normal level.

'I am glad,' said Janet. 'He's always had a great respect for you. We all have, you know.'

Alice had been still before, but now she was frozen, like a bird under the eye of a hawk. She said nothing at all.

'Well,' said Janet, since Alice was clearly not going to answer that, or even to do what she herself would have done, which would have been to ask, 'Why? You barely know me.' Since the 'well' drew no response, Janet persisted, 'Well, now, our early ripening tree is putting out more apples than we can eat or store this season.' This was not entirely true, but truth was not one of Janet's priorities. 'So we have rather a plenty of them, and I thought it might be pleasant to give some to our respected neighbours. Perhaps you would care for some?'

Alice's eyes flicked to the basket, then to Janet's face, quick and anxious. At the sight, Janet felt a more serious twinge: now she thought of it, she'd put the woman in a bind. Accepting them might place her under some kind of obligation, while rejecting them would be turning away free supplies, and she would have to make either choice without her husband's permission. Janet watched Alice's stricken face for a few more seconds before deciding that the only thing to do was tell the discreditable truth. It wasn't as if Ephraim Brady wouldn't guess it anyway; he was good at discreditable truths.

'The truth is, my dear,' she said, 'I've come to try my influence. Your husband, you know, is planning on selling the mill the Porters have worked these fifteen years, and the buyer, Mister Roger Groves, will put them out. We all have a high opinion of the Porters, and the sale will be a sad business for them. I don't wish to ask you for more than you can do, but if you have any sway with your husband, well, tonight would be a charitable time to call on it. The sale closes tomorrow, and it'll be a sad thing if it goes ahead. The Porters are fine millers, and much less trouble than a farm, truly. He might still change his mind. I think he would find it better so.'

That was the truth out, or at least as much of it as didn't touch Tobias Ware. Alice stared at her guest for another moment. Her mouth twitched as if she meant to open it, thin, dry lips almost at the point of parting. But she said nothing, and after another long minute, Janet sighed, and set the basket down at her feet. 'Well, I shan't ask what can't be done,' she said. 'I'll carry no grudge if you don't. Take the apples anyway, my dear, as neighbour to neighbour. Perhaps you'll enjoy them, they have a fine flavour.'

She turned to go. Alice cleared her throat, a dry rattle, and said, 'Thank you, Mistress Smith.'

Janet turned, but Alice had already picked up the basket and closed the door.

Janet watched from her window as the sun dragged down the sky, but if Ephraim Brady returned home that evening, she must have missed it. Nobody brought any good news.

Jedediah retired early to bed, saying nothing to anyone. He stopped long enough to give John a kiss goodnight, which so astonished the boy that he stayed awake chattering to his sisters until Molly had to promise to make him apple puffs in the morning if he would just *please* go to sleep now. Molly was a girl of some spirit, and while honestly fond of John, she would ordinarily have simply thrown a pillow at him and told him to hush up. Everyone seemed to be stepping lightly around him today, though, looking at him oddly and acting sad, and she thought perhaps he might be sickening for something.

Janet and Matthew lay hand in hand in their bed, staring up into the dark.

'Perhaps,' Matthew said, in a whisper so as not to disturb the household, 'we may still help the Porters find a place.'

'Perhaps, like enough,' said Janet, squeezing Matthew's fingers. 'They are respected folks.'

'And,' said Matthew after a pause, 'even if they must – if they can do no better than to go for jobs next Michaelmas fair, perhaps we may speak for them. Help them find a place where they could stay together. Perhaps.'

They were silent for a moment.

'And perhaps,' said Matthew, 'we may contrive a pen that does keep Tobias in. If we keep trying. It may be that he will not wander again. Then it will not matter whether he has neighbours who care to speak for him, should there be trouble.'

Janet turned on her side and laid an arm across Matthew's chest. It was a broad expanse, and she was quite a little woman, but tonight, it didn't seem quite such a shelter as it usually did. 'Perhaps you will,' she said. 'And he is a sweet boy, from what you say. Perhaps his new neighbours will care for him too.'

'Perhaps.' Matthew thought of Tobias. He hadn't called him sweet to Janet; he'd just described what he did, much of it screaming. That was what she had taken from his account. He agreed with her, but the fact that she'd heard of a touched boy and called him a sweet one spoke of a place in their souls they didn't look at straight.

There was a silence. 'Johnny is well enough,' Janet said. Her whisper had a scrape-edged quality that cut at his heart. 'He told me all about that cat, and what he did. I call that talent. Not feyness.'

Matthew took hold of her arm; he was not sure he ever

wanted her to remove it. 'I was glad he solved the problem,' he said. He blamed himself more than Janet: she wasn't a fairy-smith, and he was. He should have had his wits about him and realised she was planning something. Then he might have helped. If he'd been a man she could confide in. Or if he hadn't been so drunk that night John began. He'd never been good at resisting Janet's charms, but if he'd been sober . . . He didn't drink, these days. Though he still wasn't good at resisting Janet's charms. He might be a better man if he was, a better father, per-haps, but he couldn't stop being in love; he didn't know how.

'It was canny of him,' said Janet. 'Canny. Not uncanny. He did well there.' Why there had been no more children after Johnny was one of those questions they didn't dwell on. But she was thirty-five now; she hadn't been pregnant in ten years. Johnny was all the son they'd ever have.

'Yes,' said Matthew. Now Janet's arm didn't feel enough; he lifted her onto his chest, blanketing himself with the woman who could hear his thoughts without his having to say them. 'I hope so.' He rested his hand against her head, nestling his fingers amongst the soft, warm curls. 'But that does not do much good for Toby Ware.'

There was nothing more to say. The wind blew, clattering their windows and creeping, icy and thin, through cracks and corners, and the night fretted and gasped outside, black and deep-starred and unruly.

The sun rose white on the morning when Ephraim Brady would come to buy a farm that couldn't shelter a touched boy. The cobbles of the square held a dull gleam, and the air was full of woodsmoke; folks were rising early. Twists of grey tumbled upwards from the chimneys around Gyrford, but the sky remained clear, cloudless, empty as water.

Jedediah and his boys were up and dressed, ready for Brady and Groves to come to the smithy to make their final deal. It would be faced, and then what would follow must be faced too. Life was not meant to be easy, Jedediah's glare told Matthew, and Matthew lowered his gaze and prayed under his breath, and Janet put bread on the table and said, to the slight confusion of her children, 'We can always be good neighbours. If worse comes, we can think of what to do then.'

They waited in the smithy, but the visitor who came was not Roger Groves, nor Ephraim Brady. It was a packman, Andy Bryant, a fairly truthful fellow by the standards of his trade and an early riser by profession. Andy was a talker, who lived on charm and scraps of cloth, but this morning his voice was hoarse and his face grey as stone, and what he had to tell, he had no fine words for dressing.

Before the sun was high in the sky, word ran through Gyrford in a frantic whisper that Roger Groves had been found that morning, lying dead in Chalk Lane with his throat torn out.

## CHAPTER 8

It was a visit John was absolutely not allowed to attend. More than that, Matthew had gone to the lengths of volunteering for the task: while he had a great dislike for gore, he had a greater one for exposing Johnny to sights unfit for a child, and when it came to keeping the boy at home, Jedediah could do a much sterner job. Out on Dobbs Matthew set, answering all he passed that yes, he had heard the story, and he was going to see, and no, he had nothing more to say.

It was a cold morning, cold as winter. Up on Chalk Lane, the wind screamed.

Matthew wasn't near-sighted, but somehow it was difficult to see to the end of the road. There wasn't a mist, and the air was unclouded, but distance seemed to recede before him: places that should have been within a few yards were hazed, as if a great way away. Dobbs shied, shied again, shying at nothing. In the pale daylight, everything felt shaded and confused.

It was a long journey, too long. Away from the church clock, Matthew was usually able to tell the time by the angle of the sun, but the angle wasn't right here. He had no idea how much time had passed as he rode his whimpering horse down Chalk Lane, gravity dragging on him, the green fields either side flowing, at the corners of his eye, like the tumble of a waterfall.

But as he moved forward, the air grew clear, uncomfortably so, with a solid clarity like glass. It was there before him, suddenly: the thing he hadn't seen ten yards further back. A stocky body, chalk dust all up its boots as if they had pounded and pounded along the lane. The jacket was the one he had seen on Roger Groves yesterday, and the boots were Roger Groves', and the shirt and the belt and the hands. The face was nothing earthly, frozen and grotesque, all warp and scream. Around the body were great black footprints, burned deep into the white. There was nothing left of Roger Groves' neck but a mangled gulf of flesh, ragged threads and browning pools and the smeared gleam of bone.

It wasn't the farrier's job to convey a body to its relations, but after he'd finished being sick on the verge, Matthew knew it would have to be done. He looked up and down the road. The Porters or the Wares? He hated to trouble either of them, but there was nothing for it; the body was heavy and would need men to carry it, and while he could have lifted it himself, carrying the rigid mass down the road slung over his saddle like a slain partridge would be some kind of blasphemy. There should be a stretcher, with men to bear it.

Paul Porter would help him, but he was just one man, and then there were the little boys to think of. No, he would have to go to the Wares and hope Tobias didn't see him.

\*

It was early morning still, but the Wares would be up, if they'd slept at all. As Matthew entered the gate, he saw the oldest of the Ware sons, Peter, standing by his brother's shelter. 'Finished your coney, Toby?' Peter was saying, his voice as cheerful as if he were asking about porridge. 'Then it's time for work. Wash hands, there's a good lad . . . oh.' He turned, and saw Matthew standing at his gate. 'Oh, good day, Mister Smith. Look, Toby, here's Mister Smith come to call on us, he made you this good sleeping place, remember? I hope you are well, Mister Smith?'

Tobias gave a grinding howl and drummed his hands on the ground. It had been quite a few visits since Matthew had last tried to touch him, but the boy learned fear fast and did not forget it.

'Oh, dear,' said Peter, in a voice gently chiding. 'Oh dear, Toby. Here's Mister Smith who is your friend. Mister Smith, perhaps if you wouldn't mind, you might take an apple off that tree beside you and give it to him, I think that would— Toby, would you like an apple with your breakfast? An apple, Toby? There's a treat, see? Mister Smith has an apple for you.'

Matthew was feeling too sick to disobey anyone. He reached up and tugged at an apple, tugged at another, until he found one ripe enough to unlatch itself from the branch. Without a word he edged forward, staring more at his boots than at the boys. There was a slight smudge of dust across his toes, and he chided himself for the thought that perhaps when he got home he could burn them. Boots didn't grow on bushes. Chalk could be wiped off. And maybe the wiping cloth could be burned. Yes, nobody would blame him for that, if he used a rag.

Without a word, he held the apple out to Tobias.

Tobias looked at it. He still cringed away from Matthew, but the sight of it set him bouncing a little on his heels.

'Lovely apple, Tobias,' said Peter. 'That's from Mister Smith, because he likes you very much.'

Matthew felt the scrape of long nails flash across his palm, and then there was a crunch and some smothered half-giggles as Tobias dug his teeth into the fruit. He held it in both palms, his head shaking back and forth as he worried bites of flesh out of it.

'There, that's good,' said Peter. 'Good boy, Toby! Well done, Toby!'

Matthew, tasting acid in his mouth, couldn't manage a smile. 'Good morning, Peter Ware,' he said. 'I – I bring you some news. And some questions. I fear your landlord has met with . . . with some ill luck.'

Tobias Ware had to stay in his sleeping place late that day, as the family gathered around their kitchen table and stared at Matthew, wide-eyed in dismay as the tale was told.

'We'll make a stretcher for him, Mister Smith,' said Jonas after a long pause. 'Least we can do.'

Matthew nodded. What he really wanted to do was go home and forget all this, but no, he was bridled by duty: a fairy-smith had to know the doings of the People, and it was unthinkable he should leave without trying to learn what he could.

'Forgive me asking,' he said, 'but can you tell me what you heard last night?'

The Wares glanced at each other.

'Little enough,' said Jonas. He gave Matthew a blank look. 'We prefer not to listen out for Black Hal in this house.'

Matthew foundered. 'True, true,' he said, then felt a fool; how was he to know what was true for them? 'I don't suppose you know how Mister Groves came to be there?'

The Wares looked at each other again.

'He came by last night,' said Jonas. 'I suppose you'd know that, him being so close to us.'

'Oh – yes, yes of course,' said Matthew, feeling even more of a fool. He should have worked that out, for why else would Roger Groves have been at this end of Chalk Lane, if not to visit the Wares? All that could be said in his own defence was that the thing on the road, dense-fleshed, dressed in good cloth, and white-eyed as a boiled fish, did not invoke the image of a man who made business calls.

'Well, he came by,' said Jonas. 'Telling us the sale was to happen today. Toby was sitting in the doorway, and Mister Groves pushed at him with his boot-toe until Peter had to carry him right away.'

'He . . . was a little upset,' said Peter tightly.

'Mister Groves said he wouldn't have such a burden on him for a king's ransom, and I said Toby was a good worker and had his little ways. And Mister Groves said' – Jonas was speeding up – 'that he had his ways with other men's game, he said that twice, I think, Mister Smith, like he thought he was funny. And he said we'd better keep him in if we wanted him, for he didn't think Ephraim Brady was the man to step between a tenant and a lord, and if Toby kept poaching, then a rope would lift him off our hands comfortably enough, he was telling us between friends.'

'Oh,' said Matthew. 'My. That . . . was . . . I am sorry to think a man should have to meet his Maker so soon after such an . . . uncharitable remark.'

He was trying to be sincere, but Jonas' face was stiff. 'Yes,' he said, his voice harder than Matthew had ever heard it. 'Yes, that is a thought to think on.'

'Anyway,' Peter put in with hasty tact, 'I am sorry we cannot help you more, Mister Smith. But Toby cried for an hour after Mister Groves kicked him, and I was out with him, and after Mister Groves left we all came out to try and settle him. It took an hour. That is what we were about. With Toby as he was, that was all we could hear.'

Matthew tried to put it together. Judging by where Roger Groves had fallen in the road, he had probably not walked more than a quarter of an hour from here; maybe a little less, depending on just when he had started running for his life. The Wares, from their account, had been calming the hysterical Tobias. They could have seen nothing. Whatever had brought Black Hal to the hunt, he was not going to learn it here.

Matthew tried to be a good man. Tobias had kind brothers, but life was not a soft bed for him. The thought of Roger Groves idly harrying the poor child until he screamed for an hour was almost enough to make him commend Black Hal's judgement, and that would never do. It was time to leave.

Matthew wanted terribly to go home, to be back with his bright-faced children, his steady father, his Janet, who would give him a hug. But there was work for him; he couldn't leave this. Chalk Lane ran down to the Porters' farm, and he had to speak to them too.

The wind pressed against him as he rode, and Matthew was tired.

The Porters, when they let him in, had the grey faces of folks waiting to hear that their lives were over.

'Good day, Mister Smith,' Paul told him. Words had never come easily to the man, and today, they fell from him heavy as stones. 'Kind of you. We'll be packed soon, though.'

'Oh,' said Matthew, 'no. No, I haven't come to help you pack. I would, that is, but . . . I fear I have . . . news of a mixed nature.'

The Porters' shock looked real enough. There was a certain discomfort, but then, the death of Roger Groves had stopped the sale of their home, and who wouldn't feel relief, and the obligation to hide it?

'I don't suppose,' Matthew said, 'that you saw him last night?'

'No, Mister Smith,' said Paul Porter, and Sukie shook her head.

'He'd have passed this way,' Matthew suggested. 'To get to the Wares', he'd have to.'

'He may have,' said Sukie, her face pallid and her hands dancing in her lap. 'He didn't stop in. We were indoors, to pack our things, you see. We couldn't say more than that, Mister Smith.'

And yes, there was no reason to disbelieve her.

Matthew preferred to think well of folks, which was not the same as being naïve. There was no evidence to believe that the razing of Roger Groves was anything other than an accident, what the inquest – and there would most likely be one – would call 'death by means mysterious'. But the ways of the People were odd, and they had their fancies.

No one knew how to predict Black Hal's runs. But if anyone was placed to observe, it was the folks who lived on Chalk Lane. The Wares were facing a choice between one bad landlord or another, but the Porters stood to lose everything if this sale went through.

Matthew sighed. 'I am sorry to question you after such news,' he said. 'But it is my duty to learn what I can of this sad business – to learn more of Black Hal, if I can. Perhaps . . . if I may speak to you all, learn what you know of him, it might help us save lives another time.'

Paul Porter swallowed. 'As you say, Mister Smith.'

It was a long morning, and by the end of it, Matthew was much the wearier and little the wiser.

This was what Paul and Sukie Porter told him:

Black Hal was a sight they avoided as much as possible, and they were very grateful for the good iron hinge and lock on their front gate that the Smiths had supplied in earlier years. On dark nights, they sometimes heard him bay, and the sound went right down to your marrow. Over the years, they'd all taken to sleeping with their ears stuffed with rags, for while you never mistook his voice, it was tangled up in the sound of the wind, and the wind blew hard along Chalk Lane at night, harder some nights than others, and when you heard it rip through the trees it could sound almost like a blast in its own right.

'Once you've heard Black Hal bay, Mister Smith,' Sukie Porter mumbled, 'you never can like the sound of wind again.' She reached out for her husband's hand, and Paul took it.

Had they seen him on the hunt, Matthew asked?

Paul Porter had seen him now and then as a child, it emerged, but then, children don't always know dreams from facts, and to be sure, Black Hal would set your nightmares running. As a married couple, they'd only seen him once. It was a black night, the stars all spiked in the sky and the moonlight hissing bright, and the wind blew so hard you could hear the trees groan under it. A figure had run past their gate while they were out checking the barn door was secure, a flash of red fire and wet muscle and teeth all bared and flames bursting from his every footstep, and it was like every sound in the world was screaming together.

'Well,' said Sukie, her voice a little hoarse, 'we went in and locked the door and prayed for mercy, and that was the last time we went out at night, Mister Smith.'

Paul was letting her do most of the talking; he wasn't a chatty man even when he was happy, and on this subject, he seemed able to do little more than lend his presence, the solemnity of his face expressing his support of whatever his good wife had to say. At this, though, he spoke up.

'And we must stay in, Mister Smith,' he said. He said it with respect, but he was emphatic. 'We're sorry if that's no help. But we can't watch for him. There's the boys to think of. Maybe more young ones later, God willing. After the Wares' Tobias . . .'

Matthew managed to say, 'Of course, of course.' Of course Paul didn't want his children afflicted. Fathers were made to protect. If he'd been a better father himself . . .

'We stayed indoors, Mister Smith,' Sukie added, sounding a little nervous: Mister Smith looked upset, and she was worried Paul had displeased him, 'and we prayed that when Black Hal ran down the road, we would be looking the other way.'

Hearing her anxiety, Matthew gathered himself: he had no business fretting over his own concerns and upsetting good folks. With an effort almost physical, he assumed a calmer manner and asked about how many times had they heard Black Hal in the past year.

Well, they reckoned, from last Michaelmas, which was how Black Hal's year was reckoned – September twenty-ninth to September twenty-ninth; it had always been that way – they thought that last night had been the sixth. They were sure that they'd heard his bay five times before last night – and no, they were sure they weren't mistaken; no one ever forgot a sound like that.

Matthew took another moment to push his own feelings out of his mind. It wasn't a thing to ask harshly. 'Well now,' he said – as if it was only a question, with no shadow of accusation hanging over it – 'could you say what brings the kind friend running?'

'Hand to God, Mister Smith,' Sukie said, raising a callused palm in a gesture half-apology, half-plea, 'we wouldn't wish to know. On those bad nights, we stayed in the house and covered our ears, and all we knew was that we wanted him to pass us by.'

This was what Tommy and Bill Porter had to say to Matthew:

Tommy, who took his duties as elder brother seriously,

reported that he had looked out of his window and seen Black Hal a few times, but Bill was too scaredy.

Bill refuted the charge of being scaredy, but Tommy, whose elder obligations evidently included showing a fearless front and inspiring his younger brother to emulation, argued in its favour, because Bill would never even peek out.

'I'll tell you a secret,' Matthew intervened. 'I think I'd be scared myself. My Dada always told me a man with no fear is a man with no sense.'

'I have sense,' Tommy ventured, now worried he was open to the charge of stupidity. Matthew might have found his father a comforting presence, but Tommy felt Mister Jedediah Smith's disapproval might be a rather fearsome thing in itself.

'Of course you do,' Matthew agreed readily. 'You're a kind big brother to look out for both of you, I reckon. I'd have liked such a brother. Though I had a sort of big cousin' – he meant Franklin, who had slept many nights at the Smith house when Joe Thorpe was in one of his moods – 'and he'd have done it for me. And I'll tell you what: I think him fine to this very day. And we both grew up big strong men.'

This was a subject more to their taste, and after Matthew had dwelled upon the boys' current strength, and allowed himself to be arm-wrestled into submission by both of them, Bill and Tommy felt mutually liberated from the charge of cowardice and relaxed into their usual camaraderie. After that, they were better able to answer Matthew's questions.

What had Tommy seen? Well, Black Hal was a big dog, all fire on his feet and his mouth and eyes, and his chest was all nasty and open. Tommy had bad dreams about him, but that didn't mean he was scaredy – the dog was horrid, even Dada said so.

Was there anything different about the nights when Black Hal ran by, Matthew wondered? Tommy thought they were windier: you could hear the wind all high in the trees, going *scree scree scree*, and the dog howling too, it was all noisy and nasty.

Did they think there was any way to call Black Hal?

The reply was prompt: why would they want to do that? They might not be scaredy, but they weren't stupid.

The conversation had taken place round the side of the house, seated near the vegetable garden. As they concluded their talk, a striped brown cat came picking his delicate way amongst the cabbages like a monarch in an ornamental maze, and Bill took his thumb out of his mouth and called out, 'Puss!'

Puss turned his head to examine the group and, seeing an offending mortal sitting in undeserved dignity between his favourite boys, gave a small spit of contempt and bounded away.

Matthew headed home. Dobbs was tiptoed and frantic until they got off Chalk Lane; it was a shock to find, once they were a little ways down the hill, that in fact it was a beautiful morning. The sun shone in a clean blue sky and the air was soft, and Matthew discovered he was still a relatively young man. It appeared that he was strong and in good health; he had forgotten. Perhaps it was just the news he had to carry back – which was that he couldn't say at all what had happened to Roger Groves, or why Black Hal had set about him, but that

Roger Groves was now a stiff heap of chilling flesh, and that now nobody knew what would become of the rest of them.

John was full of far too many questions about how a fey dog went about the business of mauling folks, and Jedediah was so busy failing to suppress this ghoulish interest that he didn't notice Ephraim Brady standing his doorway until the man gave a sharp, 'Good day, Mister Smith.'

Jedediah looked up. 'So, Mister Ephraim Brady,' he said, 'have you heard the news?'

Ephraim Brady's face was as still as a statue's. 'I have heard gossip,' he said. 'I weigh it as nothing without good proof.'

'I do not know,' said Jedediah, steering John behind him with an unexpectedly gentle hand, 'why you should count worthless gossip the word of honest men. Roger Groves is dead, Ephraim Brady. My son is out there now, finding what may be made of the fey doings. But you'll have no sale for us to witness this morning. Black Hal got Roger Groves last night, and if you have no further business, perhaps you'll leave me to work at my smithy. I know you do not believe in wasting work hours.'

'Grandpa, stop pushing!' said John, worming his way back around. 'Mister Brady, if Roger Groves isn't here, you won't put the Porters out, will you? No, listen,' he insisted, not quite ducking the grab Jedediah made for him, 'Mister Brady, everyone says the Porter family are good workers. If Roger Groves didn't like them, well, Roger Groves is dead. Why should you waste money on losing good workers when there's no profit in it now?'

Ephraim gave him a look, blank and depthless as a midnight

pond. 'I need no brat to teach me what I already know, Mister Jedediah Smith,' he said. 'I hope you work iron better than you work that boy's manners.'

'Leave the boy's manners to me,' said Jedediah.

Ephraim Brady looked at them for another second, a bleak blink of contempt, and then turned and hastened out to the rest of his busy day.

## CHAPTER 9

Sensible villagers do not hold a bonfire to celebrate the death of an unpopular man of means, and the death of Roger Groves was, at least on the surface of Gyrford, greeted quietly.

Ephraim Brady went about his business with a closed mouth and a white face, and if he had been ungenial before, he was bitter now. The loss of such an ally was a great blow, and he did not chose to suffer alone: he raised rents on two families, and called in his debts, and bought his debtors' goods at heartbreaking prices when they couldn't pay them, and if folks had not sought his company before, now they would cross the road to stay out of his path. The money Jedediah had charged him for inspecting the Porter farm – which he had insisted on collecting, and which Ephraim, with his usual hostile probity, paid with his face set in an expression of dislike so rigid it troubled even Jedediah – was quite quickly dispersed. It was a good amount, but it couldn't cover everything he did; the Smiths had to eat as well, and it was becoming clear that anyone who enjoyed the protection of the Smiths against Ephraim Brady could consider themselves to have taken sides in what was becoming, at least in the eyes of Ephraim, an open feud. The Smiths did what they could, but it wasn't enough: they simply hadn't the funds to counter all the ill he was wreaking.

His one indulgence remained, as it always had been, his brother Anthony. The two of them rode together every afternoon, on new-shod horses Ephraim had brought to the smithy, with instructions for the most fey-repelling shoes ever struck. John had been going to explain to him that there was a limit to what you could expect horseshoes to do once you were out and on the move in the People's countryside, but Matthew hushed him and Jedediah quoted a price thrice their usual, and Ephraim Brady paid it.

Newly proofed, they rode together every day at one on the stroke. For the remainder of his hours, Anthony was as much at loose ends as ever; he had nothing to do but hang around Gyrford in odd places. Since no one liked to risk his company, he was always alone, with not much to do except toss crumbs to wood pigeons and scratch the backs of folks' pigs. He was even spotted attempting to make friends with the Porters' cat – which was of the wandering kind, but not fond of men these days, and spat at Anthony with lazy distaste if he got too close. Ephraim didn't take him on most of his business trips, but he did not wish his brother to dally about with rogues and idlers, wondering what to do with his afternoon.

John Smith had nothing to say, these days. He sat, and he listened.

What conversation there was never quite reached the point of saying there was something wrong with him. Dada looked at him consideringly sometimes, but when John looked back, Matthew would only pat his head or give him a kiss, and return to his work.

Instead, Dada and Grandpa were going about with grave faces, discussing lore as far back as either of them could remember, and coming up with little. Black Hal had mauled a man to death in the days of Jedediah's father, and while that man been fond of talking and prone to exaggeration, even he had spoken of it as a sight he preferred to forget. There wasn't much the smithy knew about the beast.

Could anyone have set Black Hal after Roger Groves? The problem was, however much Jedediah might dismiss and Matthew equivocate, history did show cases of the People doing favours for men.

For example: there were fey women who had fallen in love with mortal men and would come at their call – although such romances tended to end in a lost bride or a dead husband, alliances with foreigners being, as everyone knew, an unsound thing to do. (Well, unless they were sensible foreigners. Jedediah's father had been a foreigner himself, hailing from a whole county away, and had been a rather unsteady husband – but on the other hand, Jedediah had grown up friends with the son of a Moorish fellow who had tired of a life of service in the city and declared that if he had to be rained on in this wet country, he'd at least be rained on where he could watch things grow, and Mister Attic, as everyone called him, had always been very kind to his wife. But that wasn't really being foreign: he worked hard, didn't fool around with the 'afrights', and picked up a proper Gyrford accent. By now his descendants were considered settled folks; Dickon Attic, who was twelve years old and a peacemaker born and bred, was one of the main reasons John didn't get into more fights with their playmates on his most know-it-all days. So that path didn't lead anywhere useful, except to the advice that one should marry a kind soul – and when it came to the Bradys, it was too late to give such counsel to the wife who needed it.)

Then there were fey houseguests who would clean a kitchen, sweep a hearth, finish a day's work, but they did not come by invitation: on the contrary, they came as they pleased, and they had their own ideas of housekeeping besides. (Most often, they'd tidy a dirty kitchen but smash up a neat one. Some folks believed they took offence at having their work done for them, but the Smiths tended to doubt any explanation so rational. Jedediah's theory was that such People came with a plan to do housework, but that they regarded housework largely as a question of changing matters from one state to another, dirty or clean, stored or strewn, finished or unfinished, and were entirely agnostic as to which was better.)

There were stories, too, about People who lived in this or that old tree and might answer questions with riddles, but those stories came from grandfathers with an unspecified number of 'greats' before them, and the current generations of Smiths regarded them as they did much-reworked metal: there might still be some ring in them somewhere, but you'd never find the original shape by looking.

But rumours and whims aside, what Matthew and Jedediah had both known was cases where the People took a fancy to someone, and could be violent in defence of their friend. Their fancies were unswayed by whether their friend was a worthy soul — there had been that case over in Hawksdowne twenty years back, where the thing in the pond decided that the local thief was an excellent fellow because of his paddling skills, and matters had been two drownings along before the Smiths got called in. The People were also quite blithe about whether their friend wanted their championship; more than one customer in the Smiths' history had come in pleading that he'd like the freedom to quarrel with his wife or haggle with his neighbours without finding them stuck full of thistles the minute he turned his back.

Could anyone along Chalk Lane be the darling of Black Hal's flayed heart, though? It felt unlikely. Folks all stayed out of his way as best they could. Black Hal ran seven times a year, and he ran when he pleased, as far as anyone knew. Only Tobias was uncommon — and, as Jedediah put it, he was damned if he was going to look into more reasons for anyone to bother that lad.

Which was why it was only John who wanted to look into things further. He'd always been curious to see Tobias, and the more he heard of him, the more he wanted to. There were other touched folks around, but John had been thinking about what his father said, about how Mama's hands had been touched when she was carrying him. That would have to mean that whatever folks thought was wrong with him had happened before he'd been born. And that could happen; he'd seen Mama come back sad-faced from enough visits to women who'd been going to have a baby, who now weren't going to have that baby any more. Things could happen to you before you were really there, and if anyone had something against him, that must be why. He wasn't like those folks who got snatched below the ground, down into great lungs of breathing earth, and ever after their rescue tried to run up the paths the wind carved through the air, or like folks who'd felt the hag sit on their chests at night and spent the daytime panicking at the sight of anyone's knees. He'd never had any fey encounter that had led folks to sigh and say, 'He was never the same since . . .' He was just who he always had been. John didn't feel wrong in himself, he didn't feel troubled or askew. He liked his thoughts, which were interesting, and his feelings, which he considered usually justified.

But if anyone else did think him amiss, what could he do to challenge them? There was no 'since' in his life, no time before he was alive and blinking in the light and already who he was. When it came to folks touched before birth, there was just him and Tobias.

Tobias was said not to speak, and the grown folks told John to be patient and stop begging to see him, but every day that passed where Dada stroked his hair and told him he was a good boy and didn't quite reach the point of talking to him, John chafed more and more against the waiting. Something had to happen. Something had to bring him to Tobias Ware, to answer the question he couldn't formulate in his heart.

He had an idea, but he had to wait a while. And in his defence, John told himself, he might truly be of help. He reasoned that an apprentice could get away with unofficial questions that a master couldn't, and he wasn't wrong there. If there were still other motivations – if the temptation was strong on him to be back under the canopy, in the secretive heart of the woods where he could hear its life creak and whisper back and forth – he didn't mean anything bad to come of it. John never wanted to cause trouble for anyone else.

Janet had not lost her belief that any interest Anthony Brady might feel towards Francie Thorpe was best nipped in the bud. There was no possibility the brother of Ephraim Brady would be a good husband: Alice Brady's drained face swam before her at nights, drowning in silence. While as a young woman Janet had believed that parents had no business to interfere in the higher cause of love, and was slightly put out that her own parents greeted her betrothal to the thrilling paragon they insisted on calling 'a steady lad' with such dull approval, her views had undergone some natural mutation since becoming a parent herself.

She wasn't about to send John into the forest, which was the likeliest spot to find Franklin – at least if you wanted to talk to him away from interested ears, either belonging to passers-by in the Gyrford square or, in his own home, Francie herself. Instead, she chose Molly, giving her a message to memorise and instructions on finding her way, and sent her off.

John, seeing Molly set off, discovered a sudden need to deliver a talisman that should have been with customers two days ago.

'What were you about, forgetting that?' Jedediah demanded. He'd forgotten himself, so preoccupied had he been of late, but John had five-odd decades' less wear on his memory and should surely have been able to keep track.

'I . . . have no excuse,' John said with a slightly lordly air;

he hadn't thought far enough ahead to come up with one. 'I think I should just make it good now. It would be the honest thing to do.'

'All right, all right,' said Jedediah. 'No need to make a speech.' If he hadn't been so tired from worrying — about Black Hal, about Tobias Ware, who was apparently very fidgety these days since Black Hal had last roared down Chalk Lane, about who would inherit Roger Groves' estate and whether he'd have dealings with Ephraim Brady — then he might have had the wits to be suspicious. This was what he told himself later.

John ran off, saddled Dobbs, and caught Molly as she headed down the road. The parcel he carried, he'd dropped in a bush; there was nothing in it, as he'd delivered the talisman two days ago.

'Molly,' he said, 'let me carry the message. I want to speak to Mister Franklin anyway.'

Molly hesitated. She wasn't eager to go into the Bellame woods, being rather afraid of the People and not that experienced in tracking her way through forests either, but listening to John over the adults seldom ended well.

'Mama said for me to go,' she said.

'She said it's all right,' said John. 'I thought of some more things I have to ask him, and they're smithing questions.' He had thought this a simple plan when he came up with it, but he hadn't quite anticipated that everyone involved in it would ask him questions and force him to lie to them. He hadn't much of a conscience when it came to little fibs here and there, but he really was fond of his sister and was growing a bit miserable at the complications. 'I'll tell you what, you get up on Dobbs too and I'll give you a ride towards Mary Anne's. You can drop in and visit her instead.'

Mary Anne Morgan was Molly's best friend, and John had made a shrewd appeal there. It was unfortunate for everyone that, feeling the girls were too young to be worried by questions as to the soundness of their brother, nobody had told Molly that John could go a little odd in the woods.

'Well, all right,' said Molly. John was a pest sometimes, but he was actually her favourite sibling: having had neat habits dinned into him in the smithy, he made far less mess than Janet or the twins, and he was affectionate and appreciative when he wasn't preoccupied. The two of them had quite a friendly ride together before Molly dismounted and went off with a wave.

John's conscience was hurting him, but when he entered the woods, the world around him became so interesting that he forgot, for the moment, to think of anything but his surroundings and what he could learn from them.

The air was cool and brittle, the smoky scent of autumn earth all around, and the dimming leaves rattled above him as he wound his way along the paths. He was all awake, listening out: it wasn't often he got the chance to be alone in a place and really pay attention, and this forest, turning brass and garnet over his head, tattery and damp below, was like bathing in cool water. It was a *clean* place, he decided — muddy, of course, as Dobbs' hooves were already showing the smudged proof, but natural, healthy. There was nothing amiss; nothing out of kilter. Last time they'd been here, it had had a squirming, nervous quality, but of course, Dada had replanted the bush since then. Now, for all the bend of branch and straggle of bracken, it felt in good order: not quite tame, but thriving in its own clear sequence, like a garden with inoffensive ideas of growth. If Tobias had trespassed out here again, evidently the forest didn't mind.

It was cultivated, too, that much was clear: pollarded trees bristled at the height of his face, and coppiced ones lower down, great useful bouquets of wood that could be trimmed out and woven into fences, sold for kindling, maybe used for carpentry-work of the kind he knew nothing about. The birds had ordinary sorts of things to say, and ahead of him, once, he saw the flash of an ochre plume, a fox sleeking its way through the undergrowth in search of mice.

Franklin Thorpe's rounds covered quite a few miles, and John needed to find him. It wasn't exactly dignified, and probably the game wouldn't appreciate it, but after an hour or so of quiet looking, John decided enough was enough, and began to yell, 'Mister Thorpe! Hollah! Mister Thorpe!'

Franklin Thorpe did not, of course, appear immediately. John followed the paths he found, calling at intervals, and was beginning to feel fed up with it all when he heard an answer to his call: a sharp, sweet whistle, up-down-up on its notes, and, not entirely sorry to be resting his voice, John turned Dobbs and followed the sound.

Behind a cluster of bushes was Franklin Thorpe, looking interested and with a pouch of water ready to offer. 'Good afternoon, Mister John,' he said, as John took a grateful gulp. 'What brings you looking for me? I hope nothing is amiss.'

'This is a very well-kept place,' John said, not wanting to

begin by delivering what, he was remembering now, was probably not going to be a welcome message. 'I must compliment you, Mister Thorpe.'

Franklin Thorpe had been a small boy with his own yearnings to be a man that folks would listen to, and did not laugh at John's rather stately tone. 'Why, thank you,' he said. 'It's a fine place to work. I'm checking for traps today, you know, poachers' traps. I don't suppose you've seen any?'

John shook his head. 'But I wouldn't know what to look for if they were secret,' he explained; pride might have been one of his vices, but he was proud enough of his real skills to be candid about the ones he lacked.

'We all have our own trades,' Franklin agreed. 'I'm sorry I have no currants for you today. Had I been expecting you, I could have filled my pocket.'

'Oh, that's all right,' said John, with a fairly well-concealed touch of regret. 'No, I have a message to you from my mother. Look you, she made me learn the message, so I'd better just say it to you. She says: "Your Francie is a good girl, and I mean no ill of her when I send you this message. You should know that she met Anthony Brady the other day, and if I know young men, he was smitten, and ready to show it. And Francie is too natural a girl not to feel it when a handsome young man wants to court her. They always did like each other. She did nothing unbecoming, but Anthony Brady is a suitor I think a father would wish to know about. You might like a word with her." But I don't think he's all that handsome,' John added. 'He's not very tall, and you know, he looks like his brother, and nobody at all likes *him*.'

Franklin's face was very serious. 'Your mother is a good woman,' he said, as if trying to buy some time to think. 'Do give her my thanks for her kind thought.'

'All right,' said John. 'But that's not much of a message. Shall I tell her anything else?'

The breeze traced a light path through the trees, and the leaves above gave a slow sigh. 'I must take some time to put my mind to it,' said Franklin. 'Tell me, do folks know ill of Anthony Brady for himself, these days? Beyond being the brother of Ephraim Brady?'

'Well, he doesn't work,' said John, as if this explained everything: not making yourself useful or clever in a trade was, as he had been raised, a life that barely justified its own existence at all.

'Hm,' said Franklin Thorpe. 'Anything else? Is he an unkind man? Untrue to women? Dishonest?'

'He never stops his brother,' John said, a little puzzled that Franklin kept asking about what, as far as he could see, should be a settled question. 'He even *likes* him.'

'Hm,' said Franklin again. 'Stopping him . . . may not be the easiest thing to do, with a hard man.' There was a certain forlorn conviction to his words.

'He thinks Ephraim Brady is the best of men,' said John, feeling a little frantic at trying to explain something so obvious to someone so uncomprehending. 'He actually said that! I *heard* him. The best of men!'

'That is not the widest-held opinion,' Franklin said, scratching his face, and John breathed a sigh of relief that at least something seemed to be getting through.

'And that's what Anthony Brady thinks,' he added, just to make sure. 'So, do you have a message for my mother, except thank you?'

Franklin patted Dobbs' neck. 'Thank her very much,' he said. 'Tell her I will think most carefully on what she has said.'

After such a long ride, that was hardly an interesting answer, and John felt his previously high opinion of Franklin Thorpe slip a notch. 'If you like,' he said.

Franklin woke slightly from his abstraction, and gave John a smile. 'Thank you for your trouble,' he said. 'You'll find my currants ready for you, next we meet.' He knew Mister Smith was worried about the boy, and yes, he could be a little odd in his manner sometimes, but here they were in the Bellame woods, and John was being perfectly coherent. He was glad of it; he must mention it when he had a moment, as it might be a comfort to them.

'Well, thank you, Mister Thorpe,' said John. 'While I am here, I believe I should check on the bush. Would you kindly show me to it?'

Franklin knew the woods as he knew the way around his own house; it was a quick journey to find the bramble. It had nothing to say, unless a handful of saw-edged leaves flickering in the wind could be counted as a comment.

'There you are,' Franklin announced. 'Quiet as you like.'

John thanked him, bade him goodbye and turned Dobbs around. She paced quietly, and John waited until he was sure Franklin was out of hearing before he turned her back.

The bush sat there, mute and innocent. John dismounted, tapped a thorn.

There was no reaction.

John didn't have an iron ring like his father – it was a waste of metal to forge for growing fingers – so he removed one of his boots and, damp moss soaking a quiet chill into his sock, tapped one of the hobnails against a twig.

The thing gave a little snarl, and John remembered something he should have thought of before: Jedediah had promised to leave it alone if it left the folks alone.

'Good day, kind friend, by your earth my path did wend,' he told it. Jedediah often looked uncomfortable when he had to strike out couplets, but John didn't see why. 'Please forgive the iron knock, I meant you no insult or shock. I have one question, one alone: are you quite happy where you're grown? Or is there more that we should do to bring a happy end to you?'

The bush didn't bother to shape a full self; it just opened a slit on its branch and said, 'Goway.'

'Away I'll go if that will please, and leave you here among the trees. But I a boon must ask of you,' John went on. This was more questions than the 'one alone' he'd said before, but necessity was pressing on him, and he doubted the little thing's memory or haggling skills would give him much trouble. 'Can you give me an answer true?'

'Gowayway.'

John had several things to ask, but the first one rose to his lips uninvited. 'I have heard folks speak ill of me. They say that touched by fey I be. Now you be fey, and you should know. Do they speak truth when they speak so?'

The bramble gave an irritated twitch. 'Goway gowaygoway scratchity goway!' And it firmly closed its slit; every leaf turned its back on John with a rustling huff, leaving nothing but bared thorns pointing in his direction.

John felt an unmanly desire to cry; the bush was proving no more willing to answer his questions than anyone else. And he hadn't even asked it the main question. In desperation, he gave it another tap with the nail.

'Gowaygoway scratchity pull you up goway no neighbour breakityroot!' If the thing had been annoyed before, it was starting to convulse in fury now. John had the feeling that, in its own language, he was being thoroughly sworn at.

'I beg of you, I have to ask, For me it is a moral task,' said John, starting to feel desperate. 'Along the lane that's white as chalk, You know Black Hal must take his walk. There is a boy his mark's upon. He broke your twigs when by he ran.' That didn't rhyme; it was breathless work trying to make up poem-questions when there was something baring its thorns in rising enmity, flexing them like a thousand-pointed cat. 'Black Hal did kill with dreadful bite, Another man one – er – dreadful night. They ask, did someone Black Hal call? Might it have been the boy at all?'

The bush stood braced for a long, quivering moment, and then it made a frantic lurch towards John, so hard that its roots strained against the earth. John managed to leap most of the way back, but it scored a swipe across his cheek that stung far more than it should have done, a bitter, vicious burn like an icy wasp. 'Neighbour runner broke mine twig iron knock scratchity broke mine broke iron knockity goway goway goget goget goget scratchity!'

'No, no, please calm down,' John said, retreating. The scrape hurt like nothing he'd ever felt; it was like the taste of outrage scalding his face.

'Goget goget broke knock scratchity goget!'

The bush was tautening. Its roots strained against the ground, baring themselves in dull gleams as, lithe as rough-skinned grubs, they started to pull free.

John backed away, hurrying his muddy foot into his boot. 'Sorry for trouble, away I will hobble, Please forgive knocks, I meant you no shocks,' he said.

The bush was not placated. As he made his retreat, its leaves vibrated together with a sizzling hiss.

## CHAPTER 10

To begin with, matters continued quiet. Franklin dropped into the smithy and reported that Tobias had kept out of the woods, as far as he knew, for several days, although he wasn't very happy and kept biting his fingers.

'Hard?' Matthew asked.

Franklin sighed. 'I fear so,' he said. 'I saw the cuts. I brought him some leather gloves, but he just pulled them off. Wouldn't wear them for anything.'

Matthew fondled Soots' soft ears by way of solace, and accepted her sympathetic lick. It wasn't dignified for a fairy-smith to cry. 'If you bring another pair,' he said, 'we could work at that. Perhaps not iron, but I have some strips of tin. It wouldn't be our best work, but if we put some bands in the wrists, put a lock on them so he couldn't pull them off . . . I know it sounds harsh, like shackling him, but . . .'

Franklin shook his head. 'No, no, I see your point.'

'I think,' John volunteered, 'you should ask him why he's biting. I mean, if he didn't before, something must have started him.' He spoke a little quieter than usual; he'd had to account for his cut face by inventing a fall from the saddle, and he wasn't entirely sure Molly wasn't going to tell on him, so he'd been trying, for the last few days, to be as unobtrusive as possible. On the subject of Toby, though, he just couldn't keep out of the conversation; John was a boy of some skills, but melting into the background when something interesting was going on was not among them.

'You may be right, Mister John,' said Franklin, more ceremoniously than he'd been speaking to Matthew, 'but you see, he does not speak.'

'Oh, I know that,' said John. 'But you could try to think about it. Add up—' At which point, he stopped himself. He was going to suggest they added up all the events that had happened recently and see if anything had changed for Tobias, but there was a recent event that he was not at all eager for Franklin to share. Of the many problems that hadn't occurred to him when he set off into the Bellame woods, one of them was the fact that Franklin was fond of the Smith elders and would very likely mention that John had been there. 'Never mind,' he concluded. 'Perhaps I am wrong.'

This was such an unlikely statement that Matthew put a hand on John's forehead to see if he had a temperature.

Franklin was growing increasingly uneasy at paying long visits to the Smiths; Ephraim Brady's house had a view of the smithy, and it wasn't prudent to call attention. 'Mustn't linger,' he said. 'Good to see you, of course.'

'I'll come by and help you split those logs soon,' Matthew said; neither of them frequented the alehouse, so sharing everyday tasks was their main way of enjoying each other's company, and at least Franklin's home was out of Ephraim's sight. Matthew had been missing Franklin's visits; it was one of the lesser reasons to wish Ephraim Brady — well, a different man. 'Anything else of note?' He spoke a little absently; Johnny's head seemed about as cool as it ever was.

Franklin chewed his lip. 'Well,' he said, 'some of the brambles in the woods — well, I found some bushes not where I thought they were. That is, in places I had not expected to find them. Soots didn't care for them. But I cannot be quite sure; we're all a little twitchy these days. I shall keep an eye out, and tell you more if there is anything to tell.'

'Johnny?' said Matthew. 'Excuse me, Franklin. Are you quite well, Johnny? It's a mild day to be shivering.'

Janet enjoyed going to market. In her young days it had been an opportunity to put on a nice ribbon and idle her way among the stalls, fancying endless secret histories behind the folks selling their wares. Now she was a respectable matron, she could still fancy whatever she liked, but she had the added satisfaction of being 'Mistress Smith' to everyone, and haggling was one of her particular private enthusiasms. Matthew was never comfortable with it, feeling that as folks often hesitated to haggle at the forge, at least when their need for fairy-smithing was urgent, it wasn't really fair to argue prices in the marketplace. Janet had periods of guilt in which she agreed with him, but the satisfaction of a good set-to was hard to resist. It was generally understood that Mistress Smith struck better or worse bargains according to some mystic rule invisible to more sensible eyes, and that the only thing to do was to offer her something at a good high starting point and hope that you'd caught her on one of her less argumentative days – for on the days when she did feel like bargaining, she bargained with a will and could beat down the best of them.

That morning, she had it in mind to buy some late-season chicks. The smithy had had a flock last year, but feeding creatures apparently created to do little more than cackle and peck had been of only passing interest to Janet, and as a result, some days she remembered and some days she didn't. This might have gone hard with the hens if Molly hadn't decided that Janet couldn't be trusted and made sure to feed them every day, and as a result the whole lot got double rations several days a week and waxed exceptionally fat. One day a supplier for one of the grander households in the county had come in to get his horse shod, noticed the buxom brood, and offered such a good price for them that nobody had been able to resist, and all but two had ended up in some gentleman's pot.

The remaining two were Dainty and Dosie: not the best layers in the bunch but particular favourites of Molly's. Dosie would eat from her hand, and Dainty had been born with a missing toe, which always moved Molly to earnest sympathy. That was all, except for their shared husband Norrie, a rather limp-combed old swaggerer who crowed out his presence whenever the fancy took him and took umbrage every time Molly kicked him off her shoes.

It was hardly a lavish coop, and the Smith household was enjoying more of the chickens' company than their produce – which was particularly troublesome because eggs were something the Smith men could boil over the forge without relying on

Janet's uncertain cooking. It mattered less for the grown ones, but there was Johnny to think of: smithing is hard on a young frame, and it's a stupid master as well as a cruel one who doesn't look ahead to the day when an apprentice will need to be a strong man, not a sickened one. If you want to build muscle on a boy, you have to feed him properly, and the flitch of bacon they'd accepted from a farmer last winter in payment for shooing off the thing that swung on his pot-hooks was down almost to its stock-bones.

Eating the chickens, though, was not a happy thought: Molly adored them, and she was Jedediah's pet; he regarded her and Matthew as the only sensible members of the household, and besides that, she was the image of Matthew, who looked very much like his mother before him. Jedediah would say quite plainly that the twins were handsome girls, but it was Molly, in quiet moments, with whom he'd sit and talk. He didn't tend to say that she looked so much like his lost Louise, but he refused ever to hear a word against her, and, to give Molly her due, she sought out his company too. The world could be a little unstable for the daughter of a whimsical mother and a father often called away to grapple the People, and Molly took much comfort in Grandpa's patient ear for her concerns, unfaltering approval, and steadfast assurance that things could be made right, lass, never you fret. Janet was not a mother jealous of her children's love, and was glad to see Molly and Jedediah close, but she could also see he was growing rather frustrated about the business of the chickens, caught as he was between the needs of John's body and Molly's heart. It was time to replenish the flock.

With all the money they'd had to pass along, picking up some of the pieces Ephraim Brady was shattering out of folks' lives, full-grown layers were not an option. However, there were some small, scraggly cheepers on sale at Luke Morris' stall that should be within their means, and Luke had a taste for bargaining as keen as Janet's own, so they settled down with the pleasure of two experienced players.

Luke was warm on the subject of good economies, and how the chicks would grow to be fine layers fed on nothing but kitchen scraps, and also on what a particularly good laying strain these glaring little mops came from, and how, in fact, it was merely giving them away at the price he offered and it was only his respect for a good woman that allowed him to consider it, and he must hope he'd find his reward in heaven, as he certainly wouldn't be getting it in coin.

Janet, meanwhile, was resolute on the principle that good laying strains meant nothing with unproven chicks and you couldn't trust heredity: just think of Luke's beautiful children, when everyone could see that Luke himself was nothing much to look at. Luke, who was not sensitive about his appearance, grinned and replied that his own chicks took after their beautiful mother, and there was your proof of good breeding coming out in the strain, and Janet replied that for all she knew these chicks on sale took after their father, and no one could vouch for that feathered rascal's heritage, and it was pure charity on her part that she'd take in these poor orphans and raise them in a steady environment to be decent animals.

None of this was a very respectable conversation, and increasingly less so as the argument wore on, and more and more women were starting to turn from their shopping to listen in with an air of startled propriety. Being slightly shocking when her status as a farrier's lady was beyond reproach was another of Janet's pleasures in life, and she was about to say something further about the disreputable rakery of Luke Morris' cockerel, but before she had quite assembled the innocent face she would need to say it with, she saw something she hadn't expected: Alice Brady, a basket on her arm, piled neat and careful with vegetables slightly past their best and presumably all the cheaper for it, her face white and fixed.

'I'll knock a ha'penny off the price for the joke, and no more, Mistress Smith, for it's a sad shame to hear my good cock's virtue abused in the public marketplace,' said Luke Morris, still cheerful. Alice was standing very still in the crowd, her eyes fixed on Janet's face. Often when you saw Alice in the market, she might snatch a few seconds – not enough to be indecorous – to admire the living fowl on display or let a passing dog give her hand a quick sniff – but today, she didn't give the chicks so much as a glance. 'I'll have you know,' Luke added, 'that he's a bird of excellent parentage, and his mother, who laid two eggs a day every day of her saintly life, regarded him as the prop of her old age until the day she went into the pot, peace to her memory.'

'All right,' said Janet. She didn't turn her head from Alice, and Luke Morris blinked at the suddenness of the bargain.

'Can I interest you in anything further?' he said, rallying. 'There's nothing like a good fat goose, and I can sell you some eggs just warm and ready to set under your own hens, that'll—'

'No, thank you,' said Janet, only half listening. 'The chicks will be fine for me, thank you.' She put down her coins without really looking, and Luke, a little bewildered but mostly resigned to the habits of Matthew Smith's unsensible wife, set about securing the crate for her to carry.

'Good day, Mistress Brady,' Janet said. 'I hope I find you well today?'

Alice drew a quiet breath. 'You do, thank you,' she said. There was a small pause, during which her forehead crinkled as she weighed her next remark; unfortunately in that moment, Bill Morey slewed by. Sarah Morey, before she was Franklin's wife, had been the quiet and gentle one of the Morey clan; the rest of them were described by Matthew as 'meaning well', but if you weren't in the mood for some verbal knockabout, they could be a little much. Janet had loved Sarah with a partisan devotion that very well understood why she'd considered Franklin's soft voice and unfailing patience to be a blessed haven, but she herself didn't mind a bout with the Moreys now and then; after all, she was free to go home to her own gentle husband afterwards. Before she could take Bill on, though, he doffed his cap to Alice with drunken gallantry.

'Now then, Mistress,' he said, managing his consonants, just about. 'Waste of a good woman, married to that thin stick of . . .' The analogy failed him. 'Stick,' he concluded. 'You want rid of him, and he's too pious to do it, you knock on my door, Missy. Bit of adultery, best excuse in the world.'

'If Mistress Brady is too polite to slap you, Bill Morey, I'm not,' Janet snapped. Ten years ago, she remembered, Alice had had a tongue of her own and could have put Bill in his place, but today she was white and silent. 'You go home to your wife and ask her to forgive you, or I'll tell my Matthew you've been profane with women in the public square.'

'Now then, now then,' said Bill, rallying a little and touching his forelock. Matthew had no enjoyment of sparring, verbal or otherwise, but he had sometimes done Sarah the kindness of sitting in the room when she was forced to take part in family arguments, feeling tongue-tied, looking enormous, and providing enough cover that the Moreys mostly resisted the urge to drag her in. 'No need for that, now, Mister Matthew knows no harm meant. Only compliment, only compliment.'

'I'd say it was no compliment to think a woman would fancy any attentions of yours, Bill Morey, except I don't wish to heap further insult on your poor wife,' Janet said. She might have said more on the subject, only her eye caught on Alice. The woman stood with her arms wrapped tight around herself, her reddened hands growing white-knuckled as she gripped. There was a look of fear on her face, which Janet could understand – she didn't think Ephraim Brady the man to accept that his wife couldn't help it if some drunken fool made remarks to her – but there was something else, too; the downcast, frustrated look of a woman who sees herself offered a bargain she can't afford to take. And Janet doubted it was for Bill Morey's short legs and broken nose Alice pined. No doubt Ephraim Brady would leave to starve any wife he cast off for adultery, and Alice had no kin to take her in; there was only her uncle and his new family, who had no desire to know her married and respectable, never mind outcast and ruined. It looked, Janet thought with dismay, as if she'd actually had to make that calculation.

'Never you mind him, my dear,' Janet said helplessly, as Bill weaved off on his way. 'Two ales in him, and he can't tell a Christian woman from a barn door.'

Alice glanced around, reckoning up the many bodies who might have heard Bill's raillery with the same anxious eye she calculated thin-edged bargains at the stalls.

'I heard tell,' Janet went on, raising her voice, 'that one evening he stumbled home so drunk, he thought he saw a fairy maiden with snow-white skin naked beside the road, and he went down on his knees to beg for her favours, and thought in the end he'd won them. A neighbour found him the next morning, sound asleep and cuddled up to a dead sheep. Couldn't swear he hadn't had his way with it.' This story was not at all true; Janet was improvising based on an incident a couple of years ago, where Matthew had been called in by a shepherd who couldn't stop counting one sheep too many in his flock, but could never find the extra one. When Matthew finally tracked down the cause of the problem, it abandoned sheephood and became a glittering woman who made him various fleshly offers. The glitterer had probably done so, Matthew reckoned, to get him to take off his wedding ring, which had an iron core, but Janet insisted that it must have been for his personal charms, and had taken some delight in ensuring that he didn't miss out on the offers the amorous sheep-maid had tried to tempt him with. (At least, the ones physically possible to perform; the glitterer had had some slightly odd ideas about mortal anatomy.) Still, Janet felt very little compunction for Bill Morey, under the circumstances; she could see Luke already laughing at what he'd overheard, and if the story went around the market now, it'd be of Bill Morey debauching a dead sheep, not of Ephraim Brady's manhood being traduced before his unprotesting wife.

Alice looked at her, still pale. When she spoke again, her voice was subdued, and hard to hear amidst the bustle. 'I have a basket of yours I must return, Mistress Smith. From the apples. Perhaps, when your shopping is done, you'd be pleased to call on me and I can return it?'

'I— Yes, thank you, I would be obliged,' Janet said. Never in her life had Alice Brady invited her to visit. It was a warm day, one of those copper-bright autumn moments when the sunshine takes a last flourish before winter, but in the buttery light, Alice Brady's face was pale and dull as chalk.

It went against Janet's conscience to drag her scruffy new chicks around the village, so having settled with Luke Morris, she dropped back home to deposit them safely. The twins clustered around them in delight, and were busy naming them before Janet had got the crate half-open. The twins' notions of names were not conventional – 'Dainty' had been Molly's choice, and the twins thought it silly – so the chicks were in the process of acquiring such handles as 'Ropehead', 'Petticoat' and 'Madam Button' as Molly emerged from the house to shake out a duster, and caught sight of the little group.

'Let me see,' Molly said, and stepped in to investigate, lifting up one of the small scraggy bundles and looking at it with critical tenderness. 'Mama, these poor things are very underfed.'

'Really?' Janet was not the most attentive fowl-fancier, and usually deferred to her eldest daughter's expertise, but she did feel genuinely offended on their behalf. 'Well, that Luke Morris is a sharp dealer and no question! We must feed them up, poor little mites.'

'That one should be called Corn-Scuttle,' Celdie said, pointing at the hungry creature in Molly's careful grasp.

'Celdie, why in the—? Never mind,' Molly said, giving up the idea of a debate. As long as these new ones were around, there was a better chance of keeping Dainty and Dosie safe. Jedediah didn't have it in him to demand anyone cook up a chicken his Molly really set her heart on, but still, Molly decided that she might as well let the twins call these new ones whatever they wanted and nominate them for the pot next time there was a need for chicken stew; the twins' passions for new amusements were intense, but often short-lived. 'Corn-Scuttle it is.'

Janet looked at her girls, her golden-headed, ragtag twins laughing over the hatchlings, Molly's serious face and gentle hands as she lifted another little orphan out of the crate. From here, it was on to Ephraim Brady's house – it was impossible to think of it as Alice Brady's, even when it was Alice she was going to visit – and the prospect of it, even on this warm, sunlit day, struck her with a sudden chill. The place stood just across the square from the smithy: a big, fine house that looked rather handsome from the outside, but Janet preferred to ignore it at the best of times. Now, she would have to cross the square and face it, and it was not a thought she liked the flavour of.

'Molly, love,' she said, 'will you come with me now? I've an errand to run and I'd like your company.'

Molly looked at her in surprise: Janet's 'errands' usually took the form of long, meandering walks with some small excuse for a task tacked somewhere onto the beginning of them, and it wasn't common for her to volunteer for an observer. 'What's the errand?' she asked. She didn't want to have a suspicious nature, but Janet's jaunts were not something she liked to join ill-advisedly.

'Just to collect a basket I lent,' Janet said. 'But it's to see Alice Brady, you know, and . . .' She hesitated. Normally she didn't at all mind saying uncomplimentary things about the neighbours, at least if Matthew wasn't around to abash her with his superior example, but Alice Brady was something else. 'Well, she never does talk much, and it'd be pleasant to have another visitor. I'm sure she'd like to see you, lambkin, you're always so polite to folks.'

'We're polite!' Vevie declared in a cheerful, not-offended protest, and Celdie added, 'Polite as polite can be, aren't we, Madam Button?'

Madam Button, true to her baby-bird nature, was willing to cry up anyone's virtues as long as there was some food in the prospect, so Molly folded up her duster and said, 'All right, Mama. Celdie, you settle the chicks in, Vevie, you help her after you've put this away, yes? Away *properly*, do you hear?'

'Yes, yes,' said Vevie, with very little sign that she held any such domestic intentions, and Molly brushed off her hands and started down the road with her mother.

It was a short step over to the Brady house, and Janet, for a wonder, didn't cast any looks of yearning at the long, intricate lanes or the hills and fields beyond them. She was focused, serious, and it was strange enough that Molly began to feel a prick of nerves.

'Mama,' she said, 'will it be all right, visiting Mistress Brady? Only you look worried.'

Janet gave Molly a pat on the arm, less absent than usual, more firm, as if standing by some principle of family feeling. 'I'm not worried, really,' she said. 'More sad. It's a hard life, being the wife of Ephraim Brady. I never knew Alice Brady before she was married, but I never heard any harm of her to deserve it.'

Molly didn't really know what to say. Janet could have fits of grief if a swallow fell from their eaves, and her passions of offence were the stuff of everyday life, but this sober sorrow was different, and enough unlike her that it was almost frightening.

'Maybe he's a kinder man within doors,' Molly suggested. She was no adult and she knew it, but Janet was seldom as steady as an adult either, and it was unsettling to feel herself this much younger than her mother. 'After all, Grandpa speaks short to folks all the time.'

Janet patted her again, and sighed. 'Your Grandpa is a different kind of man, lovie. Ask him what he thinks of Ephraim Brady some time. You must be careful, Molly, love. Marry a man like your father, or your grandfather, but don't marry a cold man. Better a fool, or a bore, or an ugly fellow – there's many an ugly man with a good heart. Ephraim Brady's a fine-looking man, really; there's nothing wrong with his face. But whatever else someone may be, don't marry a cold man.'

'I don't know I'll have all that much choice who wants to marry me,' Molly said, feeling downcast: flirting was not a natural skill for her, and now it turned out that you could make terrible mistakes even if anyone did want you, and that ugly bores might be the best she had to look forward to.

'Oh, nonsense, darling,' Janet said, pulling herself out of her melancholy at the ridiculous suggestion that anyone wouldn't want one of her own dear children. 'Any man would be lucky to have you, that's all there is to it.'

Molly was not convinced, but by this point they'd arrived at the Bradys' door. A striped brown cat sat before it, giving it a rather baleful glare, and Molly made a brief chirrup and extended her hand – like John, she was fond of cats – but this one spat at her and turned away, scraping its back feet with a gesture remarkably evocative of burying droppings. 'Is that the cat Johnny got after?' Molly asked; she wasn't at all eager to go into the big stone house, now they stood before it, and a few more moments in the bright sunshine seemed suddenly necessary.

'Oh, who knows?' Janet loved cats, and fed a swarm of strays at her back door, but she was truly preoccupied just now. 'There are striped cats every which way. Not but that a common-looking beast mightn't be the best-tempered.' She said this to reinforce her moral; Molly wasn't over-interested in boys, but the thought of her lush-skinned, steady-eyed girl growing ashen as Alice Brady was appalling her. The cat's retreating tail gave a twitch that rather belied her praise of its temper, though whether it objected to being called common-looking, or whether it simply didn't like the scent of her, she couldn't say. Her usual skill with cats was getting lost amidst her tense sorrow, and it made the visit feel all the less propitious.

Janet sighed, and knocked the door. The knocker itself was a recent purchase from the smithy, and just such a choice as you'd expect Ephraim Brady to make: well-tempered to discourage any member of the People who came by looking for trouble, and as plain and cheap as bargaining could make it. Matthew was fond of making beautiful knockers when he had the time, and their own house had a rather nice ram's head on the door with a fine set of twisted horns, but this was a loop of cold iron and nothing more.

Alice Brady opened, and cast a quick glance around the square. Seeing no one to alarm her, perhaps, she opened the door a little wider and, with only an anxious look at the unexpected Molly, ushered the two of them in. She said no word of greeting, only some small murmurs that didn't quite rise to the boldness of speech.

'Good morning, Mistress Brady,' Molly said, mindful of her reputation for politeness to uphold. 'I hope we find you very well today?'

Alice Brady looked at her, in search of words. 'Molly Smith,' she said, as if finding the name in her memory, though the two of them had sat in the same church every Sunday of Molly's life. 'Thank you. I – I hear folks speak nothing but good of you and your good behaviour.'

It was an awkward compliment, rather strange and delivered in a half-whisper, but Molly, who wasn't used to being praised at first sight, took it gladly. 'That's very kind of you, Mistress Brady,' she said. 'I hear . . .' She struggled, trying to find a good word she'd honestly heard of Alice Brady to pass along. 'I hear folks speak so well of your housekeeping. They say you're the thriftiest and wisest woman in all Gyrford. Perhaps some time I might learn some of your methods, I'm sure they'd stand me in good stead.' 'Wisest' was Molly's own addition, but 'thrifty' didn't sound like much of a reputation.

'Oh.' Alice stood answerless, apparently lost, or perhaps stunned by hearing her thrift actually praised. She didn't manage to find anything to say in reply.

Janet glanced around her. It was a solid house, thick-walled and whitewashed and empty of items: no picture or embroidery on the wall, no rug on the floor, no ornament on any surface. The air felt odd, and it took her a moment to place it. It wasn't a strange smell, but an absence: no smell of ashes. The evenings were drawing in cold, but from this dull-scented air, there hadn't been a fire in the hearth for a long time.

'I hope you will pass along our compliments to your husband,' Janet said. The words came out extremely flat: Janet was not a good liar, and would have liked to say many things to Ephraim Brady if she hadn't thought Alice would be the one to suffer for them. But then, the whole situation was itching at her: Alice had never invited anyone into her house without her husband's permission, and that permission was never, ever offered. Indeed, he prickled at the very sight of Janet. In her long years as a midwife, there'd sometimes been women who couldn't have children who called on Janet for advice, but Alice Brady had never been among their number. Husbands varied in how embarrassed they were on the subject, of course, but she had the uncomfortable feeling that Ephraim Brady regarded her very existence as an affront to his privacy – and while some wives felt able to go behind their husbands' backs, Alice had never even tried. Could he know she was here? She watched Alice with a close eye to see how she took the pleasantry.

'I – I am sure he will be glad to hear them,' said Alice,

toneless – but not nervous: she had no air of wrongdoing or fear of discovery. Ephraim must know they'd be here.

'We see him often at the smithy,' Janet persisted, feeling that she really must tell Matthew this evening what a marvel of self-control she'd been to speak of Ephraim Brady in such heroically neutral terms. 'He continues in good health, I believe.'

'Oh. Yes,' said Alice. Something was settling on her, a slow weight in her face, as if all the muscles had lost their power to hold her expression up. She looked dazed, desolate. Then she pinched up her mouth into a smile that reached nowhere near her eyes, and said, 'Perhaps you'd like to sit down? I can offer you some . . .' She got lost in calculation for a long enough for the silence to become uncomfortable, then concluded, 'some cool water.'

It wasn't a thirsty day outside, but then, water could be offered at no expense to the host. 'That would be lovely,' Janet said. 'The very thing. Molly's been dusting at home, I'm sure a nice fresh drink would be just what she needs.'

'Thank you, Mistress Brady,' said Molly, who wasn't stupid and didn't need the look of broad hint her mother bent upon her.

'Perhaps you'd like to step into the – the kitchen,' Alice attempted. Janet and Molly followed her. There was a parlour on the way, and Janet glanced into it: two good armchairs, and a small, hard stool, and nothing more. Enough to seat them, perhaps, but Alice was hurrying by.

Janet's apple basket stood waiting for them, clean as could be, placed in the perfect centre of the kitchen table, its edges neatly aligned. Alice reached up to a shelf, where stood three cups and a jug — no more than three. She poured, and as she did, the water shivered from the spout: her hands were shaking.

'I don't suppose,' she said, her voice high and tight and as far from casual as could ever be, 'you've heard any more in the smithy about this Groves business? I — I think folks have all be wondering whether there was any . . . foul play.'

Janet looked at Alice, her care-bleached hair scraped back and her plain dress mended at the cuffs with perfect, regular stitching. Of course: Ephraim Brady would want to know whether anyone had set Black Hal upon Roger Groves. The Smiths were keeping any questioning of the Porters and Wares very quiet, at least in part because they didn't want him setting his sights upon them as possible thwarters of his plans. But if he thought that gossip on such a fatal subject flowed from woman to woman with that little trouble, he must either think nothing at all of wives, or else be prepared to try anything that might possibly work. Maybe both. After all, a cup of water cost him nothing.

Anger twisted in her throat. Janet took pride in her role as a good farrier's lady, and while she could certainly lose her temper and let her tongue run away with her on some matters, she never betrayed anything Matthew actually told her to keep quiet. What had Ephraim Brady done to this wife of his, alone in her unheated house, thin and white as a birch tree, buying second-rate vegetables out of his wealth and eating what little she could make of them, that he'd still expect her to scrape up charm enough to drag a deathly secret out of a woman he had never let her visit?

Janet remembered the look Alice had bent on the apples she'd brought before. There had been uncertainty in her face, yes, and anxiety against doing the wrong thing. Now she thought she'd seen something else. Alice Brady had looked hungry.

Janet swallowed. She was — and yes, she would use the word — she was *damned* if she was going to give Ephraim Brady a chance to blame his wife for this.

'Oh, my dear,' she said, with a passable imitation of a woman who can't resist a good prattle, 'if you only knew how complicated it is! Now on the one hand, there's the plain fact of it: the People don't do favours for the asking. But on the other, well, who can know what they'll do next?' Matthew and Jedediah, a lot of the time, was the answer to that, but for today Janet was ranking Alice's safety higher than family pride. 'My Matthew makes great study, but I'll tell you, my dear . . .' She looked around the kitchen, as if making sure they were alone. The floor was swept, the shelves polished, the stores of food and fuel nearly empty. '. . . it's a time for sensible folk to be cautious, if you ask me. The People have their fanciful seasons, and it's always best to step light.' There: that meant nothing, but Ephraim could, if he chose, take from it the hint that troubling touched boys was a bad idea.

Molly had been growing ever more uncomfortable: Ephraim Brady never shouted at anyone, for all she'd seen, but Alice Brady was *acting* shouted at. Her mother's switch from caution to volubility made her nervous, and she was about to suggest that it might be time to go home, when there was a knock on the door.

Alice Brady had been listening to Janet with a head-dropped, frozen concentration, but at the sound, she startled up like a hare. 'Excuse me,' she said, and slipped out.

'Mama,' Molly whispered, 'can we go home? I don't think we should be here.'

Janet opened her mouth to agree, but before she could, there was a clatter in the passageway, and an affable voice exclaiming, 'Oh, no, I'm sure it's all right. Ephraim never minds these things, Alice, you know how— Ah, good morning, Mistress Smith. And Miss Smith, is it?' Taking off his hat with cheerful, pleasant courtesy, Anthony Brady walked into his brother's kitchen.

Alice stood behind him, twining her fingers, her eyes darting from one side of the room to another. Anthony seated himself at the kitchen table without asking, planted his elbows, and regarded Janet with a frank interest, almost thoughtfulness, that Janet felt very much inclined to resent. 'I hope you keep well, Mistress Smith?' Anthony said. He'd greeted her already, but she hadn't said anything. There was a note of reminder in his voice, as if he was very determined she should talk to him.

'I do, thank you, Mister Brady,' said Janet, trying to feel herself as far away from him as was possible over three feet of scrubbed planking. 'I came to accept back a basket I lent to Mistress Alice Brady here. I shan't trouble you. I must thank you, Mistress Brady, for returning it in such good order. I declare, it almost looks newer than when I lent it.' If Anthony was going to sit here and hear her talk, he was going to hear good things about Alice and nothing else. Janet had no idea how much he repeated to his brother, but she didn't consider him the sort to watch his words.

'Would you . . . would you care for . . .' Alice's hands had begun wringing. She clearly had to offer Anthony refreshment, and probably better refreshment than she'd offered the Smiths, but now she had to make the offer in front of them.

'Oh, I'll have a cup of small ale well watered down, Alice,' said Anthony. His voice wasn't rude, but he didn't quite turn his head to speak to her. Alice quietly picked up her own cup from the table, took it to wash, and disappeared into the pantry.

'I wonder if we should take it to the parlour,' Anthony added as they waited, apparently moved by hospitality. 'There's my chair, and I'm sure one of you could sit in Ephraim's chair, and Miss Molly could take the stool, perhaps . . .' He stopped. Two chairs for the men, Janet thought, and the stool for Alice. But while Anthony didn't seem to have any qualms about sending Alice off to fetch him something to drink, it had evidently dawned on him that perhaps she might need to sit down too, if it was going to be a visit of any length, and that meant fitting four bodies onto three chairs. The problem appeared to be worrying him, and when Alice returned with his cup of small ale, he took it with an, 'Ah, thank you, Alice,' that was rather more considerate than his previous remarks to her, and settled himself back at the table, as if hoping his previous slip might pass unnoticed.

'I don't mean to keep you, Mister Brady,' Janet said. Staying here wasn't fair to Alice, trapping her between Anthony's blithe expectations and the reality of two more guests she wasn't allowed to feed, and it was time for them to go.

'No, no,' Anthony said, waving her down again. 'The truth of the matter is—' He stopped, blushed. The expression on his face was almost embarrassed, a look of boyish confusion. The man was all of twenty-three, and Janet was not inclined to forgive him for his family connections, but he had an air of harmlessness at that moment which was frustratingly difficult to reject. 'Well, the truth is, Mistress Smith, I was wondering if you could help me. You see, I've been— Well, there's a— Oh you see, Mistress Smith, you must understand – you must have had men longing for you in your youth,' he said in a rush.

Janet, who did not entirely like the implication that she was a hoary old grandmother, even if she was the mother of four, said nothing.

'You see, Mistress Smith, there's Francie Thorpe, and she's everything a girl could be, she's . . . she's . . . Well, you see how it is, Mistress Smith.' Anthony's face was a little damp. Janet allowed herself a private sneer; if her Matthew hadn't been able to pay her a better compliment than 'everything a girl could be', she'd have thought him a poor figure, that was all. Not that he ever would have cut such a poor figure, of course.

'Well, Mistress Smith, I've called on her from time to time, but there's her father, and I'm so often out with Ephraim, and I'm trying to find the moment to tell her how I feel, and – well, everything's so *difficult*.'

Molly looked over at her mother, whose face was set in a mask of pleasant blankness she knew presaged a contemptuous speech later in the day. She herself thought it must be rather nice to have someone stumbling over their words for love of you, but she'd heard so many bad things about the Brady family, and clearly one of them was already a bad husband, that she hardly knew what to think.

Janet gave a chilly smile. *There's her father*, indeed, as if Franklin was a ferocious guard dog, instead of a man worth fifty Ephraim Bradys all in their Sunday best.

'Love finds a way,' she said. A less carefully shielded man than Anthony might have heard the dig at his lack of initiative, but Anthony only nodded with eagerness at her sympathy.

'That's it, of course, Mistress Smith. You see, I know she comes to your smithy sometimes. I was hoping . . . well, perhaps I might leave a letter for her there? You see, I know all manner of folk come there, Ephraim's always saying it's the place where the world goes to transact. And I was thinking, if that were so, it might not be such a trouble to you if I were to leave a letter?' Anthony's face was hopeful.

If he hadn't mentioned Ephraim as the font of all village wisdom, Janet might have hesitated: Francie Thorpe, after all, was a sensible girl, and old enough to handle her own business. But she was not about to do any favours for the kith or kin of that man.

'Oh, I'm afraid we'd be no good to you, my dear boy,' she said, with an edge of sarcasm she was quite confident Anthony would miss. 'A forge is a place full of fire and water. No letter would be safe there.'

'Oh.' Anthony looked downcast, and Janet sat firm, not making any alternative suggestions.

'You could go in the forest and whistle for her,' Molly suggested; John had described hearing Franklin Thorpe whistle his greeting in the woods, and it had rather appealed to her imagination. 'Whistle a love song, so she'll hear you.' Her mother was looking very stiff at the whole subject, but Anthony's confounded romanticism was hard to spurn entirely.

'I can't whistle,' Anthony said, shame-faced. 'I never could. Oh dear.'

'Well, then it looks as if it's hopeless,' Janet said, rising and straightening out her skirt with an air of bustle. 'But never mind, perhaps you'll think of something. Mistress Brady, I must thank you for your kindness. It's been such a pleasure to see you.'

Alice had stood in the background for this conversation, mute and still as a coat hung from a peg. Janet took her hand and held it before she left. Whatever courtship Ephraim Brady had paid to her, it must have been decisive. It had had its effect.

The Ware farm, from the outside, was an unusually secret-looking place, with brambles and holly planted all around it. If you didn't know about Tobias, you might look at the great barrier hedges and think the Wares had something to hide.

Which was why, when Jedediah and John let themselves in at the gate, bringing the leather gloves they'd been adapting for Tobias, they didn't see Ephraim and Anthony Brady until they were right inside the bounds.

Anthony turned at the sound of them and raised his hat, looking a little confused at their appearance but issuing a polite, 'Good afternoon, Mister Smith.'

John cleared his throat at Anthony's apparent failure to notice him, but while he'd been practising Jedediah's formidable harrumph, he didn't have the chest for it yet and Anthony didn't mend his ways at the sound.

Ephraim Brady gave them a quick glance, and said with stiff formality, 'Good day, Jedediah Smith.' He didn't acknowledge John either.

Clearly they were interrupting a conversation. Jonas came

forward and shook Jedediah by the hand, greeting him rather more warmly than Ephraim Brady had. 'Good day, Mister Smith, and your fine lad here,' he said. 'You're always a welcome sight to us. I hope Mister Matthew is hale?'

'He's well,' Jedediah said. Being an irritable man, he tried not to irritate his own conscience to the point of discomfort, but Tobias was still in danger here, and Jedediah didn't like the sensation. He liked it even less seeing Ephraim Brady standing before him, investigating a property he was surely unable to buy now its owner was dead.

'I'll pass on your good wishes,' he said, rather angry at his own awkward tone. 'I hope you're well too. Where's that lad of yours?' It came out too sudden, and Jedediah could feel his face tightening into its habitual scowl, an expression he didn't want to display but couldn't quite prevent.

'He's up in the fields with the other boys,' Jonas said. 'Harvest beginning, you know.' They were starting a little early, Jedediah noticed; most likely, if Tobias was biting himself, they felt the need to keep his hands busy.

'I'd like to meet him some time,' John said. His voice was a little stiff, and he stared straight ahead, refusing to catch the worried look Grandpa shot at him.

'Well, that's a kind thought,' said Jonas. He knew little of this small Smith standing bold before him, but the thought pressed upon him sometimes that he wouldn't live for ever. Toby would never be able to take care of himself. Jonas was proud of what the lad could do under close supervision – all of them had sweated years of patience to teach him how to handle the tools of the farm, and the fact that Toby hadn't lost his sweet disposition under so much nagging was one reason they all loved him so much. But that sweet disposition needed a safe set of channels to run through. If Peter and the lads would take care of Toby, that'd be one weight off his mind – and they would, he was sure of that – but then Matthew Smith wouldn't live for ever either, nor probably as long as Toby, and who would come after him? If this young John was as kind as his father, that would be a great relief. 'I'm sure he'll be happy to meet you, Mister John. Your father speaks very well of you, you know.' This was a bit of a stretch, as Matthew had in fact tried to speak as little of John as possible, but he'd answered questions and shown that slight frown of concern that Jonas recognised as the stamp of a father's love.

'That's good,' John said, but before he could enquire as to the exact nature of Matthew's compliments, Ephraim Brady interrupted.

'Have you just come a-calling, Mister Smith? I have matters to discuss here.'

'I do not believe we account to you, Ephraim Brady,' Jedediah said. 'We have matters of our own.'

'I could take them round, Dada,' Peter volunteered. 'Mister Brady, Mister Anthony Brady, if you'd care to come with me, I'm sure I can answer you any questions you like to ask.'

'What questions do you come to ask?' Jedediah snapped, before Ephraim Brady could answer Peter.

'I beg your pardon?' Ephraim turned to look at him, his face still as a rock.

'Fairy-smithing business,' Jedediah said back, not moving either. 'A man of station died on this road, Ephraim Brady, as

I know you know, and if I see a man on a property not his own, visiting folks not his friends, I'll have an answer, if you please.' Let the man be on the defensive, for once. Appeals to his better nature were like pouring ale down a well; perhaps a little counter-accusation might check him.

There was a tense silence. Before Ephraim Brady could make his decision, though, Anthony Brady broke in. 'We're doing nothing against the law, Mister Smith! You must know that we wouldn't—'

'Andy, it's all right,' said Ephraim. His face didn't relax a muscle, but his voice was a little softer, just a little. 'Never you mind. There's no trouble here.'

'But if he thinks—'

'Never you mind, Andy.' Ephraim turned to Jedediah, his eyes dark and his tone growing icy. 'I'll thank you not to frighten my brother, Mister Smith. I'll tell you plain what we're doing here: we come to ask if the men here know who will be the new owner. With Mister Groves no longer with us, his heir might wish to sell some land and save himself the management of it. Jonas Ware tells me that the late Mister Groves' brother Charles has been by to visit. You do not object to my having a question answered, I hope?'

Charles Groves. He was not a Gyrford man, and the Smiths hadn't met him, but by reputation he was no pleasanter than Roger had been. Well, that was new unwelcome information. Jedediah gritted his teeth and replied, 'Thank you for your answer. I'm obliged. Now, Jonas Ware, perhaps we'll—'

'Dada!' There was a shout from behind them, and as they looked, there was a streak of fur, a quick flash to the hedge – and then the rabbit was gone. A boy was after it, faster than you'd think a boy could run. There he was, worrying at the bushes, scrabbling and snapping his teeth and giving short, high little whimpers as the holly pricked his digging fingers.

'I'm sorry, it ran by before I could—' Mark, the Wares' second son, was gasping for breath.

Jonas cut in, saying, 'It's all right, lad, no harm done.' Peter was already at the hedge, crouched down beside the flurrying figure. He didn't reach out to touch him, but his voice was soft.

'The coney's gone, Toby,' he said. 'Gone, Toby. *Gone*, Toby. Hear?'

John stared in open fascination at the boy still trying to find his way through the thorns. Nobody had been able to tell John anything tangible, just words like 'touched' that had no texture, no heft, no scent of a real soul upon them. But here was Tobias now, more real than anything rumour had been able to convey to him. He was flesh and blood, and full of movement; he was just a boy, a little taller than John, with his mind set on other things.

Tobias was thin, John thought – all the Wares were thin, they had a skinny build and no money to waste on butter, but this boy was all wrists and fingers, all angles, every part of him folding back and forth with a rapid roll. He wasn't ragged, or at least, his clothes were clean and mended and no worse than his father's or brothers', but his hair was long and ravelled, great fronds of it hanging limp from his head. His shoulders were up around his face, sharp points like elbows, and he was bouncing up and down on his haunches, wiry and weightless and resolute after the rabbit out of his reach. What was it about him? John listened, trying to feel it out, to feel the thing that was definitely present in Tobias, something he recognised without knowing why, for he'd never felt it in another man or woman. He was distantly aware, as his eyes sharpened, that he was probably getting that stare everyone was always telling him about, but this was too interesting, too vital, to worry about it now.

'Toby,' said Peter, his voice firm, 'no coney there. Time to go back to work, there's a good lad.'

'Can I say good afternoon?' John started forward, and Peter held up a hand.

'Just give him a moment to get back to himself,' he said. 'Toby, lad, no coney there now. Back to work, good lad. Come on, there's a good lad.'

The boy gave a grinding whimper, and drummed his hands on the ground, a frantic rattle of sound, as if beating out the frustrations he couldn't speak.

'I know,' said Peter. 'There's a good lad. Come on, stand up, please.'

The boy whimpered again, and Peter repeated, 'Stand up, please. *Up*, Toby,' and the boy rose to his feet with a swift, fluid motion that Peter took a few seconds of more ordinary effort to follow.

John drew forward again. He was listening hard now, trying to feel the air. There was something around Toby, a – what was it? A fluster, a tumbling disorder. The boy was fast and strong, there was no question about it, but it was as if the normal pull of the earth didn't operate on him. Something was blowing him about, gusting him this way and that faster than a common man could follow.

'Good afternoon, Toby,' he said, and the boy whipped round.

John stared, curiosity filling him to the brim. Tobias Ware's face was – well, it was entirely ordinary; there was nothing strange about it at all. He held his mouth a little open, his tongue flicking as if to taste the air, but his features weren't canine or fey. They were narrow, pleasant, the typical Ware look. Tobias looked a little drunken, perhaps, or a little tired, but he mostly just looked like his brothers.

'That's John Smith, Toby,' said Peter, his voice gentle. 'He's our friend. Would you like to wave to him?'

Tobias gave John a quick glance, then ducked his head, backed away a couple of steps.

'John Smith's our friend, Toby,' Peter said again. 'He's a good boy. We like John Smith.'

Tobias twined his limbs, then all of a sudden pressed himself against his brother. It wasn't quite an embrace: he sidled up to him, leaned his shoulder against Peter's, as if squashing them two of them together.

Peter patted his back. 'These are good folk here, Toby,' he said. 'We like them.' There was nothing of sorrow in his tone; just gentle affection, the instinctive warmth you heard in everyone's voice when someone beloved gave them a hug.

Tobias gave a small sound, a little burr in the back of his throat, and then lifted his hand. He didn't quite look at anyone, his head was down in a submissive, anxious bob, but he waved, and then he smiled too. His teeth were a bit crooked, but the smile lit him up, filling him with sweetness, everything about him suddenly bright.

John found himself smiling back, a real, bright smile. 'I'm

very happy to meet you, Toby,' he said. He would normally have said more when introducing himself, but he had the feeling that more might have been too much for Tobias to take in, and also, since Tobias' main interest seemed to be coneys and John didn't have one, he wasn't quite sure what else to say.

Peter smiled at that too, the same warm smile as Toby, though it didn't illuminate him the same way: it was just a pleasant smile, and a look of relief. 'I'm happy to meet you, John Smith,' he said.

'Ah yes, good afternoon, Peter Ware,' John said, a relief deeper than he could explain filling his own chest. Buoyed by the warmth, he remembered that he'd better make a decent showing of himself to the rest of the family. 'We're sorry to interrupt your day's work. I know time comes scarce in harvest time.'

'You're very welcome here,' Peter said. 'I hope you'll forgive Toby if he goes back to work now. It's work time, you see, isn't it, Toby? You go off with Mark, there's a good lad.'

Mark, who had been catching his breath, came over to join them. 'Good lad, Toby,' he said. He gave his brother Peter a rather weary look, and Peter gave him a glance of wry friendliness back: evidently losing track of Tobias was not something the Wares regarded as worth a reproach. 'Come on, Toby, let's go back to work. Come with me, there's a good lad.'

Toby leaned against Peter again, but when Peter patted him, he trotted over to Mark. He pressed his head into Mark, body leaning away so it wasn't a full hug, but he buried his face against Mark's shoulder and Mark patted him too, saying, 'It's all right, Toby. We all know you're a good lad. Let's go.' There was something about the gesture, John thought – he was . . . what was it? He was taking shelter, that's what it looked like, ducking under Mark's shadow as he'd ducked under Peter's. He'd been running across the field, but when he was still – yes, he'd been hunched up to the hedge as well. Dada said that Tobias wouldn't be under a roof, but outdoors, when he wasn't moving, he seemed to need to be under something.

A little more slantwise hugging, and Toby recovered himself and started heading towards the fields. As he tripped up the path, loose-jointed in his walk but limber and healthy, he looked like he'd be a good worker if he could keep his mind on the soil and not the small animals that scurried over it.

The Wares were starting to relax when the two brothers passed Anthony and Ephraim Brady. Ephraim stepped out of their way without a word, viewing Tobias with a blank, speculative eye. Anthony, however, clasped his hands together, evidently feeling the need to be polite.

'Good afternoon, Toby,' he said. 'Do you like coneys, then?'

Tobias' head flew up, and he stared at Anthony, a closer stare than he'd given to anyone present. His teeth chattered together, and his body quivered, every inch of him straining to hear a scuffle, a squeak, the word 'coney' again.

'No, no,' said Anthony, looking rather nervous now. '*I* don't have a coney. I was just asking, you know.'

Tobias continued to stare, his whole body a tense arrow of expectation.

'If you'll step back a moment, if you please, Mister Brady,' Mark Ware said. He was sounding rather nervous.

'Oh, that's all right,' Anthony said. 'I don't mean to upset him. Did I say the wrong thing? Oh dear.' He reached out to Tobias, apparently feeling that he ought to pat him by way of amends.

Tobias' hands flashed up, and then Anthony Brady's was between them. Before anyone could stop him, Tobias had his teeth in Anthony's palm, and Anthony was screaming, struggling to pull away.

'Toby!' Jonas, Peter and Mark were all clustering round, but before they could get to him, Ephraim Brady was there. His riding whip struck Tobias across the back with a dreadful dull thud, then another and another, and Tobias was crouching on the ground, arms over his head and howling, but Ephraim hit him again, again, and Peter Ware was beside him pleading, but Ephraim's face was white and set and he raised his arm.

'That's *enough*, Ephraim Brady!' Jedediah gave a bark of command, and Ephraim Brady stopped, whip still poised above him, looking at Jedediah with cold, absolute fury.

'That's enough,' Jedediah repeated, a lifetime of iron in his voice. 'Tend to your brother, if you will, Ephraim Brady. Don't waste your arm on a touched boy.'

Tobias was curled on the ground now, arms around himself, crying in a long, rending wail.

'That boy is not to be near my brother again,' Ephraim Brady told Jonas, speaking flat and sharp as a blade. 'If ever you see my brother coming, you will take that boy and lock him up, Jonas Ware, or I will know of it.' He turned, looked at Anthony, who was standing cradling his hand, rather pale and shocked, not at all certain what to do. 'Andy, let me see your hand.' The fury was gone, all at once; Ephraim's voice was almost tender.

Anthony held his hand out. There was a bite mark in it, to be sure, blood seeping out at a slow drip. 'I – I didn't think he'd do that,' he said.

'There now, Andy, never mind,' Ephraim said. He had taken a fine white handkerchief out of his pocket, and was wrapping his brother's hand with a neat, careful touch. 'We'll take you home and get that tended to, don't you worry.'

'I didn't think he'd bite me,' Anthony said. 'I don't under-stand it.'

'Well, you startled him,' John intervened. Toby was still cry-ing on the ground, with Peter and Mark beside him, both speaking to him in low, gentle voices. John took a step to stand beside his grandfather, and looked at Anthony with contempt. 'You talked of coneys, and that made him think you had one, and then you tried to touch him. Would you like it if some stranger tried to pat you just because your brother does?'

Ephraim Brady gave John the closest thing he'd ever had to a look of hatred, and John returned it. 'You should be careful of touched folks.' John planted his feet. 'And if you don't know what to do, stay away. You don't have to be in everything. You should leave it to folks who know what they're about.'

Jedediah put his hand on John's shoulder, a touch that was something between a hushing gesture and an agreement. 'I think, Ephraim Brady, perhaps you and your brother should view this place another day. Take him home.'

'And if he's touched now too?' Ephraim Brady's voice was savage. 'Who will make amends for the harm then? That crea-ture should have hanged years ago, or drowned like a whelp in a rain-barrel.'

'Ephraim?' Anthony grew pale; it was almost a plea.

Jedediah shook his head without breaking Ephraim Brady's gaze. 'A bite is just a bite, Ephraim Brady. Black Hal touched that boy and you know it. And you will be right in a day, Anthony Brady. Wash your hand in clean water – get it upstream of the smithy and boil it, mind – then put on some honey so the cut won't go bad, and don't trouble your head about it further.' There was something about Anthony Brady that made it almost impossible not to tell him not to bother himself about things. Jedediah felt the urge to shake him for standing around so helpless, yet instead, here he was giving the lad medical advice. But better Anthony than Ephraim: he wasn't going to hear Ephraim Brady's words. If he didn't notice them, if he didn't have to think of the man calling that child a whelp, a creature, he could walk away from this without doing something irreparable.

Tobias was shivering on the ground, still whimpering, covering his head against the open sky from which the whip had descended. From the looks of things, it would be a very long time before he was ready to go back to work.

'Go home, Ephraim Brady,' Jedediah said. 'You've done enough for one day.'

'I'm sure Toby will know better another time,' said Jonas. It was not the coldest of days, but his teeth chattered.

'The boy will know not to go near Ephraim Brady, that's for sure,' Jedediah said. 'Perhaps Anthony will know better another time too.'

Ephraim was not a big man, but he rose with fury, his face pale and his eyes narrow. At that moment Anthony touched his shoulder and said, 'Could you help me on my horse, Ephraim?

I don't think I can mount up alone.' John gave him a quick glance: was he trying to distract Ephraim, or was he just that useless? It was impossible to tell.

Ephraim turned, and then his voice was gentle again. 'Of course, Andy,' he said. 'You lean on me and we'll get you home.'

The Smiths had to leave the gloves they'd brought for Tobias with Peter; Toby was in no state to endure anything new. Mark had to go back to the fields alone, for work can't be left undone, while Peter took over the care of Tobias, who had still not stopped crying and didn't look set to stop any time soon. The boy insisted on returning to his sleeping-place, iron bars and all, and Peter closed the door and sat outside, his face miserable. At least no riding crop could reach in there, or that was presumably Tobias' thinking, but the boy sat near to his brother, covering his head and keening, and Peter repeated again and again, 'It's all right, Toby. You're safe, Toby,' hoarser and hoarser as the time wore on.

'Should we help you?' John asked, looking at the scene.

Jonas Ware shook his head. 'Toby'll calm in his own time, that's all. I think better leave him now. You spoke kind to him, Mister John, but better speak to him again another day. It's . . .' He trailed off, gathered himself. 'It's just how it is. Toby didn't mean to hurt that man, he just wasn't thinking. You just – you need to have the measure of Toby, is all.'

John nodded; it was quite obvious to him. Jedediah just grunted; he was too unhappy at the limits of his skills to help that lad to have anything very much to say.

'I – I hope you won't swear to it if Mister Brady wants Toby arrested,' Jonas said. His face was still, but his hands fidgeted at his sides.

'Of course not.' Jedediah gave him a glare that caused Jonas more alarm than comfort. 'I'll swear no such damn thing. It was the Bradys' own fault, and I'll say as much to any man who asks.'

Jonas sighed, and ran a thin hand through his hair. 'I – I am grateful, Mister Smith. I should ask, what brought you here today? If there's anything we can do to help you . . .'

'Don't be grateful,' Jedediah said, his voice rough. 'It's damn little we've done to help you today.'

As Jedediah spoke, John was listening. There was a soft clattering behind them, coming from the direction of the hedgerow; it had been building for a while now. He turned, but what happened was gone so fast he couldn't be quite sure he saw it. He'd thought, when he came in, that there had been several brambles in the hedge, but now there was a gap. Just in the shade beyond it, he could see a flicker of movement, like the flutter of rags in the dark. And the sound. It had a teeth-on-edge quality, like cracking knuckles, but it wasn't quite that. It was more a clapping, like delighted hands clasping together – except that it didn't sound like hands.

'John!' Jedediah shook him. 'Don't go starey now, for mercy's sake. We need to gather our wits. Forgive us, Jonas Ware. We'll be off now. Send one of your boys, or anyone you like, if you need help. Day or night, don't worry about waking us. Any time, you hear?'

## CHAPTER 12

The sky was white as John and Jedediah headed home, the warmth gone from the day. Jedediah glared at Dobbs' back and said nothing; there were things that needed explaining, but he wasn't sure how to begin.

Since Grandpa wasn't talking, John was listening to the wind around them; once the world grew interesting, it was hard to stop paying attention. Yes, it was there, blowing straight in their faces as if they were racing along at a dog's gallop. Around Toby Ware it had got all tangled up; it was as if buffets struck at him from every direction and the air was never still. John was not entirely clear on the finer points of where babies came from, but he'd seen pregnant women, and he wondered how it would be to hang suspended inside a parent and have the wind come rushing at you. Would it set you spinning, spinning so you could never stop? Black Hal had done something to Tobias Ware, and – what was it Puss had said about it? Black Hal did not turn. He ran straight along the road, leaving the world whirling behind him, and Tobias Ware, too young and unborn to stand steady on his own feet, had got caught in the wake.

'Grandpa,' he said, 'can we do anything to help Tobias?'

Jedediah grunted. 'He'd be well enough if landlords would stop harrying him and nobody hangs him,' he said. 'That boy's touched, but he can live and work. Touched folk can, sometimes.' He stared at Dobbs' back and nodded. That was a thing he needed to remember.

'I mean,' said John, 'can't we fix him?'

'If the answer was no,' Jedediah said slowly, 'what would you do?'

John frowned. The conversation was taking on a stretched quality, like thin leather over too wide a drum-top; words echoed down within it. 'The same,' he said. 'Try to help him another way. I just thought maybe there might be something we didn't think of.'

'There will be,' Jedediah said, trying to gather his thoughts. 'Many things. Maybe none of them would undo what happened to that boy. Maybe one would and we won't know it. But we don't know. He has to be who he is. So the question is, what would you do for him if you knew for sure he was touched and it couldn't be undone?'

'Well,' said John, 'try to keep him safe. I liked him. I know he bit Anthony Brady, but really, Anthony Brady was just simple about it all. And he still thinks his brother is the best of men. I think he could use a good biting.'

Jedediah gave him a glance. It was not quite flattering to hear his own tones being echoed in an authoritative little treble. 'Don't wish any man a lesson he won't learn from, lad,' he said.

'Well?' John demanded. 'What did you ask me all that for?'

He'd stopped thinking of Tobias as an image of himself: Tobias was Tobias, entirely Tobias, so much Tobias that he had difficulty hearing other folks speak. He was as different from John as any other boy in Gyrford. But that being the case, John's attention was moving to what could be done for him. Tobias had tried to be friends with him. He should stand by his friend.

'It's this way, John,' Jedediah said. 'Fixing, we can do, sometimes. Sometimes we can't. That's not the heart of what we're here for.'

'So, what is?' said John. He felt slightly cross at this upending of priorities: his short life had involved a great deal of getting told that he was doing this or that wrong about his work, and if he'd ever tried to suggest that wasn't important, Jedediah would have been on him like a dog on a grouse.

'We have to be on their side,' Jedediah said. He stopped, as if the words were so big that there wasn't room for any more of them.

'Well, we are, if you mean the Wares,' John said, still of the opinion that Grandpa was rather stating the obvious.

Jedediah took another long moment. This was the marrow of his life; it was hard to put into words what ran so deep that it never needed saying. 'Then we have to stay on their side,' he said, 'or we're not fit to be who we are. You watch, John. It's one thing for a set of poor folks to be in a man like Ephraim Brady's way. He'll knock them down if it isn't too much trouble, walk over them, dust the blood off his boots, forget them. But that boy bit his brother. He didn't know to stay down.'

'He stayed down when Mister Brady hit him,' John said, in a tone darker than his usual chirp.

'Then, he did,' said Jedediah. 'Because the man beat him. The question is, does a man know when it's time to stop the beating? I don't believe he does, lad. God knows, you've seen his wife. God knows what he does to her. But she stays down, God help her. Tobias Ware didn't know to stay down. Ephraim Brady will remember that. And he'll remember I made him stop.'

John was used to his grandfather being serious, snappish, a bedrock of kindness with a furze-bush of thorns on top. The look in his eyes now was new. He'd seen something like it before, when there was a difficult member of the People to be challenged. But as he spoke of Ephraim Brady, there was a tension, a braced readiness, as if something had dislodged before them that couldn't be held back. John was used to Jedediah considering folks unwise or tiresome. He'd never before seen him consider an enemy.

'It's all right, Grandpa, isn't it?' he said, his voice a bit smaller than usual.

Jedediah glanced down at him, saw the confounded little face. He would have liked to reassure the boy. In the end, all he could say was, 'If it isn't, we'll have to make it so. One way or another.'

'How?' John asked, feeling the evening colder than he would like.

'I don't know yet,' Jedediah told his grandson. 'We'll wait, we'll see. Just – be careful, lad. Promise me. He'll remember this day.'

John promised, though he was still a little unsure as to what he was promising: being careful was the sort of thing he was supposed to do anyway. But Grandpa had nothing else to say, so

John sat back and watched the sky turning grey. They'd be off Chalk Lane before nightfall, so there'd be no sighting of Black Hal for them. Even after everything today, he couldn't help being a little sorry about it. It must be a very remarkable creature that could stir up the world like this.

# CHAPTER 13

John had not slept well. Wind blew through his dreams, flakes of fire tumbling about him, and he'd shivered under his blankets and woken in a sweat, grabbing for something he couldn't see. His mouth felt raw today, as if he'd gnawed it in the night; there was a taste of scorching on his tongue.

And in the morning, Ephraim Brady walked into the forge — and he was not alone. Or at least, not accompanied by anything mortal. The things checked themselves as he strode past the threshold and stood wincing just outside, humped, crack-limbed, cane-ribbed, wild and thin-shanked as spiders: three bramble bushes, all thorn and angles; a crazed hedgerow crouching in the doorway. There must have been green leaves on them once, but they were shredded down to bark and spines now, scraps of berry bleeding a pulpy trail of juice across the ground. Before him they stood, twitching at the nearness of the iron smithy, whispering in a gather of voices as soft as the rub of straw on straw: 'Neighbour. Neighbour.'

Matthew crossed himself, as much at the look on Ephraim's

261

face as at the squatting brambles in the square. 'Mercy on us, Mister Brady,' he said. 'What has happened to you?'

Ephraim was scratched about the hands, his fingers swollen scarlet, but his face was grey with rage. He spoke in a slow, soft tone, as if to raise his voice would be to crack it open entirely. 'Mister Smith,' he said to Jedediah. 'I have borne with you and your . . . ways. I have been patient. But I will not endure you setting a curse on me, sir. That is malefic work. I have shown the respect due a farrier, but I will not endure malefic work, sir. I will not endure a curse.'

'Grandpa wouldn't curse anyone!' John exclaimed, feeling a little hysterical. The brambles had a nastily familiar air.

Ephraim did not bother to look at him. He raised his hands, which bore a dozen white slices amidst the scarlet. 'This is how you have injured me, sir. The things grasp at me. I will not endure it, sir. There are laws against malefic work, sir.'

'That's enough!' Jedediah snapped. Fairy-smiths were a necessary business in the countryside; maleficence was another trade entirely, one that no self-respecting farrier would have anything to do with. 'I have no dealings with demons and poisons, and well you know it, Ephraim Brady. If it's the People, I'll see to it; if it's malign work, look to your own soul.'

Ephraim's hands were too damaged to make a fist, which was probably a good thing just at that moment. 'I know you have set the People on a man before,' he said, his voice grinding like stone on stone. 'The whole county knows the tale of Adam Taunton. I will not be your next Adam Taunton, Mister Smith.'

'Oh, no,' said Matthew, in a tone of rather frantic peace-making, 'no, nothing was set on Adam Taunton. He thought there might be, but there wasn't. I don't blame you, tales twist in the telling, but it might set your mind at ease to—'

'If I wished to set my mind at ease, Matthew Smith,' Ephraim almost snarled, 'I should not look to you.'

John had crept to the edge of the smithy and was inspecting the quivering bundles. As he got near, one of them took an angry swipe at him; the air hissed as the thorns cut through it.

'Scratchity goway?' he asked it in a miserable whisper.

'Scratchity goget!' it husked back.

Which was the confirmation he needed to sink him into a freezing lake of guilt. This was his fault. Unquestionably, undeniably, this was his fault. Grandpa had promised to leave the bush in the forest alone, and he had gone and bothered it. He'd reminded it of Toby, who broke its branches. It was angry, and so too, it appeared, were its friends. And now they were following Mister Brady around.

John sat on a stool in the corner, too overwhelmed to speak. Jedediah and Matthew had told him often enough that a farrier's promise must be as iron, and he'd supposed he believed them. He should have listened. He should have stayed out of the woods.

Jedediah was bathing Ephraim's hands in quench-water – that is, water in which the hot irons had been recently cooled, a general salve against minor fey injuries. John had used it to wash his cut face when he came home from the forest, and it had helped; Ephraim's fingers were already fading from red to pink. But this didn't solve the real problem, which was the great arachnid creepers chittering away at the door.

John drew a breath. He had to say something. But Ephraim Brady was their enemy, and how was he to say it?

'Mister Brady,' he said, not managing to sound grown-up, 'has this trouble been with you since we saw you last? Since you passed the Bellame woods?'

Jedediah was busy picking spicules out of Ephraim's fingertips; to give the man his due, he didn't flinch. 'Yes,' he said, dislike constricting his voice almost to a cough.

'Well,' said Jedediah, who was not being especially gentle in removing the thorns, 'you beat a fey boy, sometimes the People don't like it.'

'Of course, we'll remedy this,' Matthew put in hastily. 'We can give you some iron to wear now, that should make them keep their distance a little. And a jug of quench-water, in case you are cut again. And a chain – if you make yourself a circle and stand in it, that will give you some space . . . And after that, we may do more. Give us a few days to . . . well . . .' In most situations they would have invited Ephraim to remain as their patient, but that was difficult to contemplate here.

'One more to remove,' said Jedediah over Ephraim's hands. 'Have to cut you a little to get it all out.' By some unknown feat of self-mastery, he managed not to sound happy at the prospect of taking a knife to the man. 'While I'm about that, Matthew, get the net, will you?'

There were three bushes out there, keenly poised and crouching. Net-throwing duties belonged to whichever man in the smithy was strongest, which made it Matthew's job: the device was made of thick twine, soaked in quench-water and dried in open sunlight, with small iron beads woven in at the joins, all adding up to a formidable weight. When Matthew cast it at the first of them, it was an easy target; so intensely had its attention been craving towards Ephraim that it didn't notice until it was tangled within the knotted coils.

Once it was caught, it shrieked, a whistling scream like a frog in the jaws of a cat. 'Help me get it out back, Johnny,' Matthew said, his teeth clamped as the thing lashed his arms; John leaped up and ran ahead, opening first the smithy's back door and then the door of a cage in the garden where they kept the extreme cases. Matthew bundled it in; it was a long moment of snapping thorns and shrilling horror before he could disentangle the net and slam the door on it.

'All right,' he said, drawing a breath between swelling lips, 'let's get after the next one.'

They managed to trap the second as it scuttled across the square, its branches flying like knotted hair. By the time they'd gone back for the third, it had fled. Matthew splashed his face with quench-water, wiped the blood out of his eyes, and said, panting a little, 'We must make a plan for the third, Mister Brady. I should stay away from the woods until—'

It should have been extremely important to Ephraim, considering the current state of his affairs, but before Matthew could finish, Ephraim's head whipped round. There was a noise coming from the square, one that didn't strike anyone else in the smithy as notable, but Ephraim turned and went straight out. Somebody was playing a pipe.

Everyone looked at one another, and, without a word, followed Ephraim Brady into the square.

It was a cheerful melody, neatly played, with a certain tenderness to its cadence as it rippled up and down the octaves. To be sure, it was less common to hear a pipe in the centre of the village than up on the hills, at least in the daytime — it was mostly shepherds who had the time to play and work at once, and a sweet tune passed the hours while you were watching over a grazing flock — but nobody had thought Ephraim Brady much of a music lover. It was only when they saw who the piper was, sitting on a bench outside Brady's house, that they realised why he had turned so fast.

It was Anthony Brady, playing a pretty little jig. And Francie Thorpe, her face alight, was dancing to it.

Ephraim crossed the square to stand before them, his head cocked a little down, like a bull sighting on a man in its field. The grey morning light cast his eyes into shadows.

'Oh!' Francie looked up, found herself with an audience of three men, and stumbled to a stop, blushing and panting a little, her smile still tentative on her face.

Anthony, who hadn't noticed their arrival until after Francie stopped dancing, looked up as well. Flushing, he greeted Ephraim with an awkward smile. 'Good day again, Ephraim,' he said. 'I . . . thought you'd be longer. I see they've taken them off you; that's a good thing. You must be glad of it.'

'We heard you play, Andy,' said Ephraim. His voice was absolutely neutral.

'Oh,' Anthony said, looking a little confused. 'Well, you see. Well. You know Francie Thorpe?'

Francie, now she'd stopped dancing, was looking abashed and rather nervous. 'Good day, Mister Brady,' she said, making a bob in Ephraim's direction. 'I . . . your brother plays very well. He tells me you gave him his pipe.'

'I did.' Ephraim faced Francie Thorpe with no expression at all.

'Well, I'm glad you did.' Francie's hands rearranged her skirt a little, although her jig hadn't untidied it. 'He must have your cleverness to play so well, Mister Brady. I've heard many things about your wits and knowledge.'

There was no sting in her words, just her father's mild politeness that always came out in the face of other folks' tension, but Ephraim did not relax. 'Francie Thorpe,' he said. 'You'll be Franklin Thorpe's daughter?' It was a question, though Ephraim's voice didn't inflect it.

'I am, sir,' said Francie; she was drawing herself together, the light going out of her face.

John, who was surrounded by adults all standing rigid, and feeling rather shorter than he liked, decided that this was a case that called for his mother: at least she was never at a loss for words. Accordingly, he slipped away, and finding Janet in the garden round the back of the house, managed to return with her before anything too drastic had happened.

Janet took in the situation with a glance: Francie facing Ephraim Brady, that despicable pinching beetle of a man. 'Francie!' she exclaimed, as if greeting an expected guest. 'I'm so glad you've come, my dear, I've a pattern I can't make out at all.' This was a rather desperate ploy, as all the village knew that Janet Smith didn't sew for fear of the People getting into her thread and growing weeds out of the cloth, but such was the situation that nobody raised an eyebrow.

Francie, grateful to be getting out of this ring of bristling men, was about to head over to Janet's house when there was a small click. In the silence, all eyes turned to it: the door of Ephraim Brady's house had opened just a crack. It closed again at once, but Ephraim turned and spoke in a flat, mild voice. 'Come out, Alice,' he said. 'We see you.'

The door unsealed. It made no sound except the click of the lock. Alice Brady stood on the step of her house, face pale and blank, hands hanging limp by her sides, looking at no one. Her hands were swollen worse than Ephraim's had been; the scratches ran all the way up her arms.

'You have been listening, Alice?' said Ephraim Brady. The words were soft, toneless.

'I . . . heard voices,' said Alice. She was hoarse; you could hardly hear her. 'I thought . . . you might like something.'

'You did?' It wasn't a question. 'And you heard music before, didn't you, Alice?'

Alice was a thin woman and her dress was not tight on her, but she still seemed to shrink inside it. 'I – I don't know,' she said.

'Really?' Ephraim's eyes were on his wife, her plain face, her white, blinking face. 'You do not know what you hear, Alice?'

'I – I was in the kitchen,' Alice said, her voice growing a little faster without getting a hair louder. 'I was in the kitchen and then I heard something and came to see, and I heard your voice and thought you might like something.'

'So you opened the door, saw me, and closed it again? Is that it, Alice?'

'I – I did not . . .'

Janet, by this time, had nudged Matthew so thoroughly that he was clearing his throat, but Jedediah had had enough too. 'If she didn't interfere with your brother playing tunes to that girl, that's good sense from her,' he said to Ephraim Brady. He was not doing as good a job as Ephraim at keeping his voice free from anger. 'That's Francie Thorpe, a respectable girl, a forester's girl. The whole county knows her father. There's not a better man in Christendom.' Anthony blinked at this and looked to Ephraim in confusion, but Jedediah was too intent to notice. 'If your brother must fix his eyes on a girl, you couldn't fault his choice.'

Jedediah sometimes found it a little difficult to talk to Francie, which was awkward; officially, he was her godfather, though she'd never seemed much in need of spiritual instruction. Pretty young girls who were silly, he had no trouble dismissing, but pretty young girls who were well-behaved, he didn't quite know how to address. Strictures were wasted upon them, and their bloom spoke of another time of life, one so long lost that when he'd gone to court his own wife, he had been another man. Nobody would ever call him Jed again. There was nothing girls wanted from him, and what he knew about pretty young women, and how you could lose them after too few years together, they did not need to hear. But he cared about Francie. Of course young men wanted lovely girls to dance for them. It didn't last.

'Why would she interfere when your Anthony was showing some sense for once?' Jedediah was not given to regretting his own words, but the 'for once', having been spoken, did not give him an entirely easy feeling.

Ephraim did not trouble to rise to the provocation. 'Perhaps you might attend to your family, and I'll attend to mine,' he said, quiet and cold as a winter stream. 'I shall be off, so you may think on how to remove this . . . inconvenience I have. If the one you failed to catch finds me again, I shall return. I suppose you will charge me yet more to remove it, that being your way. You will excuse me now.'

Janet flinched, taking hold of Matthew's arm, but Ephraim did not move towards his cowering wife. Instead, he turned on his heel and walked away to where he stabled his horse.

For three days, Ephraim Brady was not seen in the village.

Alice Brady was not seen at the market. The morning of the first day, Janet silently left a jug of quench-water and a basket of food on her front step. Then she watched from the window until she saw the door open.

Alice Brady looked at the bread and cheese and vegetables sitting on her threshold; her arms were blazing red, in dire need of quenching, but her eyes were all for the food. She stared for a long moment before she reached out to touch it, like a bird panting after a thrown crumb it doesn't quite dare make a grab for. Then, all of a sudden, she scooped up the basket. She was tearing at a roll, cramming great bites of it into her mouth, before she'd even closed the door.

## CHAPTER 14

Matthew said that he agreed someone should have a word with Franklin, and perhaps it should be Jedediah, them being such old friends.

Jedediah said that was all very well, but there was havoc all over and he'd be better manning the smithy than tramping about the countryside telling fathers who their daughters danced with, which had never been his trade. Privately he agreed that Franklin should at least know Anthony Brady was paying court to Francie – youth might be short, but unhappy marriage was long – but he was, indeed, Franklin's old friend. They knew each other widower to widower these days, and Jedediah understood better than most how much a man needed his children when there was no one else in the house. While he'd have picked up a hot brand before admitting it, he didn't quite trust himself to give Franklin any better advice than, *Don't drive your girl away*, which was perhaps not what was called for here. Besides, his own parents had married on the orders of their families and it hadn't been a success; interfering in any-one's love life made him uncomfortable.

He didn't say that, but he showed no eagerness to go and warn Franklin, and Matthew looked hardly keener. Faced with two reluctant men, Janet said she'd gladly go and give Franklin a piece of her mind: she'd told him as much before, at least by message, and if he hadn't finished thinking it over as he'd promised, it was time someone hurried him along.

Matthew said well enough, with some relief at handing the matter over to Janet, who was good at talking to folks, and added that Johnny should drive the cart.

John said hadn't he better be busy about the smithy, with all this havoc to solve?

Matthew said surely Mama would like his company, and it'd be best to have a fairy-smith with her, and with himself and Grandpa were so busy, he'd be glad to see John be a little man and go with his mother for protection.

Janet sighed, and said yes, no doubt, and Matthew said it wasn't that he didn't trust her wisdom, and Janet said it was all right, and the conversation between them ran dry.

John was not at all eager to be around Franklin Thorpe and his mother at the same time; not in the Bellame woods, where he'd set trouble running. But Mama's wordless look of sorrow was rare enough to be frightening.

Things were getting out of hand. Maybe Franklin Thorpe would say that there had been no more trouble in the woods; after all, Dada had caught two of the bushes and one of them had run away, so maybe they'd decide that they'd lost the battle. If they saw Mister Thorpe, he'd know if there had been any more disturbances, and if he had . . . well, he'd rather confess to Dada, if he had to confess to anyone. But . . . John sighed. Dada was covered in cuts from the bushes; he hadn't complained, but his face was sliced this way and that like a butcher's block. He'd got Dada hurt. Mister Brady, too, though he couldn't be very sorry about that. Mama might slap his legs, but if a few slaps stopped Dada being sliced up again ... Grandpa was always saying that a farrier had to stand between folks and harm.

'Don't be sad, Mama,' he said, putting his arms around Janet's waist. 'I'll come with you.'

The woods were dark-leaved and rich; the smoky scent of wet earth breathed around them as they drove. The presence of iron, John thought, was probably silencing some things, but it was still lovely; he still couldn't stop seeing everything. It was hard to concentrate on what folks were saying when he was in such places. Possibly that was what everyone meant when they called him starey or fey. He'd been tempted in last time, and he'd talked to that bush without remembering that Grandpa had promised they'd let it be, and now look. But he couldn't be that fey if he'd angered the bush, could he? Surely it would have liked him better if he had been?

'Mama,' he said as they drove, 'you'd still like me if I was naughty, wouldn't you?'

Janet was deeply preoccupied. 'Of course,' she said, quite automatically. 'I love you always, and you're naughty often.'

'I don't mean to be,' John said, really telling the truth.

'Just don't you go treating your wife cruelly,' said Janet. She had that set look she got when she was determined to put something right — a determination that did, sometimes, avert disaster rather than causing it.

John looked at the trees, their brown-singed heads hanging tattery and mild, and sighed. Likely Mama wasn't going to be in a hearing mood until they found Franklin, and finding him in the forest wasn't the simplest of tasks. Perhaps they could whistle for him: Franklin had a whistle that would sound out across a mile of crowded woodland, and Francie, who had learned from her father, had once shown John how to do it. It was an impressive, fingers-in-mouth shrilling, both sharp and sweet, that John greatly admired, but he had not quite mastered it, and as he was not supposed to ask her about it in public – whistling women and crowing hens being proverbially if not actually ill-fated – his progress had been slow.

It was, therefore, quite a lot of searching and a wide variety of hisses, peeps and squawks later that they found Franklin Thorpe, and by that time both John, who was annoyed by his failure to whistle like Francie, and Janet, who'd had to listen to him failing, were quite out of humour. The forest was bright, sunlight shining between the trees and spider-webs glistening among the bracken, and Janet, a little hampered by mud, marched up to Franklin.

'Franklin Thorpe,' she said, 'you've been hard enough to find, and now I'll have a word with you, if you please.'

'Er – good day, Janet,' said Franklin, a little daunted to come across critical Smiths in the midst of his quiet outdoor work.

'Good day to you too,' Janet said, 'and that's all very well, but if you ask me, which I notice you haven't, you'll keep your girl away from that young man. Francie deserves better than any Brady. Do you know what I've been about, these last three days? I've been watching the house, and since Ephraim Brady left in a temper—'

Franklin didn't interrupt, just made an uncomfortable murmur, and Janet carried on, more upset than ever, 'Oh yes, he left in a temper, we all saw him, just because he didn't raise his voice didn't mean he didn't have the devil's spite in him. He was in a temper because she didn't stop his precious brother flirting with your girl, and because the People are after him and he blames us, and his poor wife can't stop any of it, and three now days he's been gone and left Alice without a penny in the house to buy herself food, and when I left some on her doorstep yesterday she jumped on it like a beggar's dog. Only not so undignified,' Janet added, not wishing to heap insult upon a mistreated woman, 'because that Alice of his has never done anything unseemly in her life, and it's a better life she deserves than this, I can tell you that. You know how thin she is, and how afraid, and now you know why. He'll starve his wife for opening a door at the wrong moment, or just to take his spite out on someone, and that's only what we see through our own window; who knows what else he does, with her hidden away like that with no one to see? And he beat that Ware boy, you know that? He took his horsewhip to that poor boy who's never done a thing in his life out of ill will – how would you like it if it was your child? Beat him like an animal, like an *animal*. And if you think you should let your daughter hop around to the jigs of any kith or kin of that man, you're not the man I thought you were, and that's all there is to it.'

'I . . . understand you,' Franklin said, appalled in several directions at once. 'It is kind of you to let me know.'

'Will you forbid Francie to entertain that Anthony's attentions or not?' Janet demanded. 'Or do you want her going hungry if she looks at him wrong as well? Do you want your grandchildren under Ephraim Brady's whip?'

Franklin Thorpe swallowed. 'Now, Mistress Smith, I do understand you,' he said, retreating into the cautious formality he always hid behind when disturbed, and which Janet, in her less angry moments, could usually coax him out of. 'And of course I wouldn't want my Francie married to any man who wouldn't treat her kindly. God forbid. But I don't know. I've spoken to Anthony Brady a couple of times since you were so good as to warn me. Just happened on his way, you know, and spoke to the lad. I'm not sure he's so bad as you say.'

'He thinks his brother is the best of men!' John weighed in. It was a point he'd made before, but he found it hard to believe anyone could miss its importance.

'He does, Mister John,' said Franklin, a little relieved to be able to address himself to the less hostile of his two visitors, 'but you know, that's not the worst you could say of a man. Ephraim Brady's been near a father to him. You think your own father is the best of men, don't you?'

'He is!' This was exclaimed by both John and Janet simultaneously, Janet with outrage at a comparison so insulting, and John with annoyance at one so fallacious.

'Well, I don't say no to that,' Franklin said politely. 'He's a fine man. And to be sure, a man I'd rather be in company with myself than Mister Ephraim Brady. I am most fond of Mister Matthew, as you know. But then, Mister Ephraim has done much for Anthony. That Anthony, he's a loyal lad, and that's not such a bad thing.'

'He's a stupid lad, if he thinks his brother's any good,' John said. Anthony was practically old, as far as he was concerned, but he wasn't going to miss the chance to demean him to lad-hood if it came along.

'Easily led, I'd say,' said Franklin. 'But then, perhaps others might lead him in a better direction. And not so stupid either, saving your patience, Mister John. He was a bright little fellow when he was your age, and a good-tempered one. I talked to him of my work lately, you know, and he was quick enough to catch on. And he has the wish to do right by folks, if not the knowledge how. His brother . . . well, it's not so easy to know what's common sense, if you depend on those who . . . don't care for sense other than their own. Anthony Brady isn't a lad many folks talk to. They don't go near him, for his brother's sake. And he's been told nonsense about many of them, or truths overblown. He thought me fearsome at first; I had to talk to him quite a few times before he realised I wasn't going to knock his head about. But once he did, he was glad to talk to me, you know; he wants for company. But he hasn't many places to get his notions of what's going on. I have some feeling he might do better than we think, if he had a chance. Folks need chances, I think.'

The day Franklin's father had drowned, he had heard the whispers: a drunk, a wastrel, a man no loss to anyone. He had sweated many years of patience and responsibility before he'd worn that stain off his own name. And he'd never raised a hand to his wife, nor his daughter, not once. They'd never once deserved it, but that wasn't why. He would always carry his father in his bones, he knew that; that was what he had to guard against. It was tiring; on the hard days, it could leave him tired to his soul. But on those days, he would repeat to himself that his family needed him, that his friends thought well of him, that he had no right to betray those he liked better than he liked himself. From his childhood, he'd held hard to the resolution that he wouldn't disappoint Mister Smith. Who did Anthony have in his life to like?

He wished he was having this conversation with Jedediah — but then, Jedediah never let himself be thanked for the chances he'd given Franklin. And things had been simpler back then — painful, terrible, but simple. Franklin had been a child with a welted back, easy to excuse, not a grown man unable to ask the right questions. Franklin remembered moments in the smithy, back before he was safe: salve on his bruises, a gentle hand underlaying a brisk voice: *No cause to put stripes like this on you, whatever you did.* Marked skin spoke for itself. When Franklin was talked to Anthony, he saw a bruised boy, but the bruises weren't on his body, and they weren't of a kind that most folks would recognise. He'd seen the look in Anthony's eyes, the day he'd first tried to talk to him: the braced anxiety, waiting for the outside world to prove itself as hostile to you as you've always been told it would be. Franklin knew how easy it was to fear your neighbours: if Mister Smith hadn't caught him stealing food from his scrap-pail one day when he was little, and taken him into the smithy to feed him instead of hitting him . . .

And yet Anthony still tried to speak to folks, still wanted to be part of things. Even with Ephraim warning him off every friend he might ever make, Anthony wandered around from neighbour to neighbour, doing his best to find something to say to them. Franklin didn't just think him bright: he thought him brave, a braver man than anyone knew. But it wasn't easy to explain all that, and when folks were set on disliking Anthony, Franklin didn't feel the lad's private scars were something he had any right to expose.

Janet meant well, he understood, but her father was a decent fellow, and she was married to Matthew, who'd been a sweet boy and grew up to be a sweet man. She'd never lived with a hard hand twisting her understanding away from itself, and he didn't feel quite up to attempting an explanation. 'A man needn't be unkind just because he has unkind kin,' he said, keeping his voice as mild as ever. 'Sometimes he thrives better when he has a chance to leave.'

'Oh, to be sure.' Franklin was dear to Janet, but she hadn't known him growing up, only as an independent, unbruised man with no one at home to fear. The thought of Tobias had woken her throughout the night, and she couldn't keep the sarcasm from her voice. 'And to be sure, Ephraim Brady will let other men lead his precious Andy into better ways than squeezing folks and starving women and beating children and thinking Ephraim Brady the best of men. He'll just hand over the leash and let another man train his dog, no doubt about it.'

For this, Franklin had no reply.

'Mark my words,' Janet said. Looking at Franklin's tense face, she felt a prick of conscience, but there was Francie to think of. 'Your Francie can get a better man, any man she likes.

And if she likes Anthony Brady now, she'll have to learn to think better of it. If you care for your daughter – as I know you do,' she added, because now she'd said her piece she was calm enough to remember that Franklin was really the kind of father she always thought all men should be – 'then you'll give her warning. Tell her how Ephraim Brady treats his wife, and tell her Anthony will never stand up to him. Tell her she can get a better lover, Franklin. Take my advice.'

The wind sighed in the leaves overhead, and the forest rocked. It was a gentle motion, not swaying the world, and the birds cooed and chirruped to each other above them. Franklin still hadn't found an answer when they heard the sound of hooves.

The man who rode into the clearing was finely dressed, but it was the horse John noticed first. She was an astonishing creature by the name of Taygete; no one could say her name without tying his tongue in a knot, which was a sad tribute to her clean-legged grace. She was a gleaming, jewel-eyed bay, packed tight with muscle and light as a swallow, and John had never been allowed to take part in her shoeing: Lord Robert's horse was shod by the master smiths, not by an apprentice, and no amount of wheedling could persuade Dada or Grandpa to let him near her.

The fact that Lord Robert sat astride her was, therefore, something he thought about second. Having never seen Lord Robert in person, John thought of him more as a weather condition than a man – something folks talked about, sometimes with anxiety and sometimes with resignation, but with no hope whatsoever of avoiding its power to sweep through their lives. And while his clothes were certainly fancy and his face was shaven quite bald, the man himself didn't look all that remarkable to John. He was of ordinary height, had a big nose, and while he rode better than most men around Gyrford, Taygete didn't cock her ears to him as trustfully as she did to Dada.

John, therefore, was only intending to go and pat Taygete – or 'Taggity', which was what he'd settled on in his own mind, rather than going to the bother of trying to pronounce the unpronounceable – when Janet grabbed hold of his jacket and hissed at him to stay still and say nothing. It was so unlike Mama to avoid conversation with anyone that for the moment, John was startled into silence.

'Good day, Thorpe,' Lord Robert announced. And it did sound like an announcement rather than a pleasantry, as if he was declaring Franklin officially greeted.

Franklin bowed. 'Good day, my lord,' he said. To John's surprise, Franklin didn't add any wishes about him having a pleasant ride or queries after his family; usually Franklin was friendly.

'So, Haines tells me he has you looking after this Roger Groves business,' Lord Robert went on. Daniel Haines was the county sheriff, a man with an inability to show excitement about anything and an utter lack of imagination that made him, when law-breaking was to be considered, as close to a just and virtuous figure as anyone could be in the absence of charity. Janet's grip tightened on John's back, but he was too busy concentrating to pay her much mind: Lord Robert spoke a little oddly, not like normal folks, and John was absorbed in trying to understand his accent, which was rapid and clickety and very foreign-sounding. Compared with the more measured speech of Gyrford, Lord Robert was a gabbler – but folks usually gabbled when they were nervous, and Lord Robert was calm as a swan.

Franklin bowed again. It troubled John to watch him defer so deep; Mister Thorpe was a man of standing, respected by all John knew, and with good cause: he worked hard, knew his trade, and did right by his neighbours. But there was nothing on his face now; all his character seemed to have been tucked away. 'He has, my lord. I hope to do good ser—'

'What concerns me,' said Lord Robert, as if unaware he was cutting Franklin off mid-sentence, 'is what'll become of boundaries. My trappers complain there's hardly a coney to be found in these woods by the Groves borders. Village boys tramping in from all sides, I wouldn't wonder.'

'I – I do attend to the poaching, my lord,' Franklin attempted.

Franklin's opinion of his own forestry did not appear to interest Lord Robert. 'It's time those places were under proper governance,' he said. 'I hear there's a fellow negotiating with him for them, an Enoch Brady.'

'Ephraim Brady.' Janet had a grip on John's jacket, but no power she'd ever devised could keep hold of his tongue, and as he bounced into the conversation, both she and Franklin turned pale. 'But you don't want him managing, he's a very bad man.'

Lord Robert looked at the boy with the mildest of interest. 'Your son?' he asked Franklin.

'He doesn't have any sons,' John said, feeling that a man who knew that little of the families he ordered must be pretty slack about his work. 'I'm a farrier. I came to consult with Mister Thorpe on certain forestry matters.'

Lord Robert regarded John for only a brief moment before returning to his point. 'Brady,' he said to Franklin. 'They say he's thorough. Do you tell him to mend his fences. I'll look to you if he doesn't, mind.'

'But he's a bad man!' John insisted. 'You won't like him at all, nobody does!'

Lord Robert paid John's opinion about as much attention as the opinions of the birds arguing territory above. It would have ended there, except that there was a scrabble of earth, and all of them looked down the path.

Before them, hunch-backed as oxen, ragged and spined and watching, were the stooped forms of four bramble bushes. Two of them appeared to have constructed riders out of their smashed twigs, little figures with nothing much for heads, bleeding sap at their wrists and necks, swaying atop the thorns with vicious, focused concentration directed towards the mortal figures before them.

Lord Robert considered the scene. He did not look afraid; he had the placid displeasure of a man contemplating an unswept floor. 'Thorpe,' he said, 'I expect such matters to be addressed.'

John looked about him. They had an iron chain in the back of the cart; it would have to do. 'Excuse me, Mama, Mister Thorpe,' he said. 'Oh, and your lordship,' he added as an after-thought, seeing the man's eyebrows rise. He thought of the scratches Dada had taken, the sting as the thorn had cut his own skin, and swallowed. There was nothing to do but face this.

The chain weighed heavy in his hands, and as he leaped down from the cart, it almost toppled him. He stepped up towards the bushes with a cat's tread, soft-footed as he could manage. His arms were already aching from the weight of the iron.

'Kind friends I am glad to greet, Tell me, what folks would you meet?' He said it quietly; he wasn't sure he wanted this conversation overheard.

One of the little riders cocked its headless stalk at him. 'Bad friend break, kind friend beat,' it creaked. 'Find neighbour man kind friend be friend.'

John drew a deep, careful breath. He wouldn't cry; he didn't deserve to when this was all his fault. He was going to have to tell everyone the truth; he was going to have to mend this, and he didn't know how. 'You want your friend, who beat the boy who broke you?' he said. It wasn't even a question.

'Kind friend, kind friend, hitteded breaker!' This came from one of the other bushes, a riderless one that shrugged its fractured back with an eager, lopsided jolt.

The People sometimes take fancies to folks. They are unswayed by whether the object of their liking is a worthy soul.

John gathered himself, then swung out the length of chain, slashing left and right as he ran down the path shouting, 'Scratchity goway!'

The things gibbered confused invective at him, but as he kept swinging, they leaped back, snatching their branches close to their trunks like moulting birds. Then they scampered away; the effort shook flecks and chips from their limbs, but they were gone almost faster than you could reckon.

There had been four of them on the path. There had been three of them before, following Ephraim Brady to the smithy, two of which now languished in the Smiths' cages. The broken bramble was raising converts.

John turned, bowed, and said as steadily as he could, 'Excuse us, your lordship. This matter will be attended to.'

Lord Robert didn't bother to answer the small, sweating boy beneath him. 'See that it is, Thorpe,' he instructed. He touched Taggity's sides, and she was off without a murmur, picking her way through the bracken with a step light as a moth.

When he was gone, John turned back to Mama and Mister Thorpe, who were looking at him with dreadful attention. The chain weighed so heavy in his hands that he had to drop it.

'I am sorry,' he said in a small voice. 'I should have told you before.'

'John Smith, I – I *cannot tell you* how disappointed in you I am!' Janet exclaimed. She looked ready to burst into tears, even more than she looked angry, and John felt ready to cry alongside her.

'It is my fault, Mama,' he said.

Franklin clasped his hands together. Folks were shouting; Mistress Smith as shouting at her son, and he couldn't, in conscience, blame her.

'You – you go into the woods, you *lie* to us all so you can go into the woods to ask that bush a question after your Grandpa *promises* he'll leave it alone, you talk to it of poor Tobias Ware and set its mind, or whatever it has, running on a grudge, and then you just . . . just . . .'

'I did say sorry to it, Mama,' John said, with no expectation at all that this would excuse him.

'So – so let me see if I have this right,' Franklin said, with the wretched air of one who doesn't really believe that getting the conversation onto plain facts will calm things down. 'You disturbed the bush, meaning well, no doubt, if unfortunately forgetting your duty, and then, when it was angry with Toby, it witnessed Mister Ephraim Brady ... hit him. So it has decided, together with its friends it would appear, that Mister Brady is a friend – and now they follow him around?'

'I think they want to take him by the hand.' John hung his head. 'His hands were all cut up.'

'So,' Franklin said, keeping all but the slightest edge of hysteria out of his voice, 'when they follow him, they do it not to attack him, but because they ... feel fond of him?'

'The People have their fancies,' John said to his boots.

'I – I shall tell your father to take his belt to you,' said Janet, apparently lost for words.

'I don't think he knows how, Mama,' John quavered.

'*Practise makes perfect*,' Janet said grimly, but it didn't take Franklin's miserable look to change her mind on that. 'No, in fact, John Smith, I know what we shall do with you. We will take you to Mister Ephraim Brady. You will explain the matter to him, and then we will see.'

'Sh-shouldn't we ask Dada or Grandpa?' ventured John. 'I'm not supposed to act without consulting them.'

'If you think they'd tell you to do anything else,' said Janet, 'then your hopes do you more credit than your wits, my lad. Besides, Ephraim Brady dislikes them worse than he does me; I'm not the one who charges him for smithing, nor—' She stopped herself before adding, 'The one he thinks was chasing his wife'; this was not the moment to explain *that* to the boy.

'Mister Franklin can come with us, if he'll be so good.' She softened her voice as she spoke that aside; Franklin had been looking more and more wan, and it was starting to cramp her heart to have inflicted so much strain on a good man. Franklin accepted her apologetic glance with an earnest nod: Janet could speak warmly, but she was his friend, and she wasn't wrong to be worried – and besides, he couldn't bear to let Mister Smith's boy go into that place unprotected. 'It will be the best we can do,' Janet concluded, 'so you can stop dreaming up excuses and be about it.'

'I am sorry,' said Franklin, to John's terrified look, 'but I fear I agree with your mother, Mister John.'

## CHAPTER 15

John didn't mean to be a coward, but he couldn't help hoping Mister Brady might not have returned from his trip. Mama had, after all, been leaving baskets of food on his doorstep and making furious remarks about a man who'd leave his wife to go hungry. But as Janet goaded Dobbs down into the Gyrford square – at heart, she wasn't any happier at the prospect of explaining to Ephraim than John was, and felt a deep desire to get it over with – they saw a sight that drew a quiet moan from all of them. Four raggedy bushes stooped at his door, cricketing away with a whisper of a word: 'Neighbour. Neighbour. Neighbour.'

'Well,' sighed Franklin, 'I reckon we know he's home.'

Getting in took a certain amount of effort. Someone had laid a chain before the door – not a chain of Smith workmanship, by the looks of it – and the bushes were gathered as close to it as they dared, creating a spiny wall around the house no uninvited guest could step through.

John considered smacking them with his own chain, but matters were provoked enough, so he took a chance and called out, 'Kind friends at neighbour's door, I have met your friend before. I would give him service true. Please stand back and let me through?'

The bushes crackled to themselves, branches making angular squirms of confusion as they wrestled with what, for them, was evidently a complicated question. They didn't consult amongst each other, John noted; they just each debated inwardly. If one of them had been the original bush he'd bothered, it might have gone worse, but evidently it hadn't thought to inform them that John Smith was an enemy, so after a long moment of creaking speculation, they huffed back a bit, allowing John, Janet and Franklin to pick their way to the door.

John gave his mother a fearful glance, with no real hope she might have thought of some better solution between here and the woods.

'Knock the door or I'll knock your head,' said Janet, her face bearing the drawn look of a woman who couldn't spare her child.

It was Alice Brady who opened. Some of the cuts on her arms were healed by the quench-water, but there were fresh ones: evidently it was her task to clear a path for Ephraim. When she saw the three of them standing on the step, she shivered.

'Mistress Smith,' she said, her voice strained between a whisper and a carefully normal tone, 'I . . . Good day. I . . . With due respect, perhaps it must be said that your visit may be . . .' Alice could cast around without moving a muscle; only her eyes showed the fear. '. . . not convenient,' she finished.

'Oh, he'll like to hear this,' Janet said, with something like despondent humour. 'This, he can blame us for.'

There was a ghastly silence as Alice struggled to know who to disobey. Then there was a quiet step in the passage, and the trim, upright figure of Ephraim Brady walked out of the shadows.

'Mister Thorpe,' he said, slicing his eyes past Janet and John, 'I am sorry to see you in such company. I had hoped for better judgement from one of your station.'

Franklin cleared his throat, spoke with toneless rectitude. 'Well, sir, my station has brought me to intercede in disputes before. I hope to serve it now. We have here a young lad with an explanation for you.'

John wasn't afraid of Ephraim Brady, not in his own smithy with Grandpa and Dada behind him, but here in this dim house, with Mistress Brady shrinking against the wall, he felt himself shaking, just a little. It was cold in here, he told himself, that was all; he had to say his piece, or he wasn't a farrier. He had made mistakes, but if he could hammer them straight, if he could hold up his head . . . 'Mister Brady,' he said, 'I am here to correct a misunderstanding, for whom no one is to blame but myself.'

Ephraim did not move. Behind him, Alice wrapped her arms around herself; her cuffs, well-mended and neatly pressed, had spots of blood upon them.

'In the smithy, last we met,' John said, trying to keep his voice from squeaking, 'it was guessed that perhaps these People who follow you now did so because you beat a fey boy. That was my Grandpa's guess. No blame is on him, sir, for I kept matters from him. The truth is . . .' He looked at Mama, but she didn't look any calmer than him; her eyes kept slipping from him to Alice Brady, who was standing still and grey as a grave-stone. 'Sir, I acted without leave, and made some – some attempts at fairy-smithing upon a bush in the forest that had a dislike of Tobias Ware. I roused it, sir, without meaning to. When you . . . struck Tobias – it was difficult to say this as a matter of fact rather than an unforgivable evil – 'the bushes saw you, and decided to like you for it. I believe they follow you now because they regard you as a friend. It is my fault, sir. I – I beg your pardon.'

Ephraim Brady stood, regarding Janet Smith, who kept look-ing at his wife; Franklin Thorpe, father of Francie, who had come to support this tale; the scrap of a boy from the smithy who held himself so insolent in Ephraim's hallway. John was truly scared, and his stance showed the defiance of a child who has despaired of being forgiven.

Ephraim let the silence hold, and hold.

'I believe, sir,' said Franklin, only to break it, 'that with this new knowledge, it may be easier to end your current difficulty.'

'You do, do you?' Ephraim's voice held no colour, no warmth. It was smooth, and chill, and quite steady.

'I do hope so, sir,' said Franklin. He was not sounding steady himself. Ephraim was unlike his own father in manner and bearing, but Franklin could hear, all too clearly, the ring in the air when someone was getting ready to give out a beating.

'I had thought,' Ephraim said, lightly, without emphasis, 'that whatever else they were, the men of the smithy were men. Not ones to hide behind a child with tales of nonsense. But I thank you, I suppose, for confirming the Ware boy has been part of the maleficence.'

'No, no,' said John, trying and failing not to sound wild, 'Toby had nothing to do with it!'

'I shall be at the smithy in a few days with Mister Groves' heir to confirm my purchase of the farm, Mistress Smith,' Ephraim went on. 'I have spoken to men of law since I was away. I do not believe it would be hard to hang a malefic boy, not when the fairy-smiths who speak for him admit to colluding in the curse. The fairy-smiths themselves? I do not know. But a boy who trespasses, bites, and brings on curses – well, he would not be hard to hang. And if he were not, then who knows? The smiths who colluded with him would face the sheriff with it already on record that the curse was performed.'

'Mister Brady,' Franklin attempted. 'Mister Brady, surely you would like this trouble removed?'

'There is trouble I would like removed,' Ephraim said, as mild as ever. 'I would like the Smiths to stop interfering in my business. Beginning, perhaps, with Mistress Smith ceasing to pay visits to my wife.'

Ephraim was never able to speak the words 'my wife' without a flinch of the lips, as if the syllables had an ill taste to them. Janet stammered, but before she could say anything, there was a hoarse murmur from the corner.

'Ephraim,' said Alice. She spoke with sudden, terrible haste, and Franklin's peace-making dried on his tongue, because he recognised the note in her voice. It was the braced desperation you got when you knew a blow was coming that you couldn't stop, but could, with goading, draw away from others and onto yourself. 'Mistress Smith has done you no ill, nothing to kill a boy for. I do not defy you, but I advise you in all duty, you go too far.'

He did not turn fast, but slow, like an adder before sunrise. 'Say you so, Alice?' he said. His voice was quieter than ever.

'Blame me if you must,' she said. There was a click in her throat, and the words closed upon her.

Ephraim looked at her for a long, long moment. 'Perhaps I shall,' he said, softly, almost kindly. 'Consider it, Alice. You know me not an unreasonable man.'

Janet opened her mouth to say something, but Franklin caught her arm: Alice had spoken now, and if they were silent, if they didn't provoke Ephraim further, he might limit himself to something she could withstand. At the disturbance, Ephraim turned back to them again. 'Well,' he said, with dire civility, 'I believe we have a theory to test. This boy, and the People's fondness for those who are not fond of him. You will be happy to hear, Mistress Smith, that in two days, Mister Charles Groves and I will close the sale on the Ware farm. Then I shall be able to inspect my property at leisure, and put this interesting notion of yours to the test. Perhaps you might step over to the smithy and inform those men of yours of their upcoming appointment. They will be needed to witness the sale.' He bowed. Alice stood behind him, her hands pressed to her mouth. 'You will excuse us, Mister Thorpe, I am sure,' Ephraim said, quite placid now, and smooth as stone. 'I believe this is fairy-smithing business.'

None who knew the Smiths could suppose that Jedediah or Matthew were any happier than Janet at the news that John had roused the brambles against Tobias, nor that Ephraim Brady had taken it the way he had.

'Dada,' said John meekly, after the extremely long conversation that followed, 'do you mean to take your belt to me? Mama said you should.'

Matthew gave him a look so bleak that, even after his father pulled him into a hug, John felt bruised. 'No, Johnny,' Matthew said raggedly into the top of his head. 'I just don't see that it would do any good.'

It wasn't cruelly meant, but John went away and cried afterwards, for had Matthew been the most studied of tormentors instead of the most affectionate of fathers, there was hardly anything he could have said that would have crushed him more.

If it hadn't been for Alice Brady, they might have taken the desperate measure of getting Tobias into a cart, somehow, and sending him away. Exactly where was a near-impossible question – the boy had hardly been a mile away from home all his life, except for the woods, and he was not good at new situations – but it might not be safe to leave him in Ephraim Brady's path. They were debating the prospect when Franklin arrived, the day before Ephraim Brady was due to bring in Charles Groves and confirm that they were exchanging the Ware farm and the Porter mill, and Francie was with him.

Janet saw her face, and took the girl into her arms. 'Come in, dear,' she said. Francie looked at her, breathless and pale, and Janet guided her into the kitchen, saying only, 'Come now. We're hardly out of practise hearing ill news, these days.'

'It is only – Mistress Janet, you know I am fond of Anthony Brady,' Francie said once she was seated at the kitchen table. Matthew and John were with her, while Jedediah manned the smithy. Somebody had to; there were still many folks in need of ironwork. You can't lay down your duty just because those you love are under the harrow. And in truth, Jedediah was finding it hard to know what to say to John these days.

'I can't imagine why, if I am honest, dear,' Janet said. She didn't mean to rain upon the glow of young romance, and it was bad midwifery to be unapproachable to any young woman with a lover in the prospect, but recent days had exhausted her endurance.

'I know, I know, his brother is . . . not a good husband,' Francie said. There were tears starting in his eyes. 'Dada . . . Dada told me what you said, and I knew it anyway. He is like my grandfather. Not in his habits, but as a husband, he is like my grandfather. But Dada isn't, and Anthony isn't. He never was. He just thinks no one likes him, and he's not wrong, they don't. But they should; he's so kind, Mistress Janet, truly he is. I just . . . I couldn't think of Mistress Brady there alone, without food. And Dada said she had stood up to Mister Brady.'

*I do not defy you, but I advise you in all duty, you go too far.* Alice had spoken the words as if stepping off a ledge.

'So, so I brought her a pie,' Francie said. 'To see if she was all right. She was all bundled up, shawl and kerchief, she looked cold and hungry.'

'Of course,' Janet said, patting Francie's hand and privately blessing the girl for doing what, for Tobias' sake, she no longer could. 'I have done the same. Though her husband has forbidden me the house now, and his brambles could tell him if I tried. Bless you for going, lovie.'

'I was afraid for her, after what Dada said,' Francie said, help-less. 'But . . . but he came in, while I was there.'

Matthew stood up, as if to get between Francie and harm, but then finding himself on his feet to no apparent purpose, started pacing the room. Soots, who had been standing a slightly confused guard over Francie since their arrival, trotted at his heels, ears a-prick against the invisible enemy apparently threatening her family, and nobody was calm enough to reassure her.

Faltering, Francie gave her account of what followed:

Ephraim Brady had thanked her very much, with a face like a mask, for her kind and generous visit, and suggested that if she would care for an escort home, or the loan of a horse to take her, he would be happy to oblige.

Francie said she could take herself home, thank you. She had a mare of her own.

Ephraim Brady said that it was as she liked, and perhaps she should think of going soon, it being evening and the People abroad.

At this point in the telling, Francie stopped, and it was Frank-lin who repeated Ephraim Brady's next words: *It would be most unfortunate if Roger Groves' fate were to befall such a charming young woman.*

Francie had looked at the window, which was showing only an afternoon sky, but then at Alice Brady's face. She told Mister Brady that if he thought it best, she would be going.

Ephraim Brady said he would be happy to escort her, and gave her his arm.

As Francie recounted what happened next, there were tears

of doubt in her eyes: perhaps she had done wrong, but in the moment she didn't see how she could have made things worse.

She turned, speaking fast. 'Mistress Brady,' she said, 'if you must run, run to me. Never mind your uncle, we can shelter you. Run to me.'

Alice's face was a grey blank, and Ephraim turned to Francie with icicle eyes. 'I do not think I understand you, Miss Thorpe,' he said. He did not pinch or pull, but his arm under hers was as hard as bone.

Francie was not accustomed to confronting folks, and the words came out hoarse and awkward. 'I can see behind a kerchief, Mister Brady,' she said. 'I see the bruises on her throat. If you choke the life out of a woman you may hang for it, and if she vanishes, I will know what to tell the sheriff. My father can have an audience with him if I ask it, and I will know what to tell him, sir. She did not invite me here, and she did not show me her throat, and I shall say nothing to your brother if I see no more bruises, I would not shake his faith in one he loves – but I can see behind a kerchief, Mister Brady, sir.'

There was a long silence in the kitchen as Francie finished her tale.

'I thank you, dear,' Matthew said eventually. 'That is . . . knowledge we should have.'

'By your leave . . .' Franklin said. He hesitated. He'd taken so many favours from the Smiths; he owed his life to Jedediah, or at least his life as a free man with a good name and no more scars on his heart than could be avoided.

'Please,' said Matthew, 'If you need anything . . . I should be glad of your ideas.'

'I think,' said Franklin carefully, 'it might be wise if we sent Francie to stay elsewhere for a little while. I will be at our cottage in case . . . well, in case we have any visitors in want of shelter. But I think it would be best if Francie stayed out of Mister Brady's path.'

Janet had a cousin, Bessy, a mild, obliging matron who never scolded anyone, and who would doubtless be able to take in Francie as a guest for a few days if Janet asked her: Bessy had young children, and Francie was a handy lass, after all. As Janet went upstairs to lend Francie a few things for the journey, Matthew and Franklin sat together in the kitchen. John remained in the corner; he was trying to stay out of disgrace, but even if he hadn't been, this was worse than he knew how to address.

After a long silence, Matthew said to Franklin, 'Would you like some water? Something to eat? I'd offer you cider, but . . .' He made a gesture of helpless affection. Franklin didn't drink, at all. Gyrford in general held the vague assumption that forestry required a temperate man; only the Smiths knew how afraid he was of inheriting his father's thirst.

'Thanks,' said Franklin, shaking his head, 'but if you could do with a drink yourself, don't let me stop you.'

'No,' said Matthew. 'I don't much drink either.'

The room stood quiet around them.

'Do you think he wanted her dead?' Matthew asked. 'Just because she contradicted him before you and Janet?' It was his job to understand harsh realities, he knew, but this was one he struggled to bear. He knew there were men who hit their wives; he'd known it since childhood, when Franklin used to come into the smithy with bruises and Jedediah would, in between salving and feeding him, and sometimes sheltering him for the night, ask quietly, 'Your mother all right?' Matthew hadn't known how to help. Jedediah had said to just be a friend to the boy, and that had been easy; he'd always loved Franklin, and could never see why anyone would want to hit him. He'd thought Joe Thorpe must be a little mad, a man quite outside the common fold.

But as he got older, he'd had to learn more. There came a day when Nancy Torby's mother brought her into the forge asking for an iron talisman, as the People had been pinching and slapping her whenever she carried her basket home – or at least, that's how Rob Torby explained his wife's bruises. Jedediah made quiet enquiries, found a family far away who needed a housekeeper and kept a watchdog, and only once she was out of Gyrford had he told Rob that his wife wasn't coming back, and that if he went after her, there were People who'd be interested to learn that he'd been blaming them for wicked acts they never committed. Matthew had been ten years old then; he'd learned to live without his mother, but not to live without yearning, sometimes, towards the light and motion of homes that had wives in them, the bird voices and winged skirts and breakable lives of women. Joe Thorpe was the first man he'd known hit his wife, and Rob Torby wasn't the last. The thought of a home where your dearest companion was afraid of you was not, apparently, enough to scald some men's hearts.

Franklin, resting his hand on Soots' head in utter weariness, sighed. 'Likely not,' he said, 'or she'd be dead. He – if a man shows a woman he *can* kill her, he hopes she'll take the lesson and spare him the trouble of having to. Or that would be my guess. I don't think he likes her to be alive, but he doesn't care to hang for her. If she conducts herself as much like a dead woman as she can, he forgives her for breathing.'

'Why?' said Matthew in misery.

Franklin gave a dejected shrug. 'She isn't what he thinks she should be. No rich dowry, not the mother of his heirs. Not handsome enough to make a show, perhaps. Not, I don't know, a thing that makes him happy. And if he thinks a thing should be . . .'

He trailed off; there was no need to finish. It was evident to both of them: Ephraim hadn't judged foolishly when it came to Alice, at least by his own lights. There was every reason to expect she'd have a dowry, and no reason to expect she'd be barren. Or that Ephraim would, but possibly he didn't consider that. He'd made a sound calculation, and hadn't deserved to be punished by its failure; not according to his own doctrines. He had married a woman he didn't love, Franklin thought, and found she did not bring the expected compensations, and now he had to be married to her: an unrewarded sacrifice looking at him with wretched eyes every night and morning. Possibly he thought it living in hell.

Matthew stared at the floor. How could you possibly counter a man so implacable in the face of a world that wasn't as he wished, who had the money and will to transplant his feelings into the lives of others? 'I don't suppose I could hit him?' he said, without much hope.

Franklin's laugh was sad. 'Well, you could,' he said. 'She'd pay for it later, though. And, saving your presence, Matt, I don't believe it's one of your talents.'

Matthew's voice held a bitterness John had never heard before. 'I do not think I can be sorry for that.'

'Nor me,' John said from the corner. Matthew beckoned him over, and set John on his lap.

'Don't you grow up an unkind man,' he said, as John laid his head on Matthew's shoulder. 'Better your own faults than those.'

It was a mixed comfort at best, and John said nothing. Then, surrounded by the silence of the two men, he ventured, 'Couldn't Mistress Brady go to Aunt Bessy? If we helped her get away, he couldn't hurt her again.'

Matthew put his arms around him, but he didn't seem very steady. 'He is angry with us already, Johnny. And he stands to hurt Toby. Tomorrow we'll know more of what he plans.'

'But if you stop him hurting Toby, he'll hurt her,' said John. 'Won't he?' He was more interested in Toby, that was true, but he didn't want anyone hurt. It was bad fairy-smithing to let it happen, and even if it wasn't, he didn't want it.

Matthew rested his head against John's. It was a sweet sensation, holding his warm, leaning son, even if the boy had caused more trouble within the space of a month than the entire Smith clan had for a generation or more, but outside the circle of his arms, he couldn't see how to keep everyone safe. 'I know, Johnny,' he said. 'I'm sorry.'

## CHAPTER 16

Charles Groves, as he stood in the smithy, looked red-eyed and bleary, as if there had been some celebrations the night before. Ephraim Brady looked pale and tired; he was not a drinking man, regarding strong waters as both impious and extravagant, but Charles Groves wasn't the type to do business without a deal of ale to look forward to, and Ephraim hadn't got where he had without understanding the idea of self-sacrifice. Outside the door, the bushes hissed and murmured; each man had come in with his hands full of chains, but Ephraim Brady must have learned something, because he spoke to the things and they parted to let him through. A couplet, it sounded like. He must have heard John rhyming at his door.

'So this is your smithy where you do your business,' said Charles Groves, sounding a little hoarse but perfectly cheerful. 'Well, undoubtedly it's a fine thing for a man of your neat ways to spend some time among the clangs and clatters, Brady. A wise thing, to keep some home habits in your life.' The insult was all in his blitheness, the pleasant notice that Ephraim Brady, for all his rising fortune, still had nowhere grander to bring his contracts for witnessing than the Gyrford smithy. Charles Groves looked much like his brother Roger about the face, but where Roger had savoured the pleasures of coarseness, Charles had almost a parade in his courtesy, as if enjoying the sight of folks unable to find cause for their dislike in any language he used.

Ephraim Brady's face assumed a cool smile, and he bowed his head. 'As you say, sir,' he said. His voice was only a little tight.

'We're neat here!' John said. 'And we don't clatter, that's careless handling if you clatter tools about.'

Charles Groves looked at John. His expression was very like Roger's, but he didn't laugh out loud. 'An excellent thing, for a man to have some contradiction in his life,' he said. 'No doubt your father is glad of you for keeping his mind lively.'

John scowled, but Matthew, who had the feeling he'd been called dull-witted but had never been good at verbal fencing, intervened. 'I am glad of my son, sir,' he said. 'I thank you for the compliment.'

Charles Groves' eye gave an irritable twitch, but he smiled widely, his face a little redder than before. 'Well, Smith, we have a contract for you to witness,' he said, though his intonation left it provokingly unclear whether he was referring to Matthew by his name or his trade. 'We must read it to you, I suppose.'

'No, sir, thanking you for your kindness,' said Matthew. 'We can all read here, sir.'

'Remarkable,' said Charles Groves, looking further annoyed at Matthew's inability to rise to a gibe.

'That is kind of you to say, sir,' said Matthew. He didn't mean to antagonise the man, he was only floundering about in shyness and grasping what spars of good manners he could lay his hands on, but Charles Groves did not appear to like him the better for it, and Ephraim regarded him with slitted eyes.

'And you, Brady, I suppose you are an excellent reader too,' Charles Groves continued, redirecting his attention.

That did go home: most in Gyrford were lettered, at least a little bit, and being respectable, if not grand, was Ephraim Brady's foundation. His mouth worked before he managed to say, 'You are pleased to joke, sir. Most witty.'

'Ah, you'll have to learn to laugh if we do more business together,' said Charles Groves cheerfully. 'I always like to have men pleasant about me. And since the People find you so pleasant, you must have some talent for it. A man needs a sense of humour in your position, Brady.'

Ephraim Brady managed a smile. A smile cost nothing, after all.

'Well, Smith,' said Charles Groves, turning back to Matthew, 'you'll wish to exercise your powers of literacy on these documents, then. The farm to Brady, the mill, and a little sweetener, to me. I don't suppose you'll be looking for your percentage, Smiths, since the death of dear Roger was such a puzzle to you that you can't at all account for the circumstances of my little inheritance.' There was an edge of hostility in his voice – perhaps he was grieved for his brother, in his own way – and as he spoke, he cocked his head a little towards the door, where the branches mumbled.

'We take no percentage on other men's dealings, sir,' said Jedediah with stiff formality. 'Not the custom here.' If they could just get through this meeting without provoking anyone any further, perhaps afterwards they could speak to Ephraim, calm him down somehow, find some way to end this war he had declared on those they cared for.

And truly, they weren't in a position to defend their own workmanship; not unless they began by taking Johnny out and drowning him in the well. Jedediah had made a few remarks on that theme when John first made his confession, but he hadn't the energy to carry on with them. They couldn't account for Roger Groves' death, they couldn't keep Tobias from the woods, and apparently they couldn't keep their own boy from setting the People on the wander. Jedediah had always been proud of his trade, and tried to be worthy of it, but today, he was feeling his age. His own father hadn't been a Smith by birth, but by marriage; his grandfather had begotten no sons, and had to bring in a Mackem boy from the next county. That was what you did when you couldn't keep the line going: you reached out to other farrier clans with younger sons, offered them a smithy of their own instead of a life working under their older brothers, if they'd marry your girl. It hadn't been the happiest of matches: his mother was a bewildered woman and his father a strident man, and she'd been afraid of him. But the smithy had stayed manned.

Perhaps John would fail. Perhaps they all would. Molly was a fine lass, with her father's black hair and green eyes and her own sweet ways; no doubt they could find some second son from among the Gowans or the Fabers. They might even find one who'd treat her kindly.

His Molly.

You can't let the forge go out just because you feel your heart may break.

'Well, I see why you like it here, Brady,' Charles said, taking the documents back off Matthew and signing them with a flourish. 'They do cry you up as a penny-wise fellow.'

Ephraim's smile showed no teeth.

*You can't let the forge go out*, Jedediah told himself, and, drawing together all his powers of casual calm, said, 'I suppose you'll keep the miller with the mill, when it comes to the Porter place? Useful fellow, if you'll take a village man's counsel.'

Ephraim opened his mouth, but before he could speak, Charles gave an agreeable shrug. 'Sure enough. The mill's turned profit enough these past years. They must know something about it.'

'Wise thinking, sir,' said Jedediah, coming in too fast for Ephraim to interfere. 'I'll tell you plain, as I didn't like to influence you before, we've had an understanding with the Porters some time, knowing them honest folks. Ten per cent less for any work around their place, we charge. We'd be glad to keep up the same terms with you, as they'll still be there.'

John wasn't very good at hiding his feelings, but watching Grandpa's unstirred face, he decided that now was the moment he'd better get good at it. Could it be that easy, saving the Porter family just like that, a quiet word and a rich man's whim?

'Well, there's an incentive,' Charles Groves said, seeing Ephraim Brady's look at this outrage against the truth, perpetrated by men who had been doubling and tripling his bills wherever possible. 'Perhaps a wise man should learn more of village ways, eh, Brady?'

Ephraim was even better at hiding his emotions than Jedediah, but he turned a little white. 'No doubt, sir,' he said. 'I believe we are concluded here?'

'Oh, don't tell me you aren't coming to celebrate?' Charles said, mock-hurt. 'I'm sure you could out-drink me if you tried another time.'

'You will excuse me, sir,' said Ephraim. 'I have a little matter to discuss over some other properties with the Smiths. I am sure you will understand.'

'Now, it is good to know that village business goes on,' said Charles Groves. 'Does a man good to be reminded of the simple things in life.'

Matthew offered to clear a path for Mister Groves, but John volunteered for the task and, trotting out, delivered a small, improvised quatrain. His father and grandfather watched as the bushes bristled, considered, and stood aside to let Charles through. He sauntered out, whistling; while his manners were in many ways different from his brother's, they shared that tuneless, through-the-teeth squawk. The Smiths all grimaced at the noise, but Ephraim Brady remained impassive. Possibly he wasn't a music-lover, or possibly no sound, coming from a profitable business partner, could be unwelcome to him. The bushes didn't like it; there was a certain displeased cringing in their stance as Charles squeaked away.

'Never mind the off-key tune. It will be out of hearing soon,' John said, and they ruffled and settled like hawks.

Matthew and Jedediah looked at each other, past Ephraim

Brady, as John negotiated with the People. Neither of them spoke. What was there to say?

Ephraim wasn't done, though. 'I suppose it would have been too much trouble for you to set them alight,' he said with sour courtesy, indicating the bushes. 'Seeing as you are stocked with embers here.'

'No good burning the People when they mean well,' Jedediah said, too weary to speak with his usual sharpness. 'Only provokes the rest of them. We'll settle them, never you fear. Only you'd need to work with us on that. If you can stomach it.'

Ephraim looked at him for a long moment. There was nothing in his face to suggest a man who'd ever lose control of his passions.

John came in, a little breathless. 'I hung some Mackem knots on those ones,' he said – more to Matthew than to Jedediah; Grandpa was looking so tired of him these days he was becoming a little daunted. 'I've been practising making them. I had some in my pocket.'

'Do you not think,' Jedediah said, feeling as if speech involved lifting a heavy drawbridge in his throat, 'that that is the kind of idea you should ask us about before you try it?'

John tensed. 'Dada said he'd never know it do harm,' he said. 'And I have been practising.'

This was true: Mackem knots were a courtesy measure, much like leaving a gift on a neighbour's doorstep, so inoffensive that they were one of the few traditions Jedediah had learned from his father's side of the family that he'd never retuned over the years to fit better into the old Gyrford ways. But before they could get into the rights and wrongs of all that, Ephraim Brady spoke.

'So,' he said, his voice low and precise, 'I believe I own a new property. I shall take myself there now, visit my new tenants. I shall not stop you if you wish to join me. Indeed, I believe a cart would be a better transport to the Ware farm, hampered as I am by . . . my new friends in the square.'

Jedediah and Matthew froze.

'Oh, do come,' said Ephraim. Even his sarcasm had a flat propriety to it. 'There is something I would show you there.'

'What do you want, Ephraim Brady?' asked Jedediah.

Ephraim smiled at him, mirthless. 'Some things are better shown than told,' he said. 'I do suggest you come.'

There are things you don't want to witness. Nobody wanted to see what he'd do to the Wares. But if they stayed here, there'd be nobody to stand between the Wares and Ephraim. The three Smiths regarded each other for only a moment before Matthew went out to put Dobbs in her harness.

Up on Chalk Lane, the wind blew hard through the barbed tresses of Ephraim Brady's new friends. They ran behind like carriage-dogs, scuttling from limb to limb with a jagged, rippling motion, tousled but unslowed by the blast. John leaned over the edge of the cart, watching them with fixed speculation; Jedediah hadn't the strength to reprove him. Matthew, driving, kept all his focus on Dobbs, who, pursued by scrabbling bundles of grey-barked scrub, was racing along under the impression that bolting in a straight line was the only course that might save her. Beside Matthew sat Ephraim, poised, wind-whipped, entirely self-contained.

Evidently the Wares had been warned; even now, in harvest season, they had stopped their work and were gathered before the house when the cart rolled in. Or most of them were. Tobias was locked in his ken, a small, rocking figure visible through the open slats. Matthew's little silver birch and poplar, transplanted in the hopes that he might find the place more to his liking under their thin shelter, stood either side of him, pitiful saplings casting no more than a sketched line of shade.

'G-good day, sir,' Jonas Ware began, offering a quaking bow, but Ephraim did not trouble to dismount.

'Ware,' he said. 'I see you are here. You and your boys. And' – he raised his arm, pointed it straight and stiff as a weather-vane towards where Tobias hunched, digging delicate runnels in the ground with the tips of his fingers – 'the one who bites, and who breaks twigs, over there.'

At the sound of Ephraim Brady's voice, Toby looked up. He didn't shriek, as he used to do at the sight of Matthew. Shrieking had helped with Matthew, who put down unwanted objects and backed away, but he'd screamed when this man beat him and the man hadn't stopped. Toby clutched thin arms around himself, buried his face on his knees, and began to rock, keening sharp-edged, terrified whimpers.

The bushes, which had gathered behind the cart and now sat nestling towards the kind friend on the seat above, stopped their stiff-limbed ministrations and raised their hackles. On one of them sat a small rider, a flaking little poppet of stick and sap, and it craned itself sideways to Ephraim's words.

'Breaker?' It spoke out of something like a mouth, though, as it had no head to adorn with one, it had to crouch forwards and speak from a slit in its back.

Ephraim gave the Smiths a look of blithe hatred, and, with something in his voice of the sing-song John employed when he tried to rhyme bushes into reason, said, 'There sits the boy you do not like. I give you leave to cut and strike.'

There was a rustle of root on earth, and Toby's head whipped up: he was wailing even before the bushes gaped their branches up like fangs and dashed towards the ken where he sat prisoner.

'Brady! Brady, call them off, for God's sake!' Jedediah yelled.

Matthew already trying to wrestle them away; there were four of the things, and his hands were running red as he pulled one back, shouting out, 'Peter! Bring me some nails and a hammer, quick!' He was grappling as hard as he could, and John ran to help him, but they were too many and they were too spider-fast, and one limb after another reached inside the pen, cut a slash into Toby's face, his back, the hand he clutched over his head.

Toby screamed, thrashing his arms over himself, and the bushes reached in again, gouging a deep lattice into his neck, turning him ragged and red and weeping in terror beyond the mortal.

'Ephraim Brady,' Jedediah cried, wild and entirely past dignity, 'call them off now or I swear to God – *I swear to God* – I will kill you before witnesses and hang for it if I must.'

Ephraim had sat, watching, with controlled contemplation. As Jedediah broke before him, he raised his eyebrow and, slowly, patiently, as slowly as Jedediah had ever spoken to waste his time, said, 'Of course. I am sure you understand my point.'

He looked for another second at Matthew and John, flaying themselves hand and face against the bushes, and then said, 'Kind friends, rest your bough. Our turn is served for now.'

The bushes stopped, shuffled back to him in pleased compliance.

Toby was still screaming. Peter ran to him, whispering over and over, 'There now, Toby. There now, darling. There now, Toby.' There were tears on Peter's face, and his voice was a knot of pain. 'There now, Toby,' he hushed.

'I would speak to your guests alone, Ware,' said Ephraim. 'We shall speak on the road, I think.'

It would have taken a longer journey to get out of the sound of Toby's screams. On and on they went, shredding the wind, broken, unappeasable.

Jedediah spoke first; both Matthew and John were too cut about the lips to say anything clearly. 'We will call them off you, we will find a way,' he said. 'We can solve any problem you have. If it's free work you want, it's yours. You've made your point.'

Ephraim kept looking at him. In the morning light, his eyes were grey as flint.

'We could charge maleficence against you,' Jedediah said. He couldn't make the words come out evenly.

'Oh, but you yourself said it, Jedediah Smith,' said Ephraim. His voice was hoarse, the force behind it just stirring. 'This is no dabbling with demons. Only the People having their fancies.'

Jedediah swallowed, trying not to see his bleeding children, not to hear the screams beyond the hedge. 'What do you want?'

'What do I want?' Ephraim looked at him. 'What do I want? *Now*, I see, you have some concern for what I want. What I want, Jedediah Smith, is what I have wanted all along: I have wanted to be free from your interference to pursue my lawful business.'

John was trying not to cry, Jedediah realised. He put a hand on the boy's knee, but he couldn't hold it steady. John had fought bravely against the bushes; his face was slashed all over, and he was keeping his lips pressed tight. He wasn't trying to ease his cuts; instead, he was worrying at his ear, as if he couldn't bear the sound of Toby shrieking, but couldn't allow himself to shut it out. Jedediah wanted more than anything, in that moment, to pick Johnny up and forgive him: even if he'd started this, God help him, he was being punished. But he couldn't; he couldn't take the time now. The boy would have to endure. 'You have pursued it well enough, I think,' he told Ephraim Brady. 'I have never seen you not gain your ends.'

'You have not, have you?' Ephraim's voice rose, sped up. 'I have borne with your wrongs, Jedediah Smith. You cheat my tenants' debts out of my own pocket, again and again, and I say nothing. You mock me before my business partners, you mock me as I draw up my own will, and I say nothing. You rob me with your prices out of spite, and I say nothing. You cuckold me in the eyes of the world—'

'I didn't—' Matthew tried to mumble, hearing the stream of accusations turn towards him, but blood got in his mouth and he had to stop and spit.

'Oh, maybe not in my bed,' said Ephraim, his face starting to twist, 'but in the eyes of the world. You, with all you have, you had to make little of me, you had to make a show. You interfere, over and over, with my own wife, you subvert me in my own home, you and that she-cat of yours – shall I call on my friends again? Your darling Tobias is quite within their reach,' he added as Matthew started to rise, and Matthew was compelled to set his fist down. 'You connive with your friends to turn my brother against me, my only kin; you threaten me when that touched idiot on the farm turns upon him. You do nothing when my partner dies at the teeth of the People, and if that is not enough, you set the People upon me. I have borne with your wrongs, Mister Smith, I have borne and borne and borne with them, and I will bear no longer. Now you know. I can endure bushes, Mister Smith, better than I can endure you. If they are the price of you no longer checking me at every turn, they are a price I will pay. You will cease to interfere with my business dealings. You will cease to interfere with my tenants. You will cease to interfere with my wife. You will *cease*, Mister Smith. All of you. I had thought to hang that Ware creature, or try to, but now that touched boy of yours has set the People working my way, I think I shall let the creature live. I am not a man who cannot tell an asset when I see one. Tobias Ware shall live, and he shall not have a scratch on him, Mister Smith. If you stay out of my way.'

You couldn't say there was a silence. Toby's sobs rang too clearly between them.

Jedediah wanted to say, more than anything, *Is this what you have come to? Now that you finally have friends?*

He thought of the Brady tenants they had saved from impoverishment. He thought of Alice Brady, white-haired and blue-necked, starving in a cold house.

Jedediah sat in the cart as the weeping of Toby Ware harrowed the air around them.

Then he found his tongue, stirred it, forced it to say: 'I understand you, Mister Brady. Just leave the boy alone.'

CHAPTER 17

John sat in the garden, watching the cage where they kept the two bushes they'd caught, that first day they'd seen them following Ephraim Brady, before he'd realised that he, John, had, through sheer foolishness – through *touchedness*, it must be, because no one with half a grain of common sense could have created such a mess as this – handed Ephraim Brady, for free, the greatest prize anyone could ever have thought up. He could hurt his wife, he could hurt his tenants, he could do anything. And if they tried to stop him, he'd take a ride up to the farm he owned and, and . . .

John's cuts blazed upon him. They'd had to light a fire in the Wares' hearth and heat a poker to make quench-water; it was the only way to draw the fey sting. How long Toby had screamed while they worked and worked to get the iron hot, John didn't like to think.

Grandpa had later brought the Wares a new poker and pail that he'd forged to heat fast, and taught them how to make quench-water. Toby hated it; he'd writhed so desperately under the wet cloth that in the end, there'd been nothing to do but tip the whole bucket over him in a single, screaming splash. He writhed and wept as it touched his skin.

The bushes they held caged in the Smiths' garden were wounded too. The struggle against Matthew's net had taken its toll: there was little left of their leaves but raggedy scraps, and their stems were turning white.

Want of water, he supposed. Possibly earth, too; they might be starving. He could try giving them quench-water, see if that finished them off, but that would be cruel. The bushes weren't trying to be torturers. They just were a little confused.

He'd tried talking to them. One of them had no objections — it had nothing much to say at all except that it wanted to see its kind friend — but the other had said, 'Hobble trouble nailinboot goway!', which meant it must be the first bush, the one he'd woken in the Bellame woods.

He still wished he was back there, back where things were green and vibrant and writhing with life. He couldn't help it.

After a long moment, he spoke to the original bush. 'I help you live, you forgive?' he said.

'Jabbity one-footed nailinboot neighbourbad,' it said.

'I think you're thirsty,' John persisted. 'I'll water you. Then we'll be friends.'

Both the bushes cocked their crinkling bark at the thought. 'Thirstying waterme tuckin water give,' said the original. It was trying to make a mouth in its bark, but the lips of it were badly chapped.

'Forgive and be friends,' John said, 'and I'll try to do more for you. But I'll get you water.' Maybe the thing wouldn't forgive him just for a wetting; after all, it had been wronged too, dug up, broken, transplanted, then woken up after a promise to leave it alone. But either way, he couldn't let it parch. It was the wrong thing to do.

'Rain give neighbour give rain,' said the second bush, so John got a bucket – a wooden one, filled with rainwater, no iron on it anywhere – and, slipping carefully inside the cage, poured half the contents on the bush that didn't dislike him. It quivered, its roots lapping at the ground.

'Mememe,' said the first, so John, hesitant, went and tipped the rest on it.

The bush sucked and gasped at the earth. Then, apparently a little refreshed, it turned and gave John such a slap with its thorned branch that it knocked him right into the corner of the cage.

The cuts flamed on his skin. He managed not to whimper.

'Served right water neighbour,' said the bush, with evident satisfaction. Then it added, 'Water more.' Its voice was imperious, but there was something a little plaintive about it too. It had lost the note of enmity.

John got more water, and twined together a few more Mackem knots to hang on them while he was about it. The bush took no further swipes at him, just leaned its canes this way and that to catch the drops, like a cat wanting its cheek tickled. The People, at least weakish ones such as these, had trouble remembering more than one grudge at a time. It was Toby they wanted to cut.

'Yes,' John told it as he poured. 'Served me right.'

Franklin sat in the Smiths' kitchen as the sun went down that day. He took comfort in the girls' company; Francie was safe

319

with Cousin Bessy Gillam for now, and he was doing his best not to wish her back home. When Molly, picking up a hint from Janet, ushered Vevie and Celdie off to play in the garden, Franklin looked sorry. Molly was well aware that this was smithing talk – something the twins couldn't be trusted to keep discreet, and that she herself preferred to avoid, as from all she could see it was just one crisis after another – but they left behind a subdued circle.

'We managed to get all Toby's cuts washed, in the end,' Matthew said after a while. One of his eyes was swollen shut from the thorns; it was hampering his ability to judge distance, and Jedediah had banned him from any hammer work until it healed up, for fear he'd break his fingers.

Everyone sat, let the silence press.

'Alice Brady . . . continues alive,' Franklin said. He felt a little sick, unable to say more than that for her, but he couldn't think how to help her. Unquestionably he was an honorary Smith in Ephraim Brady's eyes.

Janet opened her mouth to say, *If you call it living*, but what was the point? Nobody at the table disagreed with her.

Instead, she said, 'Have you had word from Francie?' The Porter mill was about halfway between Gyrford and the Gillams', and it had been agreed that Francie would leave letters under a stone there. The Porters had no objections, not least because they no longer had to worry about Ephraim Brady as their landlord.

'Oh, yes,' said Franklin. 'She writes that your cousin has been very kind to her, and the children pretty-behaved.' He paused. 'She would like a home and children of her own, I think.'

Jedediah stared at the table, which was offering no consolations, as Matthew asked tentatively, 'Was she . . . very fond of Anthony Brady?'

Franklin shrugged, as if his shoulders were heavy to lift. 'I believe so. And truly, Matt, I don't blame her. He means well, that lad. Doesn't know the worst of what his brother does. Who would tell him? Alice can't; he just thinks her shy. He supposes she's fond of Ephraim because she doesn't dare say otherwise. And as to how his brother deals with the world, how would he hear of it? Folks see him, they think he must be part of the dealings. You don't complain to a Brady. He knows Ephraim trades, and he barely knows what that means, for no one's allowed to teach him. Ephraim's cut him off from everyone, over the years, and filled him with tales of how bad they are so Anthony wouldn't know who to believe if they told him the worst of it. He doesn't like it, you know; he wants to like folks. But Ephraim pays for him to live. He hasn't a penny of his own. If he had a trade, he could step away from it easier, but Ephraim made sure he'd stay in need of a keeper.'

'Well, none of us can 'prentice him,' said Jedediah, but he couldn't make his voice sharp. Franklin knew more than enough about depending on a hard man. 'God knows, Ephraim Brady can do as he wishes now.'

John was worrying, but he was so consumed by guilt that he hardly knew if he should speak. 'Mister Thorpe?' he said, almost in a whisper.

'Yes, lad?' said Franklin. He didn't mean to shame John by demoting him from 'Mister John' to 'lad'; he was just weary, and sitting somewhere homely, and missing his daughter. But

John hung his head, and said, even quieter than before, 'Do you think Mistress Brady will run, like Francie said to?'

'Not easy for her to do.' Franklin said it as gently as he could, but John hung his head lower.

Matthew said, in a small voice, 'I — I passed her in the marketplace yesterday. I let her know that Francie left letters at the Porters, under the stone before their gate. That is, I mentioned it to Luke Morris, where Mistress Alice could overhear me. Just in case she needed to know.'

Franklin gave him a look of concern. 'I . . . well, that might be a good thought. If her husband never suspects she knows it. I hope he does not. But . . . not easy for her. I wouldn't pin any hopes, John lad.'

Jedediah drew on his pipe. Smoke hung in the air, stinging everyone's eyes. 'Well,' he said, 'the Porters are spared, if nothing else. Roger Groves won't put them off their land, not from his grave. And Brother Charles may leave them be. I've given him a reason out of our pockets.' He puffed again. 'We can afford it. We'll manage.'

The room was dark, the rushlight throwing only the faintest of gleams. Franklin's face was drawn back from it, not clearly visible, as he spoke. 'Mister Smith.' It was a woodsman's murmur, too soft to startle a bird. 'I must ask you.'

'Go on,' said Jedediah. Franklin wasn't to blame for any of this; it was his own fault. There must have been a way to stop it, stop John, or Brady, or any of this. But he'd missed it somehow.

'Forgive me,' said Franklin. 'I would not try your patience. You know how I have always honoured you.'

Jedediah tensed a little; he'd never wanted gratitude from Franklin. The man had been demeaned enough in his early years; he would not make him a new kind of bondsman, loaded with intangible debts. 'You have no need,' he said. 'Honour yourself, if you want someone. I've made a poor enough showing.'

'Mister Smith,' said Franklin, his voice almost level, 'if it be the truth, it will die with me. But I would know. I know you a man skilled at your trade, and strong for your neighbours. When Black Hal ran down Roger Groves – it wasn't at your urging, was it?'

For once, Jedediah Smith found himself without words.

'I would understand it,' Franklin said. 'Even if it did not gain its end. Please, I mean no disrespect; you have been the kindest and best of friends to me. Only I know you can act, if need be. There was Adam Taunton . . . I was glad not to see it, but I know why it had to be done. There is no good in us if we don't try to help . . .'

*It had to be done.* That was how Franklin saw it, even now. Jedediah had been so clear, then, that he knew what needed doing, that he was wise enough to decide who should and shouldn't scar. It seemed a young man's folly now. He hadn't felt young at the time; he'd been near fifty, an elder farrier, sure of doing right. But now he felt old.

He looked at Franklin's face, which was tight around the eyes and stiff-lipped, the way it had been when, as a child, he'd limped into the smithy with bruises he couldn't explain. Jedediah had been able to help the boy, then. It had been easy: a few kind words, a little patience. Bits of food he could easily spare; salve on wounds he hadn't prevented. Franklin's gratitude shamed him.

'If the question insults you,' Franklin said, his voice hoarse and flat, 'I will understand.' He sat as if braced for a blow, waiting to hear if he'd driven away the only protector he ever had.

John looked up, ready to cry out, but Jedediah motioned him to silence. 'Never you fear, Franklin,' he said. He didn't sound strong. He sounded tired. 'Most likely, you'll not be the only man to wonder. The answer's no, if you believe me. You needn't, if you choose. Most likely others won't. But never fear I'll blame you for asking. You were always a good lad.'

## CHAPTER 18

John lay awake in the night.

*It wasn't at your urging, was it?*

That was what he'd done: created a wasteland so vast that even Franklin Thorpe, who had loved Grandpa all his life, might think him a murderer, because there wasn't any other way to end the doings of rich men.

*God knows, Ephraim Brady can do as he wishes now.*

Would Ephraim Brady even hang, if he killed his wife? No one seemed interested in stopping him, or at least, no one grand, no one with the power to do so. Why should they? He managed land and collected rents and paid taxes. What was it Lord Robert had called him? *Thorough.*

The light was rising, leaden and dry, beyond his window. He must have dozed and woken early. It would be another working day.

*Thorough.*

*God knows, Ephraim Brady can do as he wishes now.*

*Most likely, you'll not be the only man to wonder. The answer's no, if you believe me. You needn't, if you choose. Most likely others won't.*

He'd argued with Grandpa as far back as he could remember. It had been fun, really; he'd been often a little annoyed, but never for one moment had he doubted his grandfather's love or his character. Grandpa was just there, unbreakable, standing between folks and harm.

John couldn't think of any way to protect Tobias, or to protect Mistress Brady. Grandpa was at a standstill, and if he didn't know how to counter the world, then it was hardly a world any more. But if anyone thought Grandpa had had to do with Roger Groves' death . . .

No one could call on Black Hal. It just couldn't be done. He was no bramble bush; you couldn't order him to heel. Even the Porter Puss, talkative and persuadable and open to slurs on its courage, knew better than to be – what had it said? – a *rash neighbour* to Black Hal.

It had been so easy to talk to the cat. Words had piped from its throat like a blackbird calling in the morning.

*I know better than to be a rash neighbour. I have studied his form well enough; the view from the roof is a fine one.*

John sat up in his bed.

*Studied his form.*

The view from the roof was a fine one.

The cat had had plenty to say. Of course, it wasn't talking to him now, but John thought about cats, the way they perched, observed, surveyed their domains. If the cat was an observer of Black Hal – and surely it would need to be – what was the phrase? *stay ahead of his teeth* – then it must watch the road.

Suppose it had watched the road the night Roger Groves died, or the nights before? It could swear that Grandpa hadn't been anywhere near. Of course, a fey cat's chatter was hardly the testimony of a weighty man, and probably they couldn't ask it. No one needed Ephraim Brady deciding they'd lied about silencing Puss and go down the road to demonstrate his displeasure on Toby's fragile skin. But still. But still.

'Why should you go to the Porters', Johnny?' asked Matthew. 'They already know they can stay on their land. Franklin told them.'

'Well,' said John, 'I should like to leave a letter for Francie. Before, you know, before this all went wrong, she found me walking the Bellame woods.' Francie had mentioned it to Janet, and Janet had taxed him with it in the prolonged scolding that had followed his blackberry-bush confession. 'But I asked her to keep it a secret, and that was wrong of me. I — well, I have done much wrong lately, as you know.'

Matthew sighed, and Jedediah couldn't even face making a remark.

'So,' John persisted, feeling as if he was pushing a plough through a great field of disgrace, 'I feel I must become a better boy. I have been a poor apprentice, and I am sorry. And I think that if I have done wrong by others, I must begin by telling them I am sorry too. I would like to leave Francie a letter saying as much.'

Matthew looked at him with such encouragement — Matthew had a devout belief in the virtues of repentance, and this kind of talk was exactly the sort most likely to persuade him — that John's conscience goaded him to come nearer the truth. He hadn't wanted to raise hopes; he'd had quite enough of being disappointing. But he felt a need to own up, to tell at least some truth about himself to those he loved.

'Also,' he said, 'I would like to see the cat again. If you please. It was a problem I solved, and I should like to . . . to remember that there has been something in my service besides mistakes and wrongdoing. And . . . and Mister Franklin asked Grandpa . . . well, if the cat was watching, it could say he had nothing to do with Mister Groves. I could ask it. If I might.'

Matthew glanced at Jedediah, who shrugged. 'Let the boy say sorry if he's a mind to,' Jedediah said. 'And no harm in seeing the cat, as long as he doesn't get it chatting to Charles Groves or rouse it to eat the parson or some such other business. Think you can manage that, John?'

Jedediah was trying not to depress John too badly. Talking to the animal would hardly clear anyone's name: the most it had ever done was gossip and catch mice. But if the boy was to become anything, he'd have to learn to keep working in the face of failure, so they might as well let him go.

John, however, took him seriously, and said, 'All I can promise, Grandpa, is that if I do something foolish, I shall tell you at once,' in such a humble voice that Jedediah shooed him out of the smithy with instructions to take the horse and get straight along to the Porters, rather than have to look at the lad's crestfallen face another minute.

As John rode Dobbs up Chalk Lane that afternoon, the wind washed over him, cooling his skin and dandling his hair as if it had nothing more to do in the world than play. It dropped as he walked in the Porters' gate, and Mistress Porter met him, kissing him with such enthusiasm that you wouldn't know he was a burden to his family and trade. 'I hear we have your honoured grandfather to thank for us staying here,' she told him. 'I know he spoke for us. I cannot thank you, Mister John, I cannot thank any of you enough. And since your good work that day, Mister John Smith, we haven't had a word out of Puss. Well, a little hissing, but not to complain of.'

'Good, good,' John said, feeling it remarkable that rich men like Ephraim Brady and Charles Groves should be unpleasant when they feasted on such a soothing diet of deference. 'But it's best to take care over such matters, so if you wouldn't mind, Mistress Porter, I'd take it kindly if you'd let me view him. Perhaps your sons could assist.'

'Oh, of course, if you wish it,' said Sukie. 'Perhaps you'd care for a bit of bread and butter before you leave? Knock at my kitchen door.'

John bowed, and retired to a quiet spot in the garden with Tommy and Bill. The two boys were serious-faced, big-eyed lads, less appalled by life than a home beside Black Hal's road might lead you to expect. John thought back over what the Porters had said when questioned: they kept the boys inside on windy nights and stuffed their ears with rags.

Puss, when they found him, was busy after a beetle in the grass, but Tommy raised his voice and called, 'Puss, Puss, Puss!' with a note of coaxing that even the most ennobled cat could hardly object to. Puss looked over with the manner of one prepared to be courted – but then saw John, narrowed his eyes, fluffed his tail and returned his attention to the beetle with open and elaborate disdain.

'Puss, Puss,' wheedled Tommy. 'Come on, Puss, there's a pretty Puss. Come and meet John Smith.'

Puss twitched his tail as if waving aside a particularly dirty petitioner. There was something in his manner that reminded John of Lord Robert Bellamy.

'Well, that's hardly the grace I'd expect of a cat of parts,' John said. 'And after all I've said to clear your name.'

Puss did not raise his head from the beetle, but one ear flicked round in their direction.

'It's a sad business, when a cat is calum— canumli— when there's bad talk all around a cat's name, and no one to listen even to a farrier who speaks in his defence,' John carried on. He needed to fall into a grand manner in order to get Puss' attention, but after all he'd done, he didn't deserve to be having fun. On moral principle, therefore, he made an effort not to notice that he was. 'When I think of the bowls of butter I've shared with folks, trying to persuade them to understand the bravery of Puss and the slander of Old Tom.' Possibly he was starting a war amongst the cats, John thought, but the prick of conscience was only brief: if Puss was going to be this grand, he could take care of himself.

There was a small snarl from the grass; Puss was listening.

'Why,' John went on, 'I've said to folks: "Folks," I've said, "I've seen Puss myself, and a grander cat I never laid eyes upon. You should see the quickness of his eyes, the well-honed sharpness of his claws, the bright gleam of his coat, the . . . the martial markings upon his face – quite a soldier's frown in his stripes. I know cats," I say to folks, "and that Puss is the most splendid and courageous-looking cat I could ever be fortunate enough to meet. Why, he even lives on land right by Black Hal's road," I say, "and never a hair did he turn when we discussed that fearsome gentleman."'

'Hah,' Puss spat. His spitting, like his words, emerged from an open mouth; there was just a flex and ripple of muscle at his throat. '"Fearsome gentleman".'

'Oh dear,' John said. 'Did I misspeak, Puss, calling Black Hal a fearsome gentleman? I would value your view over mine, and perhaps I am cowardly myself to call him such.'

Cats as a class are given to smiling: it is in the cast of their faces, and they are not so pliable of feature as the folks who share their houses. Nevertheless, Puss managed to convey a very creditable sneer; possibly it was in the angle of his whiskers. 'Tall folks may well be cowards,' he remarked, 'when they're so slow of foot.'

'Ah, that's the sad truth,' John agreed. 'Is that the reason for your courage, Puss, the speed of your feet? I suppose you could stay ahead of Black Hal if you so chose.'

'*I*,' said Puss, 'have no need. Let cowards tremble before him; the bold have other choices.'

'Oh, my,' John exclaimed, feeling that some flattery might ease things along so he could ask Puss the question he really had in mind, 'a tale of your courage, Puss! What a pleasure it would be if I could tell it to the unworthy folks who believed the slanders of your cowardice! I am sure it would shame them. Though I suppose,' he added with a sigh, 'you do not think them worthy of it.'

'Worthy of shame, they certainly are,' Puss chirped. 'Though I hope you do not expect me to squander my time upon them should they be humble enough to change their minds. Exile from good society must be unchanging, or else how shall the remaining be deterred? I suppose,' he added, licking a thoughtful talon, 'that you could instead take an ear or two, or some other mark of distinction – perhaps their noses. Tall folks' noses are so weak that I have long supposed they must be a mere badge of display. I suggest you take noses. That might silence the calumnies.'

'Well, I shall consider your suggestion,' said John, his stomach turning over. Would it ever be possible for him to converse with the fey without getting someone mauled? This had to be fixed, and right away, otherwise he was going to have to go back to Dada and admit he'd made another mess, and then possibly go and jump down the well to save Grandpa the trouble of pushing him. 'But if you'll forgive me, Puss, I believe that shaming them with your tale of glory would be a better punishment. Noses on tall folks are so ugly and useless that I doubt it'd be much of a punishment to be deprived of them.'

'You are an unfortunate race, and that is the truth,' Puss conceded. 'It is amazing that you do not grow better fur to cover up your many failings of beauty. But then, I suppose if you are accustomed to your ill-favoured faces, shame would be the better course.'

John tried not to show any unseemly relief. He had better tell Grandpa about this, just in case – but perhaps he wouldn't come out of it looking like a permanent blight upon the country.

'Very well,' said Puss, his lipless tones taking on a slightly yowling note that John supposed must indicate the beginning of a heroic canto, 'but attend properly, kitten, for you do not deserve to hear the tale twice. You are quite right that it is a tale of courage.

'I viewed the ways of my unkempt neighbour, and I saw how it would be. A cat of discretion studies the form of his opponent before he enters the joust. So once I was quite master of my knowledge, I ran quite out ahead of him, and adorned the ground before him with an heraldic pennant of piss. And thus he understood my challenge, thus we began the contest. Ran and ran, I did, with flames tingling the hairs on my tail – but you may believe I was fast enough, and when I came to a good tree for my purpose, why, up it I ran, while down below me ran Black Hal, and I leaped – leaped with gallant grace – right over his back, and there I was, with Black Hal outwitted and myself behind his tail. And never has he bothered me since, and all through my own strategy and daring, for as I told you before, though I suppose you are too foolish to understand, Black Hal does not turn. And so I live behind his tail, and may roam as I please, and that is the tale of Puss and his grand combat against his neighbour. I hope you may profit by it.'

John sat, struggling not to gape. He had only been thinking of Puss as a witness, of sorts, who could testify that Grandpa had done nothing to call to Black Hal. But this . . . this was something he hadn't known could be. This was a tale of how to escape Black Hal altogether.

Trying to keep his look of wondering admiration, he ran his mind over the facts. And yes: they snapped together like a well-oiled latch. Puss had got Black Hal to hunt him, then dodged behind him: it fitted with that old saying, that if you got before Black Hal's teeth you'd never get behind his tail. The People could be literal-minded about their own rules. Let Black Hal hunt you, get behind his tail, and you were safe from him for ever.

'Does that mean the Porters are safe?' he asked. 'Or the Wares? He's run past their homes enough times.'

'Ignorant kit,' said Puss, his mouth set open in a small gape of disdain and his voice bearing the slow patience of one whom nobility obliges to speak to the unwashed, 'I said *plainly*, one must get behind his tail. *Get* behind, not dawdle. Call him, or challenge him. Merely standing by while he runs past you? *Pfft!*' Puss' huff denoted, with surprising expressiveness, that John's logic was a mere ball of hair, to be voided from the belly of a higher intellect. 'That is no more getting behind his tail than standing by a fight makes you the winner of it. Try standing by while two Toms challenge each other tooth and claw for a fair queen, and see if she finds you the boldest and handsomest at the end of it. You will not breed many of your lineage *that* way – and goodness knows, you tall folks have small enough litters of offspring as it is. That brown boy of yours should challenge some other Tom, if he wants to get that curly girl your mother is always fussing over into season. Sitting around cheeping about how he feared to think ill of his brother won't get her crouching, and you may tell him so from Puss.'

'Wait— What?' said John, trying desperately to sort out the rush of information. 'Do you mean Francie Thorpe? Anthony Brady and Francie Thorpe? Have you been following her?'

'*Following?* My dear kitten, when a girl disports herself all over the neighbourhood with some silly Tom of a boy, I can hardly help seeing her. She should settle herself a proper place to meet him, if she's that eager to sniff his whiskers. Though he should mewl less about the shame of misjudging her father. If I have a lady by the nape, let me tell you I do not hesitate to press home my advantage.'

'Wait,' said John again, and then, making a great effort to renew his courtly tone, 'I am eager to learn of your sagacity, Puss. You say that Francie Thorpe and Anthony Brady have been meeting in secret — but how is it you know so much of it?'

'Oh, that whistle of hers is easy to hear a mile off,' said Puss, with an air of tolerating the stupidity of those cursed with unfeline hearing. 'And that pipe he plays back to her. Any cat with half an ear could hear them. Even a noisy neighbour, though they have the sense to stay away from Chalk Lane. Nothing but the trees to call upon him for now, and those he doesn't hunt.'

'Call upon him?' said John, feeling more and more unnerved.

'Dogs have their fancies,' Puss said. 'Though why such a squeak should call him from his more accustomed home, you would have to ask him. Which I suppose you won't, having neither the fleetness of foot nor stoutness of heart.'

'Puss,' said John with great care, 'I am an admirer of your wisdom and wish to be sure I understand you as befits it. You say that Black Hal comes when he is whistled for?'

Puss shrugged, a sleek ripple of fur that ran from nape to tail.

'He comes when the wind whistles through the trees on very windy nights.' John was almost talking to himself now. 'And if he hears a whistle, he comes hunting, though he wouldn't hunt a whistling tree.'

Puss flicked a lordly, if slightly tatty ear. 'Myself, I like a good tourney, be it against living rat or plain string, but dogs are not known for their imagination.'

John had the sensation that his head might split apart like an overbaked apple if he didn't sort out his thoughts. Black Hal came when whistled for. If you challenged him, and then managed to get behind him, he'd never hunt you again. Francie was meeting Anthony Brady, whistling to let him know she was there – but surely she wouldn't meet him on Chalk Lane? She didn't know Black Hal came when he was whistled, but she must have some other place to meet him; Chalk Lane was hardly private. Surely.

'Puss,' he said, 'did you observe that man Black Hal killed earlier this month?'

'I had seen him on my turn,' Puss remarked; his face remained set in the same complacent smile.

'Your turn? You go about the neighbourhood?'

'Of course. How else am I to know matters of consequence? The burden of Puss' authority is no light one, kitten, and you show the underbelly of your ignorance to ask me such a question.'

With some regret, for cats' patience for long conversations is not notorious, John let that one go. 'But you saw him? Did you see him that night?'

Puss shrugged again; his stripes flickered dark and soft. 'To my displeasure. I knew the man by sound and smell, that squeaky whistle and sweaty jacket. A distasteful knave. If he was to die, he might have done it with some elegance. He should have studied to improve himself. That curly girl might have taught him a better sound.'

'Wait, wait,' said John, almost panting with the speed of his thoughts, 'is that why—? Puss,' more rapidly now, 'Roger Groves was whistling? Is that what called Black Hal upon him?'

'To be sure,' said Puss, washing his face with a negligent paw; its passage over his mouth did not interrupt the fluency of his speech at all.

John sat back. That irritating, tooth-squeaking whistle. A man walking bold out on a dark night, not knowing what called Black Hal to the hunt. Roger Groves had stepped out onto Chalk Lane in absolute, suicidal confidence, and he had whistled his own death upon himself.

'Puss,' John said, 'you are a cat of wisdom beyond my ken, and have enriched my mind. I must be away, to share this news as soon as possible.'

It was a quick stop to explain all this to Mistress Sukie Porter, who looked at him drop-mouthed, unable to find words to account for the sudden glut of information about the mystery that had so often galloped, flame and fang, past her door. That done, John headed for the gate as fast as he could. He must tell the Wares, no doubt of that; he must tell Dada and Grandpa. They could pass the word around the county; Black Hal would kill no one after this. He would kill no one! Sudden joy lifted him almost off his feet: he had spoken with a fey thing and had started no calamity – not he! No, he had gained information that would save lives. He shouldn't be happy, not with so much wrong, but he had done something right, he had done a good thing. There would be something in the world to show for John Smith that wasn't disaster.

Dobbs was tethered by the gate, and just before he unhitched her, he paused, lifting the stone Franklin had mentioned to leave his note for Francie. There was nothing under it, so he left the note of apology he'd brought.

He'd resolved to go straight home and report. But as he placed his letter, he thought of Francie, her kind hands and gentle voice, her sweet, piercing whistle. Francie, whistling for Anthony somewhere across the county.

Francie knew the Bellame woods; she'd never take a risk there. She'd never take a risk she knew was dangerous. But she didn't know what called Black Hal.

It was no good. He had to find her. Just in case. He'd go home after, he really would. But he had to find Francie and warn her: never whistle on Chalk Lane. Black Hal still had one run left.

The ride to Aunt Bessy's, where Francie was staying out of Ephraim Brady's sight, took him up past the Wares, so John stopped in to warn them too; goodness knows they could use the knowledge. It was the twenty-fourth of September, less than a week till Michaelmas, and on such dates farmers have time for nothing but the harvest, so when John let himself in at the gate, he wasn't surprised to find nobody in sight.

Tobias' sleeping ken lay open, the door unlocked. Perhaps in concession to the coming cold, someone had tied canvas to the top – and, surprisingly, the underside of the canvas wasn't blank, but stitched. No, more than that: it was embroidered with the rough shape of leafy branches, and some real leaves tacked on. It wasn't really like being under a tree, but more like it than being in a house. A ball rested in one corner of the ken.

What was it folks had said? He played ball with his brothers and – yes, that was it, with Francie Thorpe.

She'd known the family all her life. Janet had even said that maybe she might marry Peter Ware, but Francie had said no; they were old playmates, and she was as fond of every Ware boy as she was of Peter.

She'd been here, Francie Thorpe, making a roof for Tobias to keep him dry in the winter. John had seen that little leaf pattern trimming the sleeves of her Sunday dress. Toby had his ball there, hoping she'd come round to play.

As John headed up through the shorn fields, the light was growing a little grey. Across the wide spaces, great bronze haystacks loomed like giants. He could see the men at the corner, working in rhythm with each other. Tobias was among them, lifting bales with a spry strength, moving in time to a chant coming from Peter: 'Up and so and SO we go!' It wasn't any kind of song John had heard before; he knew plenty of work songs to sing in the smithy, and some farmers' ones as well, but they had verses set to them. This was different, simpler: a set of syllables Tobias could understand. Toby's back and face were lined with red scabs, but he laughed on the 'SO' and hefted his block of hay as if it was a familiar game.

Jonas Ware, busy in the midst of his sons, turned and greeted John with the kind of courtesy worried men show honoured guests who impede them in work that can't wait: 'Good day, Mister John. You'll excuse us if we keep on while we talk?'

'Of course,' John said. Bothering a farmer mid-harvest was very bad manners, and he knew it. 'I only have a piece of news

I think you must hear at once, as it may be safety to you. It is about Black Hal.'

Everyone stopped, except Tobias, who looked around and then shouldered Peter, stamping his foot as if to start up the lost rhythm.

'Oh, no harm has been done,' John said in haste. 'No, forgive me for worrying you. It's just that I've learned something that will help: Black Hal comes when men whistle. That, I think, is why he did as he did to Roger Groves. I reckon he comes when the wind blows so hard it makes the trees whistle – though perhaps he brings more wind with him too, that would be hard to say without further watching, which I don't suppose Dada would let me do . . .' No, he was getting distracted; he was supposed to be sticking to information they could use. 'But if a man whistles on Chalk Lane, it brings Black Hal to him, and then that is the end of that man. So I think you had better not whistle there. Or even here – not even in the daytime, if you will take my advice.'

The Ware men looked at each other. Tobias gave a whimper of frustration, and Peter said, without really turning his head, 'There's a good boy, Toby.'

'Well,' said John, feeling that his revelation really deserved more of a fuss than this, 'that is what I came to tell you. Perhaps it may save your life one day. And now I shall leave you to your work, as I know you cannot spare much time.'

Jonas looked around, and then stepped forward and took John's hand. 'Forgive us, Mister John,' he said. 'It is . . . it is great deal, to know such a thing all at once. We must not forget to thank you for telling us. As you say, it may save our lives one day. We are grateful, indeed we are.'

There was a tickle of wind around John's feet, stirring the cropped corn; little flecks of gold started pouring themselves upwards into the moving air. 'If you see Francie Thorpe,' he said, feeling his heart begin to speed up with the wind, 'do make sure you tell her too.'

Dobbs was a steady, enduring animal, but she was not fond of racing, and by the time John reached his Aunt Bessy's, the horse was puffing and out of temper with him. John dismounted and gave her some apologetic patting, but she tossed her head, evidently feeling that patting without apples or carrots was poor amends for driving a carthorse like a hunter, in clear contradiction to the terms of her indenture. John would have liked to spend more time making peace, but his nerves were pricking. The afternoon was fading, and he'd be a lot easier in his mind if he knew Francie was warned.

'Why, Johnny dear,' Aunt Bessy said as she opened the door. Much of his mother's years, if not her temperament, she was fair, plump, and fond of anyone who spoke politely. Janet and she had been close since childhood; Bessy had an admiring disposition, and was among the few who regarded it as natural that Janet would marry a clever man like the young farrier, rather than surprising that a steady, sensible fellow like the young farrier should set his heart on flighty Janet Patmore. She had always treated John with the balmy assumption that he too must be clever. 'I didn't look for you today.'

'Good day, Aunt Bessy,' John said, talking and kissing her cheek at the same time in order to move things along; he was very fond of her, which was why he called her 'Aunt' when she was technically his cousin, but the longer he went without seeing Francie, the more his back was beginning to crawl. 'I came to speak with Francie. May I see her?'

'Oh, she isn't here,' Bessy said, with placid regret. 'She went out a little while ago. You'll stop for a little visit before you go off, though, won't you dear? I've just been baking—'

'Went out where?' John said. 'Excuse me, Auntie, I do not mean to interrupt. But went out where?'

'I couldn't say,' Bessy said, a little bemused; John refusing her baking was unprecedented. 'Should I? She's a grown girl, and I don't like to harry folks if there's no need. She's been a lovely guest, I supposed that if she felt the need to—'

'Excuse me, Auntie, I beg your pardon.' John's heart was speeding up. 'Can you tell me how she left? When? Why? I beg your pardon for rushing, but if you wouldn't mind.'

'Oh, well, dear, she went out for a walk this afternoon,' said Bessy. She wasn't an unintelligent woman, but she had grown up with a scolding sister and didn't place much faith in her own judgement; Janet's appreciative nature had always been a boon to her. 'She came back with a letter and took it inside to read, then she went out again – she said she'd be back, but she didn't say when. I know she's had things on her mind; I didn't like to press.'

'Did you see the letter?'

'No, dear. It wasn't my place to ask, you know.'

'Did she leave it here?'

'Well, she might have,' said Bessy. 'She's had to share with our Betsy, so she keeps her things in a locked box. We haven't much space to give her, not but what she's welcome.' Betsy was the Gillams' little daughter, and young enough to get into all manner of things if they weren't secured.

John was about to ask if he could see the locked box, but he'd need a key or a pick to open it, and he didn't have any with him. Francie could be anywhere. He cast a look at the sky; the sun still sat above the horizon, but it was glowering brazen and dipping lower and lower. 'Did you see which way she went?' he asked, feeling a little frantic.

Bessy frowned in consternation, but before she could try to wrestle with the question, she looked up with delighted relief. 'Cousin Janet!' she exclaimed, waving happily. 'You come at a good— Ah, who's your friend?'

John's head whipped round. Janet was running up the path. 'Johnny!' she called out, before anyone could say anything, 'have you seen Francie anywhere?'

John shook his head; dread had stilled his tongue. Janet was sweat-soaked and panting – and beside her, grey and faded, wild-eyed, and bruised from jaw to collarbone, ran Alice Brady.

## CHAPTER 19

When Janet went off that afternoon, it had only been to find a quiet place to cry.

It was her fault, all of it. She had always loved her family. Folks said she was silly, light-minded, rash, that she could never carry her head so high without tripping over her feet. And they'd been right; she shouldn't have inflicted herself on fine men. Matthew had given her his heart without reservation; Jedediah had been good to her, never once reproaching her for her stupidity all those years ago that had fallowed her hands and left her son, her beautiful Johnny, with his beautiful eyes staring at the world askew. It was her fault. She had sewn with a bone needle because she hadn't been thinking, or she'd been too busy thinking of her own whims, like everyone always said. And now Johnny, her lovely, wilful, impossible, darling boy, had gone and shown himself thoughtless like her, craving after the woods and setting the People running. If she'd just accepted that life was common sense and minding out and leaving flights of fancy behind and knowing how to damn well sew . . . Matthew said he loved her flights, but he'd have been better served by a sane woman, a woman who watched her step and swept her floor and didn't yearn off into daydreams that destroyed everything. It would have been better to settle for a grey life and a colder man who wouldn't have let her be so ruinously, worthlessly stupid.

She couldn't last the day dry-eyed; she just wasn't able to do it. But she wasn't such a useless mother that she thought it acceptable to cry her eyes out where her children could see. She had to find somewhere peaceful. And she had to explain where she was going, too; she couldn't worry the girls. Franklin Thorpe's cottage was at the edge of the Bellame woods, so she told everyone she'd bring him some of her new-baked bread, because without his daughter around, he could probably do with some.

It wasn't deep in the woods, not like where Johnny had been, but the leaves were turning tawny, hushing together in the wind and drifting down from their branches in frittering spirals, letting themselves go. Yes, it was lovely here. She could see why Johnny liked to go astray, where the earth smelled crisp and rich and the trees closed round you like curtains.

Janet was dramatic by nature, but she had never really liked crying, and not like this, not raw-throated and stifling with grief and shame. It hurt, but once she got started, she couldn't stop. It wasn't helping. They said a good cry made you feel better, but it didn't.

So it was only after she'd finally wiped her eyes and was staring into the russeting thickets that she saw Alice Brady. The woman flinched at every step, clutching one swollen hand against her chest, and she stumbled as if she had never run so hard in her life.

The two women's eyes met, startled, wary. The leaves whispered around them, carrying no words of counsel.

Janet drew breath. She might be making a mistake again; she might be a fool. But she couldn't not speak to the woman staggering before her. If she turned her back, she could never again hold up her head.

'Did he do that to your hand?' she said. Her voice wasn't loud.

Alice clutched her fingers. 'Yes.' It was all she could make herself say.

'May I see?' Janet said, careful, soft. It was the left hand Ephraim had injured, she could tell that from here. Alice still had her right hand to cook and scrub with.

'The fingers are broken,' Alice said, and then, as if once she'd got her voice working, it was coming unleashed, she spoke on. 'Two of them, the smallest two. He never did that before, but, – but he knew how. He said they'd mend in a month – if he took me to get them set they'd mend, *if* – he said it could wait a day . . . I have to find Francie Thorpe, Mistress Smith. He'll hurt her. I don't know how, but he will. He would know where she left her letters, Mistress Smith, and he knew I knew. I didn't tell him till after he'd broken the second one. I'm sorry, I tried . . . He wouldn't have stopped, he . . . I have to find her, Mistress Smith. Or her father, is he nearby? She said I could run to her. I have to be away. He'll hurt her . . . I have to be away from him . . .'

Janet told herself she should think, she should weigh up the odds, she should find the sensible option. But she couldn't take Alice back to Gyrford and ask Matthew what to do; not when the Bradys' house was right opposite the smithy.

She could leave Alice alone in the woods. Or she could

stay with her and try to help, and face down whatever consequences came. Those were her choices. There would be other choices later, but now, in this moment, those were the only choices before her.

'Come with me,' she said, her voice almost steady. 'I'll take you to her.'

John looked at Mistress Brady's hand. Both fingers were askew at the joints, one overlapping the other so they'd knock together, as if gripped in a fist and bent neatly sideways. 'Grandpa or Dada can set those, if we get them here,' he said, a little queasily. 'They say you're not a smith till you've broken your own fingers three times. They've set mine before now. Though I have to tell you that it does hurt. But look, I'm all right now.' He flexed his fingers, straight and repaired, so Alice could see that she might mend. She didn't smile.

'We have to know where she went,' Janet said. 'Bessy, dear, bring Francie's box, would you? It could be she's nowhere bad, but just be a love. You can blame me if Francie's put out.'

'We haven't a pick,' John said, and then he saw, around Mistress Brady's neck, the cross Dada had given her all those weeks ago, when her husband had marked her fortieth year by signing a document that would leave her to a pauper's widowhood. 'Mistress Brady, forgive me,' he said. 'I am sure Dada will give you another one. But may I trouble you for your cross?'

Alice stood startled, looking from John to Janet.

'I feel we haven't time to waste,' said John, 'and the core of it will serve. Forgive me, Mistress Brady. I'll get you another.'

Alice glanced at Janet, and then took off the cross and handed it to John. 'Please give your father my thanks for it,' she said. 'It has been long since I had any gift.'

Bessy went for the padlocked box, and laid it before them with the confused cooperation of a woman used to assuming that the farriers had their own reasons for things. John took out his pocket-knife, and a little prying got the wooden case off. Within the cross lay two iron struts, and with handle of his knife for a hammer and the ground for an anvil, he soon had them bent into shape. Locks were delicate work and he had a great deal more still to learn about making them, but picking them was another matter. It didn't take very much prodding and twisting before he had it open.

There was a collection of letters inside, a few spare clothes, a little bunch of lavender, and a small brooch that Janet remembered seeing Sarah Thorpe wearing, before the fever took her from her husband and daughter. Janet picked up the letters and rifled through them. All of them were signed 'Anthony', and most of them were combinations of 'dearest' and 'beloved' – not particularly eloquent, Janet thought, but this was not the day to be an acrid critic of a young man's pledges – with details of where to meet: by Burnham well, at the copse on Wynn Hill, different places each time, mostly removed and out of sight.

John's hand reached out, rifled through, and pulled one out. The sun was setting and in the greying evening, there was nothing especially uncommon in its appearance.

'What is it, Johnny?' Janet said.

'I don't know.' For a moment, John looked – there wasn't even a word for it. His starey look, the world around him closing out and his eyes focused on something that might not be there, something only he could see. 'It just feels . . . look you, there's a smudge on the corner here.' He lifted it to his face. 'It smells – does that smell of sap to you? Bramble sap?'

Janet sniffed the page, then shook her head, helpless. 'I don't know, Johnny,' she said. 'I don't know any of what you're thinking when you think like this.'

John raised his head, and there was a look of hurt in his eyes, of abashed loneliness, that she could hardly bear. 'I don't mean to be odd,' he said. 'I just—'

'Wait.' It was the hoarse voice of Alice Brady that cut across them. 'Let me see.' Her broken hand lolling in her lap, she took the page between cautious fingertips and studied it for a long, long moment.

'It's Anthony's writing,' she said, 'almost. But the ink is wrong.'

'What do you mean?' Janet and John spoke together, and then looked at each other, blue eyes meeting blue eyes.

'It's grey,' Alice said. The letter shook in her hand. 'Ephraim waters down his ink, to make it go further. He doesn't make Anthony do that. Look you, the ink of all the other letters is black. The writing's almost Anthony's, but it isn't.'

Janet and John leaned in. The writing wasn't very easy to read – Ephraim's care for his brother evidently hadn't included schooling – and both of them squinted to read it aloud, each taking over when the other faltered. Together, they managed to make it out:

*Dear one, meet me on Chalk Lane tonight. I have your letter and would give you an answer that will please you as you deserve. I shall listen for your whistle. Your Anthony.*

John held the letter between his fingertips. Yes, it smelled of sap: a clean scent, fresh and green, with nothing of murder on it.

'Mistress Brady,' he said, 'I don't suppose you remember, was your husband home the night Black Hal made an end of Roger Groves?'

Alice's answer was soft. 'He was not.'

'You are sure?'

She spoke to Janet, not to the child. 'When folks said a man had been found dead on Chalk Lane, I had an hour of hope,' she said. 'Until the news came that it was not my husband they had found.'

John was on his feet. 'He told you he was away to Chalk Lane?'

'He tells me nothing,' Alice said. 'But he had dealings there. Property. I think if you guess that he went there and saw something . . .' She held up her broken hand; something almost like a laugh tangled in her throat. 'He knows how to add two and two, that man.'

'And,' Janet said, her face sickened, 'I think that now, after all that's been, he can add up that sometimes, the People might be made to serve his turn.'

Bessy was looking between them with bewildered concern; she had a new guest to find room for, by the looks of things – and John and Janet were suddenly in a tearing hurry.

'Auntie, please lend us your horse,' John said, faster than she'd thought a boy could talk. 'I had better take Dobbs, better a horse I know, but Mama—'

'I'll go for your father and grandpa,' Janet said, already running to the stables. She stopped, just for a second, turned and looked at him.

'Go, Mama,' John said. 'I'll be all right.'

Janet stared at her son. 'Promise you won't do anything foolish?' she said.

'I can't, I fear,' said John. 'It would be taking a risk with a lie on my soul. I can promise I won't act without thinking, but I think I'll have to think very fast. But we can't just stay and do nothing, can we?'

Janet ran to her, wrapped him in her arms and gave him a rapid kiss. He hugged her back, and then fidgeted out of the embrace.

'I know, I know,' Janet said. 'I'll be back with them fast as I can.' She turned her head away from John, as if dragging against an invisible force. Then she was pelting towards the stable, and she didn't let herself look back.

'Also,' John looked around a little wildly, 'I hope you will not mind if I take a few things. We can repay you. Forgive me, Auntie, but if I don't go now, I think Francie is going to die.'

## CHAPTER 20

He knew what was going to happen, knew it in his blood and in his soul. Let them call him touched, let them call him anything. Let them hand him over to Ephraim Brady, to his whip and his bushes and his bone-cracking hands. If he didn't get out there now, Francie would whistle for her lover on Chalk Lane.

As John kicked Dobbs into a canter, then a rough and unfamiliar gallop, the light settled in the west. The last few droplets of sun were trickling away through the tree branches, leaving behind a great mild wash of blue, deepening minute by minute into a broad, dark, beautiful expanse, moonless and clear and soft as a kiss.

John galloped and galloped. The earth lurched as the wind flailed around him, picking up speed, singing past his ears.

Chalk Lane was high, higher than he'd have believed, higher than it could ever be in the daytime. Dobbs struggled up the hill, heaving and sweating, and John looked around, wild with haste. There should be nowhere to hide, for the road was raised,

353

nothing but hedgerows and trees either side of it and the fields tumbling downhill in all directions.

The wind was gathering against him, great, shuddering sheets pushing him back. It was darker up here the further he rode; night was falling too fast. The verges streamed past him, everything in manic flow, and the sky was clenched, the light squeezing out of it like blood draining from pressed flesh.

John kicked Dobbs forward, down the lane, the chalk ruts blank as eye-whites beneath them, and the trees shaking, thin streams of wind slicing through with a shrill pipe. Down he rode, looking, looking, and no Francie, no Francie in sight. He should have been able to see to the end of the road, the half-mile to where the Ware farm stood and Chalk Lane started to subside downhill, but he couldn't, the air was gathered against him, struggling like an animal caught in a sack.

'Francie!' John yelled. '*Francie!*'

As he heard his voice rise, distort and twist in the deafening eddies, he knew, with a sudden grip of cold, that he shouldn't have called. There in the darkness before him, he heard the sound of a clear, sweet whistle.

The wind dropped. It dropped like a stone: there was a moment of vast, absolute stillness, the trees silent and the air vacant and the world frozen around him. Then it turned, and hard air slapped his whole body, nearly knocking him from Dobbs, and behind him, he heard another sound. It was quiet, too quiet to hear in the blast, but he could hear it just the same, close within his ears, intimate as skin.

Feet were pattering against the chalk.

John stared about himself, but he couldn't find Francie in the dark, he couldn't see his own hand. Above him were stars, white and tangled and stabbing, and behind him, along the road he'd ridden, the sound was drawing closer, a low rattle of claw and pad. And as he looked back down Chalk Lane, he saw little smudges of red, little dancing glows that grew nearer and nearer, and the darkness was untangling itself, and there in the midst of it, flames unspooling from his every step and his eyes weeping scabs of light, came the beast.

There he was, Black Hal, big as a bull, jagged-coated and dripping, coming towards John in a tumbling lope as steady and dire and inevitable as a flood. The starlight glinted white from his skinless chest, glistening against the heaving ribs, the raw meat between them all gloss and stretch and heavy, brutal muscle. His jaws were open, fangs thick as fingers gleaming red in the light from his fire-wet eyes, and he gave a howl, a great deep bay that ripped apart sound, the whole world juddering an anguished echo. Black Hal was running, an explosion of writhing flame.

Dobbs reared, but John grabbed the reins and yanked her to a stop. *I am John Smith*, he whispered in his own mind. *I am John Smith, Matthew's John, Jedediah's John, Janet's John. I am John the fairy-smith. I do not turn.*

He could hear a cry coming from ahead of him, and something was glowing, a rough orange smear in the darkness that he couldn't make out. It was Francie's cry, but no, it wasn't the moment yet. *Wait*, he whispered to himself. He didn't even know if he was afraid: the world was screaming with cold and his own flesh with it, and he could no longer remember what it felt like to be warm and safe, did not remember if he had ever known.

*Wait . . .*

Black Hal was before him. There was a long second when the beast was full alongside; John saw the gnarled jaw and the dagger-rough pelt and, between the slick bones and licking muscles of his chest, a dark gulf, darker than the sky, in which jerked, big as a head, wet as a tongue, a red, beating heart.

And then Black Hal was beyond him, racing down the road after his quarry.

John put his lips together. He couldn't do it as well as Francie, but he could do it. His first attempt failed, but he drew an icy breath and set his lips and let out a thin whistle.

It scraped across the air like chalk on slate.

The wind whirled around them, a swinging circle of force. The patter of flames before him came to a stop, slowed and stilled in the darkness, and John yelled into the gale, '*Francie, run!*' For the clawed, burning feet took a step, and then another, and they were coming towards him.

*Black Hal comes when he is whistled for.*

But Francie Thorpe was behind his tail now. Francie Thorpe would never face Black Hal's hunt again.

John felt a brief sliver of selfhood flash through his bewildered mind: if he outlived this moment, he was probably going to feel very proud of himself. But it was a distant reckoning, whirling away from him in the storm. Black Hal was running towards him now, flame splashing at every step.

John reached into his pack and threw an armful of beating wings into the air.

There was a rash, indignant crow. John had taken Aunt Bessie's cockerel Sun-Up, promising he'd give her the Smiths' Norrie in exchange, and now there he was in the air, yelling out his confusion.

'Go home, Black Hal!' John yelled. 'Your visit is ending!' It was an ancient remedy: the People vanished at cock-crow, or at least many of them did. There was no reason, John had thought, why he shouldn't engineer cock-crow a few hours early.

Just the same, though, he was doing his best to scramble up the nearest tree – no easy thing to do as it as it lurched and bucked in the wind. Dobbs bolted, leaving him stranded and alone. Black Hal was bearing down on him; through the tumbled air, he could smell the chalk singe.

Light was gathering around him, bleeding into the black in spiralling coils. From the keeling branches, John could see the road coming clear. Black Hal was cantering along it towards him, bright and relentless.

Sun-Up flapped, gave another yell: *It's morning, or it should be, and I'm the sun's great greeter, I challenge anyone to deny it . . .*

There was a snap, a squawk – and then something slashed across John's face. A feather, then another, whipping wet through the wind.

Black Hal shook a spray of blood from his jowls and ran on.

John looked down the tree at his doom coming towards him, and saw his own arms were curdling with light, his stomach and legs showing red through his clothes. A dim glow, like coals all over him, was cracking out from every pore: Black Hal's sight growing upon him like scalding moss, marking him out for the kill. He was going to die. His death was shining out through his skin.

Below him was Black Hal, worrying the air. Flakes of flame shook out around him.

Then there was a scream up ahead of him – a man's voice. It was too dark to see far, but John heard it, a cry of panic and desperate love:

'*Francie, stay there!*'

There were feet pounding the chalk, and out of the darkness ran the frantic figure of Anthony Brady. He was running straight for Black Hal, armed with nothing but a stick, which he swung in wild, useless swipes. Three blows struck against Black Hal's crouching haunches, huge and solid as stone and tall as Anthony's chest – and then the stick broke.

Black Hal stopped. His head went round, very slow. His flame-rheumed eyes rested on Anthony Brady.

Anthony backed away, his arms waving now, trying to ward off the sight of the monster he had struck.

And there was another shout. It happened very fast: the sound of a man's voice, someone racing towards them with a shout of panicked, thwarted command: '*Anthony! Andy, get back, get back!*'

There at the edge of darkness, almost swallowed up, as if the black was tearing him back into the wind, was Ephraim Brady. He was there only for a second, his eyes dashing from figure to figure: Black Hal crouched and staring, Anthony backing away.

Ephraim raised his fingers to his lips. His face was as set as ever as he blew. His whistle was sharp and precise, cutting through the wind with perfect, unbending decision.

Black Hal whirled. The light winked out of John's skin, and

started to glow in Ephraim's. Nothing changed in the man's expression as he stood, crusted with light, waiting. The wind rose to a shriek as Black Hal raced down the road, so loud that the new sounds – the scream, then a ripped, gurgling choke – faded down almost to nothing.

It was dark, and the wind blew, and John could hardly hear the sound of dying.

Jedediah and Matthew fought their way forward. At the base of the hill, darkness had grappled them, but by the time they reached Chalk Lane itself, it had started to clear, and once they'd got as far as the Ware farm, it was nothing more than a great, blustery, star-smeared night. The wind was too rough to light a candle, but there were folks holding sheltered lanterns: Jonas Ware, and his second son, Mark. They could just make out Peter, crouched and coaxing Tobias, who was howling, pounding the ground, a frantic dance on all fours. But Jonas and Mark were before the gate, holding their little light and trying to make some kind of order out of the scene before them.

Anthony Brady and Francie Thorpe stood on the road, wrapped in each other's arms. Francie was speechless as a ghost; Anthony was crying like a child.

There, on the dust and stone of Chalk Lane, blood-speckled and throatless, lay the body of Ephraim Brady.

## CHAPTER 21

When the People blaze through your vision, it can take some time before you see life normally again. Matthew spent several minutes searching wildly for John, and several more coaxing him down from the tree where he found him, clinging like a cat, apparently having rediscovered all his fear at once. When he finally did manage to get the boy out of the branches, John wrapped his arms around his father and held tight, and could not be persuaded that he was a big boy and could surely walk for himself.

It was not until they'd brought him inside, back into the Wares' dim, warm kitchen, along with Anthony Brady and Francie Thorpe, that John was able to release his grip on Matthew, though he still didn't want to stray too far from him. Not that Matthew was unwilling: he and Jedediah had caught Dobbs racing riderless down the hill as they struggled towards Chalk Lane, and it was only the fear of upsetting Johnny with his own distress that forced Matthew to set the lad on his feet.

The sight of ordinary surroundings, however, started to bring John back to himself, and while his knees knocked together with stubborn regularity, he was starting to remember that he was John Smith of Gyrford, and had, besides, just ridden out to save a girl from a dreadful fate, and that perhaps he was actually a man of dignity and courage, not a terrified little boy who'd just seen death pass him by, and that being the case – as long as Dada was in clutching reach – he should probably try to carry himself with the kind of boldness that would impress this fact on anyone who might mistake him for scared.

Janet had had little time for explanations, and Jedediah and Matthew were both nearly as confused as the Wares. Matthew was shaking with relief that Johnny was unhurt, and though Jedediah wasn't about to let anyone see his hands trembling, he wasn't quite his steady self either.

John drew a deep breath. If he didn't show his nerve now, he wasn't sure he'd ever find it again.

'Mister Ware,' he said, in a voice that was only slightly shriller than it should have been, 'what was Ephraim Brady doing here?'

Jonas Ware glanced at Anthony, sitting at the kitchen table with his hands clutched tight around Francie's. 'I don't know,' he said. 'I didn't know he was here. Only Mister Anthony Brady – he came to the gate a little while ago.'

'I . . .' Anthony sounded half-stunned. 'I had heard some things. Francie, she had been saying – been saying I should ask more about Ephraim. And . . . and he'd said Mister Thorpe was a – a rough man, and he's nothing of the sort.' As he said that, Anthony's voice grew a little stronger; he spoke as if he was relating an epiphany all at once, a little too staggered to know quite what to include and what to leave out. 'Even when I was a boy, I didn't think him so. I didn't, not in my own mind. And then

Ephraim . . . he said ill things about you, Mister Smith' – Anthony looked at Jedediah with an unaccountable sincerity – 'but you were kind too. You had no reason to be; you had every reason to think ill of both of us. But you told me how to treat my hand, after it got bit,' he clarified, seeing Jedediah's blank expression, 'and you were right, it healed quite clean. I've seen festered cuts, and I might be in a bad way now if it weren't for you. But you helped me. And you didn't ask a thing in return.'

This took Jedediah so off-guard that he could think of nothing to say but, 'My auntie was a midwife.' (Which was true, if not entirely to the purpose; Anthony's gratitude was the last thing in the world he'd ever expected, and he had no clear notion of what to do in the face of it.)

'I wished to come and thank you,' Anthony said, 'but Ephraim wouldn't have it. He . . . he didn't like it. And . . . and I thought about how I never liked to see him displeased, and how I'd heard some things of how he'd treated the boy here, with those bushes. I came to ask – there was that day, when he bit me and Ephraim was angry for me, but what I heard, those bushes, I did not . . .' He swallowed, and to give him his due, he made no attempt to sound justified in his confusion. His face was pallid, and showed a kind of pinched resolve; for all his horror and exhaustion, he suddenly looked a lot more intelligent than John had thought him. 'I wanted to think it couldn't be true,' he said. Then he swallowed. 'Or if it was . . . I needed to know what was true.'

'Was he with you when you came?' John asked.

'No,' Anthony said. 'But . . . sometimes he worries – he worried. Or he said he did, if he couldn't find me. He . . . he didn't like it. He would have asked folks if they'd seen where I was going . . .'

Light rang in John's eyes, an after-image he couldn't get away from. 'And they would have told him they saw you heading to Chalk Lane,' he said.

The wind hushed outside, lying at ease, and everyone was silent for a moment.

John turned to Francie. 'Are you all right, Francie?' he said.

Francie had not let go of Anthony's hand. 'I am alive,' she said. She spoke quietly, her voice steadfast. 'Anthony ran to save me, and I am alive.'

Anthony gave the smallest, most watery of smiles at that, and John felt a burst of outrage at Francie's ingratitude – after he'd nearly got himself eaten, and been run up that tree with Black Hal chewing flames beneath him! He was glad she was alive, of course, but the flare of pure offence restored his countenance better than anything else could have.

'Well, that's as may be,' he said, with an almost successful attempt at scornful dignity, 'but there are other matters still to settle. Grandpa, Dada, I have an idea. I shall present it to you, and you may approve it. I do not wish to be called rash.'

Out in the dark, the brambles were huddled around the gate. The wind had stripped them leafless; now, in the still air, they continued to crepitate, as if they couldn't shed the feeling of Black Hal's gale tearing through their unsheltered branches.

'Kind friends, I fear your man, has fallen foul of flame and fang,' John began. It wasn't his best rhyme, but it didn't need to be: he had their full attention. 'I should not care to see you burn, should you, like he, Black Hal's friend spurn. The boy who broke your fellow's branch, would seem to have an ally stanch.' Of course Black Hal was not about to go chasing after blackberry bushes, but the bushes didn't have much head to think with, and John's voice rang with a confidence that was evidently making its impression.

Matthew stood beside them, ready, if need be, to get between John and their thorns. It was becoming obvious, though, that this wasn't needed.

'The boy, I know, will heed my call,' John declaimed, with just a hint of his usual flourish. 'Shall I ask him to spare you all?'

There was a quivering, and a terrified mumble in the dark of, 'Neighbour spare neighbour spare spare!'

'You each may let each other live. All shall know peace, all shall forgive,' John instructed them.

His attention was on the bushes, absolutely and entirely; for all the notice he took of anything else, he might have been standing alone. Jedediah waited behind him in the night, hand on his shoulder, but the more John spoke, the lighter his grip became.

'To forest quiet we'll let you go, Tuck in your roots and slumber so,' John said, sounding less overweening than he might have, considering he was ordering the People to end a war, and apparently meeting with unquestioned surrender. 'We'll take you home to find your rest. Just mind the boy Black Hal likes best.'

There was a hush, broken only by the submissive murmur of small People grateful to be spared the attention of greater ones. John felt a little guilty, threatening them like that – goodness knows, fear of the grand was no way to make a good world – but not so guilty that he was prepared to let them savage Tobias Ware ever again. Once they were replanted in the woods, they'd be fine. Black Hal wouldn't hurt them, and neither would he.

And with that thought, he remembered that he was exhausted – so exhausted, all of a sudden, that he leaned his head against his grandpa's chest, legs sagging. Jedediah put his arm around John, and then lifted him off his feet. 'You've reason enough to be tired, lad,' he said. His voice was almost gentle.

'I think,' John said, with shaky care, 'that we had better sleep. Perhaps Mister Ware will let us have some of his floor. We should discuss matters further when it is light. Though it is probable,' he added, feeling a little better for the thought, 'that Francie and I could travel back safely – probably for ever, if the cat had the right of it. We are both behind Black Hal's tail now. Though I think it is not a method we should recommend to everyone. The inconveniences involved in getting it are probably too much.'

He managed to say it without much of a tremor, but Jedediah could feel the small body flinch in his arms. Quite tenderly, he passed John over to Matthew, who cradled him in arms that once again felt big and solid.

'Well, Johnny, that's useful knowledge,' said Matthew. 'No denying that.' He felt the need to be cautious with his praise, but his voice was soft: Johnny was alive, that was all he could care about. No doubt he'd care more for other things tomorrow, but not tonight, not with his boy's head nestled on his shoulder.

'Another time,' said Jedediah, remembering his duty as elder farrier, 'see if you can find useful knowledge without coming so close to killing yourself, boy. Use the sense God gave you.'

'I did!' John protested. 'That's how I worked it all out. Besides, if someone was to risk getting hurt, I thought it better me than Francie. That's farrier work, isn't it?'

Jedediah rested his gaze on this small oddity that had found out so much and thrown down his life before it. *Better me than Francie. That's farrier work, isn't it?*

'You thought Black Hal would turn if he heard a cock crow,' he said. Criticising the boy with normal scoldings was the only way he could think of to turn the world back to how it should be. 'You didn't work that out right.'

'No,' said John, 'but it was worth a try, I thought. And by the by, Grandpa, I am not so fey that I can see all of Black Hal's thoughts, am I? Or I would not have made that little mistake. But I didn't die of it, so there.'

There were things that could have been said, a lot of things, but with their living John there in Matthew's arms, bright with discoveries and only shivering just a little bit, neither of them felt like arguing. 'All right,' said Jedediah. 'But you'll have to keep using your head if you're to be a man of iron, boy. Don't get cock-of-the-walk, now.'

# EPILOGUE

The village of Gyrford was disturbed early the next morning. Folks sleepily beginning their days all turned in astonishment as Janet Smith ran from the smithy, shadow-eyed and fully dressed, screaming the name of her son.

His little pipe was heard down the road – 'We're alive, Mama! Dada and Grandpa too!' – and then they entered the square, and everyone stopped what they were doing. Jedediah and John rode one horse and Matthew another, and before them, there rippled a bier of brambles – brambles walking by themselves, swaying and trembling under the weight, as they carried the body of Ephraim Brady. You'd think, with so thorny a stretcher, the corpse would have been scratched to pieces, but there wasn't a mark upon him, except for his throat: open, exposed, furrowed down to the backbone.

Janet Smith gave only a glance to the ravaged carcass before hurling her arms around her son, before he'd even quite finished dismounting. They staggered together, clutching each other, and then she turned and seized her husband, pulling him into the embrace. The three stood, gripping tight, as if they'd never expected to meet again. Jedediah, who generally disapproved of making a scene, hovered next to them. Then he reached out and gave the girl a cautious pat on the shoulder, and Janet grabbed him too. He looked a little startled at being pulled into a common hug, but he didn't break away. His hand rested on John's curls, and he was heard to say, 'Well enough. It's all right.'

The living bier creaked, and Jedediah stepped free, saying, 'We'll to the sexton. A man needs burying.'

'Yes, Dada,' Matthew said into his wife's hair. It was comforting, being told to do something sensible; he felt more at home than he had for months. He just wasn't ready to let go yet.

'All right, all right,' Jedediah said. 'We're all alive, it's reason enough to be glad. But take it in the house, if you must. There's folks staring.'

Later that morning, John and Jedediah went into the Bellame woods to release the bushes. They collected the two they'd held caged in their garden, and John ran behind them like a drover, calling out obscure instructions and chasing the dark, bristling flock along. A bramble shepherd was a thing no one had ever seen before, but then, Gyrford had seen many sights in its day, and as Jedediah went along with him, giving a discouraging glare to anyone who looked like they might make a remark, the community gave up and confined themselves to discussing other matters. Black Hal, everyone told everyone else, had been on the hunt again.

Two deaths at his fangs in one year was truly remarkable, but on the happier side of things, neither man had been much loved. Besides, now folks knew that whistling called the brute down upon you, and it's always a relief to be better-informed than the dead. It was a little surprising to think that Ephraim Brady had gone about whistling at night; he'd never had a very merry manner. Still, said the more charitable folks, it went to show that you never knew, and while he hadn't been the most popular of fellows, it might at least be a comfort to think that he'd had some moments of happiness before he died.

There were matters to arrange; a man of means doesn't die without causing a certain amount of work for those who live by keeping the world tidy.

There was a body to bury, but that was quickly done: Ephraim Brady had paid for his own grave several years ago. It was plot of earth no one could object to: facing east in patient expectation of the Resurrection, not too far from the respectable grave Ephraim had bought his mother, and taking up no more space than strictly required. Some folks liked to buy a double grave, of course; Jedediah Smith, for instance, had paid for his own grave in the same purchase that buried his wife, and had instructed his son not to take too much trouble over his funeral, as he didn't much care how it went as long as his neighbours were well fed and his bones were laid to rest with hers. Evidently Ephraim Brady had felt no need to sleep in such connubial soil, but at least his wife wasn't obliged to bury him at her own expense.

There was a funeral, too, also paid for in advance. Most of the village attended; missing any event important to Ephraim Brady was the kind of rash act that nobody felt comfortable committing, even if the man himself was probably well sealed in his coffin. Anthony Brady was still and quiet during the service, and though tears rolled down his cheeks, he didn't sob or make a spectacle of himself the way folks had expected. Nobody knew quite how to comfort him, but as he'd helpfully ordered some extra viands to supplement the rather meagre feast Ephraim Brady's advance payment provided for his neighbours, it was at least easy to talk to him: folks moved quickly from regretting his loss to thanking him for providing good bacon and cakes, and Anthony, perhaps surprisingly, didn't say that his brother had been the best of men.

Eventually there was an inquest as well, although nothing like so quickly arranged as the funeral: bodies don't keep, but the will of sheriffs moves in its own stately time.

It was a fairly simple business:

Jonas Ware, farmer, testified that he'd known nothing of the matter until he heard screams, and he'd run from his house to find the body of the deceased.

John Jedediah Smith, farrier's apprentice, testified that he'd learned through various ways, which he would like to be excused from describing as they were what you might call trade secrets, that the creature unkenned known as Black Hal was given to hunt those who whistled upon Chalk Lane. The said John Jedediah Smith further testified that he had been upon Chalk Lane, eager to spread news of such great urgency and import, when he saw the deceased whistle, and fall victim to the creature unkenned known as Black Hal. The said John Jedediah Smith yet further advised the court that if it considered its duty to mankind, it would make a public proclamation regarding the fact that whistling called the creature unkenned known as Black Hal, that the news be known most widely. The said John Jedediah Smith made subsequent remarks upon the judgement of Sheriff Daniel Haines, to the effect that it might not be a legal duty to proclaim matters unkenned, but that a man who would chop logic on a point so vital was one who did not attend to his work with due diligence. At this point the said John Jedediah Smith was removed, and placed under the authority of Jedediah Smith, elder farrier.

Jedediah Smith, elder farrier, testified that the deceased was found by himself and his son, Matthew Smith, master farrier, with wounding characteristic of the creature unkenned known as Black Hal. The said Jedediah Smith stipulated further that he would keep his grandson, the said John Jedediah Smith, from any more interference with inquest proceedings, but that if anyone was to whip the boy for contempt of court it would be himself, and he would not do it.

Alice Brady, widow of the deceased, testified that she knew nothing of why her late husband had been upon Chalk Lane, she having spent the night as a guest of her friend Elizabeth Gillam, known as Bessy Gillam.

Elizabeth Gillam, goodwife, testified that she confirmed the word of Alice Brady. She added that possession of the marital home need not be the subject of any immediate dispute, as the said Alice Brady remained as her guest *pro tem*, on the grounds that the said Alice Brady had injured her hand, and between the broken bones and the shocking news, the said Elizabeth Gillam felt that Alice Brady could do with some looking after.

In conclusion, the inquest ruled that Ephraim Brady had died by means mysterious. Sheriff Daniel Haines took the opportunity to grant probate of Ephraim Brady's will to Anthony Brady, sole heir of the deceased. Anthony Brady made it known that he wished to allocate the marital home and certain parcels of land to Alice Brady, widow of the deceased, for her provision and comfort. No objections being raised to this proposition, Sheriff Daniel Haines ordered that the relevant documents be prepared.

All of which is to say, the inquest covered about as much information as the common folks felt that the grand folks needed to know. There were a couple of conversations that nobody felt obliged to report:

The morning after Ephraim Brady's death, Jedediah Smith had risen early. The Wares had insisted on the Smiths sleeping in comfort: the sons crowded top-to-tail into Peter's bed, leaving one pallet for Jedediah to enjoy in patriarchal dignity, and one for Matthew and John. The arrangements were probably for the best: John was resolute in his insistence that he was quite all right, and equally resolute that the best place for him to sit, stand or lie was extremely close to his father. In the end, the soft, low croon of Matthew's lullaby had soothed Jedediah to sleep as well, but he woke before sunrise. There would be much to do. There always was.

Matthew was deep asleep, John snuggled atop his chest with the confidence of a kitten claiming the best pillow. Jedediah didn't like to disturb them, but he wouldn't have Matthew find him gone and worry.

'Matthew,' he whispered, giving his arm a gentle shake.

'Mm,' said Matthew, half opening his eyes, then raising his head as he realised where he was.

'No need to wake,' Jedediah told him. 'I'm away to the Gillams. Break the news to the widow Brady. She'll have been on the watch. You stay here, I'll be back.'

'Do you need me to come?' The words were a little blurred; Matthew was struggling to rise through the deep shades of sleep, and hadn't fully understood.

'No, no.' Jedediah gave his shoulder a soft pat; it had been years, maybe decades, now he thought of it, since he'd woken Matthew of a morning. The lad was full-grown by anyone's standards, but somehow you never quite lost the sense you were looking at something young. 'You stay here, mind the boy. I'll be back.' Because no one was looking, Jedediah smoothed a few strands of hair that had fallen across his son's brow. Matthew said nothing, but his head relaxed back into the pallet, and Jedediah went out into a cool, clear night.

He rode through the dim lanes to reach the Gillams' house. It wasn't quite sunrise when he got there, and the garden was shadowed. At first, the figure seated by the gate looked like nothing but a bundle of blankets. Then its head came up, fast as a hare, and Alice Brady was staring out at the approaching figure.

'It's Jedediah Smith,' he said. He knew he was blunt, sometimes too much so, but here and now he couldn't but feel it would be a greater cruelty to keep her waiting than to torment her with graceful preamble. 'Your husband's dead, Mistress. No one else. Just him. Black Hal took him. I came to tell you.'

Alice's face shone pale, even in the gloom. She opened her mouth, just a little, but no words came.

'I'm sorry I can't soften it,' Jedediah said. 'I'll go and wake Bessy Gillam in a moment. If you need fuss and feathers, she's the woman for you. Always had a kind heart, that girl. I can set your fingers, though. Young John said you had need of it.'

At that, Alice Brady stood up, opened the gate. She didn't say anything, just let him in.

Jedediah sat beside her. If she wasn't ready to talk, he wouldn't force her.

It was a long, heavy moment, sitting together as the sky started to pale above them. The breath Alice drew was deep and almost level as she said, 'How?'

Jedediah rubbed his face. 'If you truly need to know,' he said, 'I'll tell you. Only there'll be an inquest. You can't testify or perjure yourself over what you don't know.'

At that, she looked at him, a quick glance of alarm.

'I'll tell you plain,' he said, 'there's nobody to blame but the dead man. And if you need answers, now or later, well, you know where I live. But I reckon you've carried secrets a long time. Might be a relief to set them down and not load yourself with any more.'

Alice voice had a drearness to it, not grief, but something near collapse, as she said, 'Francie Thorpe's alive, yes?'

'She is. Not a scratch on her.'

Alice said, 'Well, thank God for that.' Her voice shook a little.

Jedediah examined her hand, holding the fingers as lightly as he could. 'This'll likely hurt,' he said. 'Sorry, but you'll do better once it's over with.'

As he tipped one of them forwards a little, testing the joint,

Alice's head turned aside, not quick enough to hide her face from him. There wasn't a sound from her; her mouth distorted, the wail of a woman who'd learned to scream without making a tiresome noise.

At the sight, Jedediah felt a little sick. He'd learned that trick himself, when he was a young widower with Matthew to care for; even the best smith hits his own hands sometimes, and if there was anything in the world he'd bound himself to, it was the promise that he wouldn't upset his son.

He didn't want to think how she'd had to learn it.

'Could be worse,' he said, not doing a very good job at sounding cheering. 'One's broken, but the other's just out of joint. Both'll mend; the out-of-joint one'll mend quickly.'

'So I can work still?' Alice said. He recognised her tone now: it was the flat, hasty calculation of someone whose body doesn't yet know it's out of danger, and whose mind hasn't yet stopped running. 'I'll have to ask you to find me work, Mister Smith. I've heard you do such things. I'd make a housekeeper if my hands let me, or a maid, if that's what there is for me. You'd better find me something, though. I'm too old to whore.' She said this last with a kind of dismal humour, the mirthless wit of a woman suddenly free to say what she thinks.

'You won't starve,' Jedediah said.

Alice gave him a look of bleak dismissal. 'I can count,' she said. 'I've done nothing but count for a decade. If you mean you won't help me, say so.' There was a certain incredulity in her tone: not so much disbelief at his words, as at the fact that she was speaking sharp and nothing was being done to hurt her.

'Oh, I'll help you if you like to housekeep,' Jedediah said, sitting back. The bite in her voice was as gratifying as the cry of a newborn, and cheered him up immensely. 'But Anthony Brady's a rich man now. He can spare plenty of his wealth and still be rich.'

'Anthony never kept an account in his life.' Now she was allowed to direct a little forcefulness at someone, Alice was evidently finding it a relief. 'Ephraim never let the boy think straight. He'll do as the will tells him, and the will tells him to take the property.'

'He'll do some thinking now,' Jedediah said. 'If he wants to marry Francie Thorpe – and he does – he'll do more than think. I'll vouch for that,' he added with firm satisfaction. 'I know her father.'

That was one conversation nobody needed to bother the authorities with. There was another, too. Before Ephraim Brady's body was brought back to Gyrford, the Smiths had found a letter in his pocket. It wasn't public knowledge, even among the common folk. It had been quietly handed to Francie Thorpe in the Wares' kitchen.

> *Dear one,*
>
> *I swear I do not mean to come between you and your kin. Nor do I hide from you, only I cannot tell you where I stay just now. My reasons are such I cannot trust to writing, but believe me they are honest. I have said before that my feelings on Ephraim differs from yours, and while I honour the heart that honours a brother, I believe you have not all the truth on him.*

*I hold you high in my heart, but if this is to be a division between us, I must speak to you plain so you may decide. If you cannot believe me, we must part as friends. That is not my wish, but to meet in secret for ever cannot be. It cheapens my name and your word, and I hope you honour both.*

*We must meet and speak truth to each other and then know if we must part as friends or else, as I hope, link hands before the world. Name the place and I shall attend.*

*I hope I may in the face of troubles yet be,*
*Your Francie*

'What's that?' Anthony asked. He'd been unable to leave her side. Francie, holding his hand in hers, showed it to him without a word.

'Did you ever see it?' she asked.

He looked up, dazed, and shook his head.

Francie took his other hand, clasping them between her palms. 'I hope,' she said, 'you will with me to my friend Bessy Gillam. I have another letter there I believe you should see. I believe you will be seeing it for the first time.'

Travellers along Chalk Lane that autumn enjoyed a few days of confidence, as it was known that Black Hal had made his last run for that year on the twenty-fourth of September, leaving them four safe nights until Michaelmas, when his seven runs would begin again. It wasn't long, but then there is much business to do before Michaelmas, when yearly accounts are settled and everything must be made neat and ready to begin again, and any time is useful to the busy.

The bushes were replanted by John, according to Jedediah's dictum that those who make messes should clean them up. While the original bush was resolved on going back to its old spot, the rest, having only vague memories of what it was like before their friend woke them up, weren't especially attached to any location.

Toby had taken to weeping whenever he saw a bramble, and would fight for his life if you tried to bring him near one, even to show him that it wasn't fey and wouldn't hurt him. It took a certain amount of pacing and considering the angles before they found the right spots for the bushes: out of Toby's sight as long as he stayed within the bounds of the farm, but visible if he broke through the boundary hedge again.

'I don't like it,' John said, viewing the arrangement, 'hedging him in with frights like this. But it must be better than hanging.'

Jedediah put an arm around his shoulder. 'He'll have to learn to be happy at home,' he said. 'He has his father and brothers. He's luckier than some.'

The newly-planted brambles were hung at John's suggestion, with Mackem knots. Once the bushes had been watered in, and had spent a certain amount of time nuzzling the knots with their sharp-tipped stems, they settled down to nap. This had all been agreed upon before they went to the woods: Matthew and Jedediah, for once united in severity, insisted on John giving a full account of any ideas he had in mind.

Jedediah had been heard, in private, to make some remarks about the lessons to be learned from how a man might end up if he overreached, but John's spirits weren't much dampened. All he said to that was, 'If you mean Mister Brady, Grandpa, I could have told you as much. Thinking every one of the People was made to serve a man's turn. Even I'd have slapped his legs for that.'

'Let's not speak ill of the dead, Johnny,' said Matthew.

'If you wouldn't slap a man's legs for thinking the whole of the unkenned a world of hirelings, Dada,' said John, 'then I don't know what to say. Except that if I ever run that way, you have my leave to slap mine.'

Franklin Thorpe visited the Smiths on a quiet day after the harvest. He stood awkwardly; going down on your knees to a fellow-commoner is impossible to do without looking stupid, and how else was he to thank the folks who'd saved his daughter?

'Mister Smith,' he said to Jedediah, 'you'll have to forgive me. I know you prefer folks not to . . . to effuse. This is not the first time I have owed you thanks, nor the second. But for the life of my daughter, I do not know how to thank you. I cannot repay. I——'

Matthew considered giving Franklin a hug, but before he could, Jedediah stood up, waving a stiff hand. 'Save your breath, Franklin,' he said. 'There's no debt. You need help, you come again, that's all there is to it.'

'Well, I like that!' John exclaimed, bouncing into the conversation with the unstoppable buoyance of an apple dropped into water. 'As if it was you who nearly got yourself ate! You can thank me if you like, Mister Thorpe, and welcome.'

'Indeed, I do thank you,' said Franklin. His tone was almost passionate, and he would have said more if Jedediah hadn't cut in:

'Well enough, boy. We know the man has manners. Don't make him kiss your feet for not leaving his daughter to die.'

'It's quite all right,' said Franklin, a little disturbed that those he loved were arguing on his account. Matthew patted his shoulder.

'Nobody should kiss my feet,' John observed. 'I haven't cleaned my boots yet, they're all over ash.'

'Never mind your boots, boy,' said Jedediah. 'Just don't be in such a hurry to gather debts. We're down one creditor in the neighbourhood. Let's keep it that way.'

John drew himself up. It was Janet he most resembled, with a glimmer of Matthew when he smiled, but there was something in his stance now so suddenly reminiscent of Jedediah that Franklin felt an unexpected ache of delight. 'It was only a debt of thanks, Grandpa, and the good fellow has paid it already. *Of course* I don't wish to hold it over him. Why would I make debtors of my friends and neighbours?'

For a moment, Jedediah contemplated his grandson. Then he gave a nod, and something very nearly like a grin, and said, 'Good man. Now, haven't you some work to be getting on with?'

The year went on into winter, as years must, and events remained as interesting as they always are. The Porter family

stayed as millers under their new landlord, to everyone's satisfaction, as it's always a pleasure to have friendly and respectable
neighbours.

There was a certain amount of yowling from the cats around
their property for many nights, which was a little surprising
considering that the only one they had was a Tom, and you'd
have thought that such scrapping would indicate a she-cat in
season – but then cats were cats and not subject to the laws of
common sense, and as long as they continued to war upon the
rats and mice as well as each other, nobody was very worried.

Charles Groves was everything one could expect from a
landlord of his lineage, but he proved unexpectedly pleased
with his new acquisition, visiting more often than strictly
necessary, and commenting to his friends that that torn-eared
Tom of the Porters' was most enjoyable company if you ever
fancied a good set-to. Exactly what he meant by this nobody
knew, but then Charles Groves delighted in frustrating those
around him, and if the odd inexplicable remark was the worst
you had from him, then you hadn't much to complain about.

The Smiths, for their part, had no complaints at all, as the
man apparently disagreed with his late brother about their
forge being a good place to sign contracts, and kept out of their
way. Gossip reported that on his one visit to the smithy, he had
found 'that son of his' irritating. The natural assumption was
that he was referring to John, but in fact, it appeared he meant
Matthew.

Matthew was a little daunted by this, as he couldn't imagine
what he'd done to offend the man; all he could remember was
that Mister Groves had made various jabs at him, and he'd not

known quite what to say. He tried asking his father whether he should have been more polite to the gentleman, and got no better answer than, 'If you think you can be, son, don't let me stand in your path.' This confounded Matthew worse than ever, as he had no idea why Jedediah was laughing, but as it had been too long since he'd seen Dada happy, he decided to let the matter rest.

Towards Christmas, the village was entertained with a wedding announcement: Anthony Brady was to marry Francie Thorpe. Nobody had thought very highly of Anthony Brady's intelligence up until that point, but his good sense in fixing on a Gyrford lass raised him somewhat in folks' estimation, and his prospective father-in-law, Franklin Thorpe, was willing to tell anyone who asked that the lad wasn't slow when he put his mind to it, and that with all the property Anthony'd now have to manage, he, Franklin, was glad to have at least one landlord in the county who'd take his word without quarrel when it came to whose boundary was whose. And there was no question Anthony was devoted to Francie: why, he'd even driven Black Hal off her one terrible night.

That was the accepted version of events, and it did Anthony some good in the public eye. 'The tale'll twist in the telling,' Jedediah told Franklin over a quiet pipe. 'More than most tales, even. It was dark, and things were out of kilter. Black Hal went for Francie, Anthony drove him off, Ephraim Brady laid down his life for Anthony: simpler that way. But it wasn't Anthony called him off her – though he tried, to be fair. Give him credit for that. He tried. Could've been killed. But it was my boy.

My John. Francie'd've been dead before Anthony ever reached Black Hal, and Anthony'd've been dead for sure, wasn't for Johnny.'

Franklin managed not to wince, and Jedediah gave him a light clap on the arm. Then he added, 'Mind you, it won't do the boy any harm if the credit goes elsewhere. He's young to get his head swelled with folks telling the true tale, and he doesn't need any more reasons to think himself fine. Born pleased with himself, that lad.' Jedediah gazed at something that couldn't be seen, before adding, 'He knows how brave he was.'

Anthony, then, was regarded as a fellow of more substance than folks had suspected, and more than a few made an effort to congratulate him on his betrothal – and even, if they were kind, condole with him for the loss of his brother. Anthony was glad to praise his bride, and indeed his new father-in-law, but when it came to Ephraim, he was oddly mute. He would only say, with tentative but earnest courtesy, that he was most grateful for the kind thoughts of his neighbours, and he hoped that he could in the future repay them.

This was difficult to answer, especially for those who'd braced themselves for polite agreement about Ephraim's many supposed virtues, but Anthony would then thank them for their time and say he'd better be back about his work now, and it had to be said, his new-found diligence was no bad thing. Much of his time was spent with Franklin Thorpe – indeed, for the first couple of months, he was hardly away from the man, whether Francie was there to be chaperoned or not – and he was becoming a familiar sight at the farms and cottages he now visited as landlord. He could be a bit difficult to make conversation with, but he was surprisingly willing to help fix any rotting fences or broken doors, and wasn't as clumsy about it as you might have thought. He'd had a little training in carpentry before his brother ended his apprenticeship, and he was heard to say that he liked the work and must study to improve, as he was finding that things often needed mending.

This put him in a fair way towards pleasing folks, and Anthony crowned their satisfaction with his wedding gift to his wife — which was to forgive all but the wealthiest of his inherited debtors. Adding Franklin's sound advice about the utility of keeping tenants' houses fit to live in, the importance of tiding one's neighbours through hard times, the long-term benefits of funding such things as almshouses and hospitals, and the many practical advantages of exerting oneself for the common good, folks were growing quite charitable about the fact that he was sometimes rather awkward. We all have to make the best of this life, after all.

It was a winter wedding, and the snow was falling in light dabs: a lacy scattering on the ground, and little flicks of white spiralling down. Francie looked as pretty as you'd expect, and Anthony was full of delight at the sight of his bride entering the church. He had been at a loss, for a while, as to who would stand best man for him, but after some discussion, Matthew Smith had been volunteered for the position. Matthew was touched by the honour, but the ceremony cost him some anxiety despite Janet's assurances that there was no man worthier and that her only concern was that he'd outshine the groom. Janet was reliable in her loyalty, but it was not a remark that helped

Matthew relax, as the whole foundation of his nerves was that he'd have to stand in front of their fellow-villagers, and he always cried at weddings.

Alice Brady was there too; she had been very active in organising the wedding feast, and had managed to procure a remarkable amount for the money. Folks were a little surprised at the sight of her bustling around making the arrangements, partly because she wasn't usually out and about so much, and partly because she looked considerably plumper than they'd remembered her. She'd always looked such a little pick of a thing, but these days she was growing positively stout. It wasn't for want of exercise, though; much of her time these days was spent walking the lanes, her new dog Mouncie dancing at her heels.

Mouncie was a gift from her friends the Gillams, and was regarded by some as a stupid beast and others as clever, since he took his opinions very much from his mistress and had a habit of snarling at those she didn't really like. Franklin thought him an excellent addition to Alice's life, although Soots regarded him with disapproval: Mouncie was a great deal more indulged than Soots, and she thought him disorderly. Jedediah, meanwhile, had yet to meet a dog he didn't like, but John's feelings were profoundly mixed. Mouncie regarded John as one of his best friends and attempted to leap into his arms whenever they met, but for some reason, John was not over-eager to return the dog's embraces, and did not share Mouncie's opinion that all he needed was some tail-whipping and jollying along to seal their eternal bond.

(John, in fact, was rather doubtful about the merits of dogs these days, and had been seen around the Porter farm making overtures to a certain striped cat, apparently with a view to asking someone four-footed to teach Mouncie his manners. While the Porters were very glad to welcome him, his appeal didn't get very far; cats are not known for their eagerness to do us favours, and in any event, this particular cat had taken a particular liking to the widow Brady, and on its rounds about town was often seen standing on a wall, touching noses with her and exchanging civilities, to the satisfaction of both.)

So it was a spring-heeled Alice who oversaw the wedding preparations, and she bargained with fiery enthusiasm, too, saying bold as you please that she'd have nothing poor quality for the best girl in Gyrford, and she swung her basket home in her unbandaged hand with an air that was almost merry. There was some talk that Mistress Alice, who'd been as unfriendly as could be while she was a wife, was getting quite full of herself as a widow, and who'd have thought it? Possibly it was being a woman of property that did it: she'd taken management of the lands Anthony turned over to her into her own hands, and while they'd been profitable before, Alice was showing a knack with sheep and cattle, and had strong opinions about the importance of paying liberal wages, that pleasantly surprised those suddenly in her employ.

Francie Thorpe, later Francie Brady, usually made short work of any comments on Alice's new-found boldness, though: she'd have no ill talk about her sister, thank you, and she was happy to have it known that Alice had a permanent invitation if she wished to come live with Anthony and her. It was a little surprising the two women were such good friends – Alice was nearly twice Francie's age, and not known to be sociable – but they appeared devoted to each other. Alice hadn't taken up Francie's invitation yet, but perhaps when there were children in question she might like to join them; children like to have a loyal auntie around, and there was no question that Alice's housewifery was beyond equal for its prudence.

Franklin Thorpe, it was agreed, would be dividing his time between his own quiet cottage and staying with his daughter and her new husband – who was showing himself a most respectful and affectionate son-in-law. There was some gossip that, should the widow Brady decide to move in as well, perhaps she might take some marital interest in the widowed Franklin, who was a pleasant fellow of suitable age – forty-five to her forty, and after all, she had not been the happiest of wives when she married a younger man. Alice, who went about enough these days to gather plenty of talk, eventually challenged the rumour outright, stating with some firmness that, while she had great respect for her friend Mister Thorpe and was glad to count him among her kin, she was quite finished with husbands.

On that note, she tended the grave of her late husband with scrupulous propriety. Every last Sunday of the month, she went to lay flowers upon it. It might be said that the flowers weren't the best blooms from her garden – indeed, that the roses she laid were very close to being dead-heads and the snowdrops were past their best and the honeysuckle only present when it was time to prune anyway – but then, folks supposed, she'd got into an economical turn of mind, her husband having been a man who knew the value of a saved penny.

So all in all, the wedding was considered a success: the

service wasn't too tedious and the feast afterwards was tasty, and gifts were given with a good will. At a quiet moment in the celebrations, John Smith took another opportunity: his friend Peter Ware was there, although without his brother, Tobias being known to dislike long sermons, and John had a gift of his own to deliver.

'Peter Ware,' he said, ushering him into a corridor, 'how are you?'

'Oh, we're all well, thank you, Mister John,' said Peter. He very seldom had the opportunity to go out and celebrate, and he was cheerful that day, a little flushed from the cider that had been circulating, and looking quite relaxed. The farm felt safer than he could ever remember: their new landlord had actually lowered the rent that quarter-day, and indeed, he often came to visit along with Francie. There was talk of selling the place to them, even; Anthony Brady's notion of a fair price was amazingly low. He was a little wary of Tobias, that was for sure, but Francie was gradually winning him round, saying that Toby was dear to her and she hoped that he'd be dear to Anthony too, and Anthony had never been one to contradict the wishes of those close to him. Peter found he liked the fellow; not much to say for himself, but then, the Wares would never hold that against a man.

Toby himself was a little wan these days; that was the only stain on Peter's spirits. He didn't go into the forest any more. He was too afraid of the brambles. But he racketed against the bars of his ken, whined against the hedge, seemed not to feel himself at home in the place. Peter was worried. He didn't want to complain, not after the Smiths had done so much for them. He just didn't like to see the joy go out of his brother.

'Well,' said John, 'it being so cold, my mother had an idea that might be pleasant for Tobias. You know she never sews, because the People got into her hands and make her thread come up all woody? Well, it's not much use to most, but we thought if anyone might enjoy such work, Toby would be the lad.' He handed over a package, and, as Peter looked inside, his mouth fell open. It was a canvas covering – or at least, it had probably been canvas once. Tiny brackens writhed on it, hawthorn and holly and bristling beech: a great bundle of miniature woodland ready to unfold and hang over Toby's sleeping ken.

'Well, my goodness!' Peter said. 'That is very kind. Yes, I think Toby will like this very much. Why, it's quite a forest.'

'I think,' said John, in a voice of confidence calmer than his usual bounce, 'that you will find Tobias likes to be under cover. A shelter from the wind, you see. As long as it isn't a house. Houses are traps – you cannot see danger coming through their walls. He likes to be under the canopy in the woods. If you let him sleep under this, I think he will feel safe. He will not miss the woods so much. I reckon he'll still like to chase coneys, but you could breed some. We could help you make hutches. After all, if he catches them, you could all eat coney stew. Or pie; Francie makes good ones – she could teach you. I wouldn't ask Mama, if I were you. Francie's are better.'

Peter was looking at him, amazed. 'I shall try it, indeed,' he said.

'Also,' John said, 'Mama says that perhaps Tobias might like to chase chickens. They don't run away so far, and you could put them in the pot when he's done. Mister Luke Morris sold her some chicks, and then Dada went to talk to him to ask if he'd sell some to you. He said he'd sell them to you for half nothing and be glad to do it.'

This was quite true: Matthew had been surprised how easy the haggling went, and came away with the view that Luke Morris must be a generous soul with fine feelings. Which he might have been, but a more immediate reason was the fact that a man who has been making jokes about cocks in the marketplace with Matthew Smith's wife is a man who definitely feels motivated to offer low prices − and by the time Luke realised that Matthew wasn't there to punch him, he'd already made the offer and didn't quite like to withdraw it.

It had not, in fact, occurred to Matthew that Luke would suppose him angry over joking with Janet; he wasn't so foolish as to resent being married to a woman with a lively interest in congenial matters. And while Janet herself was a little puzzled to find Luke Morris so carefully respectful next time she went to bargain with him − she thought it was only a sign of Matthew's wonderful cleverness that he had struck such a bargain, and was no more likely than her husband to suppose him jealous − she managed to get Luke laughing again after a while. It attracted a few tuts from her female neighbours, but Janet rounded upon them, and said that she knew full well there'd been gossip her Matthew was prone to stray, and if anyone wished to suggest he was bored in his own bed, now was the time to say so − and that while she was on the subject, she would have it known that they had the best children in the world, and her son was a great man, and if that wasn't the sign of a virtuous father, then she was sorry to find her neighbours silly, and must do her duty as a farrier's lady by forgiving them all, and let them learn for themselves in time what a very, *very* great man her fine son was growing to be.

'So you might do a little chicken farming,' John concluded. 'Toby could have a lot of fun, I think, if you do all that. Be happy. And I'm sure Anthony Brady would be glad to set you up a coop; he likes to oblige his tenants, Dada says. I'll tell Mister Thorpe, and he'll tell Anthony it's a wise investment. You might have to let him help you build it, but he's getting handier, so that's not so bad. Only don't tell my sister Molly how you catch and slaughter them. She's tender-hearted about chickens.'

'Goodness.' Peter looked a little stunned at the flurry of advice. 'As you say, Mister John. And I must thank your mother, that is a very kind thought.'

'She'll be happy to hear it,' said John. It was quiet in the corridor, undisturbed. 'I just need to ask you one thing.'

'Of course,' Peter said, still admiring the twining mess of leaves with a delight so profound that a more scrupulous boy than John might have hesitated to cut across it.

'It's only that I'd like to know,' John said. 'That night Roger Groves stepped out on Chalk Lane. After he'd made Tobias cry so much, and I suppose it wasn't the first time, or the second. And he'd talked about Tobias' way with other men's game. You know, to tease you that he knew Toby was poaching. And joked about the rope, like he'd find it funny to hang him. Hang Toby.'

Peter did not put down the bundle, but his face became rather fixed.

'It's only that we know Black Hal runs seven times a year,' John said. He thought of that moment when he'd told the Wares, who had lived by Black Hal's road all their lives, that whistling called the hound. How unsurprised they'd seemed. He'd been too frantic to think much of it just then, but he'd had time to think since. 'You knew he'd run five times, of course, because you told us. It was what the Porters told us too. But it was late in the season, and no one else would know. No one else that didn't live by the road. If I'd been Roger Groves, I might have asked if you knew how many runs Black Hal had made that year. He'd assume you'd tell him the truth; he did assume things were made to go his way. It's just my thought, you know.'

Peter said nothing for a long moment. There was something in his face that reminded John, all at once, of his brother Tobias: that tension, that hunger for a safety that couldn't be run down.

'I don't know if I'd tell him the truth myself, if he'd asked me,' John said quietly. 'It wouldn't be murder, really. After all, Black Hal might not run him down. And I might not have known Roger Groves' whistle would call him. For sure, no one could prove I knew any such thing. Not ever. But I might have asked someone if Black Hal had finished his seven runs for the year, at least. If I'd been Roger Groves.'

Beyond the walls were the sounds of laughter and music, but between John and Peter stretched a deep, dark silence.

'Yes,' Peter said, after swallowing. 'Yes, I suppose you would. Being a farrier, you would.'

John nodded. He saw in Peter's eyes what Roger Groves must have loved to see: fear, powerless and waiting. It wasn't a sight he wished to feed upon, not ever. 'Yes,' he said, with a brisk air.

'Poor Mister Groves. What a pity he hadn't the knowledge to ask. But then, he wasn't a very wise man.'

Peter nodded, his face very pale.

'It's all right, you know,' said John. 'I only need to know such things so I'll know as much as ever I can, and that way I can help folks better another time. I'm a fairy-smith, that's all,' he added, trying and failing not to swagger about it, just a little. Then he imagined Jedediah's cynical gaze upon him, and added, 'Or I will be. Besides, some things are not my business. That's all I wished to say, Peter Ware, that I'll do my best at the business I have, and Grandpa is always saying I should know my limits. Well, I hope your brother likes the canvas. Mama says maybe she might try a blanket for him next.'

It was still snowing outside, but John stepped out to enjoy the air. He could hear the sounds coming from within, laughter, and someone singing. It was an old, cheery tune, but soon enough it was getting complicated, because Celdie and Vevie were harmonising with it, and then Janet joined in with a harmony of her own, and once they started that way they always went on for a while. The celebration would probably last into the afternoon; it was just to be hoped that no one would come along with an urgent job until it was finished, because if it did, the Smiths would have to go, and there were some cakes still to come that he'd had his eye on since yesterday.

The door creaked, and Molly slipped out. 'There you are, Johnny,' she said. 'You should put your jacket on if you're going to stand around outside. Just look at the snow.' She had it with her too, and John put it on with no more protest than a roll of his eyes.

Molly, who had wrapped up before leaving the building – Johnny always raced ahead without thinking, but she herself preferred to stay warm – breathed out a long plume of steam. 'Do you think it'll settle?' she asked, watching the white flakes dance.

John looked around, starting to feel warm again. The good, plain cobbles men had laid across the square were growing edged with crystals, sparkling and clear, too bright to be real, but there nevertheless. 'For a while, maybe,' he said, then grinned. 'As long as anything ever stays settled.'

Molly suspected she was being teased, but she let it go. Everyone had their little ways.

John Smith went walking in the Bellame woods that winter. Franklin Thorpe had another small bit of forestry that needed Smith work. He always would: the People go about their business like everyone else. It was delicate, that day, the bare limbs of the trees shawled with ice and the life of the woods held back, curled in and quiet and waiting for the cold season to pass. Hushed, but not gone; everything would bloom again.

On the way, he passed the bush they'd replanted: the bush he'd troubled, what felt like a long time ago, and set the forest running. Mackem knots still hung from its branches – but that wasn't its only adornment. Its stems had wound round and round each other, twining and dancing into unbreakable braids, a knot more elaborate than any mortal hand could weave. Thorn and twig coiled into the ground in beautiful latticework that nobody would ever be able to dig up again. On its branches gleamed blackberries, thick and glossy under their tiny featherings of frost.

John hesitated for just a moment before picking one — but it came away from its branch easy as anything, and when he put it in his mouth, it tasted sweet as honey and sharp as earth.

The End

# A NOTE ON MICHAELMAS

The events of this book take place once upon a time, and not in any specific era. However, that era is not modern. Once upon a time never really is.

Sharp-eyed readers may notice that I make reference to Michaelmas, which I describe as taking place on the 29th of September, and wonder: which Michaelmas do I mean? During the 1750s, Great Britain shifted from the Julian to the Gregorian calendar, and skipped forward eleven days, meaning that what used to be the 29th of September now took place on the 10th of October. Michaelmas was a religious festival, but it also involved secular traditions like the 'hiring fairs' where folks looking for work could go to find employers, and those fairs got moved to October 10th, ever since referred to as Old Michaelmas. The liturgical date stayed where it was, though; we still celebrate New Michaelmas on the date we now call the 29th of September. So when I say Michaelmas, do I mean the one in September, or the old festival eleven days later?

The answer is probably Old Michaelmas, but the characters would have referred to it as taking place on September the 29th.

It's neater if we suppose the festival and the fair would have happened at the same time, and I wouldn't like to confuse the People by giving them two options to pick from.

They say that after Michaelmas the Devil spits (or possibly pisses) on unpicked blackberries, and you should leave the bushes alone – but then, John Smith was never prone to go by proverbs when there was a chance before him to try something truly interesting.

## ACKNOWLEDGEMENTS

I'm very lucky to have such wonderful people to thank:

Sophie Hicks, the best agent in the world.

Everyone at JFB, especially: Jo Fletcher, Ajebowale Roberts, Ella Patel, Ellie Nightingale, Stephanie Hetherington and Leo Nickolls.

Peggy Vance, the cat's pyjamas, whose magic ears got me out of a terrible jam. (Unmix that metaphor if you can.)

Alicia Deale, who listened to me and saved me.

The staff of Heber Primary School, especially Rivka Rosenberg, Genevieve Joseph-Williams and Hannah Darkin, and even more especially, Andreea Grigorescu, who made it possible for me to think straight enough to write a book at all. If anyone ever lets me pick our next world leaders, it's going to be you.

The staff at Oldfield Forge, who patiently answered my many questions. There are other questions I doubtless didn't think to ask, so if you see a silly mistake, it's mine.

My family, for their endless love and support.

My friends, who made it feel worthwhile, and especially

those who caught some of my dafter slips and/or made good suggestions: Harriet Trustcott and Claire Bott.

All my friends, adult and child, in the special-needs community. Some of you I suspect would rather not be named, but to the adults: your spines are steel, your children are gorgeous, and your exhaustion is earned. To the kids: you're super-good, and I love you guys because you're awesome.

Gareth Thomas, husband, listener, Matthew partisan, line-by-line workshopper, orderer of take-away, and inspired asker of the wrong questions at the right times.

And Nat, my Nathaniel Rhys, my darling, my beautiful, beautiful son. You are my heart love.

## NOTE

I never set out to make this book 'about' special needs or neuro-divergence; nothing I write with an agenda comes out any good. I am, however, a member of a neurodivergent family.

As regards my own neurology . . . honestly, I couldn't say for sure. There aren't the resources to get me properly tested. I've had a couple of people suggest mild dyspraxia, and that felt like the least unlikely guess, but basically I'm one of those people who usually gets taken for neurotypical but is considered a bit 'quirky' (hands up if you're familiar with *that* word), and has an oddly high proportion of neurodivergent friends. No official diagnosis, but probably a little spice in my sauce.

One thing I do know for certain: I'm a carer. Also someone's Mummy, which is who I always wanted to be to my lovely son – but I have finally accepted that I've earned the right to my free flu shot. I'm gorily familiar with the bureaucratic death-maze that is trying to get a child's special needs met, a veteran of many days out in which people unfamiliar with autism and ADHD saw or heard my son and bestowed upon us That Look, and a woman who has a Pavlovian response to the sight of a desk fan, a Hoover, or any of the other various things that fascinate my darling lad. There's no way that didn't influence my writing. I live among the hidden things, and my normal is very far away from what most people think of when they hear the word.

If you're one of us, or if you'd like to know more, welcome aboard! This isn't anything like a comprehensive list, and nothing I suggest will be perfect for everyone; here are just a few resources that have been helpful for me, or for people I love.

## Books:

*Caged in Chaos: A Dyspraxic Guide to Breaking Free* by Victoria Biggs

*The Asperkid's (Secret) Book of Social Rules* and *Sisterhood of the Spectrum* by Jennifer Cook O'Toole

*Thinking In Pictures* by Temple Grandin

*ADHD 2.0: New Science and Essential Strategies for Thriving With Distraction* by Edward M. Hallowell and John J. Ratey

*The Reason I Jump: One Boy's Voice From the Silence of Autism* by Naoki Higashida (translated by Keiko Yoshida)

*The Selfish Pig's Guide to Caring: How to Cope With The Emotional and Practical Aspects of Caring For Someone* by Hugh Marriott (In case the title doesn't give you fair warning, please note, this is a book for carers, not people who need care, and is very frank about the less-than-noble thoughts and feelings that can go along with the role. That's what makes it useful, but it's not the book to read if you're the one who needs care, especially if you're feeling vulnerable.)

*The ADHD Effect on Marriage: Understand and Rebuild Your Relationship in Six Steps* by Melissa Orlov

*Unbroken Brain: A Revolutionary New Way of Understanding Addiction* by Maia Szalavitz
(Addiction is not my bailiwick, but Szalavitz brilliantly describes growing up neurodivergent and the vulnerabilities this can create if we don't understand each other. Her collaboration with Bruce Perry, *The Boy Who Was Raised As A Dog*, while upsetting — it's a set of case histories of traumatised children — is also very good for a description of what the developing brain needs, and I'm grateful I read it before becoming a parent.)

## Websites:

ADDitude: www.additudemag.com

How To ADHD on YouTube: https://www.youtube.com/c/HowtoADHD

Totally ADD: https://totallyadd.com

Spitting Yarn: https://spitting-yarn.com/ (Full disclosure: the author of this blog, Anoushka Yeoh, is a personal friend. Which is lucky, because she's fabulous and so is her blog. If you want a loving, honest and insightful account of the experience of parenting a child with special needs, it's a great place to start.)

I'm Not Your Inspiration, Thank You Very Much: https://www.ted.com/talks/stella_young_i_m_not_your_inspiration_thank_you_very_much

There's a lot more out there, but the truth is I have to do most of my learning on the hoof – which brings us to the next point. It's great to read up, but a few things to remember, especially if you're one of the excellent folks out there who doesn't know much about disability/divergence but would like to broaden your understanding:

- The best-informed opinions will come from the people who have these conditions or ways of being. Other people may do their best, but they should always be considered a supplement to first-hand voices, not a substitute for them. This includes me! Don't listen to me over people who know better.

- There are some people whose conditions make them unable to self-advocate, or even to talk at all. The most impaired people – those most in need of care and support – are the least able to have a public face. Let's remember they're there, and fight for anything that gives them more rights and funding.

- Divergent and/or disabled people, and those who love them, are as different from each other as anyone else, and just as likely to disagree with each other. (Possibly more so; we're all a little stressed!) The broader a range of opinions you get, the clearer your picture.

- Looking for portraits of neurodivergent people in fiction? Odds are, the best portraits will not be the ones that make a big point of the character's neurodivergence, and possibly don't identify them as neurodivergent at all. ND people are members of the public, and you meet them in everyday life – often without knowing they're ND. Writers influenced by real ND people are far more likely to create an accurate portrait than writers who stroked their chins over list of symptoms: the latter is writing a 'condition', while the former is writing a person – which is what ND people are. (In case you're wondering, I didn't decide to write neurodivergent characters when I began this book. I just wrote characters that appealed to me, and at a certain point noticed what I was doing.) Search for characters that are favourites of neurodivergent people, whether they're 'supposed to be' autistic, ADHD, &c. or not: they may surprise you.

- Meet one of us and feel worried you don't know much about the subject? Just say so! Honest open-mindedness is by far the best approach; it's so much better to ask than to insist on doing the wrong thing.

- Think you might be one of us, carer or ND person? Well, hello, you beautiful man/woman/enby/other. Best advice: find people who've been where you are, and have been doing this longer than you. I'll never stop being grateful to those who did that for me; it got me through the days better than a million 'How to . . .' pamphlets. It might just be time to make some new friends.

Kit Whitfield

2021